Writer-in-Residence

J.A. Hoskins

Nom de Plume Publishing

A catalogue record for this book is available from the National Library of Australia

Cataloguing-in-Publication Data
Creator: Hoskins, J.A., 1973-
Title: Writer-in-Residence
ISBN:
9781923595040 (Paperback (Global))
9781923595019 (eBook)
9781923595057 (Large Print Paperback (Global))

Book Cover Design by: InkWild Designs

Note to Readers: This story includes depictions of betrayal, emotional abuse, and a scene of domestic violence. These elements are included with care and narrative purpose, but may be difficult for some readers.

For DH, who always said I could... and who waits patiently for *John*.

CHAPTER 1

Rebecca Morley gazed out the airplane window as Las Vegas came into view, the sprawling city emerging from the desert like a mirage. Even in daylight, the Strip was impressive—massive hotels lined up like monuments to excess and illusion.

"Look," she said, nudging her husband's arm. "You can see the Palisade from here."

Don barely glanced over. "Hmph," he grunted.

She tried not to let his lack of enthusiasm dampen her spirit. She'd been looking forward to this trip for months—five days at the luxurious Palisade for their 25th anniversary. He said he'd chosen Sunday to Friday to avoid the crowds, but she knew it was really about cheaper rates. Even so, she wanted to believe he'd gone all-out for their celebration.

Twenty-five years of building a life and raising two children in Savannah—with Jodie just finished college and newly married, and Luke in his sophomore year, Rebecca had hoped this empty-nest phase would mean reconnecting as a couple.

"I am so excited for *Unda* tonight," she gushed as the plane began its descent, keen to see the breathtaking water spectacle at the Palisade, where bodies and waves moved as one under a blue-lit dome. "And it was such a good idea of yours to book the early show—we'll have time for a nice dinner beforehand, and still get ourselves to bed at a reasonable hour."

Don sighed with exasperation, setting his phone down and snapping an annoyed glance across at her. "Fine. You want to *chatter* the whole way?"

She studied his profile, noting the tension in his jaw, the slight furrow between his brows. He'd been unusually short and somewhat detached for days, perhaps even weeks.

"Is everything okay?" she asked. "You seem distracted."

"Just work," he replied shortly. "The Michaelson Mirrors merger is proving complicated."

Rebecca nodded, though the explanation didn't quite ring true. Her husband typically enjoyed discussing the intricacies of his cases, positioning himself as the clever problem-solver against incompetent opposing counsel.

They disembarked and collected their luggage in silence, Rebecca deliberately forcing herself to stay quiet the rest of the way.

The Palisade's grand entrance took Rebecca's breath away, with a riot of glass flowers suspended like a technicolor sky overhead. It was a luxury she had rarely experienced despite Don's comfortable income. Their suite was equally impressive, with two marble bathrooms and floor-to-ceiling windows overlooking the famous Palisade fountain.

"It's beautiful," Rebecca whispered with appreciation. "Thank you for booking this, Don. It's perfect for our anniversary."

He made a noncommittal noise, unpacking his suitcase with methodical precision.

Rebecca sighed inwardly and began her own unpacking. Perhaps he was just tired from the flight.

"I'm going to shower before dinner," she announced, selecting a navy blue patterned dress from her suitcase; Don's favorite, the one he used to say brought out the blue in her eyes.

"Fine," he replied, not bothering to look up from his phone.

By the time Rebecca emerged from the bathroom, dressed and carefully made up, Don had changed into a crisp button-down, jacket and slacks—and the same distant expression.

"Where are we going for dinner?" she asked, making conversation as she slipped on her sensible heels.

He barely glanced at her as he drummed his fingers against his leg. "There's a steakhouse downstairs—they open at five," he said. "We should have just enough time before the show."

Walking toward the elevator, Don suddenly paused, his expression softening momentarily as he looked at her. "That dress... it still looks good on you, Bec."

Her heart gave a startled jolt at the familiar nickname—one he hadn't used in months, maybe years. For a brief moment, Rebecca caught a glimpse of the man she'd married. His eyes held something like regret, or perhaps nostalgia, before the wall came back up, and he motioned impatiently toward the elevator.

Her heart lifted slightly. Maybe he was just stressed about work after all.

In the elegant restaurant, Rebecca ordered Chardonnay while Don chose vodka with a splash of soda—stronger than his usual, as if he needed fortification.

"To twenty-five years," Rebecca said, raising her glass once their drinks arrived.

His lips tightened almost imperceptibly. His glass barely touched hers, a faint clink, but no words to echo her toast.

Throughout dinner, she tried to maintain conversation about their children and landscaping plans, but Don barely engaged, his attention focused on his meal. The table shook as he jiggled his knee beneath it.

Watching him fidget with uncharacteristic nervous energy, she finally called him out.

"Don, what is going on?" she asked, setting down her fork. "You're acting really strange. If something's bothering you, can we please talk about it?"

"No," he said flatly, signaling for the check.

Rebecca's stomach tightened with dread. Whatever was wrong, it was clearly more serious than she'd initially thought.

They made their way through the casino to the *Unda* theater. As the lights dimmed and the show began, Rebecca lost herself in the magic unfolding before her.

She gasped at the artists soaring overhead and plunging gracefully into water, while beside her, Don ran his hand through his hair repeatedly, huffing with poorly concealed impatience.

When that didn't seem to satisfy his restlessness, he'd check his watch, then shift position in his seat, as if physically uncomfortable in his own skin.

Almost halfway through the show, during a particularly mesmerizing sequence, he abruptly stood up.

"Let's go," he whispered, taking her arm.

"What? But it's not over—"

"Now, Rebecca."

Bewildered and embarrassed, Rebecca allowed herself to be led out of the theater, apologizing in whispers to the other patrons as they squeezed past.

The heavy theater doors swung shut behind them, abruptly cutting off the magical underwater world, like a beautiful dream interrupted.

The transition was jarring—from the ethereal blue light and haunting music to the bright sensory overload of the casino floor. The dazzling lights and electronic symphony of sounds felt overwhelming as Don ushered her swiftly along the carpeted walkway, his thumb pressed uncomfortably into the soft flesh inside her elbow.

Rebecca blinked, trying to adjust to both the lighting and the sudden shift in mood. A nearby slot machine erupted in a cacophony of bells and whistles, the celebratory sound a discordant backdrop to the tension between them.

"Don, what is going on?" she demanded, yanking her arm from his grasp. "That was incredibly rude. I've been wanting to see that show for years, and you dragged me out like—"

He turned to face her in the aisle, arms akimbo, eyes fixed at a point somewhere beyond her shoulder.

"Don—" she ventured quietly, reaching her hand out to him.

"I want a divorce, Rebecca," he stated abruptly, stepping out of her reach.

The words landed between them like a bomb. Time slowed down as she struggled to process what she'd just heard. Eyes that had been fixed on slot machines slid their way—some curious, others openly gaping.

"What?" She stared at him, certain she had misheard over the din. "What did you say?" Her voice trembled slightly, a cold sensation washing over her.

"I want a divorce, Rebecca," he repeated.

She started to speak, then faltered. "That's not funny."

Don stood silent, his jaw working as he looked everywhere other than directly at her.

Her hands instinctively tightened on her purse strap, knuckles whitening. The floor beneath her seemed to undulate and she widened her stance to maintain her balance.

His face was set as his eyes met hers directly, for perhaps the first time that day.

"I've been meaning to tell you for a while, but I wanted to have everything arranged properly first. But now that I'm faced with this," he gesticulated wildly before continuing. "Now that I'm faced with this anniversary farce, I can't wait any longer."

"I don't understand. You can't. I mean, you can't possibly be serious," she managed, her voice barely audible. "And what do you mean, 'anniversary *farce*'?"

Don glanced around, suddenly realizing they were standing alongside the crowded casino floor.

"Our marriage, Rebecca. It's been over for a long time, in every way that matters. It's time to admit it's finished and move on with our lives."

"That's not true," she protested, though even as she spoke, memories surfaced—Don working late more often, their increasingly perfunctory conversations, the growing distance between them in bed. "We have our routines, yes, but that's what happens after twenty-five years. That doesn't mean—" Her voice caught. "Don, you know that's not true!"

"There's someone else," he said, his voice flat, emotionless.

Rebecca felt nauseous as his words slapped her. "What? Who?" The question came instinctively, even as part of her didn't want to know.

"It doesn't matter who, Rebecca," he stated belligerently.

"It does matter," she replied, biting her bottom lip.

He paused and then relented. "It's Annette. From work."

His voice moderated as he saw the impact his words were having on his wife. "You've met her. She works in accounting. We didn't mean for this to happen. It just... happened."

The name registered dimly in Rebecca's mind—a young woman, early thirties, with a sleek bob and confident manner. She had seen her at a number of company events over the past few years.

"You're having an affair? With Annette?" Her hands began to shake. "For how long? Were you—" She paused, swallowing hard as realization dawned. "How long has this affair been going on?"

Don's jaw tightened. "It's not an *affair*, Rebecca. It started as a friendship, and it's grown deeper. It's not fair to any of us for me to be here with you. I was going to wait until after the trip to tell you, but I can't continue with this—this farce."

Rebecca stood frozen, acutely aware that he'd now twice used the word 'farce' to characterize their marriage. It stung like acid.

"A farce," she repeated, almost to herself. Her eyes narrowed—how many times had he described their life that way to Annette? "Twenty-five years together, raising a family, our beautiful home... and you call it a *farce*?"

Her voice remained low, but there was a new edge to it—the first hint of anger beginning to cut through the shock.

"Let's go up to the room," Don said, his tone quiet, perhaps in response to the bewilderment evident on her face. "We'll talk there."

Like a sleepwalker, she allowed him to guide her through the casino, into an elevator, and up to their suite. The room that had seemed so luxurious and full of promise just hours ago now felt like an elaborate trap.

The door closed behind them, and Rebecca turned to face the stranger wearing her husband's face, a man who had apparently been planning this moment for months while she'd been enthusiastically preparing for their anniversary celebration.

"Why now?" she asked, her voice hollow. "Why bring me all the way to Las Vegas just to tell me this?"

Don loosened his tie, avoiding her gaze. "Well, Rebecca, the trip has been booked for six months. I guess I thought it would be easier, being away from home. A neutral location. Annette told me to cancel it, but..."

"*Annette* told you," Rebecca snorted in disgust. "Your *mistress* told you to cancel your anniversary trip with your wife of twenty-five years, but you thought it would be easier to bring me here and end it in Vegas. Have I got that quite right?"

He didn't answer.

She sank onto the edge of the bed, her legs no longer able to support her. The irony wasn't lost on Rebecca—they were in the city where people came to get married on a whim in kitschy chapels officiated by Elvis impersonators, and here was Don, ending their union with such casual indifference, as if he were cancelling a dinner reservation.

"I don't want a divorce," she admitted, the words sounding small and desperate to her own ears.

"It's not about what *you* want, Rebecca." Don's voice had regained its firm, lawyerly tone—the one he used when explaining complicated legal matters to clients. "I've made my decision. The sooner you accept that, the easier this will be for everyone."

Rebecca stared at him, this man she had loved for half her life, the father of her children, her partner in building a home and a future. How could she have missed the signs? How could she have been so blind?

Outside the window, a boom resonated through the room as the Palisade's fountains began their choreographed dance, water jets soaring into the night sky with practiced precision.

Inside the room, Rebecca felt herself dropping into the first stage of grief for a marriage that, according to Don, had been dead for longer than she'd realized.

Chapter 2

S HE SAT WATCHING AS Don packed. He talked of logistics and arrangements, but his words flowed over her without sinking in. He wouldn't make eye contact, as if he'd rehearsed not only what to say but how to appear while saying it.

"I'll stay here at the hotel tonight, in another room," he stated firmly. "I'm going to arrange to fly home tomorrow, but you should stay through to the end of the week. The room is prepaid, might as well enjoy it—use the time to sort yourself out."

Rebecca tried to swallow, but her throat closed—no passage for breath or sound. *Sort herself out?* Stay here alone? In Las Vegas? Without him? The thought floated like an absurdity.

"I'm writing down your spa appointments. They were meant to be your anniversary gift. You should keep them—it'll make you feel better." He brandished the notepad in her general direction before placing it on the nightstand.

"Feel better? Don, I don't want this," she finally ventured.

He sighed, detached and deliberate. "I've explained it as clearly as I can, Rebecca. These things happen."

She sat in silence, watching as he slid his toiletry bag neatly into the suitcase.

These things happen. As if their marriage was a weather phenomenon, something to be observed with mild interest but no control. As if it were a minor traffic accident rather than the foundation their family was built upon.

"I think that covers just about everything," Don concluded, zipping his suitcase closed with a finality that broke through her daze.

Less than an hour ago, they had been celebrating their anniversary. Now he was all packed, ready to leave her.

"No," she said, the word emerging as barely more than a whisper.

He paused, his hand still on the suitcase. "*No?* Rebecca, I've told you—"

"No," she protested, stronger this time. "Don, please. Please don't do this."

"Rebecca—"

"We can work through this," she implored, rising from the bed and moving toward him with her hands outstretched. "I can forgive the affair, or whatever it is. We can go to counseling. People overcome these things all the time. Twenty-five years, Don. That counts for something."

"It's not that simple," he countered, dismissing her plea.

"It can be," she insisted desperately. "Whatever you need from me, I can change. I'll lose weight. I'll do anything. Don, please."

He finally looked at her directly, his expression a mixture of pity and discomfort. "I don't want you to change, Rebecca. That's not the point. I've changed. My feelings have changed."

"Because of her." Rebecca uttered, unable to bring herself to say Annette's name.

"Partly," he admitted. "But it's more than that. This has been coming for a long time."

"How long?" she demanded, though she wasn't sure she wanted to know the answer.

Instead of responding, he reached into the side pocket of his carry-on bag and removed a manila folder.

"I had these prepared," he said, his tone shifting to the professional one he used when discussing business matters. "Everything you need to know is in here."

She stared at the folder, making no move to take it. "What is that?"

"Divorce papers." Don placed the folder on the bed between them. "I've been very fair. You keep the house in Savannah. There's only about a hundred thousand on the mortgage, and it's worth much more than that. Plus, I'm offering a generous alimony settlement, considering."

Considering. The implication hung in the air between them—considering she hadn't provided anything to the marriage, considering she hadn't had a career, considering she'd been, what? A burden? An ornament? A convenient housekeeper and child-raiser?

"I've had Greg Thompson draw them up," he continued, pointing toward the folder. "You know Greg. He's one of our best family law attorneys. You'll see it's all very straightforward."

She felt dizzy, struggling to process the fact that without a word to her, her husband had not only planned to leave her but had gone so far as to consult with a colleague, draw up legal papers, and make decisions about their shared property.

Typical Don—always ten steps ahead, always controlling every variable, every outcome. He'd approach the dissolution of their marriage with the same precision with which he tackled his client cases. A flicker of dark humor washed through her at the thought of him meticulously organizing the end of their life together, as if it were simply another transaction to manage.

"The kids—" she uttered, her voice sounding distant to her own ears.

"We'll break the news together when you get home," he said with maddening calm. "We'll explain that we've decided to get a divorce, but that nothing else will change. We'll stay friends. They're adults, they'll understand."

We've decided. As if this bombshell had been a mutual decision rather than his unilateral decree. As if she'd had any say at all.

She felt as if she were drowning. How could he be so composed while destroying everything they'd built?

"I'm going to head down now, go arrange another room for myself," Don said, checking his watch. "We can talk more tomorrow before my flight. I made brunch reservations at the restaurant downstairs anyway, 10:30. May as well keep the booking. You know the place, we walked by it earlier in the casino?"

He reached for the notepad, writing the name of the restaurant in clear capitals so she would make no mistake about where to be at the appointed time.

Rebecca nodded mechanically, though she had no clear memory of which restaurant he meant.

Don picked up the folder and handed it to her directly. "Look it over tonight. I'd like to take it back to Savannah signed. Every place you need to sign is flagged with pink arrows."

Pink arrows. As if she were a child who couldn't navigate an adult document without color-coded guidance.

She accepted the folder automatically, a flash of indignation cutting through her shock. The pink arrows were so patronizing, so perfectly in character for Don, who had always felt compelled to compensate for her perceived shortcomings. Her fingers closed around the manila edges with more force than necessary, a small act of resistance even as she accepted this symbol of their ending.

He lifted his suitcase from the bed and moved toward the door, his manner so matter of fact that it seemed impossible he had just shattered their entire life together.

"Don, please," she tried one last time, following him. "Don't do this. We can work it out."

He paused at the door, hand on the knob. "There's nothing to work out, Rebecca. My mind is made up."

And with that, he opened the door and strode into the hallway, rolling his suitcase behind him.

Rebecca stood frozen, staring at the door as it swung closed. Then something broke free inside her—a desperate, primal need to stop this from happening. She lunged forward, still clutching the folder, and yanked the door open again.

"Don!" she cried, hurrying after his retreating figure. "Wait!"

He didn't slow his measured pace toward the elevator bank as she followed. Her breath came in shallow gasps as she struggled to keep up.

"You can't leave like this," she begged, reaching for his arm as they approached the elevator. "We need to talk about this. *Really* talk."

Don pressed the call button, ignoring her hand on his sleeve. "Keep your voice down," he said quietly. "This isn't the place for a scene."

The elevator doors opened, and he stepped inside. Rebecca followed, unwilling to let him escape so easily. An older couple already in the elevator glanced at them with undisguised curiosity.

"Twenty-five years, Don. You don't throw that away without at least trying to save it. Please, if you ever loved me—"

"Enough, Rebecca." His interruption was low but sharp. "Not here."

She fell silent, acutely aware of the strangers witnessing her humiliation. The elderly woman pressed a tissue into her hand. Only then did she notice her face was wet with tears, shame prickling as she muttered a meek 'thank you'.

When the elevator reached the casino level, Don stepped out without looking to see if she followed. The casino swallowed her—noise, lights, chaos—assaulting her senses as she trailed behind him.

"Please, stop," she insisted, catching up to him near a row of blackjack tables.

He continued toward the lobby, his pace quickening. "Go back to your room, Rebecca. We'll talk tomorrow."

"What about counseling? People work through affairs all the time. If you'd just—"

He halted so abruptly that she nearly collided with him. He turned to face her, his expression tightening with annoyance.

"Keep your voice down. This isn't about the affair. I don't want *this* anymore," he stated, gesturing at the space between them. "I haven't been in love with you for a long time. I should have ended it years ago."

The words hit her like blows, but worse was the disgust evident on his face as he looked her up and down.

"But I still love you," she murmured hoarsely.

"It doesn't matter. It's not enough." Don glanced around, clearly uncomfortable with having this conversation in such a public environment.

His voice dropped to a near-whisper, intense and controlled.

"Pull yourself together," he instructed, his tone leaving no room for argument. "You're a disaster. We'll discuss this tomorrow when you're calmer."

"But—" she faltered as her voice caught in her throat.

"Annette is pregnant."

The words landed like the final nail in the coffin of their marriage.

Rebecca staggered back as if he'd struck her. *Pregnant.* A baby. Not just an affair, not just falling out of love, but a new family. A replacement for the one they'd built together.

Her fingers loosened on the folder she'd been trying to shove toward Don, her denial giving way to numbing shock. He was starting a new life, complete with a new child. While she—what? Faded into the background? Disappeared?

"It wasn't planned," he offered, as if this detail could somehow lessen the blow. "But it's happening."

Rebecca stared at him. How had she missed this? How had she failed to see that the man she'd built her life around was capable of such calculation, such coldness?

"Go upstairs," he ordered, spinning her around by the shoulders and giving her a gentle push. It was no harder than dozens of other nudges she'd endured, the kind that left no mark but carried an edge all the same. She'd spent years mapping his thresholds, learning the quiet signals that meant *stop*, before the gentleness became something else.

He turned away, continuing toward the front desk as if certain she would obey, like she always had.

She stood motionless for a long moment, the folder clutched against her chest like a shield. An unexpected feeling flickered through her shock—something strangely like relief. The finality of his words, the pregnancy announcement, had severed something inside her. The desperate pleading felt suddenly exhausting, pointless. Whatever they'd had, had been burned up in less than an hour in the flames of Don's revelations.

Slowly, she started walking through the casino. Her feet moved of their own accord, carrying her past the clanging slot machines and animated conversations, deeper into the casino floor rather than toward the bank of elevators that would take her to the suite.

In her daze, she wandered in a circle until she found herself at a bar nestled in the heart of the gaming floor.

Without conscious decision, she climbed the three wide carpeted steps that elevated the bar and approached the long, curved marble counter. She slid onto a leather-covered stool, setting the folder down before her.

Her mind could focus on only one reality—divorce.

CHAPTER 3

THE LEATHER STOOL FELT cool beneath her legs. Rebecca stared at the folder as if it contained something precious rather than the death certificate for her marriage.

The bartender, a middle-aged man with salt-and-pepper hair and forearms laced with faded tattoos, gave her a practiced smile. "What can I get you?"

"I don't know." She spoke quietly, her voice hollow. "My husband just left."

Catching a glimpse of herself in the mirrored backsplash—red-rimmed eyes, carefully styled hair now in disarray, she lifted a self-conscious hand to wipe away the eyeliner and mascara tracks.

He nodded, sliding a cocktail menu across the bar. "When he gets back, give me a nod," the bartender assumed, misreading her situation.

"No, you don't understand." A tear escaped and slid down her cheek. "My husband just left *me*," she clarified.

The bartender's expression shifted subtly. Without a word, he reached for a bottle on the top shelf, poured a generous shot, and slid it across to her.

She contemplated the amber liquid, then drank it in one swift motion. The liquor burned a fiery path down her throat, making her cough and gasp. "What the hell was that?" she sputtered.

Her hands trembled as she set the glass down, her special-occasion manicure marred from nervous picking.

"Bourbon. Woodford Reserve," the bartender replied. "Figured you could use something strong."

Although Rebecca rarely drank anything stronger than Chardonnay, she realized that he was right. The bourbon's warmth was spreading through her limbs now, dulling the sharp edges of her shock.

"Want another?" he offered gently.

"No. Thank you, though," she declined with a weak attempt at politeness.

She sat in stunned silence, only partially aware of the scattered patrons as the bartender moved efficiently around the bar.

Rebecca opened the folder, flipping through pages of legal terminology. Her whole life reduced to clauses and subclauses. How many meals had she cooked? How many shirts had she ironed? What was the dollar value of raising their children? None of that appeared anywhere in these cold, clinical pages.

The bartender kept a respectful distance but stayed within earshot, occasionally offering a sympathetic nod when she looked up.

"He took care of it all," she said, laying a hand on the papers. "Like he's always done. He has it all figured out—where I'll live, how much money I'll have. I just need to sign. Where the pink arrows are." She let out a bitter laugh that was halfway to a sob. "I don't even know what to do. I don't even have my purse or my room key."

She hadn't thought to grab anything as she ran after Don. Purse, keys, phone—everything essential, all left behind in her desperation to save her marriage. Now she was stranded.

The bartender placed a fresh napkin in front of her. "Hotel can sort you out with a replacement key. Check at the front desk," he suggested helpfully.

Rebecca started to nod, then shook her head, overwhelmed by even this simple advice.

"I'll give you a minute," the bartender assured her kindly, moving away to check on some new arrivals at the other end of the bar.

She slumped forward, shoulders curving inward. Someone caught her eye, sitting a few stools down—a woman playing video poker, her posture straight-backed and elegant.

Dabbing at her eyes, Rebecca caught the woman glancing her way. She was striking—Asian-American with long dark hair that tapered to a V at her lower back, the ends transitioning smoothly from black to mahogany. She wore a tailored business suit that looked both casual and formal, all the while looking expensive.

There was something commanding about her presence, an air of authority that made Rebecca conscious of her dishevelment. Her navy dress now felt like a costume, wrinkled and damp with tears.

The woman returned her attention to her game, tapping the screen with trim, manicured nails.

Trying to refocus on the divorce papers, the legal terminology swam before Rebecca's eyes. *Petitioner and respondent. Equitable distribution. Uncontested.* The words blurred together, their meanings slipping away like water through her fingers.

She had always depended on Don to handle legal and financial matters. Now she was trying to understand documents that would determine her future, feeling completely ill-equipped. Perhaps Don was counting on her *not* understanding them. Had she mistaken control for care all along?

She felt petty even thinking that way.

And yet—hadn't there always been that dynamic? Don handling the important matters because she wouldn't understand. Him making the decisions because he knew best. When had his protective attitude turned into something manipulative? Had it always been that way, and she simply hadn't noticed?

After several minutes, the woman at the video poker machine collected her winnings and made her way toward the exit. She passed Rebecca and then hesitated before sliding onto the stool one seat away.

"I'm sorry to intrude," the woman said after a pause, her voice low and measured. "I couldn't help noticing you're having a difficult night."

Rebecca looked up, surprised by the kindly approach from this composed stranger. Her hand twitched toward her hair, as if smoothing it could erase the ruin of the evening.

"I'm fine," she replied automatically, the social reflex to deflect sympathy kicking in despite everything.

The woman's eyes, dark and perceptive, flickered briefly to the divorce papers on the counter. She said nothing, respecting Rebecca's space while somehow conveying that she was available to talk if needed.

The silence between them stretched, oddly comforting rather than awkward. Then Rebecca found herself speaking, the words tumbling out before she could stop them.

"My husband just told me he wants a divorce." She lifted the folder before letting it drop back onto the counter. "Twenty-five years, and he's... *done*. He's already had the papers prepared by his attorney. He handed them to me minutes after declaring that he's having an affair—oh, and she's pregnant."

The woman nodded, her expression neutral but attentive. "That's a lot to process in one evening."

"I don't even know what I'm looking at," Rebecca admitted, pushing the folder slightly away from her. "He's always handled everything legal or financial. And now I'm supposed to just sign where he tells me to."

"Look, it's not my place to intrude, but you absolutely should not sign those papers without the benefit of a legal opinion. Signing divorce papers prepared solely by your husband's attorney would be... unwise."

Rebecca looked up, startled by the direct approach. She studied the woman warily, her defenses momentarily rising despite her vulnerable state. Who was this woman inserting herself into the most devastating moment of Rebecca's life?

She glanced down at the folder, then back up at the confident woman. Something about her certainty made Rebecca pause. "Are you a divorce lawyer or something?" she asked.

"Yes," the woman replied, with no further elaboration.

Rebecca's instinct was to politely dismiss this intrusion, to retreat into the privacy of her pain. That's what she would have done yesterday—what Don would have expected her to do. Keep things tidy, maintain appearances.

But yesterday she'd understood her place as his wife of twenty-five years. Today she was... what?

"My husband—well, I don't know what to call him now. Ex-husband. He says it's a very generous settlement," she faltered, the uncertainty evident in her voice. "And I'm sure he wouldn't try to con me. He works for a law firm. He says I just need to sign."

An expression flickered across the woman's face—a brief manifestation of skepticism so subtle it was gone almost before Rebecca registered it.

"I'm sure he believes that it's a very generous settlement," the woman remarked diplomatically. "But 'generous' is a subjective term, particularly in divorce proceedings."

The vulnerability in her tone, despite her otherwise perfect composure, made Rebecca pay attention. There was something about this woman that inspired trust—a serene authority that seemed to cut through the chaos of her thoughts.

"Would you like to go somewhere quieter to talk?" the woman proposed, eyeing the casino beyond the bar. "I'd be happy to look through these with you, if you'd be comfortable with that."

Rebecca studied the woman's face. What would Don say about her trusting a stranger with personal legal documents? She could almost hear his voice in her head, warning her about scams and opportunists who preyed on unsuspecting tourists. But Don had just blown up their life, so perhaps his judgment no longer mattered. Perhaps she could make a decision without wondering what he would think.

She glanced at the folder with its pink arrows—Don's final act of managing her life, even as he walked away from it.

She didn't know this woman at all, yet Rebecca recognized her as a lifeline she desperately needed. She represented everything Rebecca wasn't—collected, professional, in control.

Rebecca hesitated only a moment longer, then drew the folder to her chest. Don would call her naïve. Reckless. Foolish. But maybe it was time to trust her own instincts for once.

"Yes," she decided. "I'd appreciate that very much."

CHAPTER 4

"Come with me," the stranger instructed, guiding Rebecca away from the bar.

Rebecca followed, hugging the folder closely as they moved through the casino.

"Where are we going?" she asked uncertainly, her voice still unsteady.

"Somewhere we can talk privately."

They reached a discreet doorway flanked by two suited attendants.

One of the attendants straightened as they approached. "Ms. Avery," he acknowledged with a nod, immediately opening the door.

Rebecca hesitated.

"It's all right. This is the VIP lounge," the woman assured her.

Inside, Rebecca's eyes widened. The space contrasted sharply with the casino floor—dark mahogany paneling and muted lighting creating an oasis of luxury. A few occupants spoke in hushed tones over drinks from crystal decanters.

She felt like she'd stepped into another world—one where she didn't belong with her tear-stained face and department store dress.

"Ms. Avery, lovely to see you again," an elegantly dressed woman greeted. "Would you like anything?"

"Yes, thank you, Marianne. A pot of oolong, please."

"Of course," Marianne confirmed. "Right away."

"We'll sit here," the stranger said, guiding Rebecca to a secluded corner table. She invited her to sit, then settled across from her, posture perfect without seeming rigid.

"I should introduce myself properly," she began once they were seated. "I'm Justine Avery. What's your name?"

"Oh uh—it's Rebecca. Rebecca Morley." Self-conscious of her appearance, she raised a hand and smoothed her hair.

Justine nodded, then stood. "Excuse me for one moment, Rebecca."

She watched as Justine spoke briefly with the receptionist, who picked up a phone and began speaking.

When Justine returned, a waiter was arriving with a silver tea service.

"Thank you, Thomas," she said, as he withdrew discreetly.

Justine poured tea for them both, her movements graceful and precise. Rebecca's hand trembled slightly as she accepted the cup.

"Take your time," Justine advised, her voice calm but matter of fact. "There's no rush."

Rebecca's hand rested on top of the folder of papers, her fingers splayed across it protectively. She looked into Justine's eyes, searching for any hint of judgment or pity and finding none. In her darkest moment, this stranger had appeared like a guardian angel.

What did she have to lose? Don had already taken everything that mattered.

Drawing a deep breath, she slid the folder across the table.

"Thank you," Justine said simply, as if Rebecca had passed her a menu instead of the wreckage of her marriage.

Justine reached into her designer handbag and withdrew a pen that caught Rebecca's attention. It was unlike any writing instrument she'd ever seen—shiny and substantial with gold accents, radiating importance and wealth.

"May I?" Justine inquired, holding the impressive pen poised above the folder.

Rebecca nodded, gesturing for her to go ahead. "Please."

Justine opened the folder and began reading, her expression neutral and professional. Rebecca watched, transfixed, as thick black ink slashed through clause after clause without hesitation. There was no uncertainty in Justine's movements, no pause to reconsider. Each stroke of that magnificent pen made a declaration: *This is unacceptable.*

Rebecca watched in fascination, a strange mix of fear and hope rising in her chest, aware that Justine was crossing out Don's carefully constructed plan. She'd never dared question his decisions before.

"How long have you been married?" Justine queried without looking up from the documents.

"Twenty-five years," Rebecca replied.

"And your career status? Have you been working outside the home?"

"I... no. Not for years," Rebecca admitted. "I was a bank teller when we met, and going to college. I dropped out after my first year. Don insisted I stay home—he didn't want a 'working wife'. He believed women should be home for their husbands and children."

Justine nodded, making another notation. "And your husband's profession?"

"He's a partner at a law firm in Savannah. Junior partner, I should say."

"Corporate law?"

"The firm does mostly corporate law, as well as family law, ironically," Rebecca noted with a bitter laugh.

Justine's pen moved again, this time writing something in the margin. "And your bank accounts? Do you have separate accounts or joint?"

"Joint. We have the joint checking for household expenses and a joint savings. Don also has an investing account, but I don't access that at all. He says it's in both our names, but I've never had anything to do with it."

"Do you know the approximate value of your joint savings?"

Rebecca hesitated for a moment—how much should she tell this woman? Then in a sudden rush of trust, she spoke.

"Around eighty to eighty-five thousand, I think. It was meant for a lake house, or cottage, eventually."

Justine made another note.

"Are you able to check the exact balances of those two accounts as of today's date?"

"I could. I don't have online access, but I can use phone banking. Except I left my phone in the room with my purse. I'll check once I get back up there," said Rebecca.

"Yes, do that. It's important to note the balances as of the date of separation. Just write them in the margin here on page twelve," Justine instructed, tearing one of the pink arrows in half and placing it at the relevant spot in the document.

"I don't know Don," she continued, "but it's always good to be informed. And how much do you know about your husband's earnings? His partnership share?"

Rebecca's brow furrowed. What kind of wife doesn't even know? "I... I'm not sure exactly. We've always lived comfortably but not extravagantly. The house is nearly paid off—well, it *was* paid off, actually, but then just a few months ago Don pulled out a mortgage to buy his car."

Justine raised an eyebrow. "Is the house in both your names?"

"Yes. At least, I think so. It always was. Don handled all the financial matters. But I did have to sign for the mortgage, so yes, it must be."

Justine's remarkable fountain pen slashed through another section of the document as she scribbled notes in the margin.

She flipped back to the first page and looked up at Rebecca, her review complete.

"Let me walk you through the key issues here," she said, her tone professional but kind. "This settlement, while possibly generous in your husband's eyes, is quite inadequate. Three years of modest alimony, the mortgaged house, half your joint savings, none of the investments—it's significantly less than what you're entitled to, and not sufficient to maintain the standard of living you're accustomed to."

"But Don said it was more than fair," Rebecca countered, uncertainty evident in her voice.

"Maybe he believes that, and maybe he just wants you to believe that," Justine observed. "After twenty-five years of marriage, you are entitled to much more."

She pointed to specific sections she had marked.

"You should be receiving an equitable portion of marital assets, which includes these listed investments, regardless of whose name they're in. Alimony should be longer-term, given your years out of the workforce. And this mortgage arrangement puts you at a significant disadvantage—particularly since you don't have a job."

Rebecca felt a chill run through her as she realized how precarious her future would be under Don's terms.

She probably would have signed those papers without question, as she'd done with every document he had ever put in front of her. Was that what he'd counted on—her blind trust, her ignorance? The thought made her stomach clench. Had this been his intention all along—to leave her financially vulnerable while presenting it as generosity?

"What I've done," Justine continued, "is mark reasonable counter-terms." Then she walked through each change she had made to the legal documents, explaining her rationale and answering questions until Rebecca felt fully comfortable with the proposed modifications.

"If you initial these changes, you're signaling that while you're not accepting his terms, you're willing to negotiate. It's your opening move in what will likely be a series of discussions."

"Can I really do that?" Rebecca questioned, hardly believing it could be so simple to assert herself.

"Of course," Justine replied simply. "You don't have to accept what's handed to you."

The words landed like stones in a still pond, rippling through Rebecca's consciousness. She had spent so many years accepting what Don handed her without question. The idea that she could say no, that she could demand more, was something she had never dared consider.

She reached for the hotel pen sitting in a holder on the table, but Justine gently stayed her hand.

"Your signature is worth more than a plastic ballpoint, Rebecca," she stated meaningfully, extending her prestigious Montblanc.

The weight of it impressed Rebecca as she took it—solid, substantial.

Her hand hovered over the paper, trembling slightly. For decades, she'd signed wherever Don pointed without question. What would happen if she defied him now? Would he become vindictive? The pen felt heavy in her hand, weighted with consequences she couldn't fully predict.

The pen carried authority in its very weight. How strange that such a small object could make her feel different—not Don's soon-to-be ex-wife, not the woman who'd been left behind, but someone with the power to say 'no'. The sensation was foreign, almost dizzying.

Taking a deep breath, she put the nib to paper. Each initial she placed beside Justine's edits felt like a small act of rebellion, a declaration that she wouldn't fade obediently into the background of Don's new life. The scratch of ink echoed louder than the faint music as she scribed her signature at the final pink arrow.

The receptionist approached their table, carrying a small cardboard folder with a new room key tucked inside.

"Mrs. Morley?" the woman asked, her professional demeanor softened with genuine kindness. "I understand you left your key and ID in your room. Security will be ready to escort you and check your ID once you're ready to go up."

Rebecca looked up in astonishment as she accepted the new key, fresh tears springing to her eyes—but these weren't tears of despair.

A few hours ago, she'd been stranded without access to her room. Now Justine had not only analyzed her divorce papers but arranged for her practical needs to be met. The efficiency of it all made Don's controlling behavior seem so clumsy in comparison.

She glanced at Justine, who gave a small, encouraging nod.

"Thank you," Rebecca expressed warmly. "Thank you so much."

"One more thing," Justine said to the receptionist, as she helped gather the amended documents and return them to the folder. "Can you please scan and copy these documents for us?" She handed over the folder, and Rebecca noticed that she'd included a fifty-dollar bill on top.

"Of course, Ms. Avery. I'll just be a moment," the receptionist promised, disappearing with the folder.

Rebecca stared at Justine, marveling at this woman who seemed to naturally earn the respect from others that Don had always tried to demand.

"Now tomorrow," Justine said, "you can either meet your husband as agreed and firmly present your counter-terms, or leave the folder for him at the desk, and avoid a confrontation. He may be angry, so I would only advise meeting him if you feel strong enough to stand by these changes."

"Don expects compliance. I don't know how he will feel about even the suggestion of negotiation."

"It's okay, Rebecca. His anger doesn't mean you're in the wrong—it means you're taking control of your own future."

The words resonated deeply. Throughout their marriage, Don's confidence had masked his manipulation. He'd slowly narrowed her world until she depended on him for everything. Only now, standing in the wreckage, could she see the pattern clearly.

A security guard escorted Justine and Rebecca to the elevator bank, their presence an anchor in a world that still felt like it was spinning out of orbit.

"I really don't know how to thank you," Rebecca confessed sincerely as they waited for the elevator. "You've been like a life raft."

"You don't need to thank me," Justine replied kindly. "But promise you'll advocate for yourself tomorrow, and in the days to come."

She pressed a card into Rebecca's hand. "My private number is on the back. Call anytime."

Rebecca glanced at the card—a phone number written in that marvelous black ink with a no-nonsense stroke. She clutched it tightly as the elevator arrived.

"All the best, Rebecca," Justine said as the doors opened. "Remember, this isn't the end of your story—it's the start of something new."

The thought scared and intrigued her in equal measure. Tomorrow, she would need to start finding her own confidence. Not Don's bullying certainty, but something quieter and stronger—like Justine's calm authority. She wasn't sure if she had it in her, but she had no choice but to find out.

Rebecca stepped into the elevator, turning to face Justine as the doors began to close. For a brief moment, she glimpsed the woman who had entered her life at its lowest point and felt something stirring inside her that had been dormant for far too long—resolve.

As the elevator ascended toward her room, Rebecca held the divorce papers in one hand and Justine's card in the other. Both represented choices—one made for her, one she would make for herself.

The ink was barely dry, and already she wondered if she'd made the biggest mistake of her life—or the best decision in decades.

CHAPTER 5

REBECCA WOKE WITH A start, disoriented by the unfamiliar hotel room. Sunlight filtered through a gap in the heavy curtains, casting a stripe of gold across the rumpled sheets. Her hand brushed against the folder on the bed beside her, Justine's bold ink marks visible alongside her own bank balance notations and initials in the margins of the revised divorce contract.

The events of the previous day crashed into her consciousness. Don's cold declaration, Annette's pregnancy, the casino bar, Justine's unexpected intervention. Had it really been only twenty-four hours since she was home in Savannah, giving the plants a decent watering before packing for what she'd thought would be a romantic anniversary trip?

She pushed herself up against the pillows, rubbing her eyes. The hotel room felt cavernous without Don's presence, his absence a physical thing that seemed to take up space rather than leave it empty.

She carried the folder to the window armchair. Flipping through the pages, Justine's revisions leapt out—thick, decisive strokes rewriting Don's terms. The black ink radiated a certainty Rebecca lacked as she contemplated the morning ahead.

She was planning to meet Don for brunch at 10:30, present him with these revisions, and calmly inform him that these were her counter-terms. The thought alone sent nausea rolling through her. She'd never stood up to Don like this, never challenged his decisions so directly.

An hour later, showered but still anxious, Rebecca stood before the mirror assessing her reflection with newly critical eyes. Her modest, flowy blouse was designed to hide what Don called her 'donut belly'—the softness that had settled around her middle over the years. Her mom-jeans and sensible slip-ons suddenly seemed like a uniform of submission, a visual reminder of how she'd allowed herself to become invisible. Were these the clothes she would have chosen for herself, without Don's influence?

She thought of Justine in her chic tailored suit, the composed confidence she projected without saying a word. What would it feel like to possess even an ounce of that poise? To walk into a room and know that you belonged there, that your voice mattered?

With a sigh, Rebecca gathered the folder and her room key, carefully tucking the latter into her pocket. She wouldn't make the same mistake twice, locking herself out of her own room.

The elevator ride seemed endless, each floor bringing her closer to a confrontation she wasn't ready for. Her heart thumped against her ribs as the doors opened to the casino floor. Her hands trembled slightly as she clutched the folder, and she had to wipe her clammy palms against her jeans before approaching the front desk.

Rebecca greeted the clerk, forcing a smile she didn't feel. "Could I have a large envelope, please?" she requested.

The clerk handed her one without question before moving on to the next patron in line. Rebecca tucked the file inside, hesitated, then wrote 'Don Morley' on the front with a plastic ballpoint. The cheap ink seemed insulting after experiencing the gravitas of Justine's Montblanc pen, but perhaps that was fitting.

She made her way to the appointed restaurant. The hostess smiled in greeting. "Table for one?"

"Actually," Rebecca began, her voice steadier than she expected, "I need to leave this for Don Morley. He has a reservation for 10:30. Could you please give him this and let him know his guest won't be joining him?"

"Of course, ma'am," the hostess assured her, accepting the envelope.

This was supposed to be the moment she walked away, head high. But her legs carried her elsewhere, drawn by something she couldn't name—curiosity, fear, maybe both.

She drifted toward a nearby bank of slot machines, one with a clear view of the restaurant, partially obscured by a decorative column.

She kept her eyes fixed on the hostess stand, praying she was invisible.

Don arrived precisely at 10:30, his punctuality a constant characteristic. Dressed in a casual blazer and slacks, not even a hair out of place, he strode directly to the hostess, where he gave his name with the easy assurance of a man accustomed to being expected.

Rebecca watched as the hostess handed him the envelope. A slight frown crossed his features—barely noticeable to anyone who hadn't spent a quarter century studying those expressions. He glanced around the restaurant once, then allowed himself to be led to a table near the open window that looked directly out onto the casino floor.

She slid across to a different slot machine, one with a better vantage point. Her attention was fixed entirely on Don as he settled at his table and ordered coffee with a dismissive nod.

He slid the file from the envelope with a self-satisfied smirk. That expression—so familiar yet suddenly so grating—struck Rebecca in a different way. Had he always looked so smug, so condescending? For the first time, she saw him not as the powerful figure she'd built her life around, but as something smaller—petty in his certainty of his own superiority.

She held her breath, watching as he opened the file, her chest tightening until it ached. She could hear her own heartbeat, watching as confusion furrowed his brow when he encountered the first of Justine's revisions. His head reared back, and he began flipping rapidly through the pages, rage wiping out his composure. By the fourth page, his face had flushed a deep red that climbed from his collar to his hairline.

One fist lifted, hovering in the air, he glanced left and right through narrowed eyes, almost as if he sensed he was being watched. His jaw clenched so tight she could see the muscle jumping in his cheek even from across the casino floor. Instinct drove her down behind the slot machine, the impulse to retreat snapping in before she could stop it.

When she dared to peek again, he was slamming the file shut and snatching the envelope from the table, his movements sharp. He shoved his chair back and rose to his feet so abruptly he nearly knocked over a server carrying a water pitcher. The young woman stumbled aside, an apology already forming on her lips. Don stormed past her without acknowledgment, making a beeline out the door and directly toward the elevator bank.

Rebecca knew he was heading to her room, hoping to confront her there. She also knew she couldn't follow—he'd spot her immediately and be on the attack. Despite Justine's encouragement, despite the logic of the revised agreement, she felt a familiar tremor of fear cascade through her body.

Her legs felt leaden, her breath quickening to shallow gasps as a cold sweat broke along her spine. She stayed rooted to her spot, heart racing hard enough to feel a pulse in her temples.

"Is that him?" a low voice probed beside her.

Rebecca startled, pressing a hand against her chest to steady her thundering heart. Justine stood there, elegant as ever in a different suit, her expression calm but concerned.

"Oh, goodness, Justine. Yes, that's him," Rebecca blurted, her voice cracking as tears raced to her eyes. "I know I shouldn't have stuck around and watched, but I wanted to see—I don't know. Make sure he got it. See his reaction."

Rebecca heard herself rambling and bit her lip, envying how Justine never seemed to waste words, or apologize for taking up space.

"I feel like I don't even know that man," Rebecca confessed, her voice dropping to a whisper.

The admission hung in the air between them—a deeper truth: her husband had become a stranger to her. Or perhaps she was finally seeing clearly what had been there all along.

Justine nodded, no judgment in her expression.

"It's natural to want to witness his reaction," Justine acknowledged with understanding. "But right now, a confrontation won't help either of you. He's angry and you're still processing. It's best if you stay out of sight until he's left."

Rebecca noticed how Justine didn't qualify her statements with 'I think' or 'maybe'—she simply spoke her truth directly. It was a way of communicating Rebecca had never mastered, always moderating her opinions to avoid conflict.

"I won't go to the room until after he's gone. He'll have booked the 2:50 flight, so he'll want to leave for the airport at 12:30 sharp." Rebecca spoke with certainty. "He's never late."

"Then give him time to cool off," Justine suggested pragmatically. "I have to go to a meeting, but remember what we discussed. Stay calm, stay firm. This is just the beginning of the negotiation."

After Justine departed, Rebecca was at loose ends, too anxious to eat but needing somewhere to wait out the hours until Don's departure. She settled onto a plush sofa in the piano bar at the far end of the lobby, a spot that would allow her to see him leave without being immediately visible.

She ordered a club soda, hoping to quiet the riot of emotions churning inside her. Had she done the right thing in leaving him an edited document? Her fingers drummed an anxious rhythm against the sofa cushion.

The minutes crawled by, marked by the soothing notes of the piano, but Rebecca barely heard the music over the persistent knot of tension that had settled between her shoulder blades.

She checked her watch—12:20. Don would be appearing any minute, precisely on time for his airport departure. She sat up straighter, eyes fixed on the revolving lobby doors.

What she didn't see was Don striding purposefully through the casino behind her, briefcase and carry-on in hand. He paused, scanning the casino through narrowed eyes. As a man who prided himself on understanding human behavior—a skill he'd honed through years of legal practice—Don knew Rebecca's patterns. He knew her well enough to know that if she wasn't hiding out in the room, then she must be somewhere she could observe his departure without being seen herself.

He knew she wouldn't venture far from the hotel, not in her emotional state. His eyes swept across the casino floor, the restaurants, and finally settled on the piano bar.

Rebecca felt a sudden chill race down her spine. Before she could turn, she heard his voice behind her, low and controlled but vibrating with anger.

"Did you really think this little stunt would work?"

The fury in his voice—familiar from countless disagreements over the years—sent a wave of cold dread through her body. The blood rushed to her cheeks as her trembling fingers fumbled the glass onto the table.

His anger, contained but unmistakable, was somehow more frightening than if he'd shouted.

Chapter 6

Calming notes from the baby grand faltered momentarily as Don slapped the file down on the table, the sound like a gunshot in the peace of the piano bar.

Nearby patrons turned to look, conversations halting mid-sentence. The refined atmosphere shattered as the bartender made eye contact with Don, one eyebrow raised.

"What. The fuck. Is this?" he demanded through clenched teeth, swiveling his head back and forth like a snake poised to strike. "I didn't ask for your *opinion* on this, and I certainly don't agree to your changes." He leaned in, voice lowering as he spotted a couple looking their way.

"You take a very fair agreement and try to screw me for more? Keep it up, and you'll get nothing."

Rebecca shrank into her seat, a lifetime of deference taking over before she could stop it. Her pulse thundered, hands instinctively gripping the cushion beneath her, seeking an anchor against his verbal assault.

"*Triple* the alimony?" he scoffed, his face taking on an ugly, mottled red color. "What the hell is that, especially considering I'll have a new baby to support?"

The words hit her with the force of a slap. She blinked, momentarily stunned by the sheer audacity. He wanted her sympathy for the financial burden of his infidelity? Expected her to consider the needs of his child with another woman when determining what *equitable distribution* meant after twenty-five years of keeping his home?

Heat flooded through her body. The trembling in her limbs subsided, replaced by an unfamiliar stillness.

She had one opportunity to stand up to him, or it would all play out exactly as he'd planned. She straightened her spine, pulling herself up to her full height as she stood to face him, forcing him to take a step backwards in the process.

"It's not *triple* the alimony, Don," she corrected firmly, her voice remarkably steady. "It's triple *your offer*. The advice I've received is that I'm actually entitled to more. And I'm also entitled to an equal division of *all* the marital assets, not just which ones *you* decide get split."

His eyes widened slightly at her unexpected resistance. His mouth moved as if trying to form his next rebuttal, but she didn't give him the chance.

"And that would include the investments. And your 401(k)," she asserted, shocked by her own boldness but pushing forward anyway.

Several people had turned to watch the unfolding drama, and Don's gaze darted nervously to the onlookers. If there was one thing he couldn't stand, it was negative public attention. His carefully constructed image was sacred to him.

"Especially considering my role in keeping your household and raising our children," she continued, amazed at the words coming from her mouth. "Remember, I wasn't *allowed* a career—at your insistence that I stay home."

He opened his mouth to interject, but Rebecca wasn't finished.

"We got married when I was twenty and you were twenty-three," she reminded him, her voice growing stronger with each word. "And while I agree that you earned the money for the mortgage payments, don't forget that it was my unused college savings that made up the down payment for the house. And that the original mortgage was provided interest-free by *my* parents."

She couldn't believe she was standing up for herself. It felt both terrifying and exhilarating, like standing at the edge of a cliff and finally deciding to spread her wings.

"You can't possibly—" he began, but she cut him off, her voice rising.

"I *can* possibly, and I am." She felt a surge of adrenaline as she interrupted him—something she'd rarely dared to do before.

A voice in the back of her mind screamed in panic—who was this person taking over her body, challenging Don so directly? But another, newer voice whispered that this is exactly who she needed to be right now.

"Don, you made these decisions without me—about screwing Annette, about ending our marriage, about what I *deserve*. Well, now I have some thoughts on what I deserve too."

The piano player had tactfully shifted to a louder, more upbeat melody, perhaps trying to provide some auditory cover for their increasingly heated exchange.

"Keep your voice down," he commanded sharply, snatching the paperwork off the table. In a theatrical gesture of dominance, he yanked at the file, grunting as the thick folder resisted until it tore raggedly in his hands.

She watched with stunned amusement, wondering if he realized how absurd he looked. She was silently thankful that Justine had had the foresight to get a copy made before it was handed over.

"You're clearly not understanding how this works," he stated condescendingly through gritted teeth.

"I know one of us is clearly not understanding, Don, but I suspect it's not *me*," Rebecca replied coolly, stunned by the calm that had settled over her. "I'll email you a copy of my markup shortly, since you've now destroyed the original."

His expression faltered.

She stepped closer to him.

"And Don—" she spoke quietly but firmly. "If you don't file it through the proper channels, then I will find out how and I will do it myself." Her newfound determination didn't waver as she met his gaze directly—something she'd rarely ever done in the past twenty-five years.

For a brief moment, uncertainty flickered across his face. It was quickly replaced by his usual mask of authority, but she had seen it—the first crack in his confidence. A warm satisfaction spread through her chest.

Don composed himself, shoving the torn shreds of paper into his briefcase as if he'd won some important victory. He glanced ostentatiously at his wristwatch—the Rolex he'd bought himself for their 20th anniversary.

"I'll give you the next few days to come to your senses," he pronounced dismissively, his tone shifting to the patronizing one he used with difficult clients. "I know you've had a shock and you're not yourself." He waved vaguely toward the casino beyond. "Get your hair and nails done. Enjoy yourself. By Friday, you'll be back to normal."

Rebecca stared at him, marveling at his capacity for self-delusion. Did he really believe a few spa treatments would erase what he'd done?

"Will you be alright to get to the airport and onto the plane by yourself on Friday?" he inquired, the condescension so thick it was almost tangible.

She nearly laughed. She wasn't an *idiot*, despite how he'd always treated her.

"I think I can manage to board an airplane without your supervision, Don," she responded dryly.

He nodded, as though she'd confirmed some private theory. "I'll see you on Saturday then. I'll come to the house, we'll speak to the kids, and I'll bring a copy of the original paperwork for you to sign." He said it with such certainty, as if the past few hours had been merely a minor detour on his predetermined path.

He turned to go, then swiveled back for a parting shot. "But if you do want to speak to a real lawyer—not whoever came up with this mess—" he shook his briefcase at her "—then I'll arrange for another partner in the firm to represent your side. But the cost comes out of your split."

With that, he strode away, rigid with indignation, leaving Rebecca standing alone in the piano bar.

She sank down onto the sofa, suddenly drained by the confrontation. Her legs trembled. She breathed deeply, eyes closed, as the reality of what she'd done sank in.

Around her, the dignified murmur of refined conversations gradually resumed, the brief drama already fading into the background hum of the casino. The contrast between the refined atmosphere and her marriage's messy dissolution wasn't lost on her.

She sat still for several long moments, replaying the confrontation in her mind. Had she really stood up to Don? Had those words actually come from her mouth? Her body felt hollow, the momentary courage that had possessed her rapidly draining away, leaving behind a bewildering emptiness.

She raised a slightly trembling hand to signal a server. "Woodford Reserve, please? Neat." The words shocked her as they left her lips—she would have ordinarily ordered a Chardonnay, but remembered clearly how a single shot of bourbon had steadied her nerves the previous night.

As the server returned with her glass, Rebecca caught sight of her reflection in the ornate mirror on the wall. She hardly recognized herself. For a brief, shining moment, she had spoken with an authority she didn't know she possessed. But now, having watched Don walk away with such certainty, such unshakable confidence that he would ultimately get his way, doubt began to creep in.

Don was clearly furious—beyond furious. He wasn't a man who tolerated defiance, and she'd defied him publicly. He'd make her pay for that somehow, she was certain.

And yet, she had also found a tiny bit of her voice. Those words—her words—had stopped Don in his tracks, if only for a moment.

She took a long sip of the bourbon, her hand still trembling. Yes, she had stood up to Don, but what came next? He had Annette, a baby on the way, his career, his friends, his life plan. What did she have?

She reached into her pocket, her fingers finding Justine's card again. The embossed lettering felt solid, real. Perhaps it was something. A small lifeline in a sea of uncertainty.

The decisions ahead were entirely her own to make. The thought was as terrifying as it was liberating.

CHAPTER 7

R EBECCA RETURNED TO HER room, turned on the Do Not
Disturb light, closed the curtains, undressed, and climbed into
bed. For the next four days, she didn't leave the room.

The spa appointments Don had scheduled came and went. She
hadn't cancelled them, somehow beyond caring that the appointments
would be charged to the credit card anyway.

The blackout curtains plunged the room into darkness, the suite a
mausoleum—silent but for the air conditioning hum. She lost all sense
of time, never knowing if it was day or night, morning or evening.

Memories played across her mind—Jodie's wedding, Luke's first
driving lesson, family vacations where Don had been constantly
distracted with work. Had there been signs all along? Or had she
simply been too focused on maintaining their perfect life to notice its
hollowness?

Her cell phone rang, and reaching for it, she turned the ringer off
without answering. She knew it was Don without looking—who else
would call her? What was there to say?

She unplugged the digital clock, its red glow an unwelcome intrusion.
What did time matter? Her life had ceased to follow normal rhythms.

At some point during the blur of those days—perhaps it was
Wednesday, or maybe Thursday—Rebecca experienced a moment of
lucidity. She reached for the hotel phone and called the front desk.

"Could I get a wake-up call for 9:00 Friday morning, please?" she
requested, her hoarse voice sounding foreign to her own ears, rusty
from disuse.

"Of course, Mrs. Morley. We'll call you at 9 AM on Friday," the clerk
confirmed politely.

She hung up and slipped back into the shadows.

She barely ate. When hunger became actual pain rather than a hollow
sensation, she'd grab something from the minibar.

Mostly, she lay in bed, staring into the darkened room, her body impossibly heavy, the hollow ache in her chest making each breath require conscious effort.

When the wake-up call came, its cheerful ring yanked her from dreamless sleep. Her heart lurched into a panicked rhythm, her mouth dry with dehydration. Dizziness washed through her as she swung her legs over the edge of the bed.

Reality crashed in: Las Vegas, divorce, Don's betrayal, the baby.

With robotic movements, Rebecca dragged herself to the shower. The bathroom seemed obscenely bright after days spent in the dark. She avoided the mirror, turned on the water. The shower's hot spray brought her fully into her body for the first time in days, the sensation almost painful after so much numbness.

She packed mechanically, leaving nothing behind. The pristine copy of the divorce papers went into her carry-on suitcase. She smiled ruefully, visually replaying the image of Don's attempt to rip up the entire folder of originals.

The taxi ride passed in a blur of too-bright sunlight. Her outdated flip phone—Don insisting it was all she needed, because *a basic mind needs a basic phone*—showed dozens of missed calls. All from him. She flipped it closed, slid it away.

The busy airport assaulted her senses—the cavernous terminal echoing with announcements, travelers rushing in all directions. She moved through check-in and security, wandering the space like a ghost until she found her gate.

A line formed, boarding began.

She stood with her boarding pass in hand, watching as the line of travelers slowly filed through the jetway.

Panic seized in her chest. The sensation was almost painful, like a vice tightening around her ribcage. Sweat broke out along her hairline, her skin turning clammy.

Blood rushed in her ears, drowning out the boarding calls.

Images flashed through her mind in rapid succession—walking into their empty house in Savannah, the house where she'd raised their children and built what she'd thought was a life. Facing Jodie and Luke, watching their faces as they absorbed the ugly truth. Running into neighbors at the grocery store, their pitying glances following her down the aisles.

Beyond these scenarios loomed the bigger question—who was Rebecca without Don? She'd been defined by her role as his wife, her life shaped by his preferences and needs. She had no career, few independent friends, no separate identity.

Returning to Savannah meant confronting this with no preparation, no plan, no sense of who she might become. The realization struck her with perfect clarity—she wasn't ready. Maybe one day, but certainly not today.

A gate agent's voice cut through her thoughts: "Final boarding call for flight 1342 to Savannah."

Rebecca looked down at the boarding pass in her hand, then at the dwindling line of passengers.

"Ma'am? Are you boarding?" the gate agent asked.

Rebecca took a step backward. "No," she said, startled by the steadiness of her voice. "No, I'm not."

Instead of moving toward the gate, Rebecca turned and walked in the opposite direction. She wheeled her suitcase back through the terminal, past baggage claim, and out to the taxi stand.

"Where to?" the driver asked as she climbed in.

"I don't know," she admitted quietly. "Someplace on the Strip. Comfortable. Quiet."

The driver studied her in the rearview mirror. "First time in Vegas?"

"No," she murmured distantly. "But it feels like it."

He nodded, putting the car in drive. "How about the Solara? They have a beach. You look like you need some beach in your life," he suggested.

Rebecca nodded, watching as the airport slid past, the Las Vegas Strip in the distance looking somehow more honest in the daytime than its nighttime glitter.

The Solara lobby welcomed her with tropical elegance designed to evoke escape and indulgence. Through glass doors, she glimpsed the artificial beach where tourists lounged under umbrellas.

She approached the check-in desk with only the vaguest sense of what she was doing.

"Do you have any rooms available?" she inquired tentatively.

"We have a room with two queen beds available."

"That's fine," Rebecca replied listlessly. "I'd like it until next Thursday please."

The clerk looked up, holding out a hand. She paused, uncertain.

"ID and credit card, please," he prompted.

She handed over her driver's license and credit card—joint with Don, of course—and waited as the clerk processed her check-in.

In her new room, Rebecca closed the curtains, undressed, and climbed into bed. This room was different—contemporary with velvety furnishings in blues and beiges, abstract artwork suggesting ocean waves.

The darkness welcomed her back, familiar and comforting in its simplicity. No decisions to make in the dark, no futures to confront. The mattress was firm; she curled into it seeking oblivion.

She'd just pulled the blankets up when the hotel phone rang on the nightstand. It startled her—no one knew she was here. She reached for it hesitantly.

"Hello?"

"What the *fuck* is this $700 charge from the Solara?" Don exploded, jolting her fully awake. His voice triggered an immediate physical reaction—shoulders raising toward her ears, stomach clenching with dread. The familiar tang of fear flooded her mouth, metallic and bitter. Her free hand clutched the bedsheet as her body braced for verbal assault.

She silently cursed herself for not thinking this through. Of course, he would have seen the charge go through on the credit card. She raised a hand to cover her eyes.

"Don—" she began hesitantly.

"Why aren't you on the plane?" he demanded furiously. "I checked the flight status online. It's departed. You're at the fucking Solara. Now I'm going to have to book you another plane ticket, for Christ's sake!"

Rebecca sat up in bed, heart racing. "I'm not coming home yet," she stated firmly, the words surprising her as they left her mouth.

"What do you mean *'you're not coming home yet'*?" Don echoed incredulously. "What are you playing at?"

"I need some time," she asserted quietly.

Don's laugh was harsh, derisive.

"Time for what?" he scoffed. "To run up more charges on my credit card? You stupid woman. Do you have any idea how childish you are?"

The familiar pattern reasserted itself—Don's anger, her automatic impulse to apologize, to placate, to make things easier for him. For a moment, the words *'you're right, I'm sorry'* formed on her lips, the path of least resistance calling to her like a siren song.

But something stopped her this time. The memory of Justine's composure, the recollection of Don's momentary uncertainty in the piano bar when she'd refused to back down. A tiny ember of resolve flickered to life inside her.

"I'll be in touch when I'm ready," she maintained, firmness in her tone.

"*Ready*?" Don mocked. "Ready for what? This isn't up for negotiation, Rebecca. You need to get your fat ass on a plane tomorrow. I've already told the kids we're having dinner tomorrow night to discuss something important."

"Well, you'll have to tell them something else," she countered, finding unexpected resolve.

"This is ridiculous," Don's voice rose. "If this is about the settlement, fine. We can discuss it when you get home. But this little rebellion of yours—"

Rebecca disconnected the call, cutting him off mid-sentence.

A violent tremor raced through her body as she hung up. Her heart hammered with such force she could feel her pulse at her throat. Despite her gasping breath and lightheadedness, an unfamiliar warmth spread from her center—the physical sensation of power reclaimed.

Her hand shook as she immediately picked the receiver up again, calling the front desk.

"Good afternoon, Mrs. Morley. How can I help you?"

"Uh, hi. I'm wondering if it would be possible to hold my calls, or send them to voicemail, or whatever? I would like to not be disturbed. Is that something that can be done?" Aware she was babbling, Rebecca bit down on her bottom lip, waiting for the reply.

"Of course, Mrs. Morley. All calls can be diverted to the message bank," the clerk explained efficiently. "You can pick them up at your convenience when you see the red light flashing on the phone in your room. Okay?"

"Oh! Yes. That's easy. That's wonderful, thank you very much then. Have a nice day," she babbled on, hanging up the receiver and wondering what it would take to compose herself.

With a sigh, she hefted herself out of bed, rummaging in her purse for the card that Justine had given her.

Picking up the hotel phone again, she dialed.

"Justine Avery," came the smooth and measured response.

"Justine? It's Rebecca. Um, Rebecca Morley?" she ventured uncertainly.

"Of course it is. Hi Rebecca, I was hoping you'd call." Justine greeted, her calm, assured voice instantly soothing. "How are things going? I see you're calling from a Las Vegas number."

At the sound of Justine's voice, her entire body loosened—and then broke. A pressure that had been building behind her sternum suddenly released, causing her to double over as silent sobs became audible, wrenching sounds. Tears flowed freely now, not the silent streams of her isolation but forceful, body-shaking waves that left her gasping for breath between words.

"I'm still in Las Vegas," she confessed brokenly. "I couldn't—I couldn't get on the plane."

There was a brief pause. "Are you okay?" Justine inquired with evident concern. "Where are you?"

"The Solara. I just checked in. I don't know what I'm doing, Justine. I just... I couldn't go home."

"That's understandable," Justine reassured her, her tone kind but matter of fact. "Listen, I'm in Vegas too. I'm here for a poker tournament this weekend. I can be free around eight tonight. Would you like to meet for dinner? We can talk about some options for your next steps."

"Yes. Please," Rebecca responded gratefully, clutching the phone like a lifeline.

"Good. I'll meet you at the Summit restaurant at eight. It's on the top floor of your hotel."

After hanging up, Rebecca sagged back into the comfort of the bed with relief. The vast emptiness of the day ahead suddenly had a point of reference—dinner at eight. She could manage until then.

The alarm clock on the nightstand glowed 1:47 PM. She reached out and set the alarm for 7:00 PM, allowing herself enough time to shower and dress before meeting Justine.

As she drifted toward oblivion, Rebecca realized that for the first time in her life, she had hung up on Don Morley. It should have terrified her.

Instead, beneath the anxiety, she felt something unexpected—a tiny spark of satisfaction. Her spine straightened slightly and the corners of her mouth twitched upward in the ghost of a smile as she drifted into sleep.

CHAPTER 8

REBECCA ARRIVED AT THE Summit fifteen minutes early. She nearly turned back twice—once when a laughing group of tourists crowded into the elevator beside her, and again when the doors opened into the glittering lounge.

What was she doing here? She didn't belong in places like this—a woman adrift, disconnected from her former life. Her legs felt weak following the hostess, as if she'd forgotten how to navigate social spaces.

The top-floor venue was unlike anywhere she'd been before—opulent, with velvet furnishings, golden lighting, and carved wooden panels. She was led to the lounge area, where the glass walls offered a breathtaking panorama of the Strip.

From the window, she watched the lights sparkle below as dusk settled. The Strip stretched for miles, a glittering river of neon and promise, the people on the sidewalks like tiny specks.

"Beautiful view, isn't it?" a voice remarked conversationally.

Rebecca turned to find Justine approaching, elegant in a slim-fitting dress, her long hair swept up in a glossy chignon. A flood of relief washed through her. She'd been unconsciously clutching at her throat, her hand now dropping as tension eased at the sight of a familiar face.

"It's stunning," Rebecca agreed hesitantly, suddenly self-conscious of her appearance. She'd made an effort, showering and putting on fresh clothes, but she felt faded and rumpled next to Justine's polished perfection.

They were seated at a private corner table with flattering dim lighting. After ordering drinks—sparkling water for Justine, Chardonnay for Rebecca—they studied their menus in companionable silence.

"How has the week been?" Justine inquired gently.

Rebecca stared into her wine glass. "I never once left my room. Never even got dressed," she confessed. "I'd get up occasionally to use the bathroom or shower, and then climb straight back into my robe and into bed," she continued, fidgeting with her napkin. "No TV, not even any daylight. I feel so utterly useless."

Justine didn't offer immediate reassurance or platitudes. She simply nodded, acknowledging Rebecca's experience without judgment. "Any news from Don?"

"I haven't looked at his texts or listened to the voice messages," Rebecca admitted with a helpless shrug. "I just couldn't. But he called this afternoon on the Solara phone."

"How did he know you were here?" Justine asked.

"Credit card—he gets notifications for any charges," she explained, her cheeks flushing red as she remembered his ire shouted through the phone.

A waiter arrived with their first course, elaborate presentations on oversized plates. Rebecca waited until he retreated before continuing.

"So when I checked in, he got an alert, and he wasn't very pleased." She choked back a hysterical yelp, somewhere between a laugh and a sob.

"You definitely need to arrange a credit card in your own name," admonished Justine.

"I know. Yes. And a bank account," Rebecca acknowledged with newfound resolve.

Rebecca's phone began to vibrate in her purse. She pulled it out, glancing at the screen. "It's Jodie. My daughter."

"You should probably take it," Justine suggested.

Rebecca nodded and answered the call. "Hello?"

"Mom?" Jodie's voice came through clearly, a mixture of confusion and concern. "Where are you? I went to pick you guys up from the airport, but you weren't there, and Dad's not answering his phone."

She winced, realizing that Don hadn't even bothered to tell their daughter not to come to the airport. Despite arranging dinner with the children to reveal the divorce news, he hadn't bothered to tell Jodie that he'd flown back early.

"Oh honey, I'm so sorry," she apologized. "Your father didn't tell you? He flew home on Monday."

There was a pause on the other end of the line. "What? No, he didn't tell me anything. Where is he? Where are *you*?" Jodie's voice cracked, tension giving way to confusion.

Rebecca heard the worry beneath the questions, the uncertainty in her daughter's voice that made her sound younger than her years. This wasn't a conversation that should happen while she was sitting in a restaurant with Justine.

"I'm okay, honey. I'm still in Las Vegas," Rebecca reassured her. "I can't explain right now, but I'll call you tomorrow, okay?"

"Tomorrow? Mom, what's going on? When are you coming home?"

"We'll talk tomorrow, I promise."

Rebecca calmly said goodbye and ended the call, silencing the ringer. She knew her daughter well enough to know that Jodie would be soon blowing up Don's phone, demanding answers.

Rebecca looked at Justine, mortification heating her cheeks. "I'm sorry about that. And about... everything, really. Being so useless." She stared down at her hands, twisting her wedding ring unconsciously. "I don't really have any friends—I've isolated them all. Even my own kids lean toward Don. I've always been such a... such a *lump*."

The word hung in the air between them—*lump*—Don's word for her in his more cutting moments. A domestic burden. An appendage rather than a partner. Even as she voiced it, something inside her rebelled against the label. She'd raised two children, maintained a home, supported Don's career for decades. How dare he reduce all that to worthlessness?

"That isn't true," Justine countered firmly, placing a cool hand over Rebecca's. "Not a single word of it. Everyone has value. You just need time to find yourself again."

Rebecca looked up, startled by the passion in Justine's voice.

"I've seen many people lose themselves while building families or careers," Justine continued, her voice unwavering. "Sometimes their whole selves."

Rebecca nodded, wondering if she was anything but a husk without Don Morley.

"Take what you need," Justine urged. "If that's days in a dark hotel room in Vegas, so be it, but never believe you are useless."

She paused as their main courses arrived, waiting until the server had departed before leaning in.

"Some people just give and give—and I suspect that's been you for years. Now it's time for you to take what you need to heal. Until you can stand on your own."

Her dark eyes held Rebecca's with a wise intensity. "But know when enough is enough. Don't spend too long staring at the bottom of the well. No growth happens there."

Rebecca felt tears well up—not the tears of despair she'd shed all week, but cleaner ones that washed away something stagnant inside her. The pressure in her chest eased like a spring uncoiling, each breath coming a little easier than before.

Growth, she mused. When was the last time she felt she had grown in any way, other than expanding around her waistline?

Justine smiled, a hint of weariness briefly crossing her features. "You know, I should take my own advice sometimes," she admitted, tucking a stray strand of hair behind her ear. "It's always easier to know what others should do than to apply it to yourself."

It was a small moment of vulnerability, but it made Justine seem suddenly more approachable, more human. Rebecca found herself wondering about Justine's own story, what experiences had shaped her wisdom.

They finished their meal with lighter conversation, Justine guiding them toward neutral topics that let Rebecca briefly escape her immediate concerns.

Approaching the elevators outside the Summit, Rebecca surprised them both by impulsively stepping forward to hug Justine.

"Thank you," she said softly. "For everything."

Justine returned the embrace before stepping back with a small smile. "Get some rest. *Real* rest."

Rebecca marveled at how quickly she'd come to trust this woman—a stranger days ago, now something closer to a friend. Perhaps it was simply that Justine was the first person in a very long time who had truly acknowledged her.

"Justine, will you be my lawyer? Don suggested asking someone at his firm, but..." she trailed off.

"Of course," Justine replied with a gentle squeeze to Rebecca's shoulder. "We don't need to work out formalities now. Call me anytime."

"Are you staying here?" Rebecca asked.

"No, but I'm going to visit the poker tables before heading out."

Rebecca nodded, remembering how respectfully Justine had been greeted at the Palisade. There was clearly more to this woman than met the eye.

They parted at the elevators, Justine heading toward the casino while Rebecca went up to her room, feeling like something had shifted. The crushing weight of abandonment still lingered, but it felt more manageable now.

Earlier, she'd felt like an imposter in the elegant restaurant, a shadow moving through spaces meant for the living. Now she felt more substantial, as if Justine's recognition had restored something essential that she'd forgotten existed. Her reflection still looked tired and hurt, but with a flicker of light in her eyes that hadn't been there before.

She drew the curtains tightly closed, but this time the darkness felt different—chosen rather than imposed, protective rather than imprisoning.

She climbed into bed with her head full of Justine's words and her belly full of the first proper meal she had eaten all week. *Take what you need.* The phrase followed her into sleep, a new mantra replacing the harsh soundtrack of self-recrimination that had been playing on repeat in her mind for days.

Her breathing slowed as her body surrendered to true rest. For the first time since Don had handed her a folder full of legal papers and shattered her world, Rebecca slept without dreams.

CHAPTER 9

S HE WOKE IN COMPLETE darkness. Her hand groped for the edge of the bed, finding instead the cocoon of blankets she'd created. She burrowed deeper, seeking sleep's oblivion, but consciousness had taken hold.

Her mind sharpened with unwelcome clarity. Her limbs felt heavy, reluctant to commit to awakening. The thought of her promise to call Jodie sent anxiety rippling through her.

With a sigh, Rebecca struggled from the bedding and fumbled for the lamp. The sudden light made her squint. The clock read 10:23 AM, though it felt earlier in the windowless darkness she'd cultivated.

The shower cleared her head, but her mood darkened as she rummaged through her suitcase. These clothes now seemed like artifacts from another woman's life. She pulled on jeans and a blouse, noticing with surprise how loose they hung.

Before the mirror, she took inventory. Her face looked thinner, stress-carved hollows beneath her cheekbones. Dark circles shadowed her eyes, and her hair hung limp, still damp from the shower. Self-loathing rolled through her.

Her stomach knotted, a bitter taste rising as her hands gripped the sink, knuckles whitening against the weight of her harsh self-judgment.

No wonder Don had found Annette more attractive. Annette with her wide smile and flat stomach, her confident bearing and professional accomplishments. Compared to that vibrant presence, Rebecca saw herself as washed out, used up, irrelevant.

She sank onto the edge of the tub, tears spilling down her cheeks. For several minutes, she allowed herself the indulgence of crying, of feeling the full weight of her perceived inadequacy.

When the tears subsided, she splashed cold water on her face and returned to the bedroom. Her phone lay on the nightstand—a ticking time bomb of obligations. She picked it up, steeling herself to call Jodie, and noticed a text from Justine: *Hope you slept well. I'm free for lunch if you'd like some company or to talk.*

Rebecca sat on the bed, considering. Part of her craved human connection, Justine's calm presence and practical wisdom. But another part, perhaps larger, wanted only to sink into darkness, hiding from the world's expectations—a pattern that now reminded her uncomfortably of how she'd learned to retreat whenever Don was displeased.

She typed an apologetic response: *Thanks, but I think I'll stay in today. Sorry. Rain check?*

Justine's reply came almost immediately: *No apologies necessary, Rebecca. I'll be in Vegas until Sunday evening if you'd like some company.*

The simple understanding in that message brought a fresh sting of tears to her eyes. A flutter of gratitude spread through her chest, momentarily loosening the perpetual tightness that had resided there since Don's divorce announcement.

She pressed her palm against her chest, as if to hold on to the fleeting sensation of being seen and accepted. When was the last time someone had respected her needs without question? Don had always required explanations, justifications for any deviation from his expectations.

Taking a deep breath, she scrolled to Jodie's number. Best to get this over with.

Her daughter answered on the second ring, her voice a mixture of relief and accusation. "Mom? Finally! What is going on with you? I've been worried sick!"

"I'm sorry, sweetheart," Rebecca began tentatively. "I should have called sooner. I needed some time to—"

"Look, Dad told me everything," Jodie interrupted sharply, her voice taking on a harder edge. "And you're being completely unreasonable about the whole thing."

Rebecca's breath caught in her throat. "Did he tell you the circumstances?" she countered, her voice gaining strength. "That he told me during our anniversary trip that he wants a divorce? That he left me in Las Vegas? That he had the wherewithal to prepare all the divorce paperwork a month before our trip?"

"No, Mom, he told me what actually happened, and that you'd be overdramatic about it," she replied dismissively, sarcasm laced through her words. "Dad says you two have been growing apart for years, discussing divorce, and now that it's happening, you're refusing to accept it. You're hiding out in Vegas to punish him instead of coming home to deal with things like an adult."

Rebecca recognized something in her daughter's voice with a chill—Don's cadence, Don's arrogance. The familiar dynamic reasserted itself with brutal efficiency—Don setting the narrative, Jodie aligning with her father's view of the world, Rebecca cast as the irrational one. It had been this way since Jodie was a teenager: father and daughter united in their practical, linear thinking against Rebecca's more intuitive approach.

A cold weight dropped into her stomach. The familiar sensation of shrinking inward began—shoulders slouching, chest compressing. She consciously forced her spine straight, resisting her habitual posture of submission.

"It's not that simple, Jodie," Rebecca tried again, fighting to keep her voice calm.

"It never is with you, Mom," Jodie sighed, the exasperation in her voice a perfect echo of Don's. "Look, I know divorce is hard, but you can't run away from your problems. I'm going to book you a flight for this afternoon, and you better be on that damn plane," she commanded.

The crude demand—so unlike Jodie's usual careful speech, so exactly like Don at his most imperious—broke through Rebecca's habitual deference. Twenty-five years of smoothing things over, of accepting Don's framing of events, of doubting her own perceptions when they conflicted with his—all of it suddenly felt like a weight she could no longer bear.

She felt a physical sensation like ice cracking, a rigid structure giving way to allow movement where there had only been frozen stillness. Her heartbeat steadied into a stronger, more determined rhythm.

"Don't bother," she stated firmly, her voice quiet but resolute.

"Excuse me?" Jodie demanded, incredulous at her mother's audacity.

"I said, don't bother booking me a flight. I'll book my own flight when I'm ready," Rebecca maintained calmly.

"Mom, this is silly—"

"I love you, Jodie," she interrupted mildly, astonishing herself with her calmness, "but I'm done being told what to do and how to feel. I'll call you soon."

She ended the call before Jodie could respond, her heart racing despite her measured words. She'd never directly contradicted Don's narrative to the children. She'd also never hung up on her daughter before.

Her hand trembled as she set the phone down, adrenaline coursing through her. Her breath was short and shallow. She tucked her hands under her thighs, willing the tremors to subside.

The room felt too warm suddenly, too confined. She forced herself to breathe deeply, to consider her next step rather than spiral into panic over the broken norms.

She paced the length of the hotel room, her mind racing with conflicting emotions. Part of her wanted to call Jodie back immediately—to apologize and repair the breach. The lifetime habit of preserving family harmony at her own expense wasn't easily set aside.

But beneath that familiar impulse ran a deeper current—a certainty that she had done the right thing. Jodie needed to understand that there were limits to what Rebecca would tolerate, even from her beloved daughter. Even if it meant temporary discord.

She stopped pacing and held her hands over her face, trying to sort through the tangle of thoughts and feelings. What would Don do when Jodie reported this conversation to him? He would be furious, perhaps even more determined to force her return. There would be consequences for this small rebellion—there always were when she stepped outside the boundaries he had established.

The realization that she was still anticipating Don's reaction, still orienting herself around his expected response, brought her up short. Even now, miles away from him, she was trapped in patterns established over decades of marriage.

She lowered her hands and took a calming breath. One step at a time. She didn't need to figure everything out today. She didn't need to have all the answers for Don or Jodie or Luke. What she needed was a moment of peace to center herself.

Luke. She should call Luke before Don shaped his understanding of the situation too.

She dialed her son's number, but it went to voicemail.

"Hi sweetie, it's Mom," she recorded hesitantly. "Give me a call when you can, okay? Just want to say hi." She paused, then added, "Love you."

She plugged in her phone and pulled open the blackout curtains, flinching at the flood of desert light that poured into the room. The contrast between her manufactured darkness and the bright reality was jarring.

Squinting against the assault of the sudden glare, she sank into the armchair by the window, blinking as her eyes continued to adjust. The warmth of the sunlight on her skin felt alien after days of climate-control—uncomfortable yet somehow necessary, like the sting of antiseptic on a neglected wound.

Her view encompassed the airport, planes rising and descending, and beyond it the vast Las Vegas valley, rimmed by hills in various shades of rust and brown, dotted with the dark green of hardy desert vegetation and the grey of exposed rock faces.

For what seemed like hours, Rebecca sat motionless, watching the planes come and go, the hills beyond changing subtly as the angle of the sun shifted.

Each departing plane represented a choice—the choice to not return to Savannah, to not face Don and the dissolution of their marriage, to not step back into the role that had defined her for twenty-five years. Each arriving plane brought others to this liminal city—for vacation, business, weddings or gambling. How many were escaping? How many had come to reinvent themselves?

The hills drew her gaze, their ancient solidity a counterpoint to the transient activity below. They had witnessed countless arrivals and departures, unchanged as civilizations rose and fell. Whatever she decided—to stay or go, to fight or concede—those hills would remain, indifferent to her small human drama. The thought was unexpectedly comforting.

For so long, she had measured her worth by how well she met the expectations of others—Don's, the children's, the community's. But those hills didn't expect anything from her. They simply existed, as she simply existed, regardless of roles or titles or others' approval.

Her phone chimed with a text alert, breaking her reverie. Jodie again, no doubt. But when she glanced at the screen, she was surprised to see a message from Helen: *Hey! Jodie reached out. Call me when you can? No judgment, just worried about you.*

Helen's message conveyed sincerity and support, and Rebecca smiled faintly. Helen Baker had been her anchor—her best friend—since sixth grade. The two had been inseparable through high school—both spirited and adventurous, though in different ways. While Helen was loud and sometimes reckless, Rebecca had been the creative force, always dreaming up projects, planning elaborate adventures, or finding beautiful ways to transform ordinary things.

In the early years of Rebecca's marriage, Helen had been her lifeline—the one person who still treated her like the vibrant woman she'd been before Don. Helen had coaxed her into journeys with the babies in tow, refusing to accept that motherhood meant the end of Rebecca's creative spirit. Helen had seen Don's controlling tendencies from the beginning, even when she herself couldn't.

Don had always dismissed Helen as too loud, too opinionated, too 'common'. He'd said she was disruptive, an indulgence that Rebecca should outgrow.

Gradually, her contact with Helen had dwindled to random texts and occasional catch-up dinners that Rebecca had to justify for days. They'd last seen each other two years earlier at Helen's mother's funeral, which Rebecca had attended despite Don's objections.

Helen navigated tense situations well, seeing multiple perspectives without taking sides. Unlike Don, who saw every disagreement as a battle to win, Helen understood relationships were complex. And she had known Rebecca when her eyes still sparkled, and her laugh came easily—before she became Mrs. Don Morley.

She would call Helen soon, but not quite yet. For now, she turned to the window, to the unfamiliar landscape that had drawn her attention since she'd thrown open the curtains. Tomorrow, perhaps, she would find the energy to venture out again, to face the world beyond this room. For today, this quiet observation, this pause between her old life and whatever came next, was exactly what she needed.

Chapter 10

The hum of the air conditioning shrouded her in white noise, matching her mental fog. Outside, sunset painted the sky in orange and gold, gradually deepening to purple, then black. She hadn't moved for hours, hadn't eaten anything since the night before.

Thoughts danced through her mind like leaves caught in a whirlwind—memories, regrets, questions she'd never dared to ask, even of herself. Jodie's voice echoed in her memory, the accusatory tone so like Don's: *You're hiding out in Vegas to punish him.*

Was that what she was doing? Hiding? Punishing? She wasn't sure anymore. The strength she'd found to stand up to her daughter had receded like a tide, leaving her beached and uncertain in its wake.

The room had grown dark, illuminated only by the Strip's glow through the windows. She flicked on a lamp, casting shadows across contemporary furnishings. The room felt impersonal, yet oddly like a sanctuary—unmarked by memories of her life with Don.

When her stomach finally growled in protest, she stood up, suddenly aware of the stiffness in her joints from sitting so long. She felt lost, unmoored. What was she supposed to do now? What did people do when their entire identity had been stripped away?

Justine's words from their dinner floated back to her again: *Take what you need.* The phrase had seemed so wise, so freeing in the moment. But now, alone in her hotel room, Rebecca wondered—what *did* she need? After twenty-five years of responding to Don's and the children's needs, she barely recognized her own.

The irony struck her suddenly. She'd spent decades anticipating others' needs, often before they voiced them. She could tell from the slightest shift in Don's expression what he wanted before he asked. She'd known exactly when Luke needed space or when Jodie craved attention. But her own needs? Those had become so deeply buried that excavating them felt like an archaeological dig through layers of her former self.

The decision to shower again came more from a need for motion than cleanliness, for water to wash away her paralysis. The cool tile shocked her bare feet. She turned on the faucet and the sudden rush of water echoed off the bathroom walls, a sound both ordinary and somehow cleansing in itself.

She stripped off her clothes, avoiding her reflection in the bathroom mirror, and stepped under the spray. Turning the temperature up until it was just shy of scalding, the hot water pounded against her shoulders and back.

Steam billowed around her, cocooning her in a private cloud. The rainfall showerhead created a soothing rhythm.

She scrubbed her skin hard with a loofah, as if she could physically scour away the bad memories of recent events, the things she wasn't proud of, the poor decisions she had made throughout her life.

Her hands moved over her body, lingering on the soft curve of her belly, the flabby undersides of her arms. She flushed with embarrassment at how she had let herself go. She remembered her trim waist and toned legs from her twenties, how Don used to run his hands over her skin with true appreciation. When had that stopped? When had she become invisible to him?

She reached for the hotel shampoo, noting its luxurious weight, the subtle scent of bergamot. Even these small amenities felt indulgent compared to the unscented products Don preferred—products that wouldn't 'compete with his cologne'.

An image of Annette surfaced—the company picnic last summer. Annette in a sundress showing off her lightly muscled arms and tanned legs. She could almost smell the charcoal BBQ and the sunscreen, hear the laughter of children playing volleyball, feel the sticky humidity that made her own dress cling uncomfortably while Annette remained impossibly fresh.

Rebecca remembered how Don had introduced them, his dismissive glance as Annette introduced her own date for the party. Had the affair been happening even then? How long had it been going on before Don decided to officially end their marriage? Would it still secretly be going on if Annette's pregnancy hadn't forced his hand?

She tried to remember the last time Don had approached her for sex. Six months ago? Longer? And with a stab of shame, she realized she was rarely, if ever, the one to initiate intimacy. Had she contributed to the death of their marriage through her passivity? Was this all somehow her fault?

Still, she thought, as the scalding water pulsed on her shoulders, they could have talked about it. But then, it wasn't easy to talk to Don about anything. He was always so sharp, so harsh and condescending. She flinched, remembering how he'd dismiss her opinions in social gatherings with a casual *'Rebecca doesn't really understand these things,'* or *'Sorry guys—my wife isn't exactly a genius.'*

Had he always been that way? The question hung in the steam-filled bathroom, demanding an answer she wasn't sure she wanted to confront.

How much effort would it take to get him back? The thought appeared unbidden, shocking her with its persistence. Did she even *want* him back? Would it solely be for security—to allay her fears of the unknown? It was scary to contemplate starting a career in her mid-forties. She hadn't even thought about what she'd like to do professionally, having spent so many years focused on maintaining Don's home and raising their children.

She remembered bringing up the idea of a part-time job once when the kids were in high school. Don had berated her, his voice sharp with disapproval. *'What message would that send to our friends, and to my colleagues? That my wife HAS to work, that we aren't secure financially with my career? That is the WRONG message, Rebecca,'* he had thundered, scornfully attaching her name to the end of his reprimand to drive the point home.

Rebecca could still picture the way his face had tightened, how spittle had gathered at the corners of his mouth as his rant gained momentum. The memory struck her now not with the familiar pang of inadequacy, but with a sudden sense of revulsion.

He'd suggested she take up hobbies *'appropriate for a partner's wife'*—whatever that meant—if *'keeping his home'* wasn't enough to satisfy her. The condescension in his tone had been palpable, though she'd let it pass at the time.

Don truly had a low opinion of her, she realized with startling clarity. All these years, she'd been trying to please someone who fundamentally didn't respect her.

The shower spray suddenly felt too harsh against her sensitized skin, each droplet a tiny judgment. She wrenched the tap off with a decisive twist.

What struck her now wasn't only that Don had been critical—she'd always known that—but that his criticism had been strategic. Each comment about her appearance, her intelligence, her capabilities, had all served a purpose—to make her dependent on his approval, to keep her small and manageable. The pattern was suddenly so clear it took her breath away.

Don't spend too long staring at the bottom of the well, Justine had cautioned. *No growth happens there.* Was that what she'd been doing? Staring at the bottom of the well? The metaphor resonated uncomfortably. Justine was right—she couldn't hide forever, couldn't keep avoiding the situation.

She dried herself roughly with a towel, as if she could rub away the years of bad memories, self-deprecation, and disappointment along with the water droplets.

Wrapping herself in the silky robe, she padded to the bedroom. Her feet sank into the plush carpet, a small pleasure she hadn't noticed before. She picked up the room service menu, admiring the leather cover, the glossy pages. This was luxury she was choosing for herself, not experiencing as Don's accessory.

For the first time in days, she felt genuinely hungry. She called down for her favorite comfort food—poached eggs on sourdough with sliced tomato. Don had always sneered at having breakfast for dinner.

The voice on the other end of the line was friendly and unhurried, asking if she'd like to add juice or coffee to her order. The question—what did she want—momentarily caught her off guard. When had anyone last asked about her preferences without judgment?

While waiting for her food to arrive, Rebecca settled by the window, looking toward the Strip. The Vegas skyline glittered like a jewel box spilled open across the desert floor. The Eiffel Tower replica, Lady Liberty framed against the backdrop of a roller coaster, the rising spear of light from the Luxor—all of it so foreign to her. In this world, she thought, she could be anybody.

With her identity as Don Morley's wife stripped away, all that was left was a blank canvas she had no idea how to fill. But maybe, just maybe, that emptiness wasn't something to fear. Maybe it was an opportunity.

A subtle knock at the door announced her meal. Rebecca tightened the belt of her robe and answered the door. The hallway was hushed, subtle lighting creating pools of amber on the carpet—a silent corridor in this buzzing hive where thousands of other lives unfolded behind closed doors.

"Thank you," she smiled at the server—the first true smile that had crossed her face in days.

He placed the tray by the window, and she handed him a generous tip.

Taking a bite of the perfectly poached egg, yolk spilling over the sourdough, she closed her eyes in appreciation. The textures delighted her—crisp bread, soft yolk, the bright acidity of the tomato cutting through the richness. She caught herself making a sound of pleasure that Don would have mocked as overdramatic. The salt crystals crunched between her teeth, and she realized she was actually tasting her food rather than eating as a form of routine.

Don wasn't here to judge her choices, to raise an eyebrow at her pedestrian tastes or remind her about not eating carbs after 7 PM. She could eat what she wanted, when she wanted. She could wear what she wanted. Say what she wanted. Be who she wanted.

Her defiance with Jodie had unlocked something in her, small but significant. *'I'm done being told what to do and how to feel'*, she'd said. The words had come almost without thought, but they contained a truth she was only beginning to recognize. She was done being managed, done being corrected, done being made to feel 'less-than'.

For the first time since Don had uttered the word *divorce*, Rebecca felt something other than grief and uncertainty. It was small, fragile, barely formed—but unmistakable.

It was hope. A warmth spread through her entire body—not happiness, but a path in that direction. She placed her hand over her heart, as if to protect this fragile feeling.

Chapter 11

THE ROOM WAS LIGHTENING at the edges of the partially-closed blackout curtains. She lay still, taking inventory of her feelings. The crushing weight of the past days eased, leaving just enough space for something else—curiosity, perhaps.

Last night's revelation lingered with her—that startling moment when she'd realized she could make choices without Don's approval or oversight. She had gone to sleep with a fragile sense of hope, and somehow, it hadn't evaporated with the morning light.

The pain of Don's betrayal still throbbed beneath the surface, and the fear of an uncertain future hadn't disappeared. But something had changed during the night. That simple act of ordering what she wanted for dinner, of savoring flavors without judgment, had awakened a hunger for more such moments.

The thought of spending another day in darkened isolation suddenly felt intolerable. The room that was her sanctuary now felt like a self-imposed prison. She needed to move, breathe different air, see if that fleeting sense of hope could sustain itself beyond these four walls.

The bedside clock read 5:48 AM. Without overthinking it, she got up, brushed her teeth, and pulled on her clothes—the same unremarkable outfit she'd worn the day before. Grabbing her room key and purse, she headed out the door before she could talk herself out of it.

The hallway stretched before her, carpet muffling her footsteps as she made her way past identical doors to the elevator bank.

The elevator was lined with mirrors. She studied herself—face gaunt, eyes hollowed.

The descent to the ground floor was swift. The doors opened to the casino, slot machines blinking and chirping even at this early hour, players gazing at the video screens with various degrees of focus and contemplation.

Rebecca moved with purpose, though she wasn't entirely sure where she was going. All she knew was that she needed to be outside, to feel fresh air on her skin after days of being cooped up in her hotel room.

She wandered through the vast casino, looking for signs to direct her. The sheer scale of the resort was disorienting. After a few minutes of aimless searching, she approached a security guard standing near a bank of elevators.

"Excuse me," she said, her voice sounding unexpectedly confident. "How do I get outside?"

The guard looked at her with mild confusion. "Where outside, ma'am?"

"The Strip," she said decisively.

He nodded. "Best way is through those shops. Tram's not running this early." He pointed to the hallway. "Head that way, straight to the end of the mall. Then right, down the escalator to the Strip exit."

Rebecca thanked him, setting off in the direction he'd indicated.

The massive shopping hall was eerily quiet, her footsteps echoing as she navigated the winding path. Following the brightness to her right, she descended the escalator, heart lifting at the natural light ahead. She quickened her pace, desperate to be outside.

Finally pushing through the doors to Las Vegas Boulevard, the morning air hit her skin like a benediction. The Strip was relatively quiet at this hour—a few early joggers, casino workers heading home after night shift, a maintenance crew power-washing the sidewalk. Massive hotels loomed on either side, neon and LED signs still bright against the lightening sky.

Rebecca oriented herself. To the north stretched the distinctive skyline, the Stratosphere in the distance. On impulse, she headed that way, crossing a road, past a castle and over a bridge until she descended to the sidewalk below.

The air carried a coolness that would burn off within hours. Her skin prickled with goosebumps as she passed through patches of shadow between hotels. The concrete felt solid beneath her feet, each step grounding her more firmly in reality after days of floating in an emotional void.

And as she started to walk, something planted itself in the pit of her stomach. The start of something new. She pictured it as a tiny seedling that she'd need to protect at all costs, until it grew strong enough to survive on its own.

She continued walking north, looking around at the familiar brand names rendered surreal at massive scale—a giant Coca-Cola bottle and a huge Hershey bar, the enormous Titan statue of a towering bronze Atlas holding up the world. The sun rose higher, warming her shoulders through her blouse. She lost track of time, content to simply move her body, to observe the city awakening around her.

Slightly off the Strip, a sideways glance down an alley drew her eye to a small, older-looking diner. *Saddle's—OPEN 24 HOURS!* blinked in faded red letters, half the bulbs burned out.

The diner was a stark contrast to the Strip's gleaming excess—cracked vinyl booths, scratched Formica counter with swiveling stools, waitresses bustling around in sneakers. She slid onto a stool toward the end of the counter, comforted by the diner's unpretentious atmosphere.

"Coffee?" A waitress appeared almost instantly, coffeepot in hand.

"Please. And may I see a menu?"

Two cups of black coffee and a plate of poached eggs on toast with crispy bacon later, Rebecca felt fortified. The simple food was exactly what she needed—no pretense, no garnish, just honest nourishment. She paid with cash and slid off the stool, ready to continue her exploration.

Near the door, she crossed paths with a tall, wiry man in jeans and worn boots. He had leathery skin and piercing blue eyes, and he nodded politely as they passed in the entry. She paused, feeling oddly like she should say something, then realized she didn't actually have anything to say.

Shaking her head as though to clear the thought, she hit the sidewalk at a moderate pace, continuing north past the Palisade fountain, past the Aureus, the Mirage and Treasure Island. Her sensible shoes began to pinch, but she pressed on, unwilling to end her journey quite yet. When she checked her watch, she was startled to see she'd been walking for over four hours. No wonder her feet ached.

Crossing yet another pedestrian bridge, Rebecca caught a glimpse of herself in a store window. The woman staring back looked bland in loose, shapeless clothes, hair pulled up in the 'age-appropriate' ponytail Don preferred. She'd dressed exactly as he'd trained her to over the years—invisible, matronly, nothing that might draw attention or suggest confidence.

Ahead, she spotted a Macy's sign. On impulse, she headed inside, suddenly aware that her current wardrobe didn't suit her new reality. She needed practical things, comfortable things. Things she herself liked, that didn't require Don's approval.

You need something to distract the eye, he'd say, with that particular smile that managed to be both affectionate and pitying.

She chose some exercise shorts, moving through the racks with growing decisiveness before hesitating at a rack filled with long V-neck

T-shirts—plain, not patterned. *Solid colors emphasize your problem areas,* she heard Don's critical voice in her head.

As she ran her hands over a black shirt, she wondered if he'd been deliberately steering her toward clothes that made her feel frumpy. Had that been part of his plan? To keep her feeling unattractive so she wouldn't question why her husband's interest had waned? To keep her feeling inadequate while he pursued women like Annette, with her fitted clothes and lively personality? The realization sent a spark of irritation through her—one more manipulation she hadn't recognized until now.

She pulled the black shirt from the rack with sudden determination, then added a dark green one—simple colors that felt clean and uncomplicated. These weren't shirts chosen to hide or distract—they were chosen because she wanted them. The distinction felt significant in a way she couldn't fully articulate.

She added a sports bra to her selections, then made her way to the shoe department, where she chose a pair of Nike running shoes and cushioned socks. When had she last owned proper athletic shoes? Don had always dismissed her occasional mentions of taking up walking or jogging. *At your age? Not with your knees,* he'd say, as if she were ancient and decrepit at forty-five.

It was a start—a wardrobe built around her own desires, not his assessment of her flaws. Not a fashion statement, perhaps, but a declaration of independence, nonetheless.

On a whim, she grabbed a long, flowing casual dress in a soft grey and added it to her cart without trying it on. The fabric felt good between her fingers, and that was reason enough.

As she waited at checkout, she wondered what Justine might think of her adventure. The thought surprised her—when had she started measuring herself against this near-stranger's opinion? But there was something compelling about Justine's self-possession. Rebecca didn't want to become like Justine—she just wanted to rediscover herself. Yet she couldn't deny that the woman's independence had awakened something long dormant in her.

She handed over her AMEX without any anxiety about Don's reaction. A voice reminded her she'd need her own bank account soon, that she should be careful with money until the divorce settled. But that was tomorrow's problem. Today was about reclaiming herself, even if it cost a couple hundred dollars.

Making her way back to the Solara, her feet ached in her inadequate shoes, but her spirit felt lighter than it had in days. In the room, she dropped her shopping bags on the bed and opened the curtains, letting the sunlight flood in.

Her window framed a slice of the Solara Beach—wave pool, lazy river, and sand beaches. Children splashed while adults lounged with tropical drinks. The scene looked inviting, playful in a way that appealed to her newly awakened senses.

Rebecca dug through her suitcase, finding the swimsuit she'd packed for the anniversary trip—a modest one-piece in navy-and-green floral, subtle ruching to minimize her stomach and a skirt to cover her backside and thighs. She'd chosen it carefully to meet Don's approval.

She held it up, considering. Then she suddenly flung it across the room, missing the garbage bin by a foot. She reached for the hotel phone. The concierge answered on the second ring.

"Yes, I'd like to know if there's a shop in the hotel that has swimwear?"

There was, of course. Vegas seemed to be a place where every need could be met within each individual resort. The concierge directed her to a boutique near the pool.

Twenty minutes later, Rebecca stood in a dressing room, examining her reflection in a swimsuit she would never have dared to choose before—a vibrant turquoise tankini with a halter top that showed more cleavage than she was used to displaying. The bottoms were cut like shorts with a wide buckle, practical while somewhat flattering.

It wasn't the boldest suit in the shop, but it was miles from what Don would have deemed *suitable for a woman of her size and shape.* And she liked it.

She made her way to the pool complex, finding an unoccupied lounge chair in a relatively quiet corner. A familiar voice echoed in her mind—Don's disapproving tone, questioning why she'd choose something so unsuitable.

For a moment, doubt crept in. Was the swimsuit too revealing? Too youthful? She glanced around, half-expecting to see judgmental stares. But no one was looking. No one cared. The realization was both startling and liberating—her body, her choices, were simply not the center of anyone else's attention. The scrutiny she'd lived under for years had been uniquely Don's, not the entire world's.

With a deep breath, she stood and walked toward the water, conscious of the unfamiliar feeling of being so exposed. The water welcomed her, cool against the desert heat. She pushed off from the edge and began to swim with long, smooth strokes, her body remembering the motions from childhood summers.

As she cut through the water, something unfurled inside her—a physical pleasure she hadn't experienced in years. Her body moving through space, and the sensations of water and sun and effort.

For these few moments, she wasn't anyone's soon-to-be ex-wife. She wasn't a middle-aged woman whose future had been thrown into uncertainty. She wasn't defined by her failures or her fears.

She was simply a woman swimming on a beautiful day. And that was enough.

Chapter 12

FLOATING IN THE COOL blue water of the Solara pool with arms outstretched, Rebecca stared up at the green palm fronds backed by blue skies. The water muted the noise around her, her body rocked lightly on the surface.

Absorbed by the beauty of the cloudless sky and the coolness of the water against her skin, she wondered if she would have ever noticed a feeling like this if she were here with Don, and decided not likely.

She thought about Jodie's accusation that she was being childish. Unable to decide how she felt about the comment, she decided to play a little game with herself, timing how long she could go without a thought of Don, Annette, the divorce paperwork, or really anything at all to do with the situation.

Don's scowl surfaced in her mind almost immediately. Less than a minute without him. Everything reminded her of him—the families in the pool, the young couples, even the palm trees.

"GAH!" she exclaimed, standing to gather her things. But far from feeling like a failure, she was impressed with herself for not being reduced to tears from the memories.

Exhausted from walking, swimming and sun, she headed to her room for an early night.

She drew the blackout curtains closed, took a shower, and slid into the freshly made bed. Something didn't feel right, so she jumped back out of bed and flung the curtains open wide.

She didn't want to miss the sunrise, even if the alarm was set. The sunrise felt important somehow, like a small ritual she was establishing for herself.

When the alarm chimed the next morning, Rebecca rose without hesitation, pulling on her new exercise clothes with a sense of purpose. The Nike shoes felt wonderfully cushioned compared to her old slip-ons, and the plain T-shirt and shorts were comfortable in a way her usual wardrobe rarely was. Plus, they were *hers*. She'd chosen them, with no advice or opinion from anyone else.

She headed out into the morning sunshine, retracing her steps from yesterday toward the Strip. As she walked, she noticed something unexpected—she wasn't scared. Not of being alone, not of the unfamiliar surroundings, not of the day ahead. The sensation was so novel that she paused at the corner of Tropicana and Las Vegas Boulevard, just to acknowledge it.

There was a lightness in her step that hadn't been there yesterday, a subtle straightening of her spine. The physical sensation of freedom settled into her muscles, making her movements more fluid, less guarded. She took up more space on the sidewalk without unconsciously shrinking to avoid being seen. She smiled and said hello to other early-morning walkers.

Her feet automatically carried her down the side street toward Saddle's Diner. She pushed open the door, the bell jangling to announce her arrival. To her surprise, the wiry man with the piercing blue eyes was already perched on the stool at the end of the counter—the same spot where she had sat yesterday.

Rebecca chose a stool toward the middle of the counter, nodding politely to the man as she sat down.

Nodding a greeting in return, he turned his attention to his iPhone, fingers scrolling absently across the screen.

Rebecca glanced at her menu, though she already knew her choice. *I want an iPhone*, she decided suddenly, watching him navigate the screen with practiced ease. Don's snide voice badgered at the corner of her mind—*Smartphones are for smart people.*

She could picture his face so clearly—that expression of amused condescension he reserved for moments when she suggested an interest in something he deemed beyond her capabilities. It was the same look he'd given her when she'd tried to discuss a business article she'd read—*Let's not pretend you understand economics, Bec.*

Over the years, she'd learned to filter her desires through his imagined reactions, discarding most before even articulating them. Today, instead of letting his voice derail her, she felt a flicker of defiance. Maybe smartphones *were* for smart people—and maybe she was smarter than Don had ever given her credit for.

When the waitress appeared, Rebecca ordered the same breakfast as yesterday—poached eggs, crispy bacon, sourdough toast with butter.

The meal arrived quickly. She ate with enthusiasm but soon discovered her eyes were bigger than her stomach, and couldn't finish her meal.

Leaving more than enough cash to cover the bill and a generous tip, she slid somewhat clumsily off the stool and headed out to continue her walk.

The morning air was still pleasant, but she could feel the day's heat building. Halfway up the Strip, Rebecca decided to cut her walk short. Her mind was racing with all the things she needed to do—practical steps toward independence that could no longer be postponed.

She sat by the window in her hotel room with a pen and a notepad, making a list:

- *Call Don*

- *Call Jodie*

- *Bank account*

- *iPhone!!*

- *Call Helen*

- *Call Justine*

She reviewed what she'd written, the first two items making her jaw clench with anxiety. Not yet. She wasn't ready for those conversations yet. Instead, she decided to start in the middle of the list.

Rebecca tucked the notepad into her purse and went downstairs to hail a taxi.

"Where to?"

"Founders Union bank, please," Rebecca directed.

"Which one? There's a few around," the driver pointed out.

"Whichever is closest," she decided, realizing she hadn't thought that far ahead.

Twenty minutes later, Rebecca sat across from a personal banker at Founders Union, fumbling her way through opening both a checking and a savings account for herself. As the banker gathered her information, it struck her that this was the first time she'd had an account in her own name since she was twenty years old.

She wondered if Don also had a his own bank account, separate from their joint accounts. It seemed likely, given how systematically he had planned their divorce. How many other aspects of their life had been hidden from her?

"Is there anything else I can help you with today?" the banker concluded, handing her a folder with her account information.

"Yes, actually," Rebecca said, straightening in her chair. "I'd like to transfer some money. Is that possible?"

"Of course. I can show you how to do it online if you like."

"Oh! I actually don't have a computer. Or a smartphone. I've never used online banking."

The young banker looked half-startled, half-amused, as though Rebecca was a novelty on exhibit.

"Okay, no problem. I can see your accounts here," he continued, swiveling the screen around so she could see it. "Which one would you like to transfer from?"

She had already calculated slightly less than half of the balances in each account. Rounding down, she would take $8,000 from checking right away, but felt she should check with Don before moving anything from savings. She noted with curiosity that the total balance in the checking account had been reduced by $4,000 since she had checked the balances for the divorce paperwork.

"I'd like to transfer $8,000 from the joint checking to my new account, please," she stated decisively.

The banker nodded and began typing. Her confidence wavered. Was this too much—or not enough? What if Don noticed immediately and called to berate her? Her hand instinctively reached for her wedding ring, twisting it nervously. But then she remembered his face when he'd told her about Annette, the cold calculation in his eyes. If he'd been planning this for months, she had every right to protect herself now. She lowered her hand deliberately to her lap and took a deep breath.

With the transaction complete, Rebecca's heart quickened. It felt shockingly easy—both terrifying and empowering. She had never moved that much money without consulting Don before.

A tingling sensation spread from her fingertips up her arms, as if the simple act of moving money had sent an electric current through her. Even her vision seemed sharper, the colors more vivid.

As soon as she was out the door, she immediately turned around and walked back in, heading straight to the banker she'd just spoken to.

"I meant to ask," she said, "if it would be possible for me to have a credit card solely in my name as well?"

"We can check," the banker said, offering her a chair. After about 15 minutes, he advised that she'd been approved. He slid a printed page across to her with the card information.

"This is absolutely perfect," she sighed. Don wouldn't be able to check on every purchase she made from here on in.

"The physical card will be delivered to your home in about 5 to 7 business days, but in the meantime, it's active for online purchases," the banker told her. She visibly sank in the chair.

"Oh no, that won't do. I'm not going to be at home. Could I have it sent here?"

"Branch pick-up. Not a problem," he confirmed, clacking away at the keyboard. "It'll actually be quicker—here in 3 to 4 business days. We can call you when it arrives, if you like."

Relieved, she thanked him. This was all so much easier than she had thought it would be.

She headed out into the glaring Las Vegas sun, hailing a passing taxi on Maryland Parkway.

The taxi merged into traffic, and Rebecca watched the Strip slide past the window as she headed toward the Apple Store.

She froze at the entrance, then forced herself to walk in. All around her, shoppers tapped and swiped at gleaming devices with practiced ease.

You'll embarrass yourself. You won't understand a word, and they'll know it.

Don's voice, as familiar as her own thoughts.

A sales associate approached. "Can I help you find something?"

Rebecca's fingers tightened around her purse strap. "An iPhone. I'd like an iPhone. But I don't know anything about them."

"That's no problem at all." The woman's smile held no judgment. "Let's find the right one for you."

As they moved between display tables, Rebecca's attention drifted to the laptops. Refined. Beautiful. Forbidden.

What do you need a laptop for? Don's dismissive laugh echoed. *I'll be the one having to fix it every time you use it.*

"This model is very popular," the associate was saying, pointing to the phones. "It comes in several configurations and colors—"

"I like the lavender one."

"Ultramarine. Very popular choice," the associate began, but Rebecca interrupted, pointing to the MacBooks. "And one of those."

The words startled her, but the immediate lightness in her chest didn't.

The associate's eyebrows rose slightly, pleasantly. "Great! Did you have a particular model in mind?"

For fifteen minutes, Rebecca listened, asked questions, made decisions, and signed up for an introductory training—without seeking permission, without second-guessing. Each choice felt like reclaiming territory long surrendered.

The MacBook Air would fit perfectly in her handbag. Portable. Private. Hers.

The associate processed her purchase. "Will that be all?"

Rebecca glanced at the store exit, imagining herself walking through it carrying these objects Don would never have allowed her to own.

It felt strange to choose without Don's—or Jodie's—approval. Strange, but good. "Yes," she said. "That's all."

By the time she left the Apple Store, Rebecca's new bank account was significantly lighter, but she felt happily unburdened. The weight of her purchases in their crisp white bags gave her a curious sense of accomplishment as she made her way through the mall. She'd arrived by taxi but decided to walk back along the Strip—simply because she wanted to.

The distant profile of the Solara guided her south. Rebecca moved through the crowds with newfound ease. She no longer felt like a displaced visitor, but more like a temporary resident with her own rhythms and routines.

Back in her room, Rebecca unpacked her new devices, setting them on the desk. The lavender phone gleamed under the lights—a brand-new number that no one else knew, with a 702 area code.

Here, finally, was something Don couldn't control or criticize. She squared her shoulders, pressed the power button, and smiled as the screen lit up with "Welcome" in half a dozen languages she didn't speak. The word felt meant for her.

CHAPTER 13

R EBECCA STARED AT HER list. She'd successfully tackled two concrete steps toward independence. Now it was time to face the music.

She picked up her old flip phone and clicked down to Don's number. Her thumb hesitated over the call button before she pressed it, her heart quickening as the phone began to ring.

One ring. Two rings. Three. Four.

Don's voicemail picked up. "You've reached Don Morley. Leave a message and I'll return your call at my earliest convenience."

She ended the call without leaving a message. She wasn't surprised—it was a power move, making her wait. She briefly regretted not saying what she needed to on his voicemail.

Almost immediately, her phone rang. Don's name flashed on the tiny screen.

She took a deep breath and answered. "Hello, Don."

Her body tightened involuntarily, as if preparing for physical impact rather than just a conversation. The familiar tension returned to her jaw, teeth clenching slightly against words that might betray weakness.

"Rebecca." His voice sounded resigned, lacking the sharp edge of anger she'd anticipated. "Where are you? Have you finally come to your senses?"

"I'm still in Las Vegas, and very much in possession of all my senses," she countered.

"This has gone on long enough," he admonished, as though speaking to an errant child. "You need to fly home so we can discuss this rationally. I've set up a mediation for next Monday, and since you insist on having a lawyer of your own, I've asked John Rathway to represent you. He's an excellent family lawyer, one of the best in the firm—"

"Don—" The word caught in her throat as decades of conditioning urged her to stay silent. She took a deep breath, her fingers gripping the phone tighter. The hand not holding the phone had curled into a fist at her side, not in anger but as if physically gathering her courage.

"Don," she tried again, interjecting with assertiveness. A rush of heat flooded her face, her pulse quickening not with the usual anxiety but with staunch defiance.

"I have a lawyer," she continued. "Her name is Justine Avery, and if you'd like, I'll have her contact your lawyer, but I am not going to be represented by a colleague of both you and your girlfriend."

There was a moment of silence on the other end of the line. She could almost picture his face—that tight-lipped look he got when he was caught off-guard.

"Who the hell is Justine Avery?" he finally challenged. "You found a lawyer in Las Vegas?"

"It doesn't matter where I found her. What matters is that she's representing me."

Don exhaled sharply. "This is so stupid, Rebecca," he muttered. "You're making this more complicated than it needs to be."

"I'm protecting myself, Don. You can't just decide all the terms of our divorce on your own, simply because the divorce was your choice."

Another pause. Then, "What's that supposed to mean?"

"It means I have learned a bit about how divorce proceedings go," she explained, moving to the window and looking out at the Strip in the afternoon light. "Which is why I wanted to let you know that I've opened my own bank account. I've transferred half the money from our joint checking account."

"I saw the transfer, but it was quite a bit more than half," he acknowledged dryly.

"Okay. Good. Right—I noticed that you'd withdrawn $4,000 of your half *after* the date of our separation, so it was half the balance as of that date. But I wanted to speak with you before moving anything from savings."

Don let out a sound that was half-laugh, half-scoff. "Well, how very considerate of you. You realize I offered you half the savings in my settlement agreement, right?" he spat, barely controlled rage giving his voice a high-pitched edge. "So you can get off your damn high horse and take half of the damn savings."

"I'll do that," she said—then felt the old reflex of being secondary to his superiority rising within her, and let the *thank you* die in her throat.

How many times had she thanked him for allowing her to make basic decisions? How often had she expressed gratitude for things rightfully hers? The pattern was deeply ingrained—breaking it would require constant vigilance. It wasn't solely about standing up to Don in this one phone call—it was about recognizing and challenging twenty-five years of conditioning. She would need to notice these moments and deliberately choose different responses to break that pattern.

"And when are you coming home?"

"I don't know yet."

"The kids are asking questions, Rebecca. I can't keep putting them off."

She felt a pang of guilt at the mention of their children. "I've spoken to Jodie. I'll call them both again soon."

"Fine." His voice took on a businesslike tone. "Now, about the revisions you scribbled on the agreement—"

"Yes?" she asked, tensing.

"I'm not filing that bullshit," he stated flatly. "It's completely unreasonable. Triple the alimony for five more years than you're entitled to? The house free and clear? You're living in a fantasy world if you think—"

She pulled the phone away from her ear and pressed End, cutting him off mid-sentence. She stood still, waiting for the rush of anxiety that usually followed any confrontation with Don. To her amazement, it didn't come. Instead, she felt an odd sense of calm.

Her breathing remained even, shoulders loose—as if ending the call had severed more than the line.

She looked down at her list and drew a line through 'Call Don'. Then, after a moment's hesitation, she also drew a line through 'Call Jodie'. She'd had enough berating for one day. Her daughter's questions could wait until tomorrow.

She picked up her new iPhone. It was time to call someone who might actually be happy to hear from her.

Looking up Helen's number in her old flip phone, she added it in as her first iPhone contact, wondering if Helen would even want to speak to her after so much time had passed.

"Hello?" Helen's voice, slightly raspy, answered on the third ring.

"Hi, Helen. It's Rebecca."

"Rebel!" Helen exclaimed, genuine pleasure in her voice.

Something fluttered in Rebecca's chest at the sound of her old nickname—a name for someone she'd almost forgotten about. Warmth spread from her sternum outward, like armor filling in places left vulnerable for too long.

"Oh my God, what is going on? How are you, honey?" Helen's concerned voice continued.

Rebecca's eyes stung with unexpected tears. "I'm... well, I'm not great, actually."

"Tell me everything," Helen urged. "Start with, are you okay?"

"Yes, I'm okay. Don and I are getting divorced," Rebecca said, the words still strange on her tongue.

"Jodie mentioned that you had been talking about separating. She also said you'd run off to Vegas."

"Not exactly. I am in Las Vegas though. He's having a baby with his co-worker. We came to Vegas for our 25th, and he told me he wanted a divorce. On our first night here. In the middle of a show." The tears started to roll down Rebecca's cheeks, and her voice cracked. "He left me here, Helen. Flew home the next day."

There was a beat of silence, then Helen's forceful response: "Oh, good RIDDANCE!"

Rebecca laughed—actually laughed through her tears—for what felt like the first time in weeks.

The sensation was startling—her diaphragm contracting, shoulders shaking, throat open. Her body remembered how to laugh before her mind registered permission. The shared mirth connected her to a version of herself she'd nearly forgotten. Helen's unequivocal support was a balm to her raw emotions.

"You want to tell me what happened? I've only got hours before I have to be anywhere," she drawled with a chuckle, settling in for an overdue catch-up call. Helen had always set her friendship with Rebecca as 'high priority'.

Rebecca settled onto the bed, kicked off her shoes, and began to talk. She told Helen everything—the long-awaited anniversary trip to Vegas, Don's cold presentation of the divorce papers, his affair with Annette, the pregnancy. She described meeting Justine, her days of isolated depression in the hotel room, and her recent steps toward independence. Helen listened, occasionally interrupting with colorful comments about Don's character that made Rebecca both cringe and smile.

"Oh, honey, why didn't you call me?" Helen asked finally.

Rebecca hesitated. "I thought about it, but... it's been so long. I wasn't sure if—"

"If what? If I'd care?" Helen's voice softened. "Rebel, some friendships don't need upkeep. They pick up right where they left off."

Helen's kind-heartedness dissolved the last of Rebecca's reservations. She hadn't realized how much she'd feared judgment—even from Helen—for letting their friendship fade while she'd been consumed by Don's world.

"And so I'm calling you now," Rebecca replied with a smile. The response contained a hint of the playful defiance that had once been so natural to her. Where had that been hiding?

Only moments ago, she'd been falling back into old patterns with Don, and now here was this flash of her former self, emerging in conversation with Helen as if it had been lying dormant all these years, waiting for the right conditions to resurface. Perhaps reclaiming herself wouldn't require building something new so much as excavating what had been buried—uncovering pieces of 'Rebel' that Don had suppressed but never fully erased.

"He's always been such a pompous ass," Helen pronounced, her voice full of long-held conviction. "Remember that time at our housewarming party when he spent fifteen minutes lecturing Jim about the proper way to grill a steak? On Jim's own damned grill!"

"I was so embarrassed," Rebecca admitted. "I apologized to Jim for weeks afterward."

"You were always apologizing for Don. Always making excuses. It's about time you put yourself first. How are the kids handling it?"

Rebecca sighed. "Jodie's firmly on her father's side. She tore strips off me the last time we talked—just demanded that I come home."

"She's hurt," Helen observed. "Sometimes anger is easier."

"Maybe. I hear something in her voice though, beneath the anger. Confusion, maybe even fear. Her secure world is suddenly unstable, and I'm not there to help her through it." Rebecca swallowed hard. "That's the worst part."

They talked for well over an hour, moving from Don to reminiscences about college days, to updates on Helen's life—she'd split from her long-term boyfriend Jim eight years earlier, and had remained 'blissfully single' since then. She was now running a successful interior design business.

"Listen," Helen said eventually, "I have an idea. What if I flew out there to join you?"

"To Vegas?" Rebecca exclaimed.

"Hell yes, to Vegas!" Helen enthused. "When's the last time we had a girls' trip? Twenty years ago? More? Remember Virginia Beach? God that was a riot."

She smiled at the flash of memories—the two of them, barely nineteen, driving up to Virginia Beach in Helen's beat-up Volkswagen, windows down and music blasting.

Helen had convinced her to enter an impromptu dance contest at the beachfront bar, and to her surprise, Rebecca had won—spinning and laughing beneath colored lights, free in a way that seemed to belong to another lifetime now.

That trip had been the summer before she met Don. The last hurrah of the Rebecca who would do something simply because it sounded fun, who didn't calculate risks or worry about appearances.

"Listen, I could be there Thursday afternoon," Helen offered. "We'll have a proper weekend together."

"I'd love that," Rebecca admitted, realizing she meant it. "But are you sure you can get away?"

"Honey, I'm the boss. I can do whatever I want." Helen chuckled. "So stay put in Vegas, okay? I'll text you my flight details once I've booked. Wait—what is this number you're calling from? Is it your hotel?"

"No! It's my new iPhone," Rebecca said proudly. "My very first smartphone."

A few more laughs later, they ended the call and Rebecca lay down on the bed, a smile lingering on her face. She crossed 'Call Helen' off her list with a flourish.

The prospect of Helen's visit filled her with an unfamiliar feeling—anticipation. Something to look forward to, something planned purely for her own enjoyment rather than to meet someone else's expectations.

CHAPTER 14

THE LATE AFTERNOON SUN slanted through the window as Rebecca stepped out of the shower. She took her time getting ready—blow-drying her hair without Don's impatient sighs, applying makeup without his pointed glances at his watch.

She slipped into the grey maxi dress from Macy's and studied herself in the full-length mirror. The softness at her waist, the lines around her eyes, all the imperfections she usually catalogued were still there. But tonight, she didn't immediately look away.

"Not bad," she told the mirror. "Not great, but not bad."

Rather than ordering room service again, she decided to venture downstairs. The thought of dining alone sent a flutter of self-conscious doubt through her, but she pushed it aside.

She hesitated as she exited the elevator, then headed toward the restaurant precinct. Wandering past several options, she finally paused at one with a display of fun neon signs set against a stone wall.

The hostess, with a bright smile and high ponytail, seated her without ceremony. "Dining solo tonight?" she asked, her tone casual, professional.

"Yes, it's just me," Rebecca said, pleased when no flush of embarrassment followed.

She ordered the mesquite grilled fish—something Don would have dismissed as 'boring menu filler'. Around her, couples murmured over candles, friends shared appetizers, and near the window, a businessman scrolled his phone while a woman across the room read her paperback. No one was watching her. No one was judging that she was alone.

She wondered again whether Don's assumption that everyone was always watching said more about his own insecurities than reality.

The fish arrived perfectly cooked, with roasted asparagus and lemon butter sauce. She savored each bite, appreciating the smokiness of the mesquite complementing the delicate fish. Her attention remained on her meal and the modest pleasure of choosing food she actually wanted.

As she dabbed her napkin to her lips, she glanced toward the exit. The idea of spending another evening alone with her thoughts in an otherwise empty hotel room seemed overly depressing after the past week spent in darkness.

She signed the check and stood with unexpected eagerness. The casino beckoned with its lights and sounds, an adult playground she'd not yet explored.

The transition from the restaurant's muted elegance to the casino's sensory overload was jarring. Bells and electronic jingles competed with conversation and laughter. The air smelled cool and tobacco-sweet. She inhaled deeply as she wandered through the gaming floor, pausing to watch a roulette table where players crowded around, their faces tense with anticipation as the small white ball bounced and spun. She moved on to observe the intense concentration of poker players, their expressions carefully neutral as chips clicked and cards whispered across the felt.

Music drew her toward an open bar where a live band performed cover songs. The lead singer, a woman with dark curls and a vintage dress, had a velvety voice that suited the classic rock numbers. Rebecca swayed to the familiar music, songs from her youth that now carried the glow of nostalgia.

Skirting the bar, she wandered into an area with bank after bank of slot machines. She had never been much of a gambler—Don characterized it as 'throwing money away', his voice thick with contempt. She'd only played slots once, on a paddle steamer cruise years ago.

The band launched into a Tom Petty cover, the singer doing surprising justice to 'Free Fallin''. Rebecca nodded along to the beat, her feet carrying her toward a row of busy slot machines. She slid onto the stool in front of a machine with a colorful display of squares featuring various symbols. She leaned in, studying the unfamiliar buttons and pay lines.

Deciding to try her luck, she slid a twenty-dollar bill into the machine. The credit counter at the bottom of the screen jumped to 20. She pressed the 'PLAY' button and was startled to see it drop down to 15. Five dollars? Gone in an instant! Her eyes widened. Good lord, she thought, that's the minimum bet? The twenty wouldn't last long at that rate.

She hesitated, then shrugged. Three more spins before her twenty disappeared—hardly enough to consider herself a gambler. Her attention drifted to the band as she absently hit the spin button again, her foot tapping to the rhythm of the music.

A loud bell ringing drew her attention to the screen. It had filled with eight yellow sun symbols scattered across the reels. The words 'HOLD & SPIN' flashed on the screen, and below that, an invitation for her to play.

She pressed the PLAY button. Some of the empty spaces on the screen filled with additional suns, each one appearing with a small burst of light and sound. Sitting forward, eyes fixed on the display, she waited for something else to happen. After a moment, her finger hovered then pressed PLAY again.

The reels spun, and a sun landed in one of the empty spaces. Following her instincts, she pushed PLAY again. More suns landed, gradually filling the screen. With each press, the anticipation built, the music climbing to a faster pace accompanied by a drum roll. On her final press, the last empty space filled with a gleaming sun, and the screen above the machine emblazoned with the word 'GRAND'.

The slot machine erupted with flashing lights and triumphant music. 'GRAND JACKPOT' flashed across the screen while a digital counter rapidly climbed upward.

"I honestly don't know what's happening," she laughed to a couple who had rushed over, drawn by the commotion.

"Lady, you won $26,000!" the man exclaimed, his eyes wide.

Rebecca stared at the flashing screen in disbelief. "What? That must be beginner's luck!"

A casino attendant appeared at her side. "Congratulations, ma'am!"

After checking her ID and processing her winnings, he returned with a stack of hundred-dollar bills, a check for $15,000, and a tax form.

"Just under twenty thousand, after tax withholding," he explained.

Rebecca held out trembling hands as the attendant counted the cash, then tucked it into her purse with the tax form and her new rewards card. The weight of the money felt unreal. Nearly twenty thousand bucks from a five-dollar bet.

"You can resume playing now, ma'am," the attendant advised as she handed him two hundred-dollar bills, his eyebrows rising slightly as he thanked her.

She looked down at the machine, the screen still displaying her jackpot win, lights flashing around the edges. She still had ten credits in the machine. She hit the spin button twice more. Nothing happened—no bonus features, no more wins. She smiled to herself. "Well, I was right. *That* twenty didn't last long."

Making her way up to her room in a daze, she held her purse close, excitement coursing through her veins. The elevator was mercifully empty.

Back in her room, she emptied her purse onto the bed. Stacks of hundreds and a check with her name on it stared back at her. Twenty thousand. Not life-changing, but a windfall she'd never imagined.

She slipped a few bills into her wallet, locked the rest in the safe, and sat down with her iPhone, fingers still trembling as she called Helen.

"You are not going to believe what happened," she said when Helen answered groggily, the sound of rustling sheets coming through the line.

"What? Are you okay?" Helen's voice was thick with sleep but tinged with concern.

"I won twenty-six thousand dollars on a slot machine!" The words tumbled out, sounding ridiculous even to her own ears.

"Get OUT!" Helen shrieked into the phone, suddenly wide awake. "Are you serious? Twenty-six *thousand*?"

Rebecca laughed, Helen's excitement mirroring her own disbelief. "Well, after tax, it's more like twenty. I'm still in shock. I sat down with twenty bucks and hit a grand jackpot on my second spin. It's the first time I've played a slot machine in at least a decade."

"That's the best thing I've ever heard. Gotta love free money," Helen declared, her voice full of delight. "And perfect timing, too. My flight is booked—I land around two on Thursday. So you take that twenty K and book us a big old suite somewhere! Girls' weekend in Vegas!"

"A suite?" Rebecca hesitated. She had no idea what that would cost.

"Absolutely a suite!" Helen insisted, the energy in her voice infectious. "And then we'll fly home together on Monday. I already checked, and there are plenty of seats available on the afternoon flight to Savannah."

The idea of returning to Savannah sent a small ripple of anxiety through Rebecca, but the prospect of doing so with Helen at her side made it seem less daunting.

"Okay," she agreed, the word feeling like a tiny act of rebellion. "A suite it is."

After they hung up, Rebecca opened the curtains wide, letting the neon glow of the Strip fill her room. She watched the lights of cars moving below, hotels glowing against the night sky. Eventually, she tucked herself into bed, a real smile on her face as she drifted to sleep, Vegas lights making patterns on her ceiling.

For the first time in a long time, Rebecca Morley was looking forward to tomorrow.

CHAPTER 15

A SLIVER OF LIGHT on her face woke Rebecca. She blinked at the dawn visible between the curtains, then checked her phone. 6:22 AM. Annoyed she'd missed the sunrise, she sprang out of bed, muscles slightly sore from the previous days of walking. Her mind turned to Helen's visit, fingers tapping as she mentally cataloged what needed to be done.

Still riding the high of her unexpected windfall—the stack of bills in the safe a tangible reminder that it hadn't been a dream—she decided to head down to the front desk and upgrade her accommodations for the weekend.

The lobby was quiet at the early hour. A professionally dressed young man greeted her with a polite smile that didn't quite reach his tired eyes.

"Good morning. How can I help you?" he asked, straightening his posture as she approached.

"I'd like to extend my stay and upgrade to a suite for the weekend, starting Thursday," she said, her voice steady where even just a few days ago it would have wavered. "My friend is flying in, and a two-bedroom would be great, if possible."

The clerk's fingers moved swiftly over the keyboard as he checked availability, the clicking of the keys punctuating the quiet lobby. His smile faltered slightly, eyebrows drawing together.

"I'm so sorry, Mrs. Morley, but we're fully booked for the weekend," he explained, his tone shifting to practiced regret. "There's a major software conference, and both the Solara and the V hotel are completely full." He looked suitably apologetic, shoulders dropping slightly. "You do have your current room through until Thursday, though."

"Oh." Rebecca hadn't anticipated this obstacle. "I see. Thank you anyway."

The clerk turned to another guest, dismissing her with a professional smile. Deflated, she walked away, heaviness settling in her chest. Pausing by a tropical arrangement, she took a deep breath and told herself this wasn't a setback, but rather a chance to try something different. An adventure.

Back up in her room, sunlight now streaming fully through the window, she called Helen, the phone cool against her ear.

"The Solara is booked solid for the weekend," she explained, flopping back onto the bed. "Where else would you like to stay?"

"The AUREUS!" Helen's response was immediate and enthusiastic, her voice crackling with excitement through the line.

Rebecca laughed, the sound astonishing her with its lightness. "Really? It looks so ornate and fancy. I've only walked past the outside. I haven't been in."

"Honey, the Aureus is classic Vegas," Helen insisted, the words tumbling out in a rush. "Those statues, that shopping mall with the fancy ceiling? Come on, it'll be fun!"

"I'll check it out," Rebecca said, pulling up the Aureus website on her laptop, the keys smooth beneath her fingertips.

The suite she booked was more extravagant than any hotel she'd ever stayed in—a two-bedroom suite with a living room, dining area, views of the Strip, even a pool table.

When it came time to enter her payment information, her fingers hovered over the keyboard. Don had always handled anything online. What if she made a mistake? She forced herself to enter the numbers carefully, double-checking each digit, then held her breath as she clicked 'Submit'.

The confirmation page appeared moments later, bringing with it an unexpected sense of accomplishment. It was going to eat up a small chunk of her winnings, but for a reunion with her lifelong best friend, she was excited to allow herself this luxury.

Each day that week, she rose before sunrise for a long walk, covering miles while the Strip was still relatively quiet. The cool desert air would gradually heat up as the sun climbed, casting long shadows between the towering hotels. She'd stop at Saddle's for breakfast, enjoying the simple food and unpretentious atmosphere—the clatter of plates, the hiss of the grill, the murmur of conversations at nearby tables creating a comfortable backdrop to her morning.

Afternoons she spent at the Solara Beach, swimming laps or floating in the wave pool. Her skin had deepened to a golden bronze, the mirror now reflecting a woman with brighter eyes and straighter posture. She could meet her own gaze rather than quickly looking away, as had become her habit.

Each evening, she tucked a hundred into her wallet to gamble, just enough to make her pulse quicken without tipping into recklessness. Some nights she won a little and left with a pleasant buzz of satisfaction; other nights she lost it all, treating her exploratory gambling as entertainment rather than a serious endeavor. The grand jackpot, she figured, had been a once-in-a-lifetime stroke of luck.

Thursday morning arrived bright and clear, sunlight spilling through the curtains she had deliberately left partially open. She hadn't slept well, her mind cycling through plans for Helen's visit, wondering if her friend would notice the changes in her, both visible and invisible. Rising early for her usual morning walk, the now-familiar path along the Strip comfortable beneath her feet, she ended at Saddle's for breakfast.

As she slid onto her regular stool, the vinyl cool against her legs, she noticed the man in the black T-shirt had come in behind her, sitting down beside her instead of his usual spot at the far end. The scent of coffee and something like black pepper and evergreen briefly filled the space between them.

"Mornin'," he rumbled, his deep voice matching his weathered appearance.

"Good morning," Rebecca replied, fingers automatically smoothing her windblown hair.

The waitress appeared with coffee without being asked, familiar with both their routines.

"The usual?" she asked, pencil poised.

They nodded in unison.

"Noticed you've been walking the Strip pretty early most mornings," the man said, adding sugar to his coffee with hands that looked strong but moved with grace.

"It's nice before it gets crowded. And too hot."

"Smart." He extended a leathery hand. "I'm Vince."

"Rebecca." His palm was callused—a stark contrast to Don's smooth office hands.

"You here on vacation?" he asked, though something in his tone suggested he already knew the answer was more complicated.

She hesitated, then decided on honesty.

"I—*we*—came to Vegas to celebrate our 25th wedding anniversary. My husband asked for a divorce on our first night, and then he flew home. I'm staying to... figure things out. My family thinks I'm hiding," she added with an embarrassed laugh.

Vince smiled. "Vegas isn't exactly known for its healing atmosphere, but it's never done me wrong."

"Actually, it's been good for me," she said, realizing as she spoke that it was true. "No one knows me here. I can just... be."

Their food arrived and they ate in companionable silence for a few minutes.

"What about you?" she finally asked. "Do you live in Vegas?"

"Most of the time. Poker pays the bills."

"You mean you play professionally?"

"I guess you could call it that." He smiled faintly. "Been making my living at it for more than twenty years."

"That's fascinating." She leaned forward. "Do you happen to know a woman named Justine? She plays poker here too."

Her cheeks reddened as she realized what she'd just said. "Sorry, that was a silly question. Lots of people play poker in Vegas, I guess."

Vince chuckled, a warm sound that filled the space around them. "Can't say I know her. I pay attention to faces when I play, not name tags."

They talked throughout breakfast, conversation coming easily. What struck her most was how he listened. He didn't interrupt, didn't try to fix her problems, didn't offer unsolicited advice. He just listened, his blue eyes attentive, occasionally asking a question that suggested he was truly hearing what she said. His focus was complete, without the distracted glances at phones or watches that had become so common in conversations.

She had the distinct sense that he was reading her the way he read his cards at a poker table—observing, assessing, understanding—but without judgment. It was both unnerving and strangely comforting, like standing in the sun after a long winter indoors.

As they finished their coffee, she glanced at her watch. "I should go. I need to check out of my hotel and move to the Aureus. My friend Helen is flying in this afternoon."

"The Aureus is nice," he nodded, setting his empty mug down with a gentle thud. "Busy though."

She stood, suddenly feeling awkward, her movements becoming slightly jerky. "My friend and I are supposed to fly home together on Monday, so..." She trailed off, not sure why she felt the need to explain. "It's been nice talking to you. Good meeting you."

Vince smiled, the corners of his eyes crinkling in a way that suggested he did it often. "Likewise, Rebecca. Enjoy your weekend with your friend."

A strange mixture of emotions swirled through her as she stepped into the morning sunshine. Something in that conversation—a connection, a recognition—felt important, like finding a familiar book in a foreign library. She pushed the thought aside as she returned to her room, her fingers tapping with both excitement and apprehension about Helen's visit.

She packed her suitcase quickly, preparing for her move to the Aureus. When she reached the dress she'd worn during her win, she paused. Her hand smoothed over the fabric once, twice, before deciding to wear it. Among the clothes spread before her, it alone seemed worth keeping.

A taxi delivered her to the Aureus, where Roman-style columns and statues created an atmosphere of exaggerated grandeur. The lobby bustled with tourists posing for photos, shoppers laden with bags. The air was cool and scented with an expensive perfume, contrasting with the dry heat outside.

Rebecca approached the check-in desk, feeling out of place among the well-heeled guests. Her palms dampened slightly as she waited her turn.

"I'm pretty early for check-in. I have a reservation for a suite," she said to the clerk, a poised woman with immaculate makeup and perfectly coiffed hair. "Under Morley."

The clerk smiled broadly. "Ah, yes, Ms. Morley. The Orion suite. Nice choice."

Rebecca glanced around the opulent lobby with its marble columns and classical statuary while the clerk processed her check-in. A fountain splashed nearby, almost drowned by conversations in various languages.

Not even two weeks had passed since she'd been Don Morley's invisible wife, her days spent maintaining their empty home and preparing his meals—a woman whose life was defined by her relationships to others. Now she walked the Vegas Strip at dawn, won random jackpots, booked luxury suites, and shared breakfast with poker players. She examined this new self as though she were a bug under a microscope, a species that hadn't been discovered before.

Who she would ultimately become remained to be seen, but she was genuinely curious to find out, a flutter of anticipation replacing the dread that had become her constant companion.

CHAPTER 16

S TANDING JUST BEYOND BAGGAGE claim, Rebecca scanned the arriving passengers. She shifted from foot to foot, unconsciously smoothing her dress.

It had been ages since she'd last seen Helen, but she knew that it would be like old times, as though they'd only just seen each other. That's how it always was with them—time and distance irrelevant to the connection they shared.

Finally, she spotted her—Helen's unmistakable presence cutting through the crowd. Even in the sea of travelers, Helen stood out, her energy preceding her like a wave. Her jet-black hair was styled in an asymmetrical cut, shorter on one side with a dramatic sweep across her forehead, the glossy finish catching the fluorescent airport lights.

She wore slim black jeans, Italian leather ankle boots, and a white tank under a tailored leather jacket that hugged her petite but athletic frame, the sleeves pushed carelessly up to her elbows. A hammered-silver cuff bracelet matched the pendant hanging from a leather cord at her neck. The outfit was quintessential Helen—bold, unapologetic, perfectly put together.

"Rebel!" Helen shouted, her voice carrying above the airport din as she dropped her sleek carry-on and threw her arms around Rebecca, the scent of her sandalwood perfume enveloping them both. "Look at you!"

Rebecca laughed, returning the embrace, feeling the slight frame of her friend beneath the leather jacket. "Rebel—I love how you still call me that. I'm starting to feel a bit like a rebel, to be honest."

"Well, it's about time we brought Rebel back," Helen declared, looking Rebecca up and down, her dark eyes gleaming with approval as she held her out at arm's length. "And might I say, our old Rebel is making a huge comeback. You look great!"

"Okay, first off—good call on the suite at the Aureus! It's amazing," Rebecca told Helen as they collected her luggage, the hard-shell suitcase reflecting under the airport lights. "Wait until you see it."

"I still can't believe you won twenty grand," Helen shook her head in wonder, her asymmetrical hair swinging with the movement. "And that you're actually spending some of it on us! The old Rebecca would have put every penny in savings."

"The old Rebecca didn't have a soon-to-be-ex-husband with a pregnant mistress," she replied, surprised by her own candor, the words spilling out unfiltered.

Helen barked a laugh, the sound sharp and authentic. "And she's got jokes! I like this Rebel 2.0." She looped her arm through Rebecca's, their strides naturally falling into sync as they headed toward the exit.

Helen filled the taxi ride with rapid-fire updates on her life, business, and dating disasters. Her hands flew as she spoke, occasionally tapping Rebecca's knee for emphasis. Rebecca was laughing more than she had in months, her cheeks aching from the unfamiliar exercise. Helen always made the world seem brighter, more amusing, full of possibilities.

When they reached the suite, Helen let out a low whistle. Sunlight streamed through floor-to-ceiling windows, illuminating marble floors and richly upholstered furniture. A crystal chandelier hung above a large dining table, with bedrooms branching off either side. The windows offered a panoramic view of the Strip, desert mountains rising hazily in the distance.

"Now *this* is how you do Vegas," she announced, dropping her bags with a thump and spinning in a slow circle.

"Wait until you see your bathroom," Rebecca grinned, a mischievous glint in her eye as she led the way to one of the bedrooms. "The tub could fit four people."

"Don't tempt me," Helen winked, waggling her eyebrows suggestively. "I'm sure we could drum up some guys here in Vegas who'd be happy to test that theory."

They spent the afternoon settling in, unpacking Helen's extensive luggage and planning their weekend. By early evening, they were sipping margaritas in the lobby bar, the salt-rimmed glasses cold against their fingertips as they reminisced about their younger days.

Hearing Helen use her old nickname stirred something in Rebecca's chest—a flutter of recognition, a memory of who she'd been before becoming Mrs. Don Morley. She wondered when exactly she'd lost that rebellious streak, when she'd become so focused on pleasing Don that she'd forgotten how to please herself.

Her throat tightened unexpectedly, remembering how Helen's Uncle Sly had dubbed them 'Rebel' and 'Hellion' when they were teenagers, always getting into mischief together.

"Oh my God, I can't believe you remember Uncle Sly!" Helen giggled, slugging down the last sip of her drink and signaling for another.

Rebecca grinned, the tequila warming her from the inside. "You mean 'Uncle Slime'? And his creepy friend Jamie with the wandering eyes?"

"God, the way we saw grown-ups back when we were kids," Helen said, shaking her head. "Different time, different perspective."

"Speaking of kids, I still haven't really explained things to mine," she admitted, her voice dropping. "Just the basics over the phone."

"I'm sure Don is filling them up with a pack of bullshit lies, making everything out to be your fault," Helen pointed out, her dark eyes flashing with barely concealed anger. "But we're not talking about him this weekend." She reached over and squeezed Rebecca's knee. "This is about you, Rebel. About figuring out what's next."

Rebecca took a long sip of her margarita, the tartness making her momentarily pucker her lips. "I honestly have no idea what's next. That's the terrifying part." Her hand trembled slightly as she set the glass down.

"It's also the exciting part," Helen countered in a sing-song voice, a wide smile gracing her elfin face. She leaned forward with the intensity that had always characterized her approach to life. "Now, are we getting dinner or what? I'm starving, and Vegas restaurants are amazing." She bounced off her barstool in one fluid motion, extending a hand to Rebecca.

The weekend unfolded in a blur of activity. They hit the spa for massages, facials, and mani-pedis, basking in the eucalyptus-scented air and mellow music. Rebecca surrendered to the massage, feeling knots of tension melt away.

"Look at us, all blissed out," Helen said as they left the spa, skin glowing and nails freshly painted in bold colors. Rebecca had chosen a deep teal that reminded her of her new swimsuit—another small rebellion against Don's preference for traditional colors. She kept glancing at her hands, amazed by how the bold color seemed to transform them into someone else's—someone more daring.

"I need a new wardrobe," Rebecca announced, her voice laden with conviction as they entered their suite. She strode to the closet with purpose, her freshly pedicured feet padding across the carpet, and began grabbing every item of floral pattern clothing and dumping them on the couch with a satisfying whoosh of fabric. "All of that is getting donated. I hereby decree that as my first official action as Lord Mayor of My Own Life, I shall never wear floral again!"

Helen, snorting with laughter, raised an imaginary glass in salute. "Hear, hear! I fully second that motion. Let's go shopping!" She grabbed her purse with a gleeful shoulder shimmy.

The Shops beckoned, as they wandered beneath the painted sky ceiling that transitioned from day to night. Music drifted from the central fountain as they tried on clothes Rebecca would never have dared to wear before—sequined tops, leather pants, dresses with plunging necklines that made her blush.

"You should get that," Helen insisted when Rebecca emerged from a dressing room in a slimming black dress that hugged her curves, the fabric cool and smooth against her skin.

"I don't know," Rebecca hesitated, turning to examine herself in the three-way mirror, angling her body to see every perspective. Her reflection was unfamiliar—more confident, more present. "Where would I even wear it?"

"Wherever the hell you want," Helen replied, adjusting the neckline slightly. "Look at how much weight you've lost. You look amazing!"

Rebecca peered more closely at her reflection, noticing for the first time how her cheekbones seemed more pronounced, how the dress skimmed her waistline without the usual bulges she was accustomed to hiding. It was true—her face was definitely thinner, her waistline more defined. A week of being holed up in her cocoon, followed by her new routine of walking 'mad miles' along the Strip, had begun to transform her body.

"It's just water weight," she demurred, her fingers automatically reaching to pinch at her waist, an old habit.

"It's 'my husband's a cheating asshole' weight, and good riddance to it," Helen declared, gently swatting Rebecca's hand away from her waist. "We're buying the dress." Her tone brooked no argument, a throwback to high school when she would insist that Rebecca could absolutely wear that top, talk to that boy, sign up for that class.

They gambled in the evenings amid the sensory overload of the casino: Helen taught Rebecca roulette, and indulged in Rebecca's newfound enjoyment of slots.

"I can't remember the last time I had this much fun," Rebecca admitted as they returned to their suite late Saturday night, pleasantly tipsy, her feet aching from hours in new shoes. She stepped out of them as soon as they entered the suite, sighing with relief as her toes sank into the welcoming carpet.

"That's because Don was a fun-sponge," Helen said, kicking off her own heels with practiced precision, sending them flying nearly to the same spot. "Always sucking the joy out of everything with his rules and judgments."

Rebecca couldn't disagree. The image of Don frowning at their laughter, at the thought of them enjoying themselves, rose unbidden in her mind. He approached everything, even family vacations, with an agenda, frowning upon spontaneity or deviation from his plans. His disapproving eyes seemed to follow her even here, and she shook her head slightly to dispel the image.

Feeling lazy on Sunday morning, they ordered an extravagant room service breakfast on the balcony. The air was still cool from the desert night, the city stretching below in a grid, distant mountains looking hazy pink in the early light. The coffee was rich, the pastries flaky and buttery.

"So," Helen said, setting down her mimosa, the crystal glass catching the sunlight. "We've had massages, we've had mani-pedis, we've done some shopping and some gambling. All the fun stuff." Her tone shifted slightly, becoming more serious, her posture straightening. "But we haven't really talked about what happens when we get to Savannah tomorrow night."

Rebecca sighed, pushing a piece of melon around her plate with her fork, the tines scraping slightly on the fine china. "I know." Her stomach clenched at the thought of returning, of facing reality again.

"Look, I know you have to deal with Don and the divorce and all that," Helen continued, her elbows on the table. "But tell me—what do YOU want?"

The question hung in the air between them, deceptively simple yet impossibly complex. Rebecca stared out at the vista, watching a small plane trace its way across the clear blue sky, leaving a thin white trail behind it.

"I don't know," she finally answered, her voice barely audible above the distant sound of traffic below. "I've spent so many years just focused on what everyone else wants—what everyone else needs. I'm not sure I even know how to figure out what I myself want."

Helen leaned forward, resting her chin on her palm. "Start small. What sounds good for lunch today? What would you like to do tomorrow? You don't have to map out your entire future this morning. Just choose one thing."

Rebecca smiled, the simple approach cutting through her spiraling thoughts. Helen had always had that gift—breaking overwhelming situations into manageable pieces.

"Lunch at that Fusion place downstairs."

"Now we're talking," Helen smiled, tossing her napkin onto her plate with a flourish. "Decisions. Progress. One choice at a time."

"One thing I know I want is to get Don's voice out of my head. He's not even here and I still feel his critical eye watching over everything I do, his snide remarks constantly running through my mind. Maybe I need to talk to a therapist," she ventured, her hands mechanically folding and refolding her napkin into neat little triangles.

Helen reached across the table and squeezed her hand firmly, stilling the nervous movement. "Getting Don out of your head will come in time, as you start to fill up the space in there with other things. But start trusting yourself to decide on how to rebuild YOU. What makes you happy? What have you always wanted to do but never did because Don wouldn't approve?"

Rebecca nodded slowly, the questions settling into her mind like seeds. She could almost feel them taking root, tiny tendrils of possibility unfurling.

"And in the meantime," Helen continued, giving Rebecca's hand a final squeeze before releasing it, "you'll stay with me when we get back. No arguments. My guest room is yours for as long as you need it." She punctuated this declaration by stabbing a piece of fruit with her fork.

"I should probably go to the house—" Rebecca began, her brow furrowing.

"Not yet," Helen said firmly, raising a hand to cut off the protest. "You need neutral territory. Space to figure things out. Eventually you'll have to face Don, face the kids, deal with the house and all that stuff. But you need a safe base of operations, and that's with me." Her tone was resolute.

The offer brought unexpected tears to Rebecca's eyes, blurring the view of the Strip before her. She blinked rapidly, her throat constricting. "Thank you," she whispered.

"That's what friends are for," Helen asserted, lightening the moment with a playful toss of her head. "Now, what's this I hear about a roller coaster at New York New York? Because that sounds like exactly what we need to do today."

As they prepared for their final day of Vegas adventures, gathering bottles of water, sunglasses, and comfortable shoes, Rebecca turned Helen's question over in her mind with a mixture of anxiety and anticipation.

What did she want? The answer wasn't clear yet, but she was all of a sudden really keen to find out. She caught a glimpse of herself in the mirror as she slipped on her sunglasses—cheeks flushed, eyes bright, looking more alive than she had in years. In that reflection, she caught a glimpse of Rebel—the girl she used to be—waiting to emerge again.

CHAPTER 17

MONDAY MORNING ARRIVED WITH a hint of inevitability. Rebecca stood at the suite's window, her fingertips pressed lightly against the cool glass, gazing out at the Las Vegas Strip while Helen finished packing. The faint sounds of drawers opening and closing, hangers clinking against each other, and the rhythmic zip of suitcases filtered from the bedroom.

Beyond the Strip, the surrounding hills rose in rusty undulating waves, colors shifting as clouds cast moving shadows. In afternoon light, those slopes would fade to dusky grey and blue, an almost imperceptible change that always held her transfixed.

There was something about those hills that spoke to her. They represented uncharted intrigue, inspiration, mystery. Unlike the manicured perfection of Savannah's historic district with its precisely trimmed hedges and carefully preserved façades, or the calculated luxury of the Strip with its artificial landscapes and choreographed fountain displays, the hills seemed so wild, untamed, indifferent to human desires. Rebecca loved them in a way she couldn't quite articulate—they represented something beyond her grasp, something she was still reaching for. Her breath fogged the glass as she sighed.

"We should be ready to roll in about fifteen," Helen announced, emerging from her bedroom with her suitcase, the wheels rumbling against the marble floor. "You about ready?"

Rebecca turned from the window, a decision crystallizing within her, settling into her bones with certainty. The old reflex to please rose, but she let it pass. "I can't go back yet."

Helen paused, the handle of her suitcase still gripped in one hand, studying her friend's face. "Are you sure?"

Rebecca felt a familiar surge of anxiety—what would people think? What about her obligations?

The practical voice in her head listed all the reasons she should return: the house, the divorce proceedings, the children. The responsible thing would be to go back. But beneath that voice was a quieter, stronger one that had been gaining volume day by day.

"I'm sure," she said, certainty in her voice. "I'm not ready to face all of it. Not yet." Her shoulders straightened almost imperceptibly as she spoke.

Instead of arguing or expressing disappointment, Helen simply nodded, her dark eyes softening. "So don't."

"You're not upset?" Rebecca asked, her brow furrowing.

"Rebel," Helen said, setting down her carry-on and crossing the room to take Rebecca's hands, her grip warm and reassuring. "The old you would have gotten on that plane because it was expected. This is exactly what you need right now."

Relief washed over Rebecca. "Thank you for understanding."

"Promise me two things though—call your kids, and don't let Don intimidate you into coming back before you're ready."

Rebecca promised, shoving her MacBook into her handbag and following Helen out of the room, leaving her packed suitcases by the door. She shared Helen's cab to the airport, the desert heat seeping in despite the air conditioning. Their conversation turned to practical matters—how long she might stay and where she'd go next.

"I'll try calling the kids tonight," Rebecca said, her fingers unconsciously twisting her wedding ring. "Explain that I'm taking some extra time to figure things out."

"Good. And while you're 'figuring things out', get yourself a notebook and start writing down all those scattered thoughts in your head," Helen suggested, tapping a manicured finger against her temple. "Journal. Ideas. Poems. Whatever comes to mind, just WRITE. Get it all out of your head and onto paper—or even into your fancy new MacBook," she said, laying a hand on Rebecca's handbag affectionately.

"I seem to only ever surf the net on that, or make to-do lists," Rebecca laughed, the sound slightly hollow.

"You always used to write. Remember that diary of yours, with the silly lock? Maybe you should go find one of those, tell it all your innermost secrets. Trust me—it'll help."

She leaned closer, eyes narrowed, the scent of her perfume surrounding them. "You have to find yourself, Rebel, right here where you're standing. Figure out who you are when you're not being Don's wife or Jodie and Luke's mom. You don't have to have permission from anyone for anything. These decisions are solely about you now."

At the airport drop-off, they embraced tightly, Helen's small frame strong against Rebecca's.

"Call me anytime," Helen said, her voice muffled against Rebecca's shoulder. "Day or night. And remember—my guest room is waiting whenever you're ready."

Rebecca stood rooted to the curb, watching as her friend disappeared into the terminal, the automatic doors sliding closed behind her. A strange mixture of liberation and terror swirled in her stomach. She was truly on her own now, with no return ticket home, no concrete plans, just an open-ended stay in a city she barely knew.

"Where to now?" the cab driver asked, his eyes meeting hers in the rearview mirror.

"Founders Union Bank, please—the one on Maryland," she directed. Don had told her to go ahead and take half the joint savings, and that's what she'd do.

The bank branch was cool and quiet, a lovely respite from the warm morning.

"I'd like to speak with someone about online banking, please," she told the receptionist, a young man with meticulously styled hair and a crisp blue shirt. "And I need to arrange a transfer from a joint account."

Minutes later, she was seated across from a young woman with a bright smile and a nameplate reading 'Mandy Torres, Personal Banker'. The desk between them was polished to a high shine, mostly empty except for a monitor and a few items.

"So, you'd like to set up online banking?" Mandy asked, typing rapidly on her keyboard, her acrylic fingernails clicking against the keys.

"Yes," Rebecca confirmed, her hands folded neatly in her lap. "And I'd like to transfer some money from my joint savings account into my individual account."

"No problem at all. Let's do that first. Do you have your debit card?" Mandy's voice was professionally cheerful, her movements practiced and efficient.

Rebecca opened her wallet and pulled out her debit card, handing it across to Mandy. "I'd like to transfer $40,000 from the joint savings into my personal savings."

Mandy slid the card through a reader, and then typed quickly on the keyboard, frowning. The subtle change in her expression sent a warning prickle down Rebecca's spine.

"Let me verify that for you." Her friendly expression flickered momentarily, her eyes darting from the screen to Rebecca and back again. "Mrs. Morley, are you certain this is the correct account?"

"Yes, quite certain," Rebecca replied, an uneasy feeling settling in her stomach, a cold weight that seemed to grow heavier with each passing second. "Why do you ask?"

"Well..." Mandy turned her monitor so Rebecca could see it, angling it with a brisk movement. "The current balance in this account is $5,127.43."

Rebecca blinked at the screen, uncomprehending. The numbers seemed to blur before her eyes, refusing to make sense. "There must be some mistake. The balance should be over $80,000."

"Let me check the recent transaction history," Mandy said, advancing through several screens, the sound of her mouse clicks unnaturally loud in the quiet office. "Ah, I see. There was a significant withdrawal last Thursday. $78,000 was withdrawn at your home branch in Savannah, Georgia."

Rebecca felt as if the air had been sucked from the room. Her lungs seemed to collapse, her chest tightening painfully. Last Thursday. While she was preparing for Helen's visit, catching up and making plans, laughing and drinking margaritas, Don had been emptying their joint account.

"That... that can't be right," she managed to say, her voice sounding distant and unfamiliar to her own ears. "My husband—he wouldn't..."

But even as she spoke the words, she knew they weren't true. A bitter taste filled her mouth. Of course he would. Of course he *had*. The certainty settled in her gut like lead.

"I'm sorry, Ms. Morley," Mandy said, genuine concern in her voice, her professional demeanor relaxing as she leaned forward. "With a joint account, either party has full access to the funds. Would you like me to print the transaction details for you?"

Rebecca nodded mutely, her mind racing. The money wasn't a catastrophe—her jackpot winnings would keep her afloat for a while—but the violation of it, the timing, that's what made her hands shake as she accepted the printed statement, the paper crackling in her grip.

"Would you still like to set up online banking?" Mandy asked, her eyes watching Rebecca with a mixture of professional detachment and human sympathy.

"Yes," Rebecca replied, pulling herself together, straightening her spine with deliberate effort. "Yes, I definitely need to set that up."

Twenty minutes later, with her new online banking credentials established and her MacBook safely back in her bag, Rebecca stood outside the bank, blinking in the bright sunlight. The familiar tightness of anxiety squeezed her chest, but alongside it was something else—a slow-burning anger that felt almost energizing, sending heat through her veins.

"Breathe, Rebecca. One thing at a time," she told herself, the words slightly ragged, knowing that rushing to respond to the situation wouldn't help. She hailed a taxi, the hot air rushing into the vehicle as the door opened, returning to the Aureus to collect her bags and check out.

A change of scene was in order. Mentally repeating 'everything is going to be fine', a mantra that felt hollow but necessary, she sat in silence as the taxi ferried her north to Fremont Street, where Vegas had first established itself as a gambling destination.

The driver dropped her at the Gilded Horseshoe, which stood as a link between old and new Vegas—historic but updated, luxurious without the over-the-top extravagance of the newer resorts. The façade gleamed golden in the sun, living up to its name.

The Gilded Horseshoe had a different energy than the Strip resorts—more compact, with lower ceilings and closer walls. Vegas nostalgia filled the space with vintage neon and mechanical slot machines alongside the newer digital ones. She checked in for five nights, barely registering the receptionist's practiced smile.

Once in her room—comfortable, with earthy tones and plush bedding—she pulled out her phone to call Justine. The device felt unnaturally heavy in her hand.

"Rebecca, good afternoon." Justine's voice was crisp and professional even through the phone's tiny speaker.

"Don emptied our joint savings account," Rebecca said without preamble, the words tumbling out before she could arrange them into something more measured. "$78,000, withdrawn last Thursday. Left just over five thousand in the account. The withdrawal was made at the Savannah branch while I was here in Vegas. After he'd told me to transfer my half, but before I did—obviously."

Justine paused, allowing Rebecca's frantic babble to peter out.

"Okay. Legally, there's not much we can do," Justine stated in a tone that Rebecca recognized as her strategic assessment voice, the words measured and precise. "Joint accounts provide equal access to both parties, regardless of who contributed the funds."

"I know," Rebecca said, sinking onto the edge of the bed, the mattress giving slightly beneath her weight. "I'm not asking about legal action. I don't know how to handle it with Don."

"Direct confrontation," Justine advised without hesitation, the words striking Rebecca like small arrows of certainty. "Call him. Make it clear you know what he's done. Don't threaten but be firm about your disappointment and the impact on your trust during settlement negotiations. Document everything. Quick question—what did you do with the remaining balance?"

"I left it in there. Should have transferred it out?" Rebecca asked, running a hand through her hair, feeling strands come loose.

"I wouldn't, unless you need it. If this winds up in court, then all transactions will be reviewed. It may be perceived as an agreement to that division of the immediately available funds."

"Then I guess it's good I left it there. I'm okay for now, although I don't know how long Don is going to drag things out for. Should I mention that you're aware of it?"

"Absolutely. You can let him know his actions have been noted by your legal counsel," Justine replied, her tone leaving no room for doubt.

After thanking Justine and ending the call, Rebecca took a deep breath, feeling her ribcage expand and contract as she dialed Don's number. Her heart hammered, her ears rushed with sound, but her hand was steady. She was done being blindsided. Done being manipulated.

CHAPTER 18

Don answered on the third ring. "Rebecca," he said, her name emerging from his mouth like an accusation. "This is unexpected, given your lack of reply to any of my emails or calls. What can I help you with?" His voice held the cool, condescending tone she'd grown to recognize as his professional mask.

"I just left Founders Union," she informed him, her voice controlled despite the rage bubbling beneath her skin. "You withdrew $78,000 from our joint savings last Thursday."

A pause, the silence stretching between them, charged with unspoken emotions. "That's correct. I did." Don's voice was flat, offering no apology, no explanation.

"You told me last week to take my half. And when I went in today to do that, I discovered that you'd taken all of it," she countered, her free hand curling into a fist against her thigh.

"Not all of it," he corrected, his tone shifting to the condescending one she knew so well, the one that made her feel small and stupid. "I left five grand for you to fritter away in Las Vegas. You should have taken more when I offered it. Now I've had a chance to review your actions and frivolous risk-taking in Vegas, and I don't feel that my hard-earned savings should form part of my settlement offer."

His voice hardened, taking on the edge she'd heard him use with opposing counsel. "And it was necessary, Rebecca. For a downpayment on a home for Annette and the baby, since you'll be keeping the house. After all," he continued, a note of calculated emotion entering his voice, "you wouldn't want your children's new half-brother or sister to go without, would you?"

The blatant manipulation might have worked once—the appeal to family, to her maternal instincts, to her sense of responsibility for others' wellbeing. Even just a week ago, it might have left her tearful and uncertain.

Now it only crystallized her anger into something clear and sharp, a blade forming in her mind.

"Don't," she said calmly, her voice dropping to a low, controlled tone. "Don't invoke your baby to justify your actions. This isn't about the child. It's about you taking the money without discussion, without agreement."

"It's a joint account," he reminded her, a smug note entering his voice. "I don't need your agreement."

"No, you don't," she acknowledged, her fingernails digging crescents into her palm. "Legally, you're covered. Morally, you're exposed. You and I both know this was a deliberate choice—to take almost everything, to present it as *un fait accompli*."

"I needed it, Rebecca. To establish my new life," he repeated, an edge of defensiveness creeping into his voice, the smallest crack in his confident façade.

"And you didn't think I might need it too?" she asked, rising from the bed to pace the room, unable to remain still with the energy coursing through her.

"You're the one who extended your Vegas vacation," he replied dismissively, his words clipped and sharp. "If you're so concerned about finances, maybe it's time to come home and face reality."

She almost laughed at the irony, a bitter sound catching in her throat. Here in Las Vegas, facing herself honestly, and for perhaps the first time in decades, she was more in touch with reality than she'd been in years. She could almost see Don's face as he spoke—the downturn of his mouth, the way his eyes would narrow when he felt he had the upper hand.

"We'd agreed to split that money," she said, keeping her voice level with effort as she stared out the window at the Vegas skyline, so different from the view at the Aureus but no less captivating.

"You didn't sign to accept my offer, so technically you have no claim on that money anyway. And one other thing you fail to understand is that your fancy Vegas attack-dog has no standing here in Georgia. I understand family law better than you do, better than she does, and if you keep it up, you're going to get nothing more than what you've already taken from me. Not even the damn house," Don blazed, his voice rising with each word, the familiar pattern of his anger building like a predictable tide.

"And since you didn't sign to accept *my* counter-offer, technically you had no claim on that money either! And for your information, my legal advisor is based in California, and has a very good understanding of Georgia law," she corrected, a hint of satisfaction warming her chest at the knowledge that Justine was far more capable than Don assumed. "I have already informed her of this incident."

A heavy sigh came through the line, the sound of someone who believes they're being eminently reasonable in the face of idiotic opposition. "Look, Rebecca, I'm trying to prepare for a child here. A new family. You're really not making this easy for me. Whatever issues are between us, surely you understand that my baby takes precedence. And you're hiding away in Las Vegas rather than helping me sort this out." His voice was tight with annoyance, words rushing together as his temper rose. "You were supposed to be home by now, and supposed to have signed the papers I gave you."

"I decided to stay longer," she replied, the words simple but freighted with meaning—a declaration of independence that would have been unthinkable only weeks ago.

"Decided? Just like that? Without even discussing your decision with me?" Don's incredulity was palpable, his voice rising in pitch. "The kids are asking questions, Rebecca. Do you have any idea how this looks to our friends, to my colleagues?"

"I'm not particularly concerned with how it *looks*, Don," she replied, soothed by her own calmness, stillness settling over her like a shield.

"Perhaps you should be," he snapped. The sound of something hitting a hard surface—a thrown pen, perhaps—came through the line. "You're being completely irresponsible. You can't disappear in Las Vegas indefinitely. What about the house? What about your obligations? What about—"

"How are things progressing with the revised settlement?" she interrupted smoothly, her patience wearing thin as she returned to the matter at hand. "I emailed you a copy after you ripped up the original."

"I already told you I wasn't filing that bullshit," he seethed, words sharp as flint. "Is that what this is about? You're all of a sudden in some all-fired rush to get this done? You should have signed the agreement I gave you then, rather than scribble all over it with your stupid demands. You're the one dragging it out, and if this does wind up in court," he threatened menacingly, "your actions won't go unnoticed."

Rebecca felt her newfound calm beginning to fracture, heat rising to her cheeks. She pressed her palm against the cool glass of the window, grounding herself. "It's meant to be a negotiation, not only 'Don's Way'."

"I won't negotiate until you are back in Savannah," he insisted, the words clipped short.

"And I haven't decided when I'm coming back," she retorted, the words feeling dangerous and liberating as they left her mouth.

"You. Have. RESPONSIBILITIES," Don's voice rose gradually until the last word came out as a roar. He had emphasized each word as if speaking to a child—a mannerism that had once made her shrink, but now only fueled her resolve.

"Not to you," she said. "You ended that. The kids are grown. The only obligation I have now is to *myself*," she uttered with finality, the words emerging like a vow.

"You think you're so damn clever, don't you?" Don snarled, his controlled façade crumbling completely. "But I'll tell you something. You're only getting what I decide to let you have, Rebecca. I'm the one who earned the money. I'm the one who built a career while you stayed home baking cookies and knitting fucking afghans."

He paused and let the silence stretch out before speaking again, this time quieter, more snide. "You brought nothing in, Rebecca. Nothing."

Something snapped inside her, a dam breaking after years of carefully contained emotions. "Well, I'm not the one who slept with some *accountant* and got her *pregnant*, am I?" The words erupted from her, raw and unfiltered, her voice catching with the force of them.

The line went silent. She could hear his breathing, sharp and irregular, a sound she knew well from their rare but intense arguments—the sound of him processing her uncharacteristic outburst, recalibrating his approach.

"I don't like your tone," he finally said, his voice menacingly low, an attempt to reassert dominance that might once have worked, but now fell flat.

"You don't get to control me anymore, Don." The words came from some deep, previously untapped well of confidence, rising through her like a spring. "Not my tone, not my decisions, not my life."

Don's voice rose to a shout that forced her to hold the phone away from her ear. "You ungrateful bitch! After everything I've done for you? You're nothing without me. Nothing! A fat, boring, middle-aged housewife with no skills, no career, no future. You're a loser, Rebecca. Always have been, always will be. And you're clearly not understanding how this works!"

The verbal assault washed over her, but instead of crumbling as she once would have, body curling in on itself with shame, her resolve grew eerily strong. A strange clarity descended, like stepping into a peaceful room after being out in a storm. The names, the insults—they were just words, and they could only hurt her if she accepted them as truth. And in truth, Don's opinions were rapidly losing credibility with her.

"I understand that you made a unilateral decision about shared resources that we'd previously agreed to split," she replied, her voice as cold as ice. "And I understand that it confirms you are a complete asshole. Other than that, I don't understand you at all." She paused, then added, the words deliberate and precise, "I'm finished with this, Don. We don't need to speak again, ever. We're done. From now on, contact me only via email."

She ended the call before he could respond, her thumb pressing the red button with finality. She stood motionless, the phone clutched in her hand, feeling strangely calm. The anger was still there, banked into an even heat rather than extinguished, but alongside it was something that felt almost like relief—another illusion stripped away, another confirmation that the path forward lay in self-reliance rather than in any lingering trust or connection with the man she had married.

She sat on the edge of the bed, the mattress yielding beneath her as she recalculated her financial position. She pulled the elastic from her hair, loosening it, feeling strands fall around her face. She would need to consider an income source sooner rather than later.

But the money itself wasn't what lingered in her thoughts. It was the clarity that came with Don's action—the stark reminder that she was truly on her own now, for better or worse. The last threads binding her to their shared financial life had been severed, not by her choice but by his.

She felt a curious sense of lightness, as if a weight she'd grown accustomed to carrying had suddenly been lifted. The sensation was almost physical—her shoulder blades sliding together, her breath coming deeper. Don had meant to limit her options, perhaps even force her return to Savannah. Instead, he had freed her from one more obligation, one more connection to their shared past.

She was on her own—financially, practically, emotionally. Taking a deep breath, Rebecca settled at the desk with her laptop, feeling a small surge of pride as she powered it on. Learning to use technology without Don's help was its own victory; he'd always insisted such things were beyond her capabilities, punctuating her questions with condescending sighs.

Connected to the hotel Wi-Fi, she researched options for women re-entering the workforce after decades away. The results were sobering.

Most listings required qualifications she didn't have—degrees, certifications, recent experience. Even entry-level positions in retail and customer service asked for computer skills she'd never developed. The few jobs that seemed accessible offered wages that wouldn't begin to cover her expenses. Website advice assumed she'd built a network through volunteer work or maintained professional connections—neither of which she'd done.

Rebecca leaned back in her chair, the leather creaking, a shallow feeling mounting in her chest. Her volunteer experience on various community and school committees hardly counted as marketable professional experience. She'd organized bake sales and prom picnics, not managed budgets or developed strategic plans. She'd coordinated carpools, not corporate initiatives.

Rebecca opened a new document titled 'Resume' and stared at the blank page.

Education: Bachelor's degree, incomplete, English Literature.

Work Experience: bank teller, twenty-five years ago, in a world before online banking even existed.

The cursor blinked accusingly, emphasizing how little she had to offer. She'd spent two decades running a household, but what did that translate to? Who would hire someone whose technical skills were decades out of date, whose only reference was a husband who considered her incompetent?

'You couldn't handle it,' Don had said whenever she'd mentioned possibly working again. *'The business world has changed completely since you bagged groceries.'*

She hadn't corrected him about her bank job. It hadn't seemed worth the argument.

One article suggested highlighting transferable skills, but Rebecca couldn't imagine describing herself with terms like 'project management' or 'conflict resolution' without hearing Don's mocking laughter.

She closed the laptop. The available job market clearly had no place for someone like her—too old for entry-level positions, too inexperienced for everything else, and too uncertain of her own abilities to confidently pursue either.

Pacing the room, she felt the familiar weight of inadequacy settle over her. She'd never expected her intelligence to count for much—Don had made sure of that. But she'd hoped there might be some path forward, some way to support herself. Instead, it seemed her years as Don's wife had left her with nothing marketable at all. Suddenly single, and virtually unemployable.

Rebecca leaned into the window, her palms and forehead cool against the glass. Outside, the hills glowed copper and bronze in the late afternoon light, darkening to purple where shadows fell. Their ancient presence settled her, offering perspective beyond her immediate troubles.

What did the future hold? Rebecca couldn't remember the last time she had no roadmap, no expectations to fulfill, no role to play. The uncertainty was scary—but also thrilling.

She opened her laptop again and created another document, the screen illuminating her face in the dimming room. Following Helen's advice, she began to write, not knowing what would emerge but trusting the process. The words came hesitantly at first, her fingers hovering over the keys before beginning to move, a small stream of consciousness that gradually gained momentum—they were born of anger, grief, fear, but also the first tentative stirrings of joy.

Who am I? she typed as a title, the words appearing on the screen like a declaration before she sat staring at the white space below.

I am Rebecca. Not Don's Rebecca. Not Mom-Rebecca. Not even Helen's Rebel. Just Rebecca. That's all I know. That's pretty vague. But it's time to find out who that is. I can't afford NOT to find out who that is. I don't need all the answers today. I only need one honest step.

The cursor blinked steadily, waiting for what would come next.

CHAPTER 19

REBECCA ROSE BEFORE SUNRISE, eager to explore downtown in the early morning light. She dressed in her exercise clothes, laced her shoes with fingers that moved more confidently each morning, and slipped out into the pre-dawn darkness.

Fremont Street contrasted sharply with the Strip's manicured glamour. The famous canopied light show was dark, the massive LED screen dormant. The street held traces of the previous night's revelry—beer and cigarette smells lingering, promotional cards for adult services scattered on the sidewalk. Without the protective bubble of the Strip, the city's grittier reality pressed against her senses.

She passed bars shuttered until later in the day, their neon signs dark, metal grates drawn across entrances where bouncers had stood hours before. In some areas, she quickened her pace, her heart thumping a little faster. A cluster of people who looked like they'd been out all night slouched on benches, their glazed eyes tracking her as she passed. She crossed to the opposite side of the street, her fingers subconsciously tracing the closed zipper in her light jacket, where her room key and credit card were safely stowed.

Despite her mild anxiety, there was something authentic about downtown that appealed to her—a place that didn't pretend to be something it wasn't. She contemplated this as she walked, her feet finding their rhythm on the concrete. She mused on how everyone, like every city, has a seedier side. The thought made her lips curve into a small, knowing smile. Her own sharper edge had surfaced in that phone call with Don, raw words erupting after decades of careful restraint.

As the sky lightened to pearl grey, Rebecca found herself outside the Common House Eatery, just opening for breakfast. A sleepy-eyed server was flipping the sign to OPEN as she approached. On impulse, she stepped inside, the bell announcing her arrival.

The interior was inviting with exposed brick walls, rough wooden tables, and industrial lighting casting an amber wash across the space. Rebecca inhaled the aroma of coffee and fresh bread. She took a table near a window to watch the street coming to life, her fingers tracing the edge of the worn wooden surface.

A server with a sleeve of colorful tattoos and a nose ring approached with a carafe of water. "Morning," she said, her voice still husky with sleep. "Menu's on the table. I'll give you a few minutes."

When the server returned for her order, Rebecca hesitated, her stomach giving a small growl. Her usual breakfast—bacon, eggs, and toast—suddenly seemed heavy, a remnant of her old life.

"I'll try the açaí bowl," she said, the words feeling foreign yet right on her tongue. "And a cup of tea, please. Earl Grey if you have it. Black."

The bowl arrived artfully presented—honey-drizzled granola, fresh berries, thin banana slices, and chia seeds atop a purple background of açaí. Rebecca took a tentative bite and found it delicious, the flavors bright and clean, the textures varied. The honey's sweetness balanced the tartness, making her close her eyes in appreciation.

"First time with açaí?" the server asked, noticing Rebecca's reaction.

Rebecca nodded. "I usually have bacon and eggs."

The server smiled, revealing a small dimple in her left cheek. "Bold move, changing it up. How's that working out for you?"

"Better than expected," Rebecca replied truthfully, surprised by the ease of this small exchange.

"Well, enjoy," the server said, giving a small salute before moving to another table.

The brief interaction left Rebecca feeling strangely accomplished, as if she'd passed some test she hadn't known she was taking.

She resolved to start eating lighter and healthier—and simply less. It was a small change, but it felt significant—a choice made solely for herself, not to accommodate Don's preferences or maintain family traditions. With each bite her spoon moved more confidently, claiming this new pleasure.

Her mind raced as she ate, thoughts tumbling over one another like stones in a riverbed. The confrontation with Don had shifted something fundamental within her. The words she'd hurled at him—crude, raw, honest—had been so unlike the carefully modulated responses she'd cultivated during their marriage. How often had she suppressed her real feelings, she wondered, swallowing another spoonful of açaí. How many times had she bitten her tongue, nodded in agreement, deferred to his judgment even when every instinct screamed otherwise?

She was anonymous in this city, a faceless nobody among the tourists and gamblers and workers. The server didn't know her name, her history, her troubles. Yet paradoxically, she felt less a stranger to herself than she recalled being in her former life. Here, she was simply a blank canvas—undefined, unobserved, free to discover who she might become. The thought sent a small shiver of anticipation down her spine.

Rebecca headed back toward the Gilded Horseshoe, this time taking more appreciative notice of her surroundings. She watched the morning light transform Fremont Street. The shadows retreated as the sun climbed, revealing details she hadn't noticed in the dimness—vintage Vegas murals on distant buildings, a small urban garden tucked between two buildings.

She passed the neon signs of the old casinos—the El Cortez, the Four Queens—landmarks from Vegas's earlier era, before the Strip's mega-resorts claimed the spotlight.

An ABC store caught her eye, and Helen's suggestion to keep a journal echoed in her mind. She couldn't see herself sitting in front of a blank screen, typing endless thoughts and feelings on her laptop, but the physicality of writing by hand had always helped her organize her thoughts. She navigated past racks of souvenirs to a small stationery section, selecting a simple spiral-bound notebook and a pack of fine felt-tip pens.

Back outside, the heat had intensified, the sun now fully risen. Rebecca's skin prickled with sweat as she walked toward her hotel, the ABC bag swinging against her leg.

The Gilded Horseshoe's pool was famous for its waterslides—a tangle of colorful slides and tubes that wove and twisted from a great height into the magnificent pool below. She had no intention of using the slides, imagining the indignity of her body hurtling down into the pool while tourists watched, but the area seemed a peaceful place to sit with her new notebook.

She quickly changed into her swimsuit and headed poolside, settling into a lounge chair in a shaded corner and flipping the notebook open. The paper crackled, pristine and untouched.

For a long moment, she stared at the empty page, pen hovering, unsure how to begin. Her fingers tightened around the pen, then relaxed. What could she possibly write that would make sense of the upheaval in her life? Would this exercise be another waste of time, as Don would surely label it—one more self-indulgent activity with no practical purpose? She closed the notebook, then immediately reopened it, irritated at how easily his imagined criticism had seeped into her thoughts.

Finally, she wrote the date at the top of the page and the simplest truth she could think of: *I started my day with a walk.*

She paused, pen hovering against the paper, ink bleeding faintly into the page. Then, slowly, as if the pen had a mind of its own, other words began to flow:

I ordered an açaí bowl instead of bacon and eggs. The food tasted colorful, and alive. I want to eat that kind of food every day. I bought this notebook. I'm hoping it's one of many that I will fill with thoughts and feelings and plans for my future. I hung up on Don yesterday. Despite everything, a small part of me still feels guilty about it—the instinct to 'smooth things over' runs deep. But the rest of me knows it was long overdue.

I won a jackpot last week. My friend Helen came to visit. I miss my children but I'm not ready to explain any of this to them, although I know they deserve to know more.

I remember when Jodie was seven and skinned her knee badly at the playground. She had cried for me, but I went to Don first, soothing his irritation before tending to her scrape. Even then, the children seemed to sense the order of things—Luke watching Don's expression before speaking, Jodie biting her lip until the storm of his mood passed. How many times did I teach them, by my own example, that his feelings mattered more than theirs? More than mine?

I am so different than I was two weeks ago. I don't know who I am becoming. I thought I'd be more scared, but I'm not. What's the worst that could happen? Maybe the worst has ALREADY happened, and I survived.

The sentences emerged disconnected, unpolished, but honest. They tumbled onto the page like water from a tap suddenly turned on after years of disuse, spattering and irregular at first. They were small fragments of a self she was piecing together. Her handwriting, initially stiff and careful, grew looser as she continued, the blue ink flowing freely across the page.

She continued pouring random thoughts onto the pages, moving from staccato statements about recent activities to longer reflections about her marriage, about Don's betrayal, about the growing certainty that she couldn't return to her old life even if that option were offered. The words came faster as she wrote, spilling onto the pages in a stream of consciousness that bypassed her usual self-censorship.

When she finally set down the pen, her words had filled nearly twenty pages of the notebook—tiny handwriting, crowded margins. Aching slightly from the unaccustomed activity with a dull throb in her wrist, she flexed her fingers, watching the tendons move beneath her skin. She sat back, lighter somehow, as if transferring her thoughts to paper had relieved her of carrying their full weight. Closing the notebook, she leaned back in the lounge chair, the cushion warm against her skin.

Later, she would call Jodie and Luke, steeling herself for their inevitable questions and concern. Tomorrow, she would start figuring out what came next—practical matters of income and the shape of her future days. But today, she had taken a walk through downtown Vegas in the early morning light, tried something different for breakfast that had delighted her palate, and found her voice on paper after years of silence.

It wasn't much, perhaps, but it was a beginning. And beginnings, she was discovering, held their own particular kind of magic. Across the pool, a young couple leaned into each other, laughing at some private joke. They looked so certain, so unaware of how life could upturn even the most carefully laid plans. Yet there was something beautiful in their certainty too, a reminder that even after devastation, growth was possible.

Rebecca's lips curved into a smile, this one fuller and more certain than before. She tucked her journal into her bag, protecting the first fragile pages of her reinvention.

CHAPTER 20

M acBook balanced on her lap, Rebecca sat propped comfortably against the headboard. Her eyes were heavy as she stared at the login screen of her email account.

After several days of avoiding her emails, deliberately immersing herself in the physical world of Las Vegas, she had finally worked up the courage to face her inbox. She'd created a new email address but still needed to check her old account for messages.

Heaving a deep sigh of reluctance, she clicked to load her inbox.

Don's emails dominated the screen, their subject lines evolving from *When are you coming home?* to *RESPOND IMMEDIATELY!* with a progression almost comical, if it wasn't so infuriating. She deleted these without reading beyond the subject lines, each click of the delete button a small act of defiance.

A message from Jodie caught her attention—*Mom, PLEASE call me!!!*—sending a pang of guilt through her. She'd been avoiding her daughter's calls, not ready to discuss the situation or face the inevitable questions.

Among the clutter of promotional emails and notifications, their colorful subject lines blurring together as she scrolled, one made her pause: *Titan Rewards: Your Complimentary Stay Awaits*. The words seemed to pulse on the screen, drawing her attention like a neon sign.

Curious, she opened it, expecting a marketing ploy that would reveal hidden costs or impossible conditions—the kind of offer Don would have immediately dismissed as 'too good to be true'. Instead, she found what appeared to be a genuine offer:

Dear Rebecca Morley,

As a valued Titan Rewards member, we're pleased to offer you a complimentary 4-night stay at Titan Group Las Vegas Resorts.

This exclusive offer includes: - Deluxe Room for 4 nights - $100 Food and Beverage Credit - $25 Free Play

To redeem this offer, please call the number below, or book online.

Rebecca raised her eyebrows in disbelief. "Wait—WHAT?" she exclaimed aloud. A free stay at any Titan Group hotel on the Strip? She remembered the casino attendant signing her up for the rewards program after her jackpot win, but hadn't expected anything to come of it.

She quickly logged into Titan Rewards to verify the offer. Sure enough, there it was in her rewards account—a complimentary stay at any of several hotels. She scrolled through the options, her excitement growing. The non-smoking casino on the Strip particularly appealed after weeks of moving through smoke-filled gaming areas.

Rebecca checked the calendar on her laptop, the dates glowing softly on the screen. She had another four days at the Gilded Horseshoe, which would give her time to consider her next steps. Before she could talk herself out of it, she clicked through to book the Monarch at Titan Verde for the dates immediately following her current reservation. The confirmation page appeared moments later, the system verifying her booking for another four nights in Las Vegas.

The realization that she'd committed to staying away for almost another week gave her a momentary flutter of anxiety, a butterfly sensation that started in her stomach and traveled upward to constrict her throat. What was she doing? Her funds would stretch only so far, even with the jackpot money. And what about her life in Savannah? The dentist appointment she'd scheduled weeks ago seemed to be her only obligation.

But a dentist appointment could be rescheduled. She knew she wasn't ready to go to Savannah. Still not yet. The responsible Rebecca, the one who had managed the Morley household for decades, whispered warnings about financial security, practical arrangements, the complications of living in limbo.

She silenced the voice with a small shake of her head, her hair brushing against her shoulders with the movement. For once, her own healing needed to take priority over logistics and others' expectations.

A notification sound drew her attention to her email, the distinctive ping cutting through her thoughts. A message had arrived from Don's work address, with the subject line *Revised Settlement—TIME SENSITIVE*. The bold, capitalized words shouted from the screen.

Rebecca's heart thumped painfully, a rapid staccato against her ribs. Her palms dampened, leaving slight smudges on the laptop's lustrous surface. She almost closed the device, not ready to engage with Don again so soon after their heated phone confrontation, the memory of his shouting still fresh enough to make her flinch.

Something stopped her—perhaps the memory of Justine's calm certainty as she'd reviewed the original settlement, her pen marking key points with precise strokes, or Helen's encouragement to advocate for herself, her friend's voice seeming to echo in the quiet room.

Taking a deep breath, she clicked to open the email, her jaw set.

Rebecca,

Attached is a revised settlement agreement that addresses some of your apparent concerns. This is my final offer. It is overly generous, especially considering your recent behavior. I expect you to sign and return this within 48 hours. The longer this drags on, the more difficult it becomes for everyone involved. Jodie is distraught, and your continued absence is causing our family unnecessary distress.

Don

His patronizing tone made her blood simmer, heat rising to her cheeks. She could almost hear his voice, the emphasis he would place on 'apparent' and 'behavior', the disdainful manner of speech that had so often made her second-guess herself. Forcing herself to focus on the attached document, her eyes narrowed as she scrolled through the pages.

It appeared to be a barely modified version of Don's original offer, with a few token adjustments—five years of alimony instead of three, the remaining money in their joint savings acknowledged as hers, but no comment about the amount he had withdrawn. The agreement still left her with the outstanding mortgage that had been used to pay for Don's new car.

Rebecca reached for her phone, her movements deliberate, scrolling to Justine's number. The sleek device felt cool in her hand, calming her.

"Justine Avery," came the crisp response after two rings, the background noise suggesting she was in a public place.

"Justine, it's Rebecca." Her voice sounded uncertain even to her own ears, the words catching in her throat. "I—I'm sorry to bother you, but Don has sent a revised settlement, and—"

"You're not bothering me at all," Justine corrected, her tone warming. "I was wondering how things had been going, and when he'd make his next move. Can you forward the email to me?"

"Of course." Relief flowed through her at Justine's matter-of-fact response, her shoulders relaxing. "Should I do anything else?"

"You can let him know that all further communication regarding the settlement should go through me, if you'd like—alternatively, I can open that door of communication for you."

"Yes. Okay, I will let him know—although he's really riled up that I have my own legal advice. I can't thank you enough," Rebecca said, the words inadequate to express her gratitude for this lifeline of professional support.

"No thanks necessary. Just take care of yourself, Rebecca," Justine replied, the simple directive landing with unexpected weight.

After they disconnected, Rebecca forwarded Don's email to Justine, the action requiring only a few simple clicks, but feeling momentous. She then composed a brief response to her former husband, her fingers tapping against the keys with growing confidence:

Don,

I have forwarded your revised settlement proposal to my lawyer, Justine Avery. Please direct all future communication regarding our divorce to her at the email address below.

Rebecca

She CC'ed Justine and hit send before she could rethink it, the decisive click of the trackpad marking the moment. Then she sat back against the pillows, anxiety and exhilaration coursing through her veins.

Her old flip phone rang, vibrating from the depths of her purse where it had laid buried for days. Don. The name flashed like a warning. She let it go to voicemail, not ready for another confrontation. But when it rang again a minute later, she saw Jodie's name.

This call she wouldn't ignore. She took a grounding breath before answering, holding the phone to her ear.

"Jodie, hi, sweetheart," she said, trying to keep her voice light despite the tension coiling in her stomach.

"Mom!" Her daughter's voice was tight with emotion and annoyance. "Finally! I've been so worried. Are you okay? What's going on? Dad won't tell us anything except that you're hiding out in Las Vegas, and Luke says you haven't been answering his texts."

Rebecca closed her eyes, guilt washing over her in a cold wave. She hadn't even seen Luke's messages, having barely looked at the old phone these past days.

Her thoughts turned to Luke. Unlike Jodie, who approached conflict head-on like her father, Luke processed things internally, deliberating before responding. Of her two children, she worried most about how he would handle this upheaval. Their Sunday evening phone calls had been a constant throughout his college years and beyond—a tradition she'd now broken with her silence.

"I'm sorry for worrying you both," she said, her free hand coming up to rub at the space between her eyebrows where a headache was beginning to form. "I'm okay, I promise. I needed some space to think."

"Think about what?" Jodie pressed, exasperation evident in her voice. "Dad said he was very clear that you'll be well taken care of in the settlement. I know you're sad, but when are you coming home so we can sort this all out?"

Rebecca moved to the window and pulled aside the heavy curtain, looking out at the iconic neon signs of downtown Las Vegas, their glow beginning to assert itself against the fading daylight.

Was she actually *sad*? How much should she tell Jodie? The complete truth would hurt her children deeply, the revelation that their father had betrayed not only Rebecca but the entire family unit they'd built together. Yet they deserved better than the sanitized version Don had no doubt prepared, his lawyer's instinct for selective disclosure shaping the narrative to cast himself in the best possible light.

"Well, you already know that your father has asked for—no, actually, he didn't *ask*, he *informed*—that we were getting a divorce," Rebecca said, her fingers worrying the curtain's edge. "He told me on our first night here in Vegas."

"That isn't quite the story he told me," Jodie replied, her voice dropping to a more serious register. "But Sean says I should also hear your side. Tell me what you think happened."

"It's complicated, honey." Rebecca hesitated, unwilling to burden Jodie with the raw truth of Don's affair and pregnancy. The words felt stuck in her throat, reluctant to emerge. "Dad has—he's made some choices that ended our marriage."

"What does that mean?" Jodie's frustration vibrated through the line. "What *choices* ended your marriage?"

Rebecca could hear the sarcasm creeping into Jodie's tone, a trait she'd inherited from Don, along with his sharp analytical mind. "I think that's something you should discuss with your father. It's not my place to—"

"Not your *place*?" Jodie's voice rose, the words coming faster. "Mom, you're my mother. I want to know what's happened, and I want to hear it from you, not Dad's lawyer-speak version. All he says is that you've grown apart for years and that you both decided you wanted a divorce. It's completely the opposite of what you're very vaguely telling me. It doesn't make sense."

The accuracy of that characterization—*lawyer-speak*—almost made Rebecca smile despite the gravity of the conversation. How many times had she heard Don carefully construct narratives that presented facts in the most favorable light for himself or his client, while technically remaining only somewhat truthful? The familiar pattern was so obvious now that she'd stepped outside of its influence.

"Your father is in a relationship with someone else," Rebecca stated flatly, the words falling into the silence between them like stones into still water. "He plans to build a new life with her."

Another silence, this one longer and heavier, filled only by the sound of Jodie's breathing.

"What do you mean? Dad didn't tell me this. Is it someone I know?" Jodie finally asked, her voice cracking.

"Annette. She works in accounting at his firm."

"The one with the bob haircut? She was at your Christmas party? The one who brought those weird cream cheese pinwheel things? She's like, thirty?"

The strange detail Jodie remembered—those mediocre appetizers—struck Rebecca as both sad and oddly touching. Her daughter was grasping for the familiar in the midst of this revelation.

"Thirty-two, I believe," Rebecca said, amused by how little the age difference bothered her compared to the betrayal itself.

"So, when did that start? Before or after you guys split up in Vegas?" Jodie asked, clearly trying to piece together the sequence of events.

"Oh. Before. It must have started a while ago. I don't know when exactly, but long enough to get her pregnant."

"WHAT?!" Jodie's voice rang out clearly over the line, the single word almost a physical presence in the room. Then, more quietly, "Oh my God. Dad's having a baby. With someone else."

"Yes," Rebecca confirmed, waiting while Jodie processed this news. She could faintly hear Sean's soothing voice in the background.

"Oh my God, Mom. I've talked to Dad like four times this week and he didn't mention ANY of this," Jodie said, her words tumbling over each other in her shock. "Does Luke know?"

"I don't know. I left him a voicemail last week but still haven't spoken to him," Rebecca admitted, a fresh wave of guilt washing over her. "I actually left my phone in my bag for a while."

"So, what? You're just going to stay in Vegas indefinitely? I'm really having trouble wrapping my head around all this," Jodie said, audibly struggling to process the revelations.

Rebecca glanced at her laptop, still open on the bed with its confirmation of her extended booking, the dates glowing on the screen like a promise. "I'm not sure. At least another week. I need some time to figure things out before I come back to Savannah."

"Jesus Mom. I feel like I don't even know you. Or Dad. It's like we're in the Twilight Zone," Jodie said softly, vulnerability replacing the earlier anger in her voice.

The statement pierced through Rebecca, a sharp ache stabbing through her chest. "I know, sweetheart," she replied honestly. "I need some space to process everything and make plans for my future. This all happened very suddenly for me."

"Uh, yeah. For us too." Jodie's voice betrayed a tremor, suggesting she might be close to tears.

"I know, honey. I'm so sorry." Rebecca meant it with every fiber of her being. She sank onto the edge of the bed. Despite her own pain, the thought of her children suffering made her ache in a way that transcended her personal grief. "I promise I'll be more available from now on. No more avoiding calls or messages."

She could hear her daughter cursing quietly on the other side of the country, the quiet expletives almost making her smile despite everything.

"Oh, that reminds me Jodie, I'm going to give you another phone number, but I'd appreciate if you don't give it to your father," she said impulsively. She rattled off the digits for her new number, the unfamiliar 702 area code still strange on her tongue.

"A Las Vegas number? Whose is that?" Jodie asked, confusion evident in her voice.

"It's mine," Rebecca replied, a small smile forming as she glanced at the iPhone charging on the nightstand. "I have an iPhone now, and it's a lovely shade of lavender."

Jodie laughed out loud, the sound bursting through the tension like sunshine through clouds. "An iPhone? Mom! How progressive. I won't tell Dad. You sure you're trained on that machine?"

The teasing question, so normal and daughterly, made Rebecca's eyes sting with unexpected tears. "I'm learning," she said, her voice thick. "It's not so hard once you get used to it."

They talked for nearly an hour after that, the sky outside the window darkening to deep blue, then black. Rebecca answered Jodie's questions as honestly as she could without vilifying Don, choosing her words carefully but refusing to perpetuate the fiction he'd created. She corrected many untruths that Don had told their daughter, each revelation met with a mixture of disbelief and growing understanding from Jodie.

By the end of the conversation, Jodie seemed calmer, though still upset by the situation, her voice steadier as they moved from shock to practical considerations.

"You should probably try calling Luke again," Jodie said eventually. "Or I can call him, if you want. Give him the details before he hears any more from Dad."

"How about I do that," Rebecca suggested, stretching her legs. "You shouldn't have to manage this situation, Jodie. That's not your job. Your father and I should have told you both earlier. It's been—strange."

"Either way, I'm calling Dad now to rip him a new one," Jodie warned, a spark of her usual spirit returning to her voice. "He didn't need to paint you as a crazy person, or flat out lie about the situation. I mean, how was he going to explain the baby? Divine intervention?"

The comment startled a genuine laugh from Rebecca. "I love you, Jodie," she said, the words simple but heartfelt.

"Love you too, Mom," her daughter replied. "Call me tomorrow, okay?"

After they hung up, Rebecca remained by the window, watching the desert sunset complete its transformation, painting the city in hues of gold and rose that gradually ceded to the artificial glow of neon.

The conversation with Jodie had started out difficult, each revelation like navigating a minefield, but it was both necessary and refreshingly cleansing. It was the first step toward whatever relationship they would forge in the wake of her marriage's collapse, a bridge being built word by word across troubled waters.

She sent Luke a text, her fingers tapping out the message with growing confidence on the new device: *Hi Honey, it's Mom! Would love to have a chat—when is good for you?*

Her phone pinged with a text notification almost immediately. Expecting a response from Luke, she was surprised to see a message from Justine instead: *Reviewed the revised settlement. Still inadequate. Will send through counter-proposal suggestions tomorrow. Don't sign anything.*

Rebecca smiled faintly, the expression relaxing her features in the dim light of the hotel room. Between Justine's professional guidance, her direct language cutting through legal complexities, Helen's friendship, warm and unwavering even across the distance, and now the beginning of honest communication with her children, clearing away Don's carefully constructed narratives, she was building her own independent support network.

It wasn't the life she'd planned—her carefully tended future now scattered like seeds in the wind—but perhaps she could make a life worth living, nonetheless.

She grabbed her notebook from the nightstand and settled in on the couch, the leather cool against her bare legs. Uncapping her pen, she added an entry beneath her earlier thoughts, the ink flowing smoothly across the page:

Today I booked more time in Vegas. Today I talked to Jodie about the divorce.

Small steps. Or maybe giant leaps. Either way, the world isn't ending.

Chapter 21

THE NEXT FEW DAYS at the Gilded Horseshoe took on the quality of a meditative tour. Each morning, she rose early for her walk, but something had changed in her stride. What had begun as aimless wandering had evolved into purposeful movement.

She started adding brief sprints between landmarks, racing from one vintage neon sign to the next, pushing herself until her lungs burned and her calves protested. The physical exertion felt like a metaphor, as if she were racing toward the future, or perhaps even the present that she had been missing out on during years of blind stagnation.

After one particularly vigorous burst of speed she paused, hands to knees, catching her breath outside the El Cortez. A passing jogger gave her an encouraging nod, one athlete to another. The notion almost made her laugh—Rebecca Morley, athlete? Yet her body had been changing, responding to the miles she logged each day and the healthier food choices she'd been making. Her clothes hung looser now; her wedding ring had begun to slip on her finger. She questioned why she was still wearing it.

Back at the hotel, she showered and changed, slipping her ring into a side pocket of her toiletry bag—no longer on her finger, and no longer in plain sight.

She settled on the bed with her phone. She'd tried to contact Luke, leaving both voice and text messages, but still hadn't managed to connect with her son.

This time, Luke answered on the fourth ring, his voice cautious. "Hey Mom. I got your messages. You okay?"

"Hi sweetheart," Rebecca said, her throat tightening. "I'm okay. But I wanted to talk to you about something important."

"I already talked to Jodie. And Dad," Luke said quietly.

Rebecca closed her eyes briefly. "I'm sorry we didn't talk sooner."

"It's okay." His voice held the careful neutrality he'd adopted in adolescence, the tone that masked whatever emotions churned beneath. "Dad told me some stuff. Jodie explained what she knows."

"What did they tell you?"

"Well, Dad said that you're refusing to leave Las Vegas after you guys decided to get a divorce. Then Jodie told me that Dad actually left you in Las Vegas after dropping the news on you like a bomb. That he's leaving you for someone at his office. That she's knocked up. That he told you on your first night in Vegas." The neutrality slipped, revealing a thread of anger. Luke's voice dropped almost to a whisper. "Jesus, Mom. I can't even—"

He cleared his throat. "That's pretty cold, even for Dad. How are you even functioning right now?"

Rebecca wasn't sure how to respond. She'd never encouraged her children to criticize their father, even when his strict parenting style had chafed against their teenage independence.

"It was... unexpected," she said carefully.

"So, are you coming home soon? I want to see you." Luke asked.

"Not yet. I'm staying in Vegas a bit longer. I need some time to figure things out."

A pause. "Do you think that's kind of weird, Mom?"

She couldn't help but smile at his bluntness. "Well, honey, the whole situation is kind of weird. I know it probably seems like I'm hiding or running away. But this is something I need to do for myself. Vegas is like a cocoon."

"Okay. If you say so, Mom. But listen, it's also kind of cool, because Jake and I were thinking about coming out to Vegas next weekend," Luke said, his tone lightening. "His cousin's getting married at one of those Elvis chapels on Saturday, and he's got tickets for the basketball championships. He asked if I wanted to come along and I was thinking if you were still there, maybe I could see you? If you want to see me."

Rebecca felt a surge of both excitement and anxiety. "I would *love* that," she said honestly. "Of course I want to see you! Do you want me to organize a hotel for you guys?"

"Hell yeah," Luke commented, and she could hear him telling Jake in the background.

"Hey Mom, can we stay at the Titan Royale? That's where the game is."

"Of course, I can book that. I can't believe you're coming here."

"I know, right? I can't believe my Mom is hanging out in Sin City," he joked. "Who are you and what have you done with my risk-averse mother?"

She laughed. "I'm still figuring that out myself."

They spoke for another twenty minutes, the conversation shifting to the architectural firm where Luke had been doing work experience. Promising to book the room and send details, she was overwhelmed by the excitement of seeing her son on what she now thought of as 'her territory'.

By the time they finished the call, she felt lighter, reassured that her relationship with her son would weather this transition. She set a reminder to book Titan Royale for Luke and Jake and text them the details.

Feeling restless and noticing how most of her clothes now hung loosely on her frame, it was time to do something about her wardrobe. She needed more than her walking clothes and a couple of dresses. The concierge suggested the Las Vegas North Premium Outlets, accessible by a short taxi ride.

The sprawling outdoor mall was bustling even on a weekday afternoon. She wandered from store to store until a boutique caught her eye. In the window, a mannequin wore slim dark jeans with a studded belt, ankle boots with a substantial heel, and a tank top under a fitted silk blazer.

It was the antithesis of the 'Rebecca Morley uniform' of modest necklines, sensible shoes, and loose-fitting clothes in the matronly patterns that she'd worn for years.

Before she could talk herself out of it, she entered the store.

"Can I help you find something?" asked a salesperson with a shaved head and multiple ear piercings.

"Those jeans in the window," she heard herself say. "Would you have them in my size?"

The salesperson assessed her with a professional eye. "Try these," the salesperson said, handing her sizes 14 and 12, along with a belt and several tops.

In the fitting room mirror, Rebecca barely recognized herself. Shocked that the size 12 jeans even slid on at all, she turned from side-to-side in the mirror, noting that they hugged curves she'd been hiding for years. The belt emphasized her newly narrowed waist, and the deep V-neck revealed more décolletage than she normally showed in public. The black leather ankle boots transformed her posture, making her stand taller, shoulders back.

She froze, Don's voice momentarily echoing in her head—*a bit much for someone your age, don't you think?*—before she silenced it with deliberate finality. The woman in the mirror looked confident, almost defiant—nothing like the accommodating, invisible Rebecca who had dressed to fade into the background.

"I'll take it all," she said, a thrill running through her at her own boldness.

That first purchase broke a dam. Store by store, she assembled a new wardrobe—a silky blazer, a form-fitting dress, casual wear in fabrics she'd never allowed herself before: raw silk and cashmere. Her color palette shifted to dramatic blacks, earthy neutrals, and splashes of deep jewel tones.

By sunset, she returned to the Gilded Horseshoe laden with shopping bags. She spread her purchases across the bed, marveling at the colors and unfamiliar styles. Nothing resembled the clothes she'd worn in the past.

On impulse, she gathered everything she'd brought from Savannah—the modest blouses, the mom-jeans, the sensible shoes, as well as some of the new exercise clothes that she had already shrunk out of, and stuffed it all into three large shopping bags. Following the concierge's directions, she carried them to a nearby donation center, dropping the bags in silence into the after-hours bin.

It was her second-to-last evening downtown, and feeling restless, Rebecca decided to dress up and explore a few classic casinos she hadn't yet visited. She chose one of her more daring new outfits—slim jeans with the studded belt, a low-cut silk tank in deep crimson, and the heeled boots. She finished with a black silk blazer, sleeves rolled up, pleased with the transformation in the mirror.

Binion's casino greeted her with the sounds of slot machines, murmurs around gaming tables, and the scent of perfume in the air. As she wandered through, she noticed a poker room in the far corner with a crowd gathered around one table.

She approached curiously, peering over the spectators' shoulders. There were three men at the table. Her breath caught when she recognized Vince, the poker player she'd met at Saddle's. He looked different here—more focused, almost predatory in his concentration, yet utterly at ease as he arranged his chips and studied his cards.

She watched, fascinated by the subtle psychological warfare playing out. Vince seemed to read his opponents' thoughts from the smallest tell—a finger tap, a change in breathing, a too-casual glance at chips. He won a hand, then looked up as he collected his winnings.

His eyes met hers across the room, and his composure slipped for a brief moment in clear recognition. She saw surprise register on his face—not just at her presence, but at her appearance. It was a look she was unaccustomed to receiving—one of genuine appreciation.

She felt herself blush and gave a small wave, suddenly uncertain. Should she approach? Leave?

Vince made the decision for her, saying something to the dealer and rising from the table. He made his way through the spectators toward her.

"Rebecca," he said, her name somehow both a greeting and a question.

"Hello, Vince," she replied, pleased at how assured her voice sounded. "I didn't expect to see you here."

"I could say the same." His blue eyes took in her appearance with undisguised admiration. "I almost didn't recognize you."

"Good unrecognizable or bad unrecognizable?" The words slipped out before she could stop them.

A smile crinkled the corners of his eyes. "Very good unrecognizable. Like seeing a flower bloom." He paused. "Not that there's anything wrong with how you normally look. I've only ever seen you in your walking clothes."

The compliment pleased her more than it should have. "Thank you."

"I thought you were heading home to Savannah. What brings you downtown?"

"I decided to explore Vegas a bit more. I move back to the Strip tomorrow," she replied.

"You're not heading home yet?"

"Not yet. I'm staying at the Monarch next."

He nodded. "Really nice place. Very different from most of the big hotels. I think you'll like it."

A voice called from the poker table, signaling the break was ending.

"I have to get back," he said, glancing over his shoulder. "But it was good to see you, Rebecca."

"You too." She hesitated, then added, "Good luck with the game."

With a small nod that somehow conveyed both respect and friendship, he returned to the table.

Rebecca left Binion's feeling strangely energized by the brief encounter. It wasn't only Vince's obvious appreciation of her appearance—though that was admittedly flattering—but the way he'd spoken to her, as one independent adult to another. No condescension, no assumption that she wouldn't understand the subtleties of his profession, no hint that she was somehow inferior. It was refreshingly uplifting.

On her final morning at the Gilded Horseshoe, she woke early, packed her new wardrobe into her suitcase, and prepared to leave downtown behind. Strolling through the familiar streets one last time, she marveled at how much had changed in the span of a few weeks.

A taxi delivered her to the Monarch at Titan Verde entrance. Unlike the bright casino entrances of most Strip hotels, the Monarch lobby was an oasis of understated elegance with rich woods and lowkey lighting. The walls were lined with bookshelves containing real volumes, and original artwork hung in careful arrangements.

"Welcome to Monarch Las Vegas," the receptionist greeted her. "Checking in?"

Presenting her ID, she took in the finer details of the lobby, appreciating the fresh flowers and the subtle woodsy scent in the lobby. The receptionist slid over a folio confirming the details of her stay—four free nights, $100 dining credit, and $25 free play. Rebecca smiled gratefully and wheeled her bag toward the elevator.

Her room continued the theme of refined comfort—a cloud-like king bed with a leather-wrapped headboard, a freestanding copper bathtub visible through French doors leading to the bathroom, artwork that managed to be both soothing and thought-provoking. It felt more like a well-appointed guest room in a stylish home than a hotel room.

She unpacked her clothes, hanging them carefully in the closet, then stood by the window. The view encompassed a section of the Strip, with the mountains visible in the distance.

On the desk, she noticed a small pad of paper embossed with the Monarch logo and a slim pen. She sat down, picked up the pen, and wrote the date at the top of the page. She traced the logo with the pen, lost in thought. Instead of her usual 'Today I...' statement, different words flowed:

The woman stood at the window, watching the desert light transform the mountains from rust to purple. Behind her, a suitcase lay open, filled with clothes she'd never worn. Ahead of her stretched days she'd never planned for, in a city that had no claim on her past. She laid a hand on the blank page in front of her. For the first time in decades, she could feel the contours of her own life beneath her fingertips, like a sculpture emerging from unworked stone.

Rebecca set down the pen, startled by what had appeared on the page. Not a journal entry but the beginning of something else—a story, perhaps. Her story, though cast in the third person, as if she needed that slight distance to see it clearly.

She glanced up at the artwork gracing the room's walls, at the carefully curated images chosen to inspire and comfort travelers. The Monarch's atmosphere seemed to be working its creative magic already.

CHAPTER 22

REBECCA WOKE BEFORE HER alarm, soothed by the unfamiliar luxury of her new surroundings. The copper bathtub caught the morning light, scattering reflections across the ceiling. Despite the comfort of the plush bed, her body craved the morning walk that had become her ritual, muscles already anticipating the familiar stretch.

She dressed in new exercise clothes—form-fitting activewear rather than the baggy tees and shorts she'd been wearing. The woman in the mirror looked like she belonged in this elegant room, like someone who valued herself enough to invest in both appearance and comfort. She noted a slight definition beginning to show in her arms, a physical manifestation of her daily walks. She did a quick shadow-box in the mirror before laughing at herself, and headed out to walk the Strip.

On impulse, she turned down the alley toward Saddle's as she was nearing the end of her walk, her feet carrying her there without conscious decision. A bell jingled as she pushed open the door, and the scent of coffee and frying bacon enveloped her—comforting, though now faintly off-putting after days of lighter meals. The vinyl seat squeaked as she slid onto a stool at the counter.

Darlene, her pen already poised over her order pad, gave her a familiar smile. "Welcome back. The usual, hon?"

Rebecca shook her head, unconsciously sitting up straighter. "Not today. Could I please have one poached egg on multigrain toast, no butter? And maybe sliced tomato instead of bacon. And black tea too, please."

She glanced at her bare hand on the counter. The absence of the ring felt more significant than its presence ever had.

Halfway through her breakfast, savoring the fresh tomato with the crisp toast and egg, the bell over the door jingled. Vince walked in, his presence somehow both relaxed and alert. His gaze swept the diner with practiced efficiency, then landed on her.

"Mornin'," he said, his voice a rough timbre as he settled onto the stool beside her. "How's the Monarch?"

"Beautiful. Really classy," she replied, her fingers curling around the warm mug of tea.

"I'm happy you like it," he said simply, accepting coffee with a nod of thanks.

As Darlene moved away, Rebecca relaxed into the conversation, the ease of it pleasing after years of carefully measured exchanges with Don, where every word felt weighted.

"So, what are you really still doing in Vegas?" he asked, adding sugar to his coffee with a practiced motion.

She stared into her mug of tea before looking up to meet his eyes. "I've been here over three weeks now. Don is moving his belongings out of our house in Savannah, and I know I should probably be there, but I don't feel strong enough yet. It's like I'll lose some of the footing I've gained here." She hadn't meant to be so honest, but the words flowed naturally.

Vince nodded, his expression neutral, giving her space to continue, his silence an invitation rather than a void to be filled.

"My son is coming to visit this weekend with his college roommate," she added, her mouth curving into a smile that reached her eyes. "They have a wedding to go to, and tickets for the basketball championships. I've booked rooms for us at the Titan Royale."

"Good choice," he observed, raising his mug slightly in approval. "Lots of action."

Her gaze drifted toward the window and the hills visible in the distance, their contours softened by morning haze. Her shoulders relaxed as she looked at them. "I've become fascinated by those hills. They call to me more each day, and I don't even know what they're called."

He followed her gaze, leaning slightly to see from her perspective. "The Spring Mountains are to the west, with Mount Charleston at the highest point. The McCullough Hills are to the southeast. The reddish ones to the northeast are part of the Muddy Mountains and the Valley of Fire. You should check them out."

"Valley of Fire," she repeated, tasting the words, liking the sound of it. "Sounds dramatic."

"It is. Red sandstone that looks like it's on fire when the sun hits just right." He seemed to make a decision, setting his mug down with a clink. "I can show you, if you have time today."

She blinked, stunned. Her fork pausing halfway to her mouth, suspended as if the whole diner were waiting on her answer. "Show me what?"

"Some of those hills you've been staring at," he clarified, gesturing vaguely toward the window. "But you'd want to change into jeans, bring a jacket. Meet me back here in an hour?"

The invitation hung in the air between them—spontaneous, unexpected. The old Rebecca would have hesitated, made excuses, found reasons to say no.

"Okay," she said instead, her pulse quickening slightly. "See you in one hour."

She walked briskly to the Monarch, morning air cool against her flushed cheeks. In her room, she changed into jeans, a lightweight sweater, and lavender Doc Martens—an impulse-buy that she knew Jodie would likely steal as soon as she laid eyes on them. She added mascara and lip gloss, fingers steadier than they once would have been at the prospect of an unplanned day spent with a near-stranger, then grabbed her new lambskin jacket.

The Strip was coming to life as she strode back toward Saddle's, tourists emerging from hotels in search of coffee and breakfast. Vince was already waiting outside, leaning against a motorcycle that gleamed black and chrome in the morning sun, its metal surfaces reflecting pinpoints of light.

When he saw her, he straightened, unfolding his tall frame from its casual pose, and held out a helmet. "Right on time," he noted.

Rebecca stared at the helmet, then at the motorcycle, her heartbeat suddenly loud in her ears. "I've never been on a motorcycle before," she admitted, her voice small. Don's voice echoed in her memory: *Death traps. Only fools and teenagers ride those things.* She'd never questioned his pronouncement before.

"I figured," Vince said matter-of-factly, no judgment in his voice. "We don't have to go if you're not comfortable. I can bring the car another day."

Something about the way he phrased it—offering an alternative without pressure—made her decision easier. The old Rebecca would have retreated to safety.

"I'd like to try," she decided, reaching for the helmet. "Just tell me what to do."

He gave her a quick rundown on motorcycle etiquette—how to mount the bike, where to put her feet, how to lean into turns with him. His instructions were clear, hands demonstrating as he spoke. "And hold on," he finished, first tapping his waist and then the steel rail behind the seat.

She nodded, trying to commit the instructions to memory while her heart hammered with nervousness and excitement. She fumbled with the helmet strap, fingers suddenly clumsy, until Vince reached over to help her adjust it, his movements efficient.

"There," he said, stepping back to assess his work. "Ready? You look like my kid sister," he laughed, the sound warm and authentic.

She wasn't ready, but she nodded anyway, lifting her chin with determination. He swung a leg over the bike with the ease of long practice, the suspension dipping slightly under his weight. Taking a deep breath, she climbed up onto the seat, settling inelegantly behind him.

The motorcycle came to life with a rumble she felt through every point of contact with the machine, vibrations traveling up through her legs and spine. She hesitantly placed her hands on Vince's waist, keeping a respectful distance, feeling the solid presence of another human being close to her for the first time in weeks.

"If you get scared, tap me," he said over his shoulder, voice raised to be heard over the engine, before pulling away from the curb with a smooth acceleration.

She tightened her grip, fingers curling into the leather of his jacket as they merged onto Las Vegas Boulevard. The first few minutes were terrifying—the exposure to the elements, the proximity to other vehicles, the vulnerability of being unprotected. Wind tugged at her clothes, the helmet heavy on her head.

As they left the congested Strip and picked up speed on the highway heading northeast, something loosened inside her. The rush of air and the desert landscape opening up around them combined into an unexpected sense of freedom. Rebecca gradually relaxed, her white-knuckled grip easing, her tense shoulders dropping. She found herself instinctively leaning with Vince into each curve, their bodies moving in synchrony as the bike carved through space. The motorcycle responded to the smallest shifts in weight, alive beneath them. The frantic tension that she had come to accept as her constant companion melted with each mile.

The city fell away, replaced by the stark beauty of the Nevada desert, the mountains rising in the distance like giant sentinels. The brisk morning air made her grateful for the jacket.

They turned onto a narrow road marked 'Valley of Fire State Park'. The landscape changed dramatically, with massive red rock formations jutting from the earth like the spines of ancient creatures, their color deepening from orange to crimson in the sun. The scent of sun-toasted stone and desert plants surrounded her.

Vince slowed the bike, allowing her to take in the scenery, the engine's roar quieting to a purr. They followed the winding road through a landscape that seemed alien, primordial. At a scenic overlook, he pulled over, gravel crunching beneath the tires.

"What do you think?" he asked as they dismounted, his voice sounding strange in the sudden quiet after the constant wind and engine noise.

"It's... incredible," she breathed, removing her helmet and running fingers through her flattened hair. Her eyes widened as she took in the panorama. "Like being on another planet."

They walked to the edge of the overlook, their boots raising small puffs of dust with each step. The vastness of the landscape made Rebecca feel simultaneously insignificant and expansive, her chest opening with each breath of the clear desert air. This was what she'd been seeing in those distant hills—this wild, untamed beauty existing just beyond the manufactured glitz of the Vegas Strip.

They continued their journey, stopping occasionally to take in the striking formations. At one stop, Vince led her down a short trail to a hidden alcove where the red rock formed a natural amphitheater, petroglyphs etched into the stone.

"These are thousands of years old," he explained, running his fingertips reverently near but not on the ancient markings. "The Ancestral Puebloans and later the Paiute people left their marks here."

She studied the mysterious symbols of bighorn sheep, human figures, and spirals, tracing their outlines in the air without touching them. "So people have been passing through here, leaving traces of themselves, for thousands of years," she murmured, her voice hushed as if in a sacred space.

"And most of them were simply traveling through, like us," he said, his voice taking on a contemplative quality. "Moving from one phase of life to another."

The observation hit close to home, making her breath catch. She wondered if this trip was more thoughtfully planned than she'd assumed, if Vince understood more about her situation than he let on.

They rode deeper into the park, the landscape revealing arches carved by wind and water and balanced rocks defying gravity. The beauty was raw and honest, so unlike anyplace else she'd ever been.

As they rounded a curve facing a spectacular vista—an enormous rock arch framing the far-off mountains against a sky so blue it hurt to look at—something unexpected rose within Rebecca: pure, unfiltered joy. Without thinking, she threw out both arms, tilting her head back and hollering a "*Woo-hoo!*" that echoed off the sandstone cliffs, returning to her like a gift.

Vince's shoulders shook with silent laughter. "That's the spirit," he called, his words carried away by the wind.

She was weightless, unburdened by expectations or appearances or the careful dance of her impending divorce. She was simply experiencing joy without qualification or apology, her body feeling more alive than it had in years, every sense heightened.

"Thank you for showing me this place," Rebecca said as they sat on a rock outcropping, sharing sandwiches and water Vince had packed in the saddlebags.

"I spent a lot of time in Nevada when I was young," he replied, brushing crumbs from his jeans. "Not Vegas—a small town north of here. My grandfather had a repair shop there. I spent summers helping him fix motorcycles. We used to ride out here. Now I come out here when I need to clear my head." He gestured to the landscape around them. "Something about this area puts things in perspective. The red sandstone offset by the grey limestone. It's like no place else."

"You're right," she agreed, tilting her face up to the sun, feeling its heat sink into her skin, feeling the essence of the hills under her hands. "Makes my problems seem very small."

"Not small," he corrected, "just... right-sized. These rocks have been here for millions of years. They've seen civilizations rise and fall. But that doesn't make individual lives any less significant."

There was something about his presence that invited honesty without expectation. Unlike Don, who had always pushed for immediate solutions, or Helen, whose loving support sometimes came with implicit advice, Vince simply listened, creating space for her thoughts without trying to shape them.

"I'm not sure who I am anymore," she opened up, shedding light on the fear circling within her mind for weeks. "For twenty-five years, I was a wife and mother. I knew what every day would hold. Now I'm... what? A middle-aged divorcée? A tourist?" Her hands moved restlessly before settling back onto the stone by her sides, her legs dangling over the edge of the rock. "I look in the mirror sometimes and don't recognize the person looking back. I'm different every day now."

Vince stood quietly, watching a hawk circle overhead. "Maybe not recognizing yourself isn't such a bad thing," he finally said, his tone thoughtful. "Getting the chance to discover yourself again."

"What if there's nothing to discover?" The question emerged as barely more than a whisper, a fear she hadn't articulated even to herself.

"Not possible," he said simply, certainty in his voice. "Every day you make choices. Those choices, more than anything that happens to you, are what define who you are. Lots of folks in your position would just let themselves stagnate. I think you're doing great."

They rode back toward the city in the late afternoon, the city's skyline gradually materializing from the desert haze like a mirage. Rebecca felt the transition physically—her chest tightened as reality reasserted itself, and her arms instinctively held onto Vince as they rejoined heavier traffic.

She realized that what was settling in wasn't the same crushing weight she'd carried before. Something had changed during their day in the Valley of Fire, some understanding that had been beyond her grasp. The realization that boundaries—whether geographic or personal—were more permeable than she'd believed. That she could move beyond them when she chose.

As Vince pulled up outside the Monarch she felt profound gratitude for the day. Her legs wobbled slightly as she dismounted, unused to the hours of riding.

"Thank you, Vince," she said, her voice rich with sincerity as she removed the helmet and shook out her hair. "I needed this more than I realized."

He nodded, a simple acknowledgment, his eyes crinkling at the corners. "Sometimes we need to get outside ourselves to find ourselves, if that makes sense. Seeing new things can wake us up."

She felt a sudden reluctance to end the day. The thought of returning to her empty hotel room after the day's sense of connection felt almost painful.

"Dinner," she blurted, the word escaping before she'd fully formed the thought. She felt herself blush, but hurriedly continued, "I mean, not a date, but can I buy you dinner? I'd like to thank you for today."

Vince smiled, a flash of surprise crossing his face before he nodded. "Not-a-date dinner sounds great. I know a casual place—one of my favorites. Italian. What do you think?"

Rebecca put the helmet back on, its weight now familiar, and swung her leg over the seat with newfound confidence.

Chapter 23

Joe's Ristorante was nothing like Rebecca had expected. Nestled in a converted house downtown, it had the unassuming appearance of a place known only to locals. The small red-brick building seemed almost defiantly ordinary amid Las Vegas's carefully cultivated spectacle.

Inside, however, was a different world—cozy, intimate, with red-checkered tablecloths and walls covered in photographs, memorabilia, and vintage wine bottles wrapped in straw. The scent of tomatoes, garlic, and fresh herbs enveloped them as they entered, along with the low hum of conversation and the clink of silverware against plates.

"Vince!" A tall, sturdy man with olive skin and salt-and-pepper hair approached, arms outstretched, his face lighting up. "Where have you been hiding?"

"Joe," Vince embraced him amiably, their handshake turning into a back-slapping hug. "Been hiding right here in plain sight. This is my friend Rebecca."

"Any friend of Vince's is always welcome here," Joe said, sizing her up with frank curiosity. "Come on in, I have the perfect table."

He led them to a corner booth, partially secluded by a wooden partition. "Chianti?" he suggested, one eyebrow raised, and Vince nodded.

Vince leaned forward after Joe had disappeared into the kitchen, the wooden booth creaking slightly. "Trust me, everything here is authentic," he told her, as if sharing a secret. "Joe's parents opened this place in the seventies. The recipes are all passed down through family. Everything is delicious."

She settled into the booth, the worn leather seat conforming to her shape, amazed by how comfortable she felt. This place was truly authentic, unpretentious—where the food and company were what mattered, not the appearance or status.

"I can see why you like it here," she said, unwrapping her silverware from a crisp white napkin. "It feels real."

He nodded, understanding immediately. "That's exactly it. In a city built on illusion, this place has never pretended to be anything but what it is."

A young woman arrived with wine and two glasses, depositing them with practiced efficiency. "What can I get you?" she asked, looking directly at Rebecca. "The special today is osso buco, but Vince always has the lasagna," she announced in a Southern drawl, pen poised over her order pad.

"Because it's the best in Nevada," he confirmed with a grin that made him look years younger.

"Then I'll have the lasagna too," Rebecca decided, charmed by his enthusiasm.

Vince poured the wine, its ruby color catching the candlelight, the rich aroma of berries and oak rising from the glass. "To new experiences," he offered, raising his glass in a toast.

"To new experiences," she echoed, the crystal rim cool against her lips as she sipped.

"So you liked the Valley of Fire?" he asked after a moment, leaning back against the booth.

"I loved it. It was transformative, in a way I was not expecting," she replied, searching for words adequate to describe the day. "Those ancient formations, the colors, the vastness—it really did put things in perspective. A break from being stuck in the same thought patterns. I mean, it got me thinking of things other than my immediate situation."

He nodded in agreement, his expression showing he understood exactly what she meant.

"I've been dwelling on what you said out there," she continued, turning the stem of her wineglass between her fingers. "I've realized there are no hard and fast rules about how long it should take to recover from rejection, or divorce. And while I'm going to be in a difficult position, having not worked for twenty-five years, these weeks have shown me that I am resilient. I can bounce."

She paused, gaze fixed on the dancing candle flame. "Today I learned something important—that even if I don't get it right on the first try, it's okay. Making an effort is better than lying in bed wallowing in self-pity—which I did for more days than I care to admit," she added with a self-deprecating laugh. "The world keeps spinning, making my problems seem proportional—important, but without the power to consume me. They only matter to the extent that I can change them."

Vince studied her with quiet appreciation, his blue eyes reflecting the candlelight. "Well done, Rebecca," he said, his voice filled with respect. "Most people see only emptiness in the desert. They miss the life, the history, the beauty. And most people see only difficulty in their problems. They miss the opportunities, the future, the gifts."

"I think I've spent too much of my life not really seeing," she admitted, the confession easier than she'd expected. "Following prescribed paths, meeting expectations. Today felt like... waking up."

Their conversation paused as Joe returned with steaming plates of lasagna, the aroma making her stomach growl. The first bite was a revelation. Her eyes closed as she savored the layers of pasta, cheese and sauce in perfect harmony, rich and comforting.

"Oh my God," she said after swallowing, her eyes widening. "You weren't exaggerating."

Vince laughed, the sound rolling from deep in his chest. "Never exaggerate about food or cards."

As they ate, their conversation flowed easily from topic to topic—his early years learning poker from his grandfather and his uncle, books they'd both enjoyed, places they hoped to visit someday. Their forks punctuated points, wine refilled without asking, the restaurant's ambient noise a comfortable backdrop. Not the careful exchange of people on a date, but the comfortable dialogue of two individuals interested in each other's perspectives.

"Can I ask you something personal?" she ventured as they lingered over tiramisu and espresso, scraping the last of the mascarpone cream from her plate.

"Sure," Vince replied, setting down his espresso cup with a clink, seeming neither eager nor reluctant—simply open.

"Why Las Vegas? I mean, I know the professional poker explanation, but... is there more to it?" She tilted her head, curious.

He considered the question before answering, fingertips tapping lightly on the tablecloth. "There is. I came here after my own divorce, actually. Nearly twenty years ago."

"Twenty years—that's a long time."

"We were married seven years. No kids," he stated matter-of-factly, his expression neutral but not closed. "She was a rancher's daughter. Brilliant, ambitious. I was playing poker professionally, traveling the circuit. For a while, it worked—we were both independent, respected each other's paths." His gaze grew distant, remembering. "Then she inherited the ranch, and suddenly there was pressure to settle down, to be someone I wasn't."

Rebecca nodded, understanding immediately, responding to the familiar story. "The *expectations.*"

"Exactly," he agreed, gratitude flashing briefly in his eyes at her comprehension. "One night—after sixteen hours of mending fences in the rain—my hands were raw, bleeding through my gloves. She wanted to talk about the fences, about more work to be done. I dealt out a few hands on the kitchen table and she said, '*Can't you just be present here instead of escaping to your games?*' She saw cards as an escape for me, not who I essentially *was.*"

He shook his head. "I tried managing livestock, tending the land. But it was like wearing someone else's skin. The more I changed, the more I disappeared. I became a shadow version of myself, and she recognized it was time to set each other free. Her voice broke when she said it, but she meant it. And she was right."

"What happened?"

"I packed a bag and left." He lifted his shoulders in a small shrug. "We stayed in touch briefly. She remarried quickly, and we disappeared from each other's lives. I went to Reno first—I have family there. Then Vegas because I could make a living playing cards, but also because..."

"Because it's a place where you can redefine yourself on your own terms," she finished, the realization dawning as she spoke the words.

Vince grinned widely, his entire face transforming. "Exactly. No one here cares about your past or your pedigree. The only thing matters is who you are now."

"I'm starting to understand that," she realized, fingers twisting the napkin in her lap.

"So then, how long do you think you'll stay?" he asked.

She considered his question seriously, searching for honesty rather than a convenient answer. "I think Vegas is helping me discover who I am when I'm not defined by my marriage, by my life in Savannah. Being somewhere else helps—I'm forced into changing fast. Here, I'm just me—on my own. I'm someone I barely know but would like to know better, if that makes sense."

He nodded sagely, understanding in his eyes. "It's a worthwhile journey. Getting to know yourself."

"A scary one, too," she admitted, her voice catching slightly. "There are days when I wonder what I'm doing, if I'm being foolish, if I should go back to what's familiar."

"The familiar isn't always safe," he observed, his gaze steady. "Sometimes it's a comfortable prison."

The blatant truth of his statement struck her deeply, raising goosebumps along her arms. How many years had she spent in that comfortable prison? How many compromises, accommodations, silent surrenders of her own needs?

"Thank you," she said after a moment, reaching across the table to briefly touch his forearm, the gesture spontaneous. "Not just for today, but for really seeing me. For your friendship. Your kindness."

"The real you is worth seeing," he replied simply, no artificial flattery in his tone.

Leaving the restaurant, the evening air cool against her skin, Rebecca felt a connection that had nothing to do with romance or attraction. It was something richer: a rare understanding between two people at similar junctures in their lives. Something she wasn't ready to label but valued deeply.

"Not-a-date dinner was nice," he said with a slight smile as he swung a leg over the motorcycle seat, the leather creaking beneath him. "We should do it again sometime."

"I'd like that," she agreed, meaning it completely as she secured her helmet.

He dropped her at the hotel entrance, where the doorman helped her off the motorcycle. Rebecca watched as his taillight receded into the night.

If Don hadn't left her in Las Vegas, she would never have met Vince, never ridden into the desert for a life-altering day. Her shoulders straightened as she entered the Monarch, her steps purposeful.

Don and the kids expected she'd be returning to Savannah, a place that represented only the ruins of her former life. But change, she realized with a quickening pulse, was only one decision away.

Chapter 24

Rebecca's body was pleasantly tired from the day's adventures, her mind more awake than it had been in weeks. The exhilaration of the Valley of Fire still lingered as she showered away the desert dust, letting hot water soothe muscles unaccustomed to motorcycle riding. Toweling her hair dry, she caught her reflection, cheeks flushed with color, eyes brighter than they'd been in months.

Wrapped in the hotel robe, she settled on the bed with her laptop. The lessons from the desert left her ready to strike while the iron was hot. It was time to advance the divorce paperwork and close that chapter of her life. She opened her inbox to see two new messages at the top of her email.

The first, from Justine, carried the subject line *Small Win*. The second, from Don, was more cryptic: *You Win*. Her eyebrows arched as she studied the contrasting messages, her pulse quickening slightly. Curious, she opened Justine's email first.

Rebecca,

I've received a revised settlement offer from Don's attorney that addresses some of our key concerns. While he hasn't agreed to everything we proposed, there's significant movement in the right direction.

Key points:

1) Alimony: Don has offered $2,500 per month for 6 years (our request was $4,500 monthly for 8 years; his original offer was $1,500 monthly for 3 years).

2) Alternative lump sum option: $150,000 as spousal support, which would free him from monthly obligations and will apparently help him with a better mortgage rate.

3) House: Don will cover 50% of the outstanding mortgage ($50,000), leaving you with the remaining $50,000 to pay off.

4) Joint savings split is now $5000 to you, remaining balance to Don.

I think we can push back on this, as he is effectively claiming the savings as an offset to the increase in the offered alimony. I also believe we can push for better on the house, given that the mortgage was taken out for his vehicle purchase. Let's discuss further before we respond.

Are you available for a Zoom call with Don and his attorney tomorrow at 10 AM?

I'm driving to Vegas this evening and can be with you in person for the meeting, though I suggest you remain off-screen but present in the room.

Let me know your thoughts.

Justine

Rebecca reread the email, a mixture of emotions swirling. Relief that progress was being made, indignation at Don's assumption that she should pay for half of his car loan, and gratitude that Justine was on her side. The mention of a lump sum payment was particularly interesting—$150,000 all at once would provide a substantial cushion as she figured out her next steps.

With a deep breath, she opened Don's email, her jaw already tensing in anticipation.

Rebecca,

Because you've been somewhat reasonable in not asking for my 401(k) or other investments, I've decided to meet your demands halfway. The revised settlement reflects what I believe is fair given our circumstances. With the baby coming in five months, I'm facing significant financial responsibilities. I need this to be over so I can move forward with Annette. I'd prefer you take the lump sum spousal support to make things a bit easier for me when the baby arrives.

I trust you'll see wisdom in this, so we can all move on with our lives.

Don

She barked out a short laugh. The wisdom, as always, was all his. His implication that she should be grateful for his 'fair' offer, and his assumption that her primary concern should be facilitating his life with Annette, caused heat to rise to her cheeks. She recognized the familiar tactics, Don trying to get his way through condescension.

She snapped the laptop shut, then reopened it almost at once to respond to Justine, her fingers tapping a determined rhythm on the keys.

Justine,

Thank you so much for your advice.

I agree that the mortgage arrangement isn't fair—Don took out that mortgage last year specifically to buy his BMW, and I don't see why I should be responsible for half of his car. And you're right—looks like the money Don took from the savings is indeed reflective of his increased alimony offer—good catch!

I'd like to discuss the lump sum option further. Having a significant amount upfront might give me more flexibility as I figure out next steps, and also not tie me to Don for the long-haul. And it helps Don and Annette, which is not my primary concern, but I get it (and I'm not a monster, despite how Don is framing me).

10 AM tomorrow works for me and I'm looking forward to seeing you! The Monarch can arrange a meeting room if needed, or we can use my suite.

Rebecca

She went to the window, looking out as evening deepened into night. The neon signs glowed over the city, a stark contrast to the Valley of Fire she'd experienced earlier.

Almost a month had passed since Don had handed her that manila folder at the Palisade. A month of shock, grief, anger, and finally, the first tentative steps toward something new.

Her phone rang, the sound startling in the quiet room. Justine's name flashed on the screen.

"I'm about an hour outside Vegas," Justine said without preamble, road noise faintly audible in the background. "I've been thinking more about the settlement terms. Are you free to talk through some strategy now?"

"Of course," she replied, sitting on the sofa and reaching for the notepad on the side table.

"Great. The offer has improved but is still well below what would likely be awarded in court," Justine explained, her voice taking on a precise, measured tone. "Georgia generally favors the spouse who sacrificed career opportunities in a long-term marriage—and they take a particularly dim view of adultery. But of course, it also depends on the judge."

Rebecca crossed and uncrossed her ankles, rearranging her seating position. "I'm not sure I want to go to court. I cringe at the thought of sitting across from Don's belligerence in that setting."

"I understand," Justine assured her. "And litigation is always a last resort. But sometimes the threat alone is effective."

"What do you suggest?"

"I'm going to draft a petition tonight, insurance in case they keep stalling," Justine stated. "We'll offer them a week to reach settlement terms for an uncontested agreement, or we'll file the petition ourselves, on the grounds of adultery, proposing an equal split. Don clearly wants to speed this up—a public filing will motivate him to stop playing games."

"He'll flip if you even mention that," Rebecca predicted, picturing Don's face reddening. "I honestly think he just wants to feel like he's *won.*

He expected that I'd take whatever he offered and probably can't stand the thought that he might lose the battle he started."

"Agreed. It's been stalled for almost a month now since we submitted the counter-offer, and Don's attorney is acting like you've been the hold-up," Justine pointed out. "The mortgage is also a contentious issue. Borrowing against shared equity specifically for his personal benefit, and then leaving the marriage shortly after—we'll push for him to assume full responsibility for that loan."

Rebecca nodded, jotting down a note. "What about the lump sum option? Is that a good idea?" Her pen tapped against the paper as she listened.

"It can be, depending on your circumstances and plans. The advantage is immediate access to funds, which provides flexibility. The disadvantage is losing the security of guaranteed monthly income for a longer period of time. If you run through the lump sum and haven't established a sustainable income source, you'd be in a vulnerable position. And don't forget about the residual mortgage—you'd need to use part of the lump sum to pay off whatever remains, to avoid trying to qualify on your own—particularly with no income history and no monthly spousal support."

The practical assessment helped Rebecca think more clearly. "Right. I'm not exactly known to be frivolous with money. Well. Not usually, anyway," she said, cringing as she thought of her recent splurges. "And what about the savings? Is that a lost cause?"

"Not at all," Justine assured her, conviction in her voice. "We can negotiate a settlement that includes the money he took from savings as part of the marital assets to be split, and I think we do have an excellent chance of getting some of that back. Especially considering we haven't asked for any share of the 401(k) or the investment savings. Those balances are considerable, and they would be viewed as marital assets by the court."

A brief pause, then, "What are your thoughts about the future? Are you planning to return to Savannah soon?"

The question caught Rebecca off-guard, her breath catching momentarily. "I'm not sure," she admitted, gazing toward the window. "My son is visiting this weekend. After that..." She trailed off, realizing she truly didn't know.

"That's perfectly fine," Justine said, her voice reassuring. "You don't need all the answers yet. Anyway, we can prep over breakfast. I'll meet you in Arbor—it's in the lobby of the Titan Verde—at eight sharp. The goal of tomorrow's negotiation is to secure your options, not limit them."

CHAPTER 25

J USTINE WAS ALREADY SEATED at Arbor in an impeccable suit when Rebecca arrived. Documents were spread across the table, her Montblanc pen poised over a legal pad filled with tidy notes.

"You look ready for battle," Rebecca observed as she approached the table.

"And you look fantastic!" Justine stood to embrace her, genuine warmth lighting her professional demeanor. "Wow, Rebecca, you're like a whole new woman."

Rebecca brushed off the compliment, realizing that Justine hadn't seen her in person since her first week in Vegas, when she was falling apart and spending entire days wrapped in the cocoon of darkened hotel rooms. She shuddered at the memory, her shoulders tensing briefly.

They settled at the table, Rebecca eyeing the documents warily before studying the menu. The bright morning light streaming in and the restaurant's soft music created a bubble of calm.

The waitress arrived and Rebecca said, "You know, I'd really love a bagel with cream cheese. But not with the salmon that's on the menu. Can I do that? Maybe a side of sliced tomato? And an Earl Grey tea please."

"Of course," the waitress replied, noting the order down on her pad as Justine looked on, amused.

After ordering a granola bowl, Justine observed, "You know, Rebecca, you seem amazed that you can order what you want, even if it's not written that way on the menu."

Realizing she was right, Rebecca laughed. "I'm not used to asking for what I want, I guess."

Justine smiled before turning her attention to the legal pad, her expression shifting to focused determination. "Okay, first off, negotiations aren't battles, but they do require strategic positioning. Don's attorney is his colleague and friend Gregory Thompson—he's experienced and somewhat aggressive, but ultimately pragmatic."

Rebecca nodded, absorbing the assessment, her fingers smoothing the table edge. "I know Greg. Not that well, but we've met. What's our strategy?"

"If they leave the ball in our court, we'll acknowledge progress and express appreciation for compromise. Then we address the remaining issues, particularly the mortgage and savings, and acknowledge the significant balances in the investment and 401(k) that Don has tried to conveniently ignore. I'll present a counteroffer with Don assuming full responsibility for the mortgage, and increase the lump sum offer to include the savings," she explained, making precise marks on her pad. "However, I suspect Gregory is the kind of guy who'll want to take the lead."

"I'd agree, from what I remember of him. Don certainly is. And so, we let them talk first, and then we respond? What if they refuse to negotiate?"

"They won't," Justine said with quiet confidence, her posture relaxed but alert. "Everything we are asking for is more than defensible from any legal standpoint. Don's attorney knows this, and he would also know that Don is shooting blanks, hoping to bully you into compliance."

Rebecca raised her eyebrows, acknowledging that that was indeed Don's style.

"So, I've considered Don's revised offer in detail, as well as his actions over the past month," Justine continued, flipping to a fresh page in her notepad with practiced efficiency. "The $2,500 a month for six years is better than their original offer, but still inadequate for a marriage of this duration and the underlying circumstances. They're trying to position it as generous, but it's still well below what you're entitled to."

Rebecca sipped her tea, the warm liquid soothing her suddenly dry throat. "Honestly, if I had an income right now, I wouldn't even want any alimony. I just want to get it over with." She was shocked by the admission.

Justine leaned forward, her expression serious, eyes focused intently on Rebecca's face. "Rebecca, Don is making a base salary of $180,000 a year. That doesn't include his partner share. For a twenty-five year marriage where you supported his career as a homemaker, Georgia courts would typically award a third or more of his income for at least ten, maybe twelve years. Possibly even permanent alimony given your age and circumstances."

"That much?" Rebecca's eyes widened, her teacup stilling halfway to her lips.

"Absolutely. Even at the lower end of the range, we're talking at least four thousand a month for potentially a decade or more. That's upwards of half a million dollars in financial support before we even discuss the investment and retirement accounts." Justine tapped her pen against her notepad, the sound punctuating her words. "On that basis, Don's initial offer was insulting, and while this revised offer is an improvement, it's still far from fair."

"What do you think we should counter with?" Rebecca asked, setting down her cup with a small clink.

"We should hold firm at $4,500 monthly for eight years, or a $400,000 lump sum payment. Along with the house clear of mortgage, and the return of the money Don took from savings. Anchor high and expect movement. But that's still less than 30% of the investment accounts. Honestly, a court would probably award you more."

"Umm... that's—a lot of money," Rebecca said, her eyes wide as she processed the numbers.

"It's at least what you've earned through twenty-five years of partnership," Justine corrected. "I know you don't want to drag this out, and it's admirable that you don't want to be spiteful. But being reasonable doesn't mean giving everything away. This is about your future security. And on the topic of that, I want you to think about those investment accounts, because you are entitled to a fair division."

Rebecca's brow furrowed as she absorbed the information. "I trust your judgment, but I'd be happy with the lump sum and the house. He does have a new family to start. And Annette and the baby didn't create this mess, Don did. God, the house. I can't even imagine living in that house anymore. In any case, let's do what you think is right."

Breakfast arrived, and as Rebecca bit into the perfectly toasted bagel with cream cheese and tomato, she was on cloud nine. The combination of flavors was exactly what she wanted. She moaned out loud, closing her eyes briefly in appreciation, the sound breaking through the mounting tension.

After breakfast, they convened in Rebecca's suite, discussing potential scenarios with the documents spread out across the coffee table. Justine was thorough but efficient, explaining various legal points without condescension and asking direct questions about Rebecca's priorities.

When Justine's alarm rang at 9:55, Rebecca felt prepared and unusually calm. The negotiation that had once seemed overwhelming now felt like just another hurdle to clear—one that would bring her closer to true independence. And this time, she wasn't afraid of the fight.

CHAPTER 26

JUSTINE POSITIONED HER LAPTOP on the desk, adjusting the camera to show only herself. Rebecca took a seat slightly out of frame, close enough to see and hear but invisible to the others. The suite felt suddenly too cool, a stark contrast to the heat of anxiety building in her chest.

Precisely at ten, the Zoom call connected. Gregory Thompson appeared first, a polished man in his fifties with silver hair and wire-rimmed glasses. His background was clearly a law office, with leather-bound volumes visible on shelves behind him. A moment later, Don entered the screen, taking the seat beside Gregory. Despite her preparation, Don's familiar features caused a jolt in Rebecca's chest, her heart racing momentarily before settling.

"Good afternoon, Ms. Avery," Gregory began, his tone a shade too patronizing to be truly cordial. "I trust you've had time to review our revised offer with your client, and we appreciate your flexibility in scheduling this discussion."

"Good morning, and likewise, Mr. Thompson," Justine replied, her posture relaxed but attentive. "I believe this call shows good progress toward resolution. Mrs. Morley is here in the room with me, and I believe we are in a good position to agree on a settlement today."

"Before we begin," Gregory said, straightening his tie with practiced precision, "I should note that we want to make it clear that this is our final response to the rather excessive markup of the original settlement. We've made significant concessions in the spirit of compromise."

Don nodded firmly beside him, leaning back in his chair, arms crossed over his chest.

"Shall we review what we've put on the table?" Gregory continued, reaching for a document. His tone suggested he was explaining something to a child rather than addressing a fellow attorney.

He proceeded to read through the terms, his voice laced with sarcasm as he offered the remaining $5000 from the joint savings to cover 'Mrs.

Morley's ongoing holiday in Las Vegas', and magnanimously noting that each party would keep their respective vehicles—Rebecca's eight-year-old Honda, and Don's fairly new BMW.

"As you can surely see, this represents extraordinary generosity on Mr. Morley's part, given that Mrs. Morley contributed nothing to the household during the marriage," Gregory concluded with a self-satisfied smile, adjusting his glasses with one finger.

Rebecca's hands balled into fists on her thighs as she watched, her body remembering years of similar negotiations across their kitchen table. The familiar dismissal of her contributions sent a rush of anger through her chest, but she stayed silent, as agreed.

Justine's expression remained perfectly neutral, not a hair out of place. "Thank you for that summary, Mr. Thompson. However, I need to inform you that we are not prepared to accept the offer as presented."

Gregory's expression hardened instantly, his smile vanishing. "Ms. Avery, I'm not sure you understand the situation. My client has already demonstrated considerable flexibility. If your client persists in making unreasonable demands—"

"We can end this call right now," Don interrupted, pushing his face forward with a scowl, the familiar crease appearing between his eyebrows. "If Rebecca is going to be ridiculous, we can let a judge decide. I'm building a new life here. I've been more than generous." His voice strained with barely controlled frustration.

"*Unreasonable*, *ridiculous*, and *generous*, are all matters of opinion," Justine stated, her tone even despite Don's provocative tone. "I assure you, Mr. Thompson, that Mrs. Morley is ready to negotiate this very fairly right now. She has no desire to prolong the process unnecessarily, especially given Mr. Morley's impending, ah—delivery."

She paused, allowing her words to sink in. "However, should we need to pursue this through litigation, I should point out that in this case, the majority of alimony eligibility factors have been triggered."

Gregory shifted slightly in his chair as he licked his lips, a subtle tell that Justine had struck a nerve.

"These factors," she continued, her voice gathering momentum like a river, "include a marriage of more than twenty years; a significant income disparity; a spouse who was a homemaker, and who, while very willing to begin a new career, needs time to develop job skills; a divorce that was very unexpected; and, last but not least, the conduct of the parties—specifically Mr. Morley's adultery, which is clearly evident given that Annette Peters is pregnant, and your client blatantly admitted the affair to his wife when he abandoned her, alone, in Las Vegas, on the eve of their 25th wedding anniversary."

With the last point delivered effectively, Justine primly folded her hands and awaited a response. A flutter of vindication had risen in Rebecca as Justine systematically dismantled Don's arguments, putting words to truths she would have never been able to articulate. She pressed her lips together to suppress a smile.

Don's face flushed and he leaned forward to reply, his complexion reddening visibly, but Gregory placed a warning hand on his arm.

With no response forthcoming, Justine continued. "You know as well as I do, Mr. Thompson, that the likely award if brought to court would be around forty percent of Mr. Morley's net income for a minimum period of ten to twelve years, as well as an equitable portion of the marital assets—and those would include, as you of course know, the investment account and the 401(k)."

She let the numbers hang in the air. Don visibly paled, clearly uncomfortable at that prospect, the color draining from his face as swiftly as it had risen. He whispered something to his attorney, who gave a slight shake of his head.

Gregory paused, recalibrating, his fingers steepling in front of him. "Alright, Ms. Avery, your point is taken. Let's get your team there back on track. Tell me what aspects of the offer you specifically find problematic."

"Quite a few things. First, the mortgage arrangement," Justine said, her tone brisk but professional. "As I outlined in my response, the outstanding mortgage on the marital home was taken out for the sole purpose of financing Mr. Morley's BMW purchase. We propose that Mr. Morley assume full responsibility for this loan prior to signing the house over to my client, as it represents a personal asset he retained in the separation."

Don leaned forward. "That's not going to happen. The house mortgage is a joint obligation. I've offered to pay my half." His voice had the sharp edge Rebecca knew all too well.

"Don," Gregory cautioned, clearly not wanting his client to speak directly, his expression tightening.

Justine addressed her response to Gregory rather than Don. "The timing and purpose of the loan are well-documented. The BMW is in Mr. Morley's possession and was purchased for his exclusive use only a few months ago. Asking her to pay half the debt for his new car is inequitable by any standard."

Don, who had been increasingly agitated during Justine's systematic dismantling of their position, could no longer contain himself. "You're out of your fucking minds, both of you. If she's going to be so petty, then I'll adjust my lump-sum offer—reduce it by $50,000. She'll get a hundred grand and not a penny more, but the house will be *free and clear of mortgage.*"

His lawyer's hand shot up in warning, but Don ignored him. "No! We're done here. End the call!"

Rebecca watched the exchange with a strange sense of detachment. Don's face, once the center of her world, now seemed like that of a stranger—familiar features twisted from the expression she recognized as his 'negotiation face', to one of uncontrolled anger.

How many times had she seen that face across their kitchen table, dictating their vacation plans or major purchases? She'd always yielded then, believing his judgment superior to hers. The realization that she now saw through his tactics so clearly felt like waking from a long, confusing dream.

Gregory conferred briefly with Don, their muted discussion inaudible. When they returned their attention to the call, Gregory's expression had shifted subtly.

"We might be amenable to adjusting the mortgage arrangement," he conceded, his fingers smoothing his tie. "Perhaps Mr. Morley could assume a larger percentage of the outstanding balance, given the circumstances."

"One hundred percent to Mr. Morley is appropriate, given the circumstances," Justine countered calmly, not giving an inch. "Now, let's discuss the joint savings account, which Mr. Morley has essentially emptied, just days after taunting my client to withdraw $40,000 from."

Gregory's eyes narrowed slightly—the only indication that this information was new to him. He glanced briefly at Don before smoothly pivoting, his professional mask never fully slipping.

"Alright, Ms. Avery, your points have been noted. What's your counter-offer?"

"We remain at $4,500 monthly for eight years, however, in order to allow Mr. Morley to qualify for a mortgage, my client would be willing to accept a lump sum spousal support payment."

Rebecca could see Don nod at Greg, showing that finally, she was thinking sensibly.

"We'd accept a $400,000 non-tax-deductible lump sum payment plus $30,000 for legal expenses," Justine stated firmly, her voice clear and confident. "Along with the house free and clear of mortgage, and the entirety of the joint savings as of the date of separation, the balance of which was $83,172. In addition, Mr. Morley will continue to cover the health insurance premium for my client at an equivalent level of coverage to what she has enjoyed through his corporate insurance plan, for a period of five years. This represents considerable compromise on Mrs. Morley's part."

"That's outrageous," Gregory sputtered, his professional veneer cracking. "The offer was $150,000 lump sum."

"I'm aware of what your offer was," Justine replied coolly. "I'm telling you what would make this acceptable to my client. And I assure you, it's far less than what she'd receive if we litigate. And we do have a few more points to discuss."

"What *more points*? I'm offering her the damn house!" Don exploded, shoving his face toward the screen again, veins visible at his temples.

"And we note that the investment accounts are worth considerably more than the house," Justine countered smoothly, one eyebrow arching slightly.

"I worked damn hard for those," Don snapped, jabbing a finger toward the screen.

"And Mrs. Morley worked hard keeping your house and raising your family for twenty-five years," Justine replied, her tone sharpening for the first time. "Let's also remember that it was her savings that paid the down payment on the house, and her parents' generosity that allowed you to have an interest-free mortgage for ten years."

Gregory shot a glance at Don, his eyes wide. This appeared to be more information that he hadn't been made aware of by his client.

"Furthermore," Justine rolled on, "We note that Mr. Morley wouldn't *allow* Mrs. Morley to work, based on his misconception and insecurities." She punctuated this with a barely perceptible eye roll.

Gregory raised a finger to the screen and muted the call, signaling that he needed a moment with his client.

Rebecca stared at the screen intently, as if observing a stage play about people she used to know. The Don on-screen, his face contorted with indignation, seemed like a caricature of the man she'd been married to—his worst qualities magnified by stress and opposition.

Don and his lawyer returned to the call, Gregory looking considerably more composed than his client. But Justine didn't wait for them to speak before continuing. "I would like to also emphasize that Mr. Morley will have no claim on my client's future earnings."

Don snorted with derision, a sound so dismissive that Rebecca felt a flash of anger break through her detachment. The implicit message was clear—he didn't think she was capable of meaningful earnings.

The Valley of Fire mountains flashed through her mind, ancient and enduring. There was a version of herself emerging that Don couldn't see or comprehend, and somehow that made her feel powerful rather than diminished. In that moment, the last remnants of any attachment to him dissolved completely, like ice melting in warm water.

Don's lawyer finally managed to regain control of the situation, placing a restraining hand on Don's shoulder. "Ms. Avery, we will take a brief recess to consider your position."

"Of course," Justine agreed, nodding graciously. "And to be perfectly clear, Mr. Thompson—you know as well as I do that Mrs. Morley is being very reasonable here. She has no interest in dragging this out, and she's not asking for anything approaching what she might be awarded in court."

"We'll call you in fifteen minutes," Gregory said tersely, ending the call without a goodbye.

CHAPTER 27

WHEN THE SCREEN WENT black, Rebecca released a breath she hadn't realized she had been holding, her entire body slumping into the chair.

"You were incredible," she told Justine, leaning back. "Thank you for saying all the things I never could."

Justine turned to her with a small smile, the professional mask loosening. "I was stating facts. And I'm relatively certain they'll come back with an improved offer. We've established a strong position. They'll likely counter with something between their original offer and our demands."

"I can't believe you asked for *all* of the joint savings back! Did you see Don's face?" Rebecca exclaimed, half laughing, half shocked.

"I did. Sorry. That was a spur of the moment ad-lib reaction to his smugness," Justine admitted with a cheeky grin, her professional demeanor cracking momentarily.

"And if we reach an agreement, this will be over?"

"Once we agree on terms, the paperwork can be filed as soon as it's signed. Georgia has a thirty-one-day waiting period for uncontested divorces, so within a month or so, it'll be finalized."

The thought brought a sense of relief, a weight lifted from Rebecca's chest. The marriage that had defined more than half of her life would soon be legally dissolved, leaving her free to discover who she might become without the title of 'Don's wife' attached to her identity.

The laptop chimed, signaling an incoming call. Justine straightened her jacket with a swift, practiced movement and answered.

Gregory appeared alone on the screen, his expression carefully neutral, his silver hair catching the light. "Ms. Avery, my client is requesting that Mrs. Morley returns to Savannah in order to continue negotiations. He will not accept the terms as offered, and in fact has instructed me to revert to, ah—to the original offer."

Shocked by this turn of events, Rebecca straightened in her seat, a rolling sensation spreading through her stomach. She expected Justine to confer with her before responding. But without a glimmer of emotion, Justine nodded and swiftly pulled another file forward.

"Then thank you for your time today, Mr. Thompson. My client has no interest in returning to Savannah to continue these negotiations, and I'm confident that you can understand, Mr. Morley's original offer was grossly undervalued and insulting. Therefore, we have no choice but to file for fault-based divorce on grounds of adultery, which as you know will take much longer than a negotiated settlement. I have the petition prepared here and will file it by next Wednesday at noon, if we have not received a fair and reasonable offer in writing from you by that time. Good day to you."

Justine clicked the red button to disconnect the call, Rebecca watching in awe. She knew she would have never had the cold hard steel in her nerves to have pulled that off.

Justine picked up the hotel phone and ordered a pot of tea to be brought up, her voice as calm as if they were only pausing for a break, not executing a high-stakes legal strategy. She curled up on the sofa, serene, while Rebecca still vibrated with adrenaline.

As the tea arrived, fragrant steam rising from the porcelain pot, Justine's laptop chimed again.

"That was quick," Rebecca whispered, raising an eyebrow.

"I expected it," Justine murmured, straightening in her seat. "Don needs this resolved before the baby comes. He's running out of time to posture."

Gregory Thompson appeared on screen, looking somewhat satisfied, more relaxed than before. Don was notably absent.

"Ms. Avery, it was quite a battle, but I've managed to convince my client that it is in everybody's best interest to continue negotiations. As such, we're ready to present a counterproposal."

"I'm listening," Justine said, her expression attentive but revealing nothing.

"Mr. Morley will pay the outstanding mortgage on the marital home prior to transfer," Gregory began, consulting a document off-screen.

Justine nodded but didn't interrupt, her pen poised over her notepad.

"Regarding alimony, we are prepared to offer $3,000 per month for eight years, or a lump sum payment of $225,000. We will not cover any legal expenses, as Mrs. Morley was offered legal support by my client, and instead chose to engage her own. Furthermore, there will be no concession for health insurance premiums, as this would be considered Mrs. Morley's responsibility, with the alimony more than sufficient to cover the cost."

Rebecca could see Justine mentally calculating, her eyes narrowing slightly as she processed the numbers.

Justine tapped her pen against her notepad thoughtfully, the rhythm filling the pause before she looked up. "Let's split the difference on the lump sum, as well as half of the health insurance premium, and the return of the savings withdrawn by Mr. Morley. That comes up to a total $425,000 payment, the mortgage cleared and the house transferred into my client's name within fourteen days of finalization. Mr. Morley keeps the cemetery plots, his BMW, and whatever personal belongings he has already removed from the marital home. Those terms would be acceptable to my client," she said. "With the addition of a non-disparagement clause regarding both parties and a mutual waiver of all future claims."

Gregory tilted his head to one side, considering, his fingers adjusting his glasses. "As you say, let's split the difference. We'll agree to a total inclusive payment of $375,000, the mortgage cleared, and the remaining terms as discussed."

Justine looked over at Rebecca, who both nodded and shrugged at the same time, her heart beating faster with the realization that this was actually happening. $375,000—enough to sustain her for several years while she figured out her next steps, possibly even seed money for some kind of business venture or education.

Combined with the house free and clear, it meant real financial independence, not just symbolic freedom. Letting Justine steer the negotiations had resulted in future security for herself, in a way that she could never had expected if she had handled it on her own.

Justine considered, her expression professional but with a hint of satisfaction in her eyes. "Round it up to $400,000 and we have a deal."

Gregory slumped in his chair, sighing to show his exasperation with Justine's apparent splitting-of-hairs. "Fine. I'll have the revised agreement drafted and sent to you early next week."

"My client appreciates the reasonable resolution," Justine confirmed as she ended the call.

Rebecca relaxed in her chair, a complex mix of emotions washing over her, making her skin tingle. Relief predominated—that the negotiation was over, that a fair settlement had been reached, that this chapter of her life was closing with dignity rather than further acrimony.

"We did well," Justine said, making notes on her legal pad, the scratch of her pen audible in the quiet room. "The house free and clear, plus a fair lump sum—it's a solid foundation for your next chapter. Without dragging it out through court."

"*You* did well. There was no 'we' about it. And that last bump in value, I can't believe that happened. And so quickly," Rebecca said with heartfelt gratitude, leaning forward in her seat. "I can't thank you enough. Not just for the negotiation, but for… everything. For understanding what I needed even when I didn't."

Justine looked up, her expression softening, the lines around her eyes crinkling. "That's the most important part of what I do, especially with clients at your stage of life. Divorce after a long marriage isn't simply a legal proceeding—it's an identity transition."

The phrase struck Rebecca as particularly apt, resonating in her chest. An identity transition. That's exactly what she'd been experiencing these past weeks in Las Vegas—not only the end of her marriage, but the beginning of discovering who she was without it.

"What happens next?"

"I'll review the agreement when it arrives next week, then send it to you for signature," she explained, closing her notepad with a decisive movement. "Once both parties have signed, the papers will be filed in Georgia and the waiting period begins. Thirty-one days later, you'll be divorced. And I'll be here throughout the whole process, Rebecca. You don't need to worry."

Thirty-one days. After twenty-five years of marriage, it seemed both an eternity and the blink of an eye. Rebecca felt the paradox of it settle in her bones. She nodded, absorbing the information, her fingers lacing and unlacing in her lap.

Justine studied her, her gaze both professional and compassionate. "How do you feel?"

Rebecca considered the question, searching for the pain or panic she might have expected. Instead, she found a new sense of resolution, the closing of a door that had been left ajar too long. The sound of it clicking shut was strangely satisfying.

"Like I can start looking forward instead of backward," she said finally.

"That's exactly the perspective you need. Many of my clients get stuck looking at divorce as an ending. The healthiest approach is to see it as a transition—not an ending, but a beginning."

Rebecca glanced toward the window, where the desert hills were visible, their outline sharp against the clear sky, calling to her with their ancient patience. A beginning. The word sat in her chest, not fragile but solid, as if it belonged to her now.

"Okay! Let's go get lunch to celebrate," Justine suggested, closing her laptop with a satisfying click. "There's a French bistro I know that's quite good."

Rebecca jumped up, realizing she was both hungry and wanting company, the knot that had been in her stomach all morning finally loosening. "I'd love that. I think we've earned it."

Chapter 28

REBECCA CHECKED INTO THE Titan Royale shortly after noon, rolling her suitcase through the vast casino floor. The familiar cacophony of slot machines washed over her like white noise. Having spent nearly a month in Las Vegas, she'd become accustomed to navigating the labyrinthine resorts, no longer overwhelmed by their scale.

She nervously got ready to pick up Luke and his friend Jake at the airport. Her outfit was carefully chosen—the dark slim jeans and ankle boots that added inches to her height, topped with a loose silk V-neck T-shirt. Her hair, freshly colored and cut, now fell in smooth dark chocolate waves, framing her face in a way her previous shapeless cut never had. She applied her makeup with a lighter hand than she once would have, having learned that sometimes less was more.

The woman in the mirror looked at least five years younger than she had a month ago, and certainly nothing like the shell-shocked wife Don had abandoned at the Palisade. Her reflection blinked at her, almost a stranger with her straight posture and confident gaze.

The thought of seeing Luke sent a flutter of nervous excitement through her. They'd spoken only briefly since she'd extended her stay in Vegas, and while he'd seemed supportive, there was a world of difference between phone approval and seeing the reality of her transformation in person.

At the airport, she positioned herself past the security exit. The terminal buzzed with activity, the announcements over the PA system barely registering. Luke's flight had landed fifteen minutes earlier, and she scanned the crowd for his familiar frame.

Then she spotted him—her son, tall like his father, walking alongside Jake, a compact young man with a ready smile whom she'd met several times during college visits. And then—her heart stuttered in her chest, her breath catching as her pulse raced ahead—there was Jodie, trailing slightly behind the boys, her attention on her phone, the overhead lights glinting off her blonde hair.

Jodie? Rebecca's mind whirled with confusion and delight. Despite their phone conversations, she'd assumed her daughter was still somewhat in Don's camp, on the fence about her side of the situation. Yet here she was, striding through the airport without warning.

Rebecca raised her hand in greeting, a wide smile spreading across her face as joy bubbled up inside her. The three young people walked straight past her, continuing toward baggage claim without a glance in her direction.

She stood frozen, arm still half-raised, smile faltering as heat rose to her cheeks and her stomach dropped. She lowered her arm awkwardly.

"Dude," she heard Jake say as he paused and turned to look at her, nudging Luke with his elbow. "Isn't that your mom right there?"

Luke and Jodie whipped around simultaneously, identical expressions of confusion crossing their faces as they scanned the area Jake was indicating.

"MOM?" Luke's eyes widened comically as recognition dawned. "Is that *you*?"

She couldn't help but laugh at their shock, a strange mix of pride and amusement washing over her. Her own children hadn't recognized her. "Last time I checked," she confirmed, enjoying their stunned expressions.

"Oh my God," Jodie breathed, rushing forward to close the distance between them. "Mom, you look... wow!"

"I can't believe you're here," Rebecca cried as Jodie reached her, pulling her into a fierce hug that squeezed the air from her lungs.

"You didn't think I was going to let Luke come see you without me, did you?" Jodie whispered, her voice breaking slightly. When she withdrew, Rebecca was startled to see tears glistening in her daughter's eyes, turning them a deep shade of blue.

"I'm so glad to see you," Rebecca murmured, her own vision blurring with emotion as she blinked away tears. "Both of you."

Luke joined them, looking her up and down with undisguised astonishment, running a hand through his hair. "Mom, you look totally different."

"I feel totally different. But I'm still Mom. And I'll take that as a compliment," she quipped, folding her arms around her son, inhaling his familiar scent.

Jake hung back slightly, rocking on his heels, watching the family reunion. "Told you it was her," he said to Luke, punching him lightly on the shoulder. "Can't believe you didn't even know your own Mom," he joked, earning a playful shove from his friend.

"Come on," Rebecca urged, including Jake in her smile as she gestured toward the baggage claim. "Let's get your bags and head to the hotel. I've got us all checked in at the Titan Royale. Jodes, you can bunk with me."

Jodie linked her arm through Rebecca's, leaning in to examine her more closely. Her daughter's warmth against her side felt both familiar and different.

"I almost didn't come," she confessed, her voice barely above a whisper, her fingers digging into Rebecca's forearm. "I've been so confused, so mad at you and then so sad for you. But then I kept thinking about Dad telling you he wants a divorce and leaving you here."

Her throat worked visibly as she swallowed. "So at the last minute I called Luke to pick me up on his way to the airport, and booked the ticket while I was waiting. I realized that no matter what happens between you and Dad, I needed to see you. To understand. Because all I could think about was how alone you must have felt in that moment."

Rebecca squeezed her daughter's arm gently, feeling the smoothness of her skin beneath her fingertips. "There's a lot we should talk about, but not right this minute. Let's enjoy being together, okay?"

Jodie nodded, straightening her shoulders and composing herself as Luke and Jake approached with their bags, the wheels rumbling across the polished floor.

"So! What's the plan?" Jodie asked, her voice steadier now, some of her usual briskness returning. "Hopefully we can think of something more exciting than watching these two cheer for sweaty basketball guys tomorrow night."

Rebecca laughed, the sound echoing off the high terminal ceiling. "I've planned a few things if you're all up for it, and maybe tomorrow while the boys are at the wedding and the game, you and I could do some shopping, then visit the Neon Museum, and maybe get some Italian food afterward? Girls' night?"

"That sounds perfect," Jodie agreed, her smile erasing the tension from her face.

Rebecca fell naturally into the role of tour guide, showing them some of her favorite spots and hidden gems she'd discovered during her extended stay.

"How do you know all this? I didn't even know Vegas had places like this," Luke marveled after she led them through the flower displays in the Wynn and down to a small lakeside bar. The afternoon sunlight danced on the water, casting golden reflections onto their faces.

"I've had a bit of time to explore," she replied simply, lifting her mojito to catch the light. The cool condensation from the glass trickled down her wrist, leaving a damp trail on her skin.

Later that evening, they enjoyed dinner at a steakhouse in the Titan Royale. The conversation flowed more easily than she had dared hope, the initial shock of her appearance having given way to comfortable camaraderie, with Luke and Jodie genuinely pleased by the changes they saw in their mother.

"So," Luke ventured, tapping his water glass as they lingered over dessert, "let's talk about Dad. He's acting weird as hell, but wasn't this whole thing his decision?"

Jodie shot him a warning look, her eyes narrowing. "Luke..."

"What?" he challenged, straightening in his seat. "I'm just asking. He's always all moody and tense, and he keeps talking shit about Mom, but then he'll suddenly get all like 'your mother and I made this decision together, we want what's best for everyone', like we can't see through his bullshit."

Rebecca took a sip of her water as she carefully considered her response. She'd promised herself she wouldn't disparage Don to the kids, regardless of how justified it might feel.

"We definitely did not make this decision together," she stated finally, keeping her voice measured despite the surge of anger that threatened to color her words. "But there is no going back. It took me a little while to realize that change, even though it wasn't part of the original plan, has really been a good thing for me. I'm liking who I'm becoming but I still have lots to sort out. I know it's a difficult time—for you both, for me, even for your father."

"He is being truly annoying," Jodie admitted, unable to contain herself, her cheeks flushing with emotion. "Calling me three times a day to ask if I've heard from you, then trying to make it sound like you've got mental problems and he's concerned." She stabbed at her cheesecake with unnecessary force, the tines of her fork scraping against the plate.

Luke snorted, leaning back in his chair. "And it's like he expects that he can remove you and slot Annette into our lives, like we won't notice a difference. I've just been ignoring him," he declared, crossing his arms over his chest as he leaned back in his chair.

Rebecca felt a pang of guilt twist in her stomach. Despite everything, Don was still their father, and Annette would soon be the mother of their half-sibling. "He's adjusting too," she said, amazing herself with her capacity for generosity. "This is new territory for all of us."

Jake, who had been quietly observing the family dynamic, raised his beer, the amber liquid catching the light. "To new territory," he offered, lightening the moment.

"To new territory," they echoed, clinking glasses around the table, the crystal singing with each contact.

Later that night, after the boys had headed out to explore the nightlife, Rebecca and Jodie returned to their room, a cool sanctuary from the warm desert night outside. Jodie curled up on the queen bed closest to the window, looking younger than her twenty-three years with her makeup scrubbed away.

"I'm sorry about being such a bitch to you. You know, at first," she confessed, hugging a pillow to her chest.

"Language, Jodie," Rebecca scolded automatically, then laughed. "Sorry—habit."

"You've really changed, Mom," Jodie mused, her expression thoughtful as she studied her mother's face in the dim lamplight. "And I don't just mean how you look, although that's a pretty spectacular change."

"Thank you," Rebecca murmured, feeling a blush rise to her cheeks as she sat cross-legged on her own bed, the crisp sheets cool beneath her.

"What happened? I mean, I know what Dad did, but... what's happened with you? It's like you're a familiar stranger."

Rebecca settled deeper into the plush pillows, tucking her legs beneath her. "I *am* a familiar stranger. To myself as well." Her throat tightened around the words as she spoke, her fingers absently tracing patterns on the bedspread.

"I'm still figuring things out. I went on a motorcycle ride the other day. I went shopping by myself, made my own choices. Every one of those things has made an impression on me. Shaping me. But it hasn't all been fun. I cried for days at first. I sank into some serious darkness—I could barely even get out of bed. Those days shaped me too. But that's not really all of it."

She paused, trying to articulate the transformation she'd experienced, feeling the weight of her daughter's gaze. "I think... I think I just started taking up space in my own life. And I'm not sure if that would have happened if I'd come back to Savannah."

Jodie's brow furrowed, creating a small crease between her eyebrows. "What do you mean?"

"I just..." Rebecca hesitated, looking down at her hands. The pale band where her wedding ring had been was barely visible now. "When your father told me he was leaving, it was like the floor disappeared. I realized I'd forgotten who I was outside of being a wife and a mom." She gave a small, rueful smile. "Turns out I'm someone who likes adventure and emerald green shirts and making her own decisions. I'm still getting to know this new me."

Jodie was quiet for a long moment. "I never realized that you were unhappy," she finally said, her voice small.

"I wasn't unhappy! Or maybe I was, but I didn't even know it," Rebecca corrected, feeling her way through the realization even as she spoke it. "Just... invisible, sometimes. In retrospect. Even to myself. Your father used to call me a *lump*. Back then I just laughed it off, hoping he was joking. Now, looking back, I wonder if part of me believed him." The admission hung in the air between them, heavier than she'd intended.

"Oh my God, Mom. That's so horrible." Jodie's voice hardened, her knuckles whitening as she gripped the pillow tighter. "What an ass. He says you're being stubborn about the settlement and forcing him to drag things out in court."

Rebecca's jaw clenched, a muscle twitching in her cheek as she fought to keep her expression neutral. "The details of our divorce settlement should be between your father and me," she said firmly, hearing the steel in her own voice. "But I will say that I am being fair, not stubborn. Your father just doesn't like not getting his way. He's not impressed that I have my own lawyer, and that I'm standing up to him."

Jodie nodded, seeming to accept this boundary. "I've never seen you stand up to him before," she observed, a hint of admiration creeping into her tone. "It's weird. Good-weird, but weird."

They talked late into the night, the conversation winding through memories, current events, and tentative plans for the future, their voices growing quieter as the hours passed. When Jodie finally drifted off to sleep in the other bed, Rebecca lay awake for a while, savoring the comfort of her daughter's presence and the unexpected gift of reconciliation, listening to the gentle rhythm of Jodie's breathing in the darkness.

CHAPTER 29

THE NEXT MORNING, REBECCA rose early as usual and was surprised to find Jodie already dressed in workout clothes when she emerged from the bathroom.

"I thought I'd join you for your morning walk," Jodie announced, straightening up and bouncing lightly on her toes.

They set out as dawn was breaking, the Strip unusually quiet and bathed in the golden light of sunrise. The air still held the coolness of night as Rebecca fell into her usual pace, Jodie matching her stride for stride, their footfalls creating a steady rhythm on the concrete.

"You're fast, Mom," Jodie commented after they'd covered several blocks, the faintest sheen of sweat appearing on her forehead.

"I've been practicing," Rebecca replied with a small smile, enjoying the burn in her muscles, the strong thump of her heart.

As they walked, Rebecca added in the short sprints between landmarks while Jodie kept pace, her athletic build giving her an advantage despite Rebecca's head start. The morning air rushed past her face, filling her lungs with each deep breath.

"Since when did you become a runner?" Jodie asked, barely winded as they paused near the Venetian.

"I'm not a runner, really," Rebecca laughed, pressing a hand to her pounding heart. "But I really like how those sprints feel."

"Don't sell yourself short, Mom," Jodie insisted, nudging her with an elbow. "If you run, you're a runner."

They continued their tour of the early morning Strip, conversation flowing easily between sprints as the city slowly stirred to life around them.

"Breakfast?" Rebecca gasped as they sprinted toward the alley where Saddle's was tucked away.

"I could eat two breakfasts," Jodie quipped, her cheeks flushed with exertion as they stepped inside the diner, the bell above the door announcing their arrival with a cheerful jingle. Rebecca waved as she saw Vince sitting on his usual stool.

"Jodie, meet my friend Vince," she said, walking over to join him on the stools at the far end of the counter, the worn vinyl squeaking beneath her. "Vince, this is my daughter Jodie!"

"Hi Vince," said Jodie, raising an eyebrow at her mother, who smiled sweetly in return as she ordered two bagels with cream cheese, sliced tomato on the side, and Jodie added in a request for scrambled eggs. The sizzle from the grill and clink of dishes created a comforting background noise.

"I hate to ask, because the situation keeps getting weirder, but..." Jodie leaned forward, lowering her voice to a stage whisper, her eyes darting between Rebecca and Vince, "you two aren't dating, are you?"

"No, not dating," Vince's deep voice rumbled like distant thunder, his tanned face crinkling into a smile. "Just a friend in the right place at the right time, when your mother needed one."

Jodie nodded, sizing him up. Apparently deciding he was a good guy, she was animated and friendly throughout breakfast, peppering him with questions about local hidden gems.

By the time they returned to the hotel, Rebecca felt a deeper connection with her daughter than she had in years. Their shoulders bumped as they walked side by side, comfortable in their shared silence.

"I mean, he seems nice, Mom. You could date him if you wanted to," Jodie finally blurted out as they rode the elevator up to their floor.

Rebecca laughed, shaking her head. "Jodie, I'm not looking to date anyone, for heaven's sake. I still need to figure out what I'm going to do with myself," she explained, watching the floor numbers light up one by one. Then she leaned in with a conspiratorial smile. "Plus, I'm saving Vince for Helen."

"Oh my God, he's perfect for Aunt Helen," Jodie breathed, her eyes widening with delight, the two of them giggling like schoolgirls as the elevator doors slid open.

The rest of the day unfolded like a perfect family vacation—the kind Rebecca had rarely experienced with Don's rigid itineraries. She'd rented a Suburban, and after breakfast, they all piled in for the drive to Valley of Fire State Park.

Leaving the city behind, the landscape gradually transformed from urban sprawl to open desert, the colors shifting from muted greys to vibrant rusts and reds. She felt confident behind the wheel of the large vehicle, guiding it along the winding road with ease.

"Mom, this is incredible," Luke marveled as they wandered among the fiery red rock formations, the intense heat radiating from the stone even as a dry breeze carried the scent of sage and dust. The brilliant blue sky arched overhead, making the rocks seem even more vibrant in contrast. "How did you even find this place?"

Rebecca sized up her son and then replied truthfully, "A high-stakes poker-player named Vince brought me here on his Harley-Davidson."

Luke snorted, shaking his head in disbelief. "Yeah right, Mom. As if."

They spent hours exploring the park, climbing rocks and marveling at the petroglyphs. The physical freedom of scrambling over boulders with her adult children felt symbolic—a new way of being together, unburdened by old dynamics.

That afternoon, Luke and Jake headed off to the wedding, their excited chatter echoing down the hotel corridor as they left, and Rebecca and Jodie hit the shops. As evening approached, they made their way to the Neon Museum for a night tour, wandering among the illuminated signs of Vegas' past, their faces bathed in the multicolored glow.

"It's so nostalgic," Jodie mused as they gazed up at a massive vintage casino sign, its buzzing neon casting an electric blue tint over her features. "These were all considered so modern and cutting-edge once."

"Now they're history," Rebecca agreed, watching the lights pulse and flicker. "But still beautiful in their way."

After the museum, they headed to Joe's Ristorante. Jodie's eyes lit up at the first bite of her favorite—chicken parmigiana.

"Yum, this is delicious," she declared, closing her eyes briefly to savor the flavors. "Mom, what a great find!"

Rebecca laughed, twirling pasta around her fork. "Actually, Vince brought me here too, and they make the best lasagna I've ever had."

"Good ol' Vince," Jodie winked, lifting her wine glass to clink against her mother's.

As they lingered over dessert, Jodie grew more serious, her spoon pausing midway to her mouth. "Do you think you'll ever forgive Dad?" she asked abruptly, the question hanging heavy in the air.

Rebecca set down her fork, considering the question. "I think forgiveness is something that happens gradually," she said finally, her voice measured. "Right now, I'm still working through hurt, insecurity, and anger. Some days I think I'm making progress, and then something reminds me of how he deceived me, and it all comes rushing back."

She tapped a fingernail against her water glass, gathering her thoughts. "But I don't want to carry this weight forever. I hope someday I'll get past all that, if only for my own peace of mind."

Jodie nodded slowly. "I'm still mad at him," she admitted. "For what he did to you, but also for how he's handling everything. He's all business on the surface, but then he'll throw out these little digs about you, and it's just... it's gross. Especially considering he's the one who cheated."

"There's always two sides," Rebecca conceded. "I could have done things differently too. You're allowed to be angry. But try not to let it consume you."

"That's very evolved of you, Mom," Jodie marveled.

"I'm working on evolving," she remarked, feeling lighter somehow for having voiced the complicated tangle of her emotions.

Returning to the hotel, they joined Luke and Jake in the casino, still buzzing with energy from the game. Their faces were animated as they talked over each other, recounting the final game minutes.

"It was INSANE!" Luke exclaimed, his voice carrying over the ambient casino noise. Rebecca listened with interest, if not complete understanding. His excitement was infectious, his eyes bright as he relived the game's highlights.

As they moved toward the elevator, Jake fell into step beside Rebecca. "You know, Luke," he remarked, winking back at his friend, "your mom is kind of a MILF now."

Rebecca nearly choked on her surprise, a startled laugh escaping before she could suppress it. Heat rushed to her face; the off-color compliment landed awkwardly, ridiculous and—annoyingly—somewhat flattering.

"DUDE," Luke interjected, his face contorting with horror as he punched Jake's arm with enough force to make his friend wince. "That's my *Mom*. That's so not right!"

"Just saying," Jake shrugged, unrepentant, raising his hands in mock surrender. "No offense, Mrs. Morley."

Despite his outward show of disgust, Rebecca caught the flash of pride in Luke's eyes—pride in her transformation, in having his mother elicit such a reaction, as inappropriate as it might be. The subtle straightening of his posture did not escape her notice.

Their final morning together arrived too quickly. Over breakfast, a quiet melancholy settled over the group, the impending separation dampening their spirits like a physical weight.

"So, when are you coming home, Mom?" Luke asked, the question that had been hovering unspoken throughout the weekend finally finding voice.

Rebecca looked at her children's expectant faces, Jake's politely interested expression. She set down her teacup, the porcelain making a faint sound against the saucer. "I'm not sure yet," she answered honestly, feeling the weight of their gaze. "I have some things I need to figure out first."

"But you will come home, right?" Jodie pressed, her breakfast forgotten. "To Savannah, I mean."

"Of course," Rebecca said, though the small shock resonating in her chest made her realize that she wasn't entirely certain. The house in Savannah would soon be hers, but was it still home? "I mean, I think so. That's where my house is. Where else would I go?"

The question hung in the air, more significant than she'd intended, filling the space between them. Where else, indeed? The answer wasn't predetermined by Don's career, the children's schools, or any of the other factors that had anchored her to one place. The realization left her feeling both liberated and unmoored, like a boat slipped from its dock.

"Wherever you go, make sure it's someplace we can easily visit," Luke said, breaking the momentary tension with a generous smile, reaching across to squeeze her hand briefly.

Rebecca smiled, grateful for his easy acceptance, the knot in her chest loosening. "Deal."

The goodbye at the airport was emotional despite their efforts to keep it light. Rebecca hugged each of them tightly, lingering especially with Jodie, whose former hostility had transformed into fierce protectiveness over the weekend. She memorized the feel of her children in her arms, the scent of Jodie's shampoo, the way Luke's chin rested on the top of her head when they embraced.

"I'll come visit again soon," Jodie whispered, her breath warm against Rebecca's ear, her grip almost painful in its intensity. "And ignore Dad's bullshit."

"Language," Rebecca replied automatically, making them both laugh through their tears.

As she watched them disappear beyond the security checkpoint, Rebecca felt a complex mix of emotions—sadness at their departure, joy at their reconnection, and a strange, growing sense of independence.

The weekend had shown her something crucial: her relationships with her children could evolve and deepen outside the structure of her marriage. She didn't have to be Don's wife to be Luke and Jodie's mother. And equally important, she could be more than either of those roles.

On the way back to Titan Royale, Rebecca realized how much she was enjoying driving the big Suburban. Instead of pulling into the parking lot to return the car, she kept driving west on Tropicana, the road stretching out ahead of her.

Tomorrow, she'd move to another hotel and start thinking seriously about a career for herself, but for today, the open road stretched out for miles in front of her.

CHAPTER 30

C HECKING OUT OF THE Titan Royale the next morning, Rebecca felt a hollowness in her chest. The weekend spent with her children had left her both energized and drained. She paused in the lobby, caught between the impulse to linger and the need to move forward.

Instead of heading to the taxi stand, she walked north along the Strip, wheeling her suitcase behind her. Navigating the crowded sidewalks and occasional uneven pavement would have overwhelmed her a few weeks ago, but today it felt like just another small challenge to overcome. Her legs carried her effortlessly—a reminder of how much her body had changed in such a short time.

She hadn't booked anything but found herself drawn once again to the Monarch. The literary atmosphere and elegant design had resonated with her during her previous stay in a way no other place ever had. She had felt at home there. As she approached the entrance, her steps quickened with purpose.

The understated elegance of the lobby welcomed her back, the hushed atmosphere worlds away from the casino floor's constant stimulation.

"Hi," she said, approaching the front desk. "I stayed here last week, and I'm wondering if I could book in and stay a little longer this time. Maybe two weeks?"

Her fingers drummed lightly against the polished marble counter, betraying an anticipation she hadn't expected to feel. Two weeks seemed right—enough time to make meaningful progress on her next steps but not so long that she'd feel untethered. The divorce paperwork would likely be signed and submitted by then, giving her a natural transition point for whatever came next.

The receptionist smiled, offering Rebecca a choice of available rooms.

"That Grande Suite looks lovely," she advised, pointing toward the screen. "The extra space will be nice for a longer stay."

The receptionist busily clicked away at her keyboard. "I do have one available for a two week stay. It's on the 31st floor."

"I would love that—do you know which direction the window faces?" she asked, keen for a view of the hills that pulled her so strongly.

The receptionist's fingers danced across the keyboard again. "It faces west. Strip view. It's ready now, if you'd like an early check-in?"

"That's wonderful, thank you," Rebecca replied, warmth spreading through her chest at this small kindness.

The Grande Suite exceeded her expectations. While maintaining the Monarch's signature old-world sophistication, the accommodation featured a separate living area that instantly captured her imagination. This space offered distinct areas for different aspects of her life.

The mahogany table positioned by the window overlooking the Strip, the distant hills framing the background, presented a new possibility. This wouldn't be just her hotel room, but also an office—a place where she could reinvent her entire approach to daily life.

She wandered through the suite, mentally arranging the space. The living area would be her workspace. The bedroom would be strictly for rest and relaxation—a sanctuary, not a hiding place. No more staying in bed with the curtains drawn, no more aimless drifting.

A routine, she decided. This space would bring some normalcy into her life—a routine different to what she'd ever had before. She made a mental commitment to be regimented and stick to her work.

The only question was: work on what? The thought landed heavily, momentarily dampening her enthusiasm. Her first project would be to figure that out.

With her clothes neatly hung, Rebecca opened her laptop and began organizing her digital life. She created folders for finances, divorce paperwork, and random journal entries. She set up a calendar with recurring events—morning run, breakfast, work sessions, breaks. The familiarity transported her back to when she'd created schedules for the kids, using magnets to hold them in place on the side of the fridge, giving structure to shapeless days.

The following morning, she woke before her alarm, now acclimated to early rising. She dressed quickly, her running clothes no longer feeling foreign. She tied her shoelaces with practiced efficiency, the motions now ritual rather than novelty.

She added an extra mile to her route now that sprinting felt natural rather than punishing, completing her run before most of the tourists had even thought about climbing out of bed.

After stretching, she showered and dressed in a slim black dress and low heels—appropriate for her first day at her new 'job'. She closed the double doors to the bedroom, symbolically separating living space from workspace, and headed down to Arbor for breakfast.

The garden atmosphere in the restaurant was beginning to fill with morning guests as Rebecca was seated at a small table near the hotel lobby. She ordered her now-favorite breakfast—the sesame bagel toasted perfectly, whipped cream cheese, whisper-thin slices of tomato, and a pot of Earl Grey. As she ate, she mentally reviewed her schedule, treating the meal as if she were stopping for breakfast on the way to an actual office.

At precisely 9 AM, she seated herself at the mahogany table by the window, opened her laptop, and called Helen.

"Well, if it isn't the woman of mystery," Helen greeted her, her face appearing on the screen. "And now technology wizard, look at you using FaceTime! How was the family reunion?"

"Better than I could have hoped," Rebecca replied, unable to hide her smile. "Jodie tagged along with the boys too. We had a fantastic weekend."

"I love hearing that. And how are you feeling about everything else? Any progress with the divorce stuff?"

"Well, the settlement was verbally agreed upon, now we're waiting on the final paperwork, which should come through this week. After that, it'll take around a month to finalize, Justine says. But if they renege, she's prepared the paperwork to file a fault-based divorce, which could take up to a year to settle, and she says I'd probably wind up with more than what I asked for, but things'll be tight in the meantime."

Helen nodded, her expression turning thoughtful as she mentally replayed Rebecca's report. "You know, Rebel, I'm really proud of you. You've come such a long way in what, a month? Some people spend years picking themselves up after a fall like you've been through, hanging onto the bitterness."

Rebecca felt her throat tighten at Helen's words. When was the last time someone had said they were proud of her?

"So what's next?" Helen pressed on, not allowing Rebecca to get maudlin. "What are the plans for *life after Don*?"

"That's actually why I called," Rebecca said, gesturing to the space around her. "I need to figure out what I'm going to do career-wise. I've set up a proper workspace here in my new room. I'm determined to be productive, to have a real routine. It's my first day at my new job of... *WHAT'S NEXT.*"

Her voice faltered as she took note of Helen's raised eyebrow. "I'm excited, but I... well, I don't know what I should be working on. Thought you might have some ideas."

"Look, once you're back, I could use some help with my business," Helen offered immediately. "Client care follow-ups, filing, maybe some bookkeeping, that sort of thing. I've been contemplating hiring an assistant anyway. The paperwork is honestly drowning me these days."

Rebecca smiled at her friend's generosity but felt a twinge of hesitation. "That's really kind of you, Helen, but I'm not sure that's the right fit. No offense, but I don't want you to create a position just to give me something to do."

"Not at all offended," Helen chided with a grin. "And trust me, I wouldn't offer if I didn't need the help. But I also get that filing my insurance paperwork isn't exactly a dream job. So, what are you thinking? Are you making lists of what you're good at and what you love to do?"

"That's the million-dollar question," Rebecca sighed, holding up her notebook. "I've got 90 minutes assigned here on my schedule for brainstorming possibilities."

"Hit me," Helen said, leaning back with her elbows on the armrests, positioning her pen in both hands like a tiny bridge.

"Well, I've always loved baking. Maybe I could open a small bakery."

Helen tilted her head, considering. "You do make the best scones I've ever tasted. But running a bakery is physically demanding, with crazy early hours, and you're tied in for as many days as you are open. Is that really what you want?"

Rebecca nodded, looking down at her notebook. "Good point. What about real estate? I've always loved going through open houses, imagining families that would suit the spaces."

"That could work. You've got the people skills, and you've always had a good eye for properties. Would need licensing, though. And there's no shortage of agents out there now—it's pretty competitive. Maybe not as competitive as a bakery though," Helen announced with a slightly raised eyebrow, and Rebecca knew she was thinking of Baker's Pride, one of their favorite haunts in Savannah. She could almost smell the fresh bread baking as she continued.

"Then there's college," Rebecca continued. "Maybe I could finish my degree."

"Or, more practically, you could work with me part-time while taking interior design or business courses that would apply to whatever you eventually decide."

Rebecca straightened. "Helen, do you actually want me to work with you? Or are you offering because I'll need a job and it seems logical?"

"Well, I haven't wanted to ask, but—*what about the money, honey*?" Helen point-blanked her.

"I'll be okay financially, for a while," Rebecca replied, meeting Helen's gaze. "I've decided to take the lump sum option rather than alimony. It's a smaller total, but so much less hassle than dealing with Don every month. It won't last forever, obviously, but it's enough to get me a solid footing on a new path—if I can figure out the right one."

"Okay, so what's that path going to be?" Helen asked, pulling her on track.

The question caught Rebecca off guard, even though figuring that out was exactly the task she had set for herself. "I think I'm feeling overwhelmed with possibilities. After twenty-five years of having my path determined for me, suddenly having to choose a new one is paralyzing. Not to mention my complete lack of qualifications."

"That makes total sense," Helen assured her. "So don't rush into anything. Take some time to discover what you actually enjoy, not just what you *think* you should do, and then figure out what you need to learn to be able to make it happen."

As they continued talking, Rebecca jotted down more options and crossed others off. After ending the call, she paged through her notes, feeling no closer to a decision.

She pushed away from the desk, feeling restless despite her determination to stick to her schedule. Maybe what she needed wasn't more options but a way to narrow them down.

Something that she enjoyed, rather than grasping at the first job that came along. How many people get the opportunity to do what they enjoy, rather than what they need to do to pay the bills? Rather than stick with a career they fell into when young, and just stuck with? Not many, she decided. And what had she truly enjoyed doing before marriage and motherhood had become her whole identity? What activities had made her lose track of time, energizing rather than depleting her?

Her reflection stared at her from the window. Behind it, a memory stirred. Her younger self, maybe nine or ten, hunched over a notebook at her desk in elementary school. Stories had spilled from her imagination faster than her hand could capture them.

The memory shifted to high school—the flutter in her stomach as she watched from a corner of the auditorium, her classmates bringing her words to life. She'd gripped the seat in front of her, hardly daring to breathe as they spoke lines she had written.

Another memory surfaced—her college dorm room, filling journals with stories and poems late into the night. The satisfaction of a page filled with words that had existed only in her mind just hours before.

She remembered her creative writing professor, Dr. Levine, stopping her after class. "You have a gift, Rebecca," he'd said, tapping her latest short story. "You create worlds that feel as real than reality." She'd carried those words with her for years, a small ember of pride even as she'd set aside her writing dreams to raise a family.

The memories hit her with physical force. She had once been creative—intensely, passionately so. That spark hadn't been extinguished after all, just buried beneath layers of other people's expectations. She could feel it flickering to life again, warm and insistent.

She returned to her laptop and opened a fresh document. Instead of listing potential careers, she began typing memories—specific moments when she'd felt fully alive, completely herself. Her fingers clunked across the keys, the clicking creating a rhythm that barely kept up with her racing thoughts. A pattern emerged, so obvious that a laugh escaped her, startling in the quiet room.

Writing. It had always been writing.

The realization brought both clarity and unease. Writing wasn't a practical career, per se—it lacked the clear trajectory of real estate or retail, or even opening a small bakery. Writing was uncertain, subjective, vulnerable. Her stomach clenched at the thought of sharing her words again after so many years, of exposing them to the judgment of others.

She still had some of those old plays and stories she'd written, tucked away in boxes in the attic of the Savannah house, despite Don pointing out the amount of space they wasted. Works she'd carefully preserved, never quite ready to part with them despite their apparent lack of practical value. While Savannah loomed in her mind as a nearly impassable hurdle to overcome, unearthing those old creations would help her to reclaim the creative spirit she had packed away along with those yellowing pages.

She sat straight and gazed out the window, considering the possibility of writing as more than a part-time hobby. Journalism? Fiction? Copywriting? Each path presented different challenges and opportunities.

She could write from anywhere. The realization landed with a delicious freedom.

The afternoon passed in a blur of research. Despite her intention to stick to her schedule, she acknowledged that this detour had been necessary. Her restlessness gave way to focus. The possibilities expanded before her like roads on a map, but this time she felt excited rather than paralyzed. Her fingertips tingled with the urge to create, to shape thoughts into words, words into stories.

As evening approached, she realized she had kept to her schedule after all, just differently than planned. She had worked productively and with focus.

Tomorrow, she would run again, have breakfast at Arbor, and return to this mahogany table by the window for another workday. She would explore what it meant to be a writer at forty-five, with no formal training and decades of dormant creativity. She would research, practice, learn—and most importantly, she decided, she would start a habit of writing every single day, whether inspiration struck or not, building the skills that would carry her forward.

Closing her laptop, she pulled her notebook closer and flipped to a fresh page.

DECISION, she lettered across the top, the letters bold and definitive. Beneath them, she wrote, *I won't return to Savannah until the house is officially mine. And until then, I will write every day.*

Her hand stilled, hovering over the page. The pen's tip created a small dot of ink as she considered what she'd written. Then as she added the next line, she spoke the words aloud: *I will write every day for the rest of my life.*

She capped the pen. Tomorrow at nine, she'd be at the table—on time, on task, and writing.

CHAPTER 31

R EBECCA HAD BEEN SITTING by the window for hours, typing steadily since returning from breakfast. Research on writing courses had given way to her own tentative attempts at creative expression. The words came more easily today than yesterday, though she still found herself pausing frequently to question a phrase or reconsider an approach.

She re-read the paragraph she'd just written: *Margaret stood at the edge of the desert highway, her thumb extended toward the approaching headlights. The wind whipped her hair across her face, and she pushed it away with her free hand, refusing to lower her gaze as dust stung her eyes. She had exactly twenty-seven dollars in her pocket and no plan beyond getting as far from Carson City as possible.*

Not perfect, but a rhythm was forming—a voice that felt authentically hers after years of silence.

Her phone rang, breaking her concentration. Justine's name appeared on the screen.

"Justine, hello," she answered, setting aside her laptop with a mixture of anticipation and nervousness.

"Rebecca, good news" Justine's voice was crisp and efficient as always. "The final settlement documents are ready for your signature. No surprises, everything is as we agreed on the call. Don has already signed."

A flutter of nerves stirred in her stomach. "So this is it? The last step?"

"For the settlement portion, yes. After it's filed, the thirty-one day waiting period starts. The deed to the house will be transferred to your name once the paperwork is finalized. Don can prepare the financial transfers anytime, but he'll likely wait until everything is complete. Are you okay money-wise for the time being?"

"Yes, absolutely. All good here, as long as I don't do anything crazy," she laughed, thinking of her sensible budget spreadsheet and the modest routine she'd established. "When do you need me to sign?" she asked, already mentally reviewing her schedule—a novel feeling after weeks of unstructured days.

"That's partly why I'm calling. I'll be heading up for some meetings tomorrow morning, and I thought I'd bring the paperwork in person. Some things should be done face-to-face."

She was touched by the gesture. "That would be wonderful. Thank you."

"How about dinner tomorrow evening? Say, seven o'clock?"

"Perfect," she agreed. "There's a restaurant here at the Monarch called the Library. It seems fitting, given what I've been working on."

"Oh?" Justine's tone shifted from professional to curious. "What have you been working on?"

Rebecca hadn't planned to mention her newly discovered direction but found herself eager to share. "I was exploring some career options, trying to figure out my next steps, and I realized—well, I used to write, before I got married. Stories, plays, poems. I loved it. I was actually pretty good at it." Her fingers drifted to the laptop screen where her character Margaret waited, frozen in her moment of decision.

"That doesn't surprise me at all," Justine said. "You have a natural way with words. Is this something you're seriously considering pursuing? A career as an author is not an easy road. No guarantees on income, although with the settlement you should be well-positioned for a little while."

"I think I'm serious. It's all I can think about," Rebecca admitted with conviction. "I've been researching writing courses, but also testing the waters, writing a bit. I was thinking of copywriting, but instead I'm finding myself drawn to fiction. It still feels a bit indulgent, I guess. Not practical, like a job working for someone else."

"Well, 'practical' isn't always fulfilling," Justine observed. "And writing isn't as impractical as you might think. There are many ways to build a career around it."

"That's what I'm discovering. It's intimidating to think about starting something new at forty-five, but also exciting."

"I look forward to hearing more about your plans tomorrow at the Library, then," Justine said, wrapping up the call.

Rebecca returned to her writing with renewed focus. The impending signing of the settlement documents lent momentum to her day—the longest chapter of her life officially closing, making space for the next to begin. She placed her hands on the keyboard, letting Margaret's story continue.

The approaching car slowed, its headlights illuminating the determination on Margaret's face. She'd spent fifteen years on the run. Now it was time to find her way home.

She smiled. Perhaps there was a bit of herself in Margaret.

Rebecca arrived early at the Library restaurant. The space lived up to its name—floor-to-ceiling bookshelves, leather chairs, and subdued lighting gave it an air of literary sophistication. The hostess led her to a corner alcove surrounded by antique volumes. She ran her fingers along the spines, drawing strength from their presence.

At seven sharp, Justine appeared, immaculately dressed as always in a midnight-blue suit that managed to be both authoritative and feminine. Rebecca had chosen her outfit with care: a deep-purple dress that skimmed her figure and caught the light at her collarbones. For the first time since meeting Justine and her tailored perfection, Rebecca didn't feel drab by comparison. She looked—and felt—like she belonged at the table.

Justine set her briefcase on the spare chair and placed a small gift bag tied with a gold ribbon in front of her.

"Rebecca," she said warmly, leaning in for a quick embrace.

Rebecca smiled, rising to meet her.

"What's this?" Rebecca asked, looking down at the gift bag. "You didn't need to—"

"It's a small thing," Justine insisted. "Consider it a graduation present."

Curious, Rebecca opened the bag and withdrew a glossy black box embossed with a white star logo. With a small intake of breath, she lifted the lid to reveal a Montblanc pen—a deep forest green with gold accents, similar to Justine's pen but uniquely its own, with a slightly feminine silhouette.

"Justine," Rebecca began, momentarily at a loss for words. She remembered watching Justine use her own Montblanc to slash through Don's initial settlement terms, the power and authority it had symbolized. "This is... this is too much."

"Not at all," Justine replied simply. "Remember what I told you when we first met—your signature matters. I thought you should have the proper tool for such important occasions. And when you told me you'd started writing again, and were thinking about it as a career move, I knew it was the perfect gift for you."

The dual symbolism wasn't lost on Rebecca.

"Thank you," she said, lifting the pen from its velvet nest. It felt substantial in her hand, the weight both unfamiliar and right somehow. "This means more than I can say."

Justine nodded, understanding in her eyes. "Now, let's get these documents out of the way before we order dinner."

She opened her briefcase and removed a folder containing the settlement documents, sticky flags marking the signature lines. Justine walked her through each section, confirming that Rebecca was in agreement before she signed, even though the terms were already familiar.

"I'm happy for a clean break, not years of financial ties." Rebecca confirmed, "And it also frees Don up to move on with his life."

"It's a smart choice, in my opinion," Justine agreed. "The division of the rest of the personal property has been outlined according to our discussions. I've had confirmation that Don has already removed the rest of his belongings from the house and given his keys to Greg Thompson."

Rebecca absorbed this information with a curious detachment. Imagining Don moving through and taking things from their shared home should perhaps have felt more emotional. Instead, it seemed like random news about a stranger, a story happening to someone else. She could picture him now, sorting through their accumulated possessions, but the image carried no pain—just the distance of a scene observed rather than experienced.

Rebecca picked up her new Montblanc pen, feeling its weight and balance as she poised it over the first signature line. The green barrel caught the light, its gold accents gleaming in the restaurant's amber lighting.

"This feels significant," she said quietly.

"It is significant," Justine agreed. "Take your time."

Rebecca nodded and signed her name at the first flag, the shimmering dark green ink flowing smoothly onto the page. Her signature looked different somehow—more confident, more intentional—though it was the same name she'd been writing for decades.

She continued through the document, signing and initialing where indicated. When she reached the final signature line, she paused, acknowledging the magnitude of the moment.

"Twenty-five years," she murmured, more to herself than to Justine.

Rebecca signed her name one last time, then capped the pen and set it down beside the completed documents. The click of the cap was punctuation—the period at the end of a very long sentence.

"Done! What's next?" she asked, flexing her fingers as if they'd accomplished something physical rather than symbolic.

"We eat!" Justine joked as she gathered the documents and slid them into the briefcase. "I'll FedEx these to Greg Thompson tomorrow for filing with the Georgia court. His office will handle all the details of the house transfer as well. You shouldn't have to deal with any of the administrative aspects."

"I've decided that once the house is transferred to my name, that's when I'll return to Savannah," Rebecca declared. "Not before."

"And in the meantime?"

"In the meantime, I stay here in the Monarch, and I write," Rebecca said simply. "I practice, I learn, I get better. I may take some online courses. Figure out what kind of writer I am."

Their food arrived, and they paused the business discussion to enjoy the meal. The Library's cuisine matched its sophisticated ambiance—simple dishes elevated by perfect preparation and thoughtful presentation.

"So—writing," Justine inquired as they ate, cutting into a perfectly seared scallop. "Tell me more about this new direction."

Rebecca shared her rediscovery of her old passion and her tentative steps toward creative writing, her research into potential programs and courses. As she spoke, her enthusiasm grew, the words flowing easily.

"I've started a short story," she admitted, wanting to share this private creation. "Just a few pages so far, about a woman changing direction after having been on the run. It's fiction, but," she smiled, "there might be some autobiographical elements."

"Your face is lighting up even talking about it," Justine observed.

"I know! I feel addicted to it already," Rebecca gushed, her fork pausing midway to her mouth. "Though I have so much to learn, so much catching up to do. Some of what I wrote back in the day," she paused with a laugh, "I'm sure it was nothing but drivel. I've given myself two full years from the date of the divorce to see if I can make something of it, and if I haven't earned a penny through writing by that time, I'll still have some time to try a different direction."

"We all start somewhere," Justine said. "And you're not starting from zero. You have life experience, perspective, a voice shaped by everything you've been through. Those are valuable assets for a writer."

Preparing to leave the restaurant, Rebecca slid the Montblanc pen into her purse. It felt like a talisman, a physical reminder of her evolution from the woman who had been abandoned in Las Vegas, left shocked and shattered, to the woman who now faced the future with curious optimism.

"Thank you, Justine," she said as they parted in the Monarch lobby. "Not only for handling the legal aspects, but for... well, for everything, really."

"Rebecca, watching you grow and change and step into yourself has been my pleasure," Justine replied, hugging her tightly. "I'm so happy to provide a little perspective, and a little legal guidance."

Rebecca watched as Justine crossed the elegant lobby toward the exit. She was about to turn toward the elevators when a familiar voice froze her in place.

"Rebecca?"

The floor dropped out from under her. Her stomach plummeted as if she'd missed a step on a staircase. She turned slowly, unable to believe what she was hearing. Don stood there, staring at her with undisguised shock.

"Don," she managed, despite the sudden hammering of her heart. With conscious effort, she straightened her spine and pulled back her shoulders, reclaiming her physical presence even as old patterns threatened to reassert themselves. "What are you doing here?"

He moved toward her, his gaze traveling from her trim dress to her new hairstyle, taking in the transformation with widening eyes. She was struck by how different he looked—his face puffy yet more lined, with shadows under his eyes. His sport jacket hung on him awkwardly, as if he'd lost weight in the wrong places.

"I... I had to see you. In person."

"How did you know where to find me?" she asked, acutely aware they were standing in the middle of the lobby. She moved her purse, holding it low in both hands, almost like a barrier.

"Jodie told me you'd be at the Monarch. I thought I'd have to ask at the front desk, but here you are," he replied, waving his hand to demonstrate her location. "Rebecca, I..." His voice broke. "I've made a terrible mistake."

Something in his expression—a vulnerability she'd rarely seen—caught her off-guard. He looked disheveled, his usually impeccable appearance showing signs of strain. His eyes were bloodshot, his shirt slightly rumpled.

"Cleaning my things out of the house," he continued, "being there without you, seeing the spaces you'd always filled... it hit me, what I've thrown away. Twenty-five years. Our family. You."

She stood motionless, unable to process the surreal nature of the moment. After everything—the paperwork, the negotiations, the plans—here was Don, apparently having flown across the country to find her.

"Let's call the whole thing off," he said, stepping closer. The familiar scent of his cologne reached her—once comforting, now cloying. "The paperwork isn't filed yet. We can tear up the settlement. Start fresh."

"What about Annette?" she asked, the question automatic. "Your new house. The baby?"

His face shifted, something cold briefly visible before he arranged his features into what she recognized as his 'let's be reasonable' look—the one he used when presenting difficult compromises to clients. The transformation was so familiar that Rebecca almost laughed at how transparent it now seemed.

"I'll support the child, of course. That's my responsibility. But Annette and I..." he shook his head. "We won't be together. I realized it was a mistake, Rebecca. A midlife crisis, a moment of weakness. It's you I love. It's always been you."

His eyes traveled over her again, lingering in a way that made her skin crawl. "And God, Bec, you look amazing. What have you been doing to yourself?"

Without waiting for an answer, he closed the distance between them, one hand reaching for her waist while the other brushed her hair back from her face. "Let's go up to your room. Catch up. Talk things through."

The touch of his fingers against her skin sent a wave of revulsion through her. Her body tensed, and she stepped back hard, breaking the contact. Where once his touch had been familiar, now it felt like an invasion.

"Don, stop."

"I know you're angry," he said, misreading her reaction. "You have every right to be. But we can work through this. For better or worse, remember?"

To her astonishment, she saw tears forming in his eyes. Don, who prided himself on emotional control, who had mocked what he called her 'excessive sensitivity' throughout their marriage, was crying in the lobby of the Monarch.

"I've been such a fool," he pleaded, his voice cracking. "Please, Bec. Give me another chance."

She stared at him, this man she had once built her life around, and felt nothing. No desire to comfort, no lingering love, not even the anger that had sustained her through the early days of their separation. Just a clear, calm certainty.

"No," she replied flatly.

He blinked, not expecting such a direct refusal. "What?"

"No," Rebecca repeated, her voice firm. "I don't want to give you another chance, Don. I don't even want to consider it."

"You're saying that because you're hurt, and you want to hurt me in return," he insisted, reaching for her again. "I understand. I deserve it. But I know you still love me, Rebecca. You've loved me for twenty-five years. That doesn't just disappear."

"It didn't *just disappear*, Don," she corrected him, standing her ground rather than stepping away again. "It withered. Slowly, over years of being dismissed and diminished and treated like an accessory to your life rather than a partner in it. And then you delivered the final death blow in the middle of the Palisade casino, on our anniversary."

Don flinched at the precision of her words but recovered quickly. "I was wrong. I made a mistake. People make mistakes, Rebecca. You've always been the forgiving one, the one who sees the best in people."

"I've forgiven your actions that led to this point," she conceded, surprised to find it was true. The realization lightened something in her chest, a burden she hadn't known she was still carrying. "But that doesn't mean I want you in my life. And forgiveness was more for my own healing than it was benediction for you."

Disbelief spread across his features, followed by the first flickers of anger. "Is there someone else? Is that what this is about?"

The question was so absurd that she nearly laughed. "No, Don. There's no one else. Well, actually, there is. There are a few *someone elses*."

He reeled back as if slapped, his face darkening with shock and betrayal. She had to stop herself from actually laughing out loud at his misunderstanding.

"Not in that way, Don," she placated. "There's Annette. There's your baby. And then there's me, finally understanding what I really want. And it isn't you."

His expression changed, the vulnerability draining away as if a mask had slipped. He struggled for a moment, visibly battling between maintaining the pleading façade and revealing his true feelings. His jaw worked silently as his eyes hardened.

"You'll regret this," he warned quietly, his voice taking on the cold, controlled tone she knew so well. "When the excitement of playing dress-up in Las Vegas wears off, when you're alone in that house with no purpose, no identity beyond being my wife, you'll realize what you've thrown away. The same as I have."

She felt the supple leather of her purse in her hands and visualized the Montblanc pen snuggled there in its velvet sleeve.

"I have plenty of purpose," she said. "And my identity has nothing to do with being your wife—or your ex-wife."

His jaw tightened, a muscle twitching visibly beneath the skin. "This isn't *you*, Rebecca. This," he gestured at her appearance, her confident stance, "this is some kind of phase. A reaction. You'll come to your senses."

"This is exactly me," she corrected him. "The real me. The one that's been buried under years of trying to be who you wanted me to be."

Uncertainty flickered in his eyes—the disorientation of a man who had always seemed so certain of his place in the world suddenly finding the map redrawn.

"I signed the papers tonight," she continued. "They'll be sent for filing tomorrow. It's over, Don."

"Papers can be torn up," he insisted, though with less conviction than before. "Legal processes can be stopped."

"Not this one," she stated with finality. "Goodbye, Don."

She turned and walked toward the elevators, half-expecting him to follow, to make another attempt at persuasion. But when she glanced around from the hallway to the elevator bank, he was still standing in the middle of the lobby, looking small, diminished by the elegance of his surroundings and the failure of his mission.

As the elevator doors closed, a curious lightness spread through her chest—not the weightlessness of the motorcycle ride, but something equally freeing. The last thread binding her to her old life had been cut, not by legal documents or property transfers, but by her own clear-eyed choice.

In her suite, Rebecca moved to the window, gathering strength from the familiar view of the Strip. The city glittered below, striking against the darkness of the desert night.

She retrieved her new pen from her purse and sat down at the mahogany desk. Opening her notebook to a fresh page, she uncapped the pen and watched the amber light gleam on its polished surface. She had signed her name today to the end of one story. Now she would begin writing the next—with her own pen, in her own hand, on her own terms.

And no one, not even Don Morley, could change that narrative now.

CHAPTER 32

R EBECCA ROLLED OVER, UNSETTLED. It was before sunrise, the confrontation with Don playing on a loop in her mind. Despite her firm stance, doubts and questions had crept in during the night. Why would Jodie tell him where she was staying? What had really happened with Annette? Was he still in Las Vegas?

She reached for her phone, knowing there was one person who might have answers. Her fingers flew across the screen as she composed a text to her daughter:

Hi Sweetheart—sorry for the language, but why the HELL would you tell your father where I am? He showed up here last night! He wants to call off the divorce, said he was through with Annette.

She added three 'face screaming in horror' emojis and hit send. The message went with a decisive whoosh. She set the phone down and crossed to the window, enjoying the morning light spreading across the skyline as she pulled on her exercise gear and did a quick stretch. The hills that had become so familiar were hazy this morning, as if reflecting her own clouded thoughts.

Her phone chimed with Jodie's response less than a minute later:

WHAT??? I didn't tell him ANYTHING about where you are! I swear, Mom.

Before Rebecca could reply, another message appeared:

And he is NOT through with Annette. It's the other way around. She kicked him out last Friday. He's been staying in the house FYI.

Rebecca sighed, processing the information. Annette had kicked him out? That didn't align with his tearful plea about realizing what he'd thrown away. And he was back in the house? She made a note to have the locks changed before returning to Savannah.

The pieces clicked into place. Don's sudden appearance, his tears, his desire to reconcile—it wasn't about love or regret. It was about being rejected, about needing someone to fall back on. And he had assumed, as he always had, that she would be there, waiting for him.

Did you know he was coming to Vegas? she texted.

No! I'll text him and find out what he's doing.

She considered this.

No, maybe leave it, she texted. *Just shocked me when he said that you'd told him where to find me.*

She placed her phone on the table and then immediately scooped it up:

Actually YES! Find out if you can—I don't want to be looking over my shoulder every five minutes.

You ok, Mom?

The concern in those two simple words touched her. *I'm fine. A bit annoyed. Heading for a run. Talk later?*

She set her phone aside and tied up her running shoes, determined not to let Don's presence disrupt her routine. As she ran, her mind churned with Jodie's revelations, the burn in her muscles dislodging the growing uneasiness she felt.

She felt almost back on track as she returned to the hotel, aligned with her plan for the day, but as she walked through the casino, a familiar figure stepped into her path.

Don wore rumpled golf attire with a faint scruff of beard—something she'd never seen on him before. Dark circles shadowed his eyes, his skin had a sallow tint, and his hair stuck up awkwardly on one side. He looked tired and disheveled, but no less determined.

She stopped short, her heart sinking. "Don. You're still here."

"We need to talk," he said, moving toward her. "About last night. I didn't explain myself well."

Glancing around, she noted that the area was relatively quiet, but not empty. A few other guests moved through the space, and staff members were visible at their stations. Not an ideal place for a confrontation, but at least she wasn't alone with him.

"I think you explained yourself perfectly well," she replied, keeping her voice level. "And I gave you my answer."

He ran a hand through his hair, a gesture of frustration she recognized from countless arguments over the years. "Can we at least sit down? Let's go up to your room and talk. Or mine. I have a room too," he said, inviting her toward the bank of elevators.

Part of her wanted to simply walk away, to continue with her morning as planned. But another part—curiosity perhaps—wanted to understand what game he was playing.

"Fine," she conceded. "In the restaurant, not up in a room."

Annoyance flashed across his features. "Rebecca, we need the privacy. I don't want to talk in a public restaurant." Patronizing, once again. *Don's way* was the only way.

"That's all that's on offer, Don. You're not coming to my room; I'm not going to your room. I'll meet you in Arbor in twenty minutes. If you're there, then we can talk. One-time-only offer."

"Fine. I'll see you there."

She walked in silence to the Monarch elevators, aware that he was closely shadowing her.

"Don, stop following me. Otherwise, I will march directly over to that security desk and report harassment."

"You would," he muttered, and she could have sworn that she heard him tack on 'bitch' under his breath, as he turned away.

Wondering why she was even entertaining having a conversation with him, she quickly showered and dressed in a pair of jeans and a T-shirt. She didn't bother with makeup, or blow-drying her hair. She didn't want him to think she'd made an effort for him, especially not after his ogling and attempted groping the previous night.

She headed down to Arbor, where he was already seated at a small table near the front.

"I've already ordered the food," he said, as if he had done her a favor. The waitress carried over a stack of brioche French toast that smelled delicious, as well as a platter of eggs and meat for Don.

"I'm really sorry," she said to the waitress, "I'm happy to pay for that, but it was ordered in error. And while it looks and smells absolutely divine, I'd like my usual, please," she stated, sliding the coffee back toward the waitress.

Don, taken aback, watched in silence as the waitress said, "Of course, Miss Rebecca, I'll get your tea right away."

"Your *usual*? *Miss* Rebecca?" he mimicked. "What a load of pretentious bullshit. And since when don't you eat French toast with all that sticky stuff on it?"

"Since about a month ago, actually. So, tell me Don, how did you really find me?" she asked point-blank, not bothering with any more preliminaries. "And don't say Jodie told you. I know that's not true."

He had the grace to look slightly abashed. "The credit card, of course," he admitted.

"Hmm. Interesting. You tracked me through the credit card account," she said flatly. It wasn't a question.

The waitress stepped forward with Rebecca's bagel and cream cheese, sliding the breakfast onto the table without interrupting their tense conversation.

"I was worried about you," he defended, shoveling a forkful of eggs and bacon into his mouth between sentences. "You've been away for weeks, Rebecca. Acting irrationally. I needed to make sure you were okay."

"I'm fine," she said. "As you can see. However, Don, you're still lying. I have my own credit card now, and it is not linked to our joint accounts."

His expression hardened slightly. "All of the online banking shows up on my profile, Rebecca, even if the account is in your name. I have a right to—"

Horrified, she interrupted, "No, you have *NO RIGHT*! Not anymore. Not since I opened my own accounts. The bank would not have made a mistake like that. So now I would like to understand how you got access to my private accounts, or this conversation is over."

"Private accounts," he snorted disdainfully. "Fine. A copy of the bank's 'welcome letter' came to the house."

"And you opened my mail?" she asked, incredulous. "You're crossing the line, Don. How did you get my password?"

"Please," he scoffed. "Your password pattern hasn't changed in fifteen years. Birthday plus maiden name plus a question mark. You always use the same formula." He tapped the table with smug confidence, leaning back with a smirk.

A chill ran through her. It was true, she'd used variations of the same password formula for years. Something he'd mocked her for, but now wielded against her. Another boundary she hadn't even thought to establish.

Don leaned across the table, shoulders squaring, his voice deceptively even while his presence pressed her back in her chair. He didn't need to raise his voice to make her feel cornered, caged.

"And by the way, I saw that $15,000 deposit. Where were you hiding that?"

"I'm not hiding anything," she said, anger flaring. "The money is sitting in my account, in my name. That's hardly hiding it."

"Maybe not legally hiding it," he conceded, "but you certainly didn't disclose it as a shared asset. Seems like it should have been split fairly and squarely. Which makes me wonder where you transferred that money from and what else you might be concealing."

"I'm concealing nothing," she insisted, annoyed with herself for sounding so defensive. "Unlike some people at this table, I don't make a habit of lying. And speaking of things that aren't true," she continued, "I know Annette kicked you out. You didn't end the relationship because you 'chose me and felt sad about throwing us away'. *She* ended it."

Don's expression hardened. "Careful, Rebecca. I'm trying to be reasonable here, but if you're going to be hostile—"

"Hostile?" she repeated, her voice incredulous. "You tracked my location using my private financial information, used unauthorized access to look at my personal accounts, showed up unannounced and accosted me at my hotel, and now you're accusing me of hiding assets—and *I'm* the one being hostile?"

Several diners at nearby tables glanced their way, but she was past caring about making a scene.

"Let's get something straight," she continued, leaning forward. "I won that money fair and square *after* you abandoned me in Las Vegas. It was never 'marital property'. You lost any right to question my financial decisions when you handed me a folder full of divorce papers with sticky pink arrows on our anniversary trip!"

The color had drained from Don's face, then returned in a flush of anger. "You think you're so clever now, don't you? With your fancy hotel life and your new clothes and your sudden independence. It's pathetic, Rebecca. A sad middle-aged woman trying to reinvent herself. You're all alike, a dime-a-dozen."

Each word was precisely targeted, designed to strike at her deepest insecurities. A month ago, the words would have landed like physical blows. Even now, she felt their sting. A familiar tension began spreading across her shoulders and up her neck, squeezing like a vise at the base of her skull. She caught herself shrinking in her seat, unconsciously trying to make herself smaller under his verbal assault, and instead forced herself to sit straight against the chair.

"You're nothing without me," he continued, his voice low but intense. "This whole woman-power reinvention thing—the clothes, the haircut, the attitude—it's so lame. You have no right. You're trying to be something you're not, and everyone can see through it. Like mutton dressed as lamb. You disgust me. You're forty-five. You have no career, no skills, no prospects," he jabbed his finger toward her face for emphasis. "Nobody's going to want you. No one will hire you. You're useless. Just bloody *useless*. Just a *lump*—like you've always been."

Rebecca sat very still, absorbing the verbal assault as she casually finished her bagel, trying to stop tears from springing to her eyes. Her hand slipped to her purse, fingers finding the hard outline of the Montblanc pen nestled inside. She gripped it tightly, drawing strength from its solid weight.

As Don's finger stabbed the air between them, she caught herself visualizing how satisfying it would be to grab that finger and bend it backward, or better yet, to take her elegant pen and drive it straight through his pointing hand, pinning it to the table like an insect specimen. The violent image was shocking, but steadying.

This was the real Don—not the tearful, regretful man from last night, but the cruel, calculating one who had always known exactly how to diminish her.

"You'll fail at whatever you do," he rolled on, gaining momentum as well as volume as she remained silent, his finger still jabbing rhythmically with each point. "You'll crawl back to Savannah with your tail between your legs, and everyone will know what a fool you made of yourself."

"Are you done?" she asked quietly when he finally paused for breath.

Don blinked, clearly expecting a different reaction—tears, perhaps, or angry denials. For a heartbeat, something feral flickered behind his eyes, there and gone.

"Because if you are," she continued, "I'd like to get on with my day. I have things to do. And you should probably head home to Savannah. I'm sure you have plenty to attend to there. Making amends with your pregnant girlfriend, for instance."

She stood, placing enough cash on the table to cover all three breakfasts that had been ordered. "Goodbye, Don."

She stepped away from the table, and he reached out, grabbing her arm firm enough to bruise. "Rebecca—wait."

"Don't touch me," she spat, loud enough that several nearby diners turned to look as she wrenched her arm from his grasp.

Don immediately released her, too aware of appearances to create even more of a scene. "You're making a mistake," he said, his words tight with anger. "You're going to regret this."

"I doubt that very much," she replied tersely, and walked away.

Crossing the restaurant and making her way through the hotel lobby, she managed to maintain her composure, but by the time she reached the elevator, her hands were shaking. The confrontation had taken more out of her than she wanted to admit.

In her suite, she locked the door behind her and leaned against it, breathing deeply to steady herself. His words echoed in her mind, each carefully crafted barb finding its target despite her best efforts to deflect them.

You have no career, no skills, no prospects. You're nothing without me. You're trying to be something you're not, and everyone can see through it.

She pushed away from the door, suddenly unable to bear the surroundings that had felt so empowering yesterday. Her workspace, laptop, and books on writing—all seemed phony now, artifices of a life she was playing at rather than living.

She stripped off her clothes, leaving them in a heap on the floor. Her hands trembled so badly she could barely work the zipper of her jeans. A cold sweat had broken out across her skin, and her stomach churned violently. She barely made it to the bathroom before heaving up her breakfast, throat burning as she knelt on the cold tile floor. The spasms left her weak and shaking, a rushing sound filling her ears as black spots danced at the edges of her vision.

She crawled into the shower, turning the water as hot as she could stand it, as if it might somehow wash away Don's words along with her tears. She kept her eyes firmly away from the mirror, not wanting to see the person Don had so thoroughly dismantled, afraid his cutting assessment might be visibly true: *mutton dressed as lamb, pathetic, disgusting.*

The bed welcomed her as she crawled beneath the covers, drawing the sheets over her head as she had during those first dark days after Don's announcement. She reached for the control panel and closed the blackout curtains with the push of a button, plunging the room into artificial night.

Who was she to think she could build a new life? Become a writer at forty-five?

A part of her—a small, fierce part that refused to be completely silenced—whispered that she'd already started building that life. That she'd already taken steps no one could take away from her. But his words had found every crack in her newfound confidence and pried them wide open.

Maybe he was right. Maybe this had all been an elaborate fantasy, fueled by the artificial environment of Las Vegas and the unexpected windfall of the jackpot.

The Montblanc pen that had been her talisman now felt like a toy. A prop in a game of make-believe.

Maybe reality was waiting in Savannah—the reality of being a middle-aged divorcée with no real prospects. Pitied by her social circle. Defined by her failed marriage.

She curled tighter beneath the covers, her thoughts spiraling into self-doubt. The structured day she had planned dissolved into darkness. Drifting in and out of fitful sleep, haunted by dreams where she was lost in a desert, searching for something she couldn't name, she would wake only to cry and feel like a failure.

The hours blurred together, marked only by the occasional chime of her phone as messages arrived—from Jodie, from Helen, even one from Justine confirming the paperwork had been sent to Savannah. She ignored them all, too drained to engage, too afraid that any response would reveal how thoroughly Don had shaken her newfound confidence.

Who was she kidding? She wasn't strong. She wasn't independent. She wasn't a writer. She was exactly what Don had always told her she was—limited, incapable, defined by her relationship to him.

Maybe, she thought as she drifted into another restless sleep, she should go home. Back to the life she knew, back to being Don's wife.

CHAPTER 33

D ARKNESS ENVELOPED THE ROOM, the blackout curtains doing their job with ruthless efficiency. Rebecca had no idea how much time had passed since she'd crawled into bed. The digital clock displayed 6:17, but whether evening or morning, she couldn't say.

Don's words echoed in her mind, a poisonous loop she couldn't silence. *You're nothing without me. You're trying to be something you're not. Everyone can see through it.*

She dragged the blankets over her head, a dull ache spreading through her chest. Was he right? Had this all been an elaborate fantasy—the clothes, the writing ambitions, the carefully structured days? Was she just a middle-aged woman playing dress-up?

Who was she to believe she could build a life on her own? Perhaps Don was right—

NO.

The word slammed into her consciousness with unexpected force. Don wasn't right. And she didn't want him back in her life. The papers were signed. The die was cast. Even in this moment of doubt, she knew that much with absolute certainty. Why did *Don* always get what he wanted, even at the expense of what she wanted?

No. She did not have to go back.

"What an ASSHOLE!" she shouted into the empty room, her hands balling into fists.

She could make choices for herself, the past month had well proven that. The realization offered cold comfort against the reality of what lay ahead. Without Don, without the shelter of marriage and the identity of wife, she would have to stand on her own two feet. Create her own life. Become self-sufficient in ways she had never been before.

The prospect loomed like a mountain before her—daunting, seemingly insurmountable. Maybe not impossible, but GOOD LORD, it was going to be hard.

She drifted back into fitful sleep, her dreams a disjointed mess of anxiety. Don's face morphed into shadows. Mountain paths crumbled beneath her feet. The children turned away, their expressions unreadable. She tried to call their names, but couldn't find her voice.

A faint sound penetrated her troubled dreams. A robotic beep followed by a metallic noise—a keycard held against the electronic lock, the mechanism turning with a low snick.

Rebecca's eyes flew open, instantly alert despite the disorientation of awakening from deep sleep. Her mouth went dry, the metallic tang of fear coating her tongue. The suite remained in darkness, but her senses were suddenly, acutely alive, skin prickling with goosebumps as though the temperature had plummeted. She sat bolt upright in bed as the door pushed inward—bumping the security latch with a thud.

A narrow slice of hallway light cut through the darkness. She pulled the blankets up to her neck, her heart hammering against her ribs. This wasn't hotel staff. They would knock first.

"Oh *Re-bec-ca*..." A familiar voice filtered through the gap, cajoling, intimate. "Open up..."

Don. It was Don.

Fear flooded her system, a cold rush of adrenaline that momentarily paralyzed her. How had he gotten a key to her room? How had he even known which room was hers?

"Re-*bec*-ca," he sing-songed as the door was shoved against the latch again, more forcefully this time.

"I know you're in there," Don called, his tone shifting from wheedling to irritated. "Open the door and talk to me, you *fucking coward*."

She scrambled out of bed, her bare feet landing on the plush rug. Still disoriented from sleep and darkness, she made her way toward the bathroom, her gaze catching on her purse sitting on the desk. The Montblanc pen was still inside—the elegant weapon she'd fantasized about driving through Don's hand just hours ago. For a split second, she considered grabbing it, the instinct to have something to defend herself almost overwhelming.

His voice grew louder, and she hurried to the bathroom instead, fumbling for the door handle. Once inside, she locked the door behind her, flipped on the light, and leaned against the vanity, trying to slow her breathing, her empty hands trembling against the cool marble.

The main door to the suite rattled again, followed by the sound of Don's voice, now pitched lower but still audible. "This is childish, Rebecca. Open the door. I want to talk."

She pressed her hands against her ears, willing him to go away. This wasn't happening. Couldn't be happening. Don had always been controlling, manipulative, even cruel at times—but this? Breaking into her hotel room? It crossed a line she hadn't imagined even he would transgress.

The thumping of the door against the latch continued, punctuated by moments of silence that were somehow worse than the noise. Had he given up? Was he still there, laying in wait?

An eternity passed before she heard the door slam completely closed. Silence settled over the suite, heavy and ominous. She remained frozen in the bathroom, straining to hear any movement in the outer room. Nothing.

Had he left? Or was he in the room, waiting in silence, hoping she would emerge?

Her eyes fell on the hotel phone mounted on the bathroom wall. She'd always wondered why there were phones in hotel bathrooms, and now she knew. With shaking fingers, she lifted the receiver and pressed the button for the front desk.

"Front desk, how may I assist you?" a cheerful voice answered.

She swallowed, trying to find her voice. "This is Rebecca Morley in suite 3123. My, uh, my husband was up here trying to open the door to my room."

"Oh, Mrs. Morley, of course. Is there a problem with his key?"

A cold wave washed over her. "No, the problem is, he shouldn't *have* a key. We're in the process of getting divorced. He isn't staying here with me."

"Oh, my goodness, I am so sorry." The clerk's voice shifted from cheerful to concerned. "I see here that he had a key printed about thirty minutes ago. Looks like he showed his ID with the same address and last name, and said he'd left his key up in the room. I am so sorry about that. I can't apologize enough."

Rebecca closed her eyes, leaning her forehead against the wall. Of course. So simple. Same last name, confident demeanor, and the assumption of a shared room between spouses.

"It's not your fault," she said with a sigh. "He's very persuasive when he wants to be."

"I'm cancelling all of the room keys right away, so your key won't work either, and I'm sending security up to check the room. I'll file an incident report and alert the shift manager. I'm also adding a do-not-issue flag—keys only with your photo ID."

"Thank you," Rebecca said, her voice steadier now that action was being taken.

She hung up, remaining in the bathroom until a knock came at the main door, followed by a male voice identifying himself as hotel security. Only then did she emerge, wrapping her robe tightly around herself before approaching the door.

"Mrs. Morley? Security. The front desk called about an unauthorized person attempting to enter your room."

Rebecca peered through the peephole to see a uniformed security officer in the hallway—alone, no sign of Don. She listened for an extra moment before releasing the security latch and partially opening the door.

"Is he still out there?" she asked.

"No, ma'am. I've checked the hallway and the elevator bay. No one's there. Would you like me to come in and ensure everything is secure?"

She stepped aside, allowing the officer to enter and conduct a brief sweep of the suite.

"Everything appears to be in order, ma'am," the officer reported. "If you'd like to get dressed, I'll stand outside and escort you down to get a new key."

"Oh! Yes, thank you," Rebecca said. "I'll get dressed right away."

While the officer waited, she turned on every light, banishing the threatening shadows. She dressed hurriedly in jeans and a sweater, concerned only with feeling protected. Her fingers fumbled with the zipper, compromised by the lingering tremor of adrenaline.

She grabbed her purse and went out into the hall to join the security guard, who stayed close as he escorted her down to the lobby.

Declining an offer to change rooms, or to contact the police, Rebecca thanked the front desk for their thorough security response, and tucked the new key in her back pocket. The guard walked her back to her room, conducting another sweep before allowing her to enter the suite. The routine should have been reassuring but instead reinforced the reality of her situation. How quickly this fear had entered her life—looking over her shoulder, suspecting danger in every shadow.

"All clear in here, Mrs. Morley. I'll do extra checks on the floor tonight. No one will be allowed access without your explicit authorization. We'll also be keeping an eye out for Mr. Morley in and around the casino. And if you do decide to change rooms, the front desk will be happy to accommodate."

She thanked the guard, closing the door and engaging the security latch.

She needed to talk to someone. Someone who would understand the gravity of what had happened without minimizing it or, worse, suggesting she was overreacting.

Her phone lay on the nightstand where she'd abandoned it hours earlier. She picked it up, seeing a series of missed calls and texts.

She called Jodie.

"Mom?" Her daughter answered on the second ring, her voice thick with sleep. "It's like one in the morning. Is everything okay?"

"I'm sorry to wake you," Rebecca said, suddenly conscious of the time. "It's not... I mean, I'm okay, but..." She paused, taking a steadying breath. "Your father tried to break into my hotel room."

"He *WHAT*?" All traces of sleep vanished from Jodie's voice, replaced by sharp alarm.

Rebecca explained what had happened—Don showing up at breakfast, their confrontation, her retreat to the room, and the frightening escalation.

"He got a key by telling them he was my husband and had left his upstairs," she finished. "If I hadn't had the security latch on..."

"That is so far over the line," Jodie said, her voice tight with anger. "What the hell is he thinking?"

"I don't know. He's acting a bit erratic," Rebecca mused, though part of her wondered. Was this really so out of character? Or had Don always been capable of this level of boundary violation, but she'd simply never created boundaries for him to violate before?

"I'm going to call him," Jodie declared. "Right now. See what the hell he's playing at."

"Jodie, no, you don't have to—"

"Yes, I do, Mom. This is stalking. It's harassment. It's not okay." Her daughter's protective fury was both touching and slightly alarming. "Are you safe now? Does the hotel know?"

"Yes. They've changed the key and added a security flag to my room. They're also keeping an eye out for him."

"That's good. I'll call you after I speak to Dad, okay? I need to know you're safe. And Mom? Don't answer if he calls. Don't engage at all. This is seriously messed up behavior."

Jodie ended the call. Rebecca spun around in the center of the suite, surveying the space that had been her sanctuary, her office, her fresh start. Now it felt almost tainted by Don's intrusion—another piece of herself he had claimed ownership of without permission.

She caught a glimpse of herself in the mirror—pale, disheveled, eyes wide with lingering fear. But beneath the fear, she saw something harder, more resolute. She pulled the Montblanc from her purse, its weight substantial in her palm.

Don had attempted to invade her physical space just as he had invaded her mental space for years. But this time, there had been a latch on the door. This time, she had called for help instead of accommodating his demands. This time, she had stood her ground.

Her fingers tightened around the pen—no longer a fantasy weapon to stab through Don's hand, but an instrument of her own agency. She uncapped it and found her notepad on the desk, her hand steadier now as she wrote three words—bold, deliberate: *I AM ENOUGH.*

The small act of resistance suggested that perhaps she wasn't as helpless, as 'nothing without him', as Don wanted her to believe. She tore off the page and smoothed it flat on the nightstand where she would see it first thing in the morning—a talisman, a reminder that even the smallest boundaries were worth defending.

CHAPTER 34

REBECCA WATCHED AS THE morning light crept through the gap in the curtains, but made no move to open them. With the security latch engaged and a chair pushed against the door, she had fallen into an exhausted, dreamless sleep.

The elegant room felt different this morning, carrying shadows of invasion. The memory of that sound—the metallic snick, the heavy thud—was still fresh in her mind. Everything seemed altered, as though Don's presence had seeped through the crack in the door.

The thought of venturing out—of potentially encountering Don in the lobby, the elevator, the restaurant—sent terror rolling through her. He had crossed a line she hadn't imagined even he would transgress.

She reached for the hotel phone and ordered room service, annoyed that her breakfast now had to be delivered to her door instead of enjoyed in the peaceful garden setting at Arbor. She hated the feeling of fear—hated that Don had disrupted her routine, her independence, her hard-won progress.

She sat at the mahogany table by the window and opened her laptop. Margaret's story stared back at her, the cursor blinking in silent accusation. She had abandoned her schedule—her discipline—after the confrontation with Don. She had let his words drive her into darkness and doubt.

But today, despite the lingering anxiety, she felt something else stirring beneath the surface. A quiet anger, not the explosive kind that flares hot and fast, but the slow-burning type that could, perhaps, fuel something productive.

Her fingers brushed against the pen lying beside her laptop—the pen she'd used to sign her divorce papers, the pen that had momentarily steadied her during Don's verbal assault. Almost unconsciously, she picked it up, its solid weight grounding as she tapped it lightly against her chest, thinking.

She opened a new document and titled it: *FEAR*.

The words came tentatively at first, then with growing confidence:

Fear has a sound. Not the dramatic crash of thunder or the sudden screech of tires that make you jump. Not the rising crescendo of eerie music in the movies. Real fear is the sound of a key opening a lock, when no key should be there. Like a door pushing against a latch that wasn't designed to withstand much force. Like your heartbeat in your ears, drowning out rational thought. Fear has a taste—metallic and sharp, coating your tongue as your mouth goes dry. It has a smell—your own sweat, but altered, carrying chemical signals from a brain in fight-or-flight. But most of all, fear has a voice. Sometimes it's the voice of a stranger, speaking threats from the shadows. Sometimes it's the voice of someone who once promised to love you, now twisted with entitlement and anger. And sometimes—perhaps most terrifyingly—it's your own voice, whispering that you deserve this, that you brought it on yourself, that you are too weak to escape it.

She paused, fingers hovering over the keyboard. This wasn't fiction, not entirely. But it wasn't just a recounting of the previous night's events either. It was something in between—taking the raw material of her experience and shaping it into something that could be examined from a distance, something she could potentially control.

She continued writing, losing track of time until a knock startled her. Her heart rate spiked before a voice called out, "Room service."

Verifying through the peephole that it was hotel staff, she accepted her breakfast and returned to the table, eating absently as she reread what she had written. It wasn't polished or perfect, but it felt honest in a way her previous writing attempts hadn't quite achieved.

Her phone rang, Jodie's name flashing on the screen.

"Mom? How are you this morning?" Her daughter's voice was tense with concern.

"I'm okay," she said, stunned by how true it felt. "Better than last night, anyway. I'm sorry I woke you at such an ungodly hour. I hope you and Sean got back to sleep."

"Nothing could keep Sean awake, but I didn't sleep much more," Jodie admitted. "I was too angry. Dad wouldn't answer when I called, but I've just spoken to him now. He's feeling pretty sheepish."

Rebecca winced. "Honey, I wish you didn't have to do that."

"Well, someone needed to tell him how completely out of line he was." Jodie's voice took on an edge Rebecca rarely heard from her typically composed daughter. "I tore a strip off him, Mom. Told him he was acting like a stalker, that he'd scared you, that what he did was probably illegal."

"How did he react?" she couldn't help asking, although part of her didn't want to know.

"He was defensive at first—you know how Dad gets. He blamed you for not listening, for blowing things out of proportion. But then..." Jodie paused. "He actually seemed to get it. Said he realized how scary it must have been for you. That he wasn't thinking clearly."

Rebecca made a noncommittal sound. Don's moments of self-awareness were typically short-lived, usually followed by justifications and deflections.

"He feels really foolish, Mom. He wanted to either call you or come see you to apologize in person, but I told him absolutely not. It's too soon, and the whole thing was too awful."

"Thank you for that," she murmured quietly, recognizing the familiar pattern. Don's remorse always arrived after he'd pushed too far—a tactical retreat, not a change of heart. She'd seen this cycle many times—transgression, apology, temporary restraint, then another escalation. The apology was a form of control, designed to make her doubt her own boundaries.

"Anyway, he said he's flying back to Savannah this afternoon," Jodie continued. "His flight leaves at three. He wanted me to tell you he's really sorry."

"I appreciate you running interference. And I'm sorry that you had to, Jodie. You shouldn't have to manage your father's behavior."

"I know, but it seems like someone has to," Jodie replied with a sigh. "I told Luke about it too. Luke and I have been talking about this a bit—Dad's been losing control ever since Annette kicked him out. Not just with you, with everyone. Like he's having some kind of midlife meltdown."

They said goodbye with promises to talk again soon. She sat still, processing the conversation. Don's behavior was concerning enough that even the children had noticed. That didn't excuse what he'd done, but it at least suggested it wasn't specifically aimed at terrorizing her.

Her next call was to Helen, who responded to the news with an explosive string of profanities that made Rebecca laugh despite herself.

"That absolute piece of garbage," Helen fumed when she'd exhausted her more colorful vocabulary. "Are you okay? Do you need me to come out there? Because I will be on the next flight if you say the word."

"No, I'm okay," Rebecca assured her. "Shaken up, but okay. And apparently he's flying back to Savannah today."

"He better be," Helen growled. "If I find out he's still lurking around Vegas, I will personally come out there and kick his ass around the desert. Maybe tie him to a cactus."

The fierce protectiveness in her friend's voice warmed something in Rebecca's chest. For so many years, Don had systematically isolated her from people like Helen—people who would have challenged his authority, who would have encouraged her independence. Now, rebuilding those connections felt like recovering forgotten pieces of herself.

"How are you really, though?" Helen asked, her tone gentle. "And don't give me the 'I'm fine' line."

Rebecca considered the question. "I'm... processing. Part of me is still scared. Part of me is angry. But I'm also writing again this morning, so that's something."

She wrapped up the conversation with Helen and immediately dialed Justine. The attorney's response to the situation was predictably more measured than Helen's, but no less concerned.

"This is completely unacceptable behavior," Justine said, her voice cool with professional anger. "I wish you had called me the moment he appeared in the lobby, we could have put a stop to a lot of this. Do you want to press charges? Or request a protection order?"

Rebecca considered the options, weighing the potential consequences. A protection order seemed so over-the-top. It would mean court appearances, documentation, explanations. It would pull the children further into their conflict and create another battle when she was already emotionally drained from the ones she'd fought. And a part of her—the practical part—knew that legal paperwork wouldn't necessarily stop someone determined to cross boundaries.

"No," Rebecca said after a moment's consideration. "He's leaving town anyways, I don't want to make the whole situation worse."

"I understand," Justine replied, though she sounded unconvinced. "But I'll be calling Greg Thompson immediately. His client needs to stay in line. And if you change your mind, just say the word and I'll file *ex parte*."

The practical, strategic aspect of Justine's response was comforting—a reminder that there would be penalties for Don if he persisted.

Disconnecting the call, Rebecca took a deep breath. Safe in her suite, she sat down with her laptop and returned to her writing, adding to the short piece she'd begun that morning.

The story evolved into an almost mythological examination of fear as an entity. She was surprised by the way her mind transformed raw emotion into something tangible yet separate from herself.

In her narrative, fear became a creature—ancient and cunning, yet alarmingly fragile. It fed on doubt but withered in the light of scrutiny. It slipped through locked doors but couldn't withstand confrontation. It wielded power only when unacknowledged, becoming oddly vulnerable when named and faced. It whispered with familiar voices—sometimes Don's, sometimes her own—but fell silent when challenged aloud.

As she wrote, Rebecca realized she was creating a map of her emotional landscape. There was power in naming the shapeless dread that was surrounding her.

She wasn't sure if it was good writing, but it felt necessary—a way of processing her experience that neither minimized it nor allowed it to overwhelm her. The act of creation itself was reclaiming power, one sentence at a time.

Just shy of 3 PM, her phone chimed with a text from Jodie:

Dad called from the airport. He's boarding his flight now. It's safe to come out of hiding.

The attempt at lightness didn't quite land, but the message itself was reassuring. Don was leaving Las Vegas, heading far across the country.

With a deep breath, she crossed to the windows and pulled open the curtains. Sunlight flooded the room, illuminating every corner. The view was breathtaking as always—the Strip giving way to the mountains, their contours understated by afternoon haze.

She moved through the space, running her fingers along the desk, straightening her books on creative writing. The suite had been her sanctuary long before Don's intrusion, and she'd be damned if she'd let his actions change that. Still, as she approached the window, her hand hesitated on the curtain, feeling the smoothness of the luxurious fabric. A fleeting image of Don watching from somewhere below made her stomach tighten.

"No," she said aloud, her voice firm in the quiet room. "He doesn't get to take this from me."

She opened the slider on the window, letting desert air circulate into the room. There was something cleansing about the act. She moved the chair she'd pushed against the door back to its rightful place, her movements measured. The security latch would stay, but she wouldn't live behind furniture barricades.

The beautiful suite began to feel like hers again—not through denial of what had happened, but through deliberate reclamation of the space. This room had witnessed her first steps as a writer, had sheltered her transformation, had represented a crucial and conscious life decision. One frightening incident couldn't erase all that meaning.

Though her routine had been disrupted, she had completed a rough draft of a short story, and felt steady enough to leave her room for a swim.

There was a new resolve in her demeanor that hadn't been there before. Not confidence exactly, but its precursor: determination—the kind that digs its heels in when fear threatens to take ground.

Only yesterday, Don's verbal assault had sent her spiraling into darkness, doubting everything about herself and her journey, and surrendering to despair. Today, after an even more direct violation, she had reached for her computer and written. She had made calls, accepted help, taken concrete steps to protect herself. The difference was subtle but significant—she hadn't bounced back completely, but she hadn't broken either.

Her phone chimed with a text from Justine:

Phone call and follow-up email sent to Thompson. Quite pointed. Received immediate response assuring your ex-husband is on a flight to Savannah and will have no further contact. Let me know if anything else occurs.

Rebecca set the phone down, a weight lifted from her shoulders. Don was gone.

CHAPTER 35

IT WAS TWENTY-TWO MINUTES before sunrise. Rebecca dressed in her running gear, determined to get back on track after the setback of the past forty-eight hours. She was determined not to let it derail everything she'd been building. The familiar ritual of stretching her muscles felt like an act of defiance, a statement: *Don had not won.*

The Strip was eerily quiet in the pre-dawn light as she headed out through the main doors.

Her mind raced as her feet pounded the concrete. The man who had once been so controlled had become increasingly erratic—from showing up unannounced, to tearful pleas to reconcile, then a vicious verbal attack, and finally the frightening attempt to enter her room. Each escalation more disturbing than the last.

The rhythmic impact of her feet on the pavement grounded her, and gradually, the tangle of thoughts began to loosen. She was almost oblivious to the slowly waking world around her, locked in the bubble of her momentum.

Approaching the alley near Saddle's Diner, a flash of motion caught the corner of her eye, something in the shadowed space between buildings. She hesitated for a split second, her instincts signaling danger even before her mind could process it. That moment of awareness wasn't quick enough to save her.

The impact came from her right side—the entire weight of a full-grown man slamming into her with deliberate force. The collision drove the air from her lungs in a sharp gasp as she was propelled sideways into the alley. Her momentum carried her forward until she slammed against the brick wall, palms scraping against the rough surface as she instinctively tried to break her fall.

Before she could regain her balance or cry out, a gloved hand clamped over her mouth, the pressure bruising as her head was wrenched backwards. The attacker's body pressed against her from behind, pinning her to the wall with his weight. The abruptness of the attack left her disoriented, her mind unable to process what was happening to her body.

Her face was shoved sharply against the wall, the rough brick skinning her cheek. Gloved fingers laced tightly into her hair, twisting painfully at the roots, yanking her head back and then smashing her forehead into the wall with sickening force. The impact sent a flash of white light across her vision, her knees buckling momentarily. Pain exploded through her skull as the attacker's free hand grabbed her wrist, wrenching her arm up behind her at an unnatural angle. Something in her shoulder gave way with an explosion of pain.

Through her panic, a scent registered—sharp, expensive cologne, wildly out of place in the stale air of the alley. Recognition flickered at the edges of her mind, but she shoved it away. Impossible. Her brain was scrambling, desperate for order in the chaos.

A hiss burned hot against her ear. *"Fucking bitch."*

The words were warped, guttural, the voice low and strangled with rage. It tugged at something deep in her memory, horrifyingly familiar, yet too distorted for her to trust what she thought she heard.

"No," she whispered, the word breaking out of her like a reflex, disbelief warring with terror.

A knee drove into her lower back, and her arm was wrenched further upward, sending white-hot pain searing through her. Warm blood trickled into her eye, blinding her.

Her body recognized the attacker long before her mind would allow it. The cadence, the phrasing, even the rhythm of his breath—details that made her stomach clench with nauseating certainty. But still her mind rebelled. It couldn't be him. Not the man who had stood beside her at church every week. Not the man who had brushed away her tears at their daughter's wedding. Not the father of her children.

This isn't happening. This can't be him.

Yet the pain in her arm, the blood on her face, the fury in his words—those were real. Terrifyingly real.

Then, from the mouth of the alley, another voice thundered:

"What the—HEY!"

The weight was torn from her, the pressure lifted in an instant. She spun clumsily against the wall, disoriented, blood dripping into her vision. Her attacker was on the ground, clad entirely in black, a mask over his face and a ball cap pulled low. Standing over him was a familiar figure—Vince, perfectly timing his exit from Saddle's, his leathery face contorted with fury as he drove his well-worn boot into the attacker's gut with brutal precision.

"You." Kick.

"Don't." Kick.

"Touch." Kick.

"Her!"

The last word was punctuated by another savage kick, the attacker rolling onto his side and drawing his knees up for protection against the blows.

She watched as Vince reached down, yanking away the mask and cap in one vicious motion.

Her world tilted.

She had already *known*, in some terrible, half-denied way—but seeing his face, red with rage and exertion, made her knees buckle.

Don.

His eyes were wild, his hair disheveled. This was not the man she had loved for twenty-five years. This was someone—something—else entirely.

What terrified her most wasn't the violence itself, but what she saw in his eyes. Where there had been calculation, even during his angriest moments, now there was something fractured and unhinged—a disconnection from reality. In that moment, she understood that Don wasn't just angry or jealous or controlling—he was dangerous in a way she had never comprehended before.

"Don," she breathed as her vision swam.

Vince turned toward her, flabbergasted, one boot still firmly planted on Don's chest. "This piece of garbage is your ex?"

She nodded, unable to form words. Blood from the gash on her forehead trickled towards her ear, and she wiped it away with a shaking hand.

The world began to swirl, darkness creeping in from the edges of her vision as she heard Vince calling 911.

Don's crumpled form, Vince's weathered face, the coarse brick wall she leaned against—all began to blur and fade. The last thing she heard was Vince's voice, suddenly closer, laced with concern: "Hey, hey, stay with me. Don't close your—"

Then nothing.

"—coming around. Ma'am? Can you hear me?"

Rebecca's eyes fluttered open to harsh sunlight and the rhythmic jostling of movement. She was lying down, a blanket tucked tightly around her legs. A face hovered above her—young, female, concerned.

"There you are," the woman said. "I'm Tara, a paramedic. Can you tell me your name?"

"Rebecca," she managed, her voice a rasp. "Rebecca Morley."

"Good. Do you know what day it is, Rebecca?"

She struggled to focus, the pounding in her head making it difficult to think. "Friday? Morning."

"That's right. You took some nasty hits to the head, but your vitals are stable. I'm going to check you out, okay?"

As her awareness sharpened, Rebecca realized she was on a stretcher just outside an ambulance, the doors open wide. To her left stood Vince, his face etched with concern. Every heartbeat shot pain through her skull. Her right cheek felt hot and swollen. When she tried to move her head, the world tilted sickeningly. Her shoulder raged with agony.

"Vince," she said, relieved to see a familiar face, her voice sounding strange and far away in her own ears.

"Right here," he confirmed. "How are you feeling?"

"Like I've been hit by a truck," she admitted, gingerly touching her temple where a gauze pad had been taped. The memory of what had happened came rushing in—Don's attack, Vince's intervention, the moments before she'd lost consciousness. The recollection had a dreamlike quality, as though she were remembering a particularly vivid nightmare rather than events that had happened to her own body. "Where's Don?"

"Police took him," Vince said, his expression hardening briefly. "He didn't put up any resistance. Just kept saying he didn't mean it. Pathetic."

Tara continued her examination, checking Rebecca's pupils with a penlight, gently probing the wound on her forehead. "You've got a laceration that I'm going to clean and Steri-Strip, and you might have a mild concussion. Shoulder injury—might be a rotator cuff. You'll need some imaging, for sure. I do recommend going to the hospital for a proper evaluation, maybe a CT scan."

Rebecca shook her head, then immediately regretted the movement as pain lanced through her skull. "No hospital. Please."

Tara frowned. "It's really recommended with head injuries—"

"I know," Rebecca acknowledged. "I know it's not the wisest choice, but I can't... I can't deal with that right now." The thought of the emergency room was overwhelming—bright lights, endless paperwork, and hours of waiting while feeling exposed and vulnerable.

Vince stepped forward, his tone respectful but firm. "I'll make sure she sees a doc for follow-up."

Tara gave him an appraising look. "You're family?"

"Friend," Vince clarified. "I'll look after her."

"Ma'am?" A police officer appeared at the ambulance doors. "When you're cleared by medical, we'll need to take your statement."

Rebecca closed her eyes briefly, fighting a wave of dizziness.

Vince spoke up. "Is there any way you could take her statement at her hotel? She's staying at the Monarch. I can take her there, get her settled."

The officer hesitated, then nodded. "Given the circumstances, we can do that. We'll need your statement as well, sir."

"Of course," Vince agreed, then provided his phone number. "You can reach me at that number to coordinate."

Tara reluctantly agreed to release Rebecca into Vince's care, with strict instructions. "No more than two hours of sleep at a time," she emphasized, handing Vince a sheet of warning signs. "If she vomits, shows confusion, or her pupils become uneven, get her to an ER immediately."

The short ride to the Monarch passed in a blur, the morning's events seeming both hyper-real and strangely distant. She was vaguely aware of Vince speaking with the front desk, of being guided through the lobby, of him helping her to her suite and settling her on the bed.

"I'll be right out here," he said, gesturing to the living area of the suite. "You rest, but I'll need to wake you in a couple of hours. Doctor's orders."

She nodded, wincing at the pain the movement caused. "Thank you," she said, the words wholly inadequate for what she owed him.

He waved away her gratitude. "Just rest. The police will be by later for statements."

"Could I have my phone? I'd like to call Helen. And Jodie."

Vince located her phone on the dresser, handed it to her, then quietly closed the door, giving her privacy for the difficult calls ahead.

She called Helen first, her fingers trembling slightly.

"Hello?" Helen's voice was bright and professional—it was three hours later in Savannah, Rebecca realized with a pang of guilt about interrupting her at work.

"Helen, it's me," she said, stunned by how calm she sounded. "Don attacked me."

"WHAT?" All traces of professionalism vanished from Helen's voice. "Where are you? Are you hurt? Where is he now?"

"I'm at the hotel. I'm... I've been better. Don is with the police. A friend—my friend Vince, he helped me."

"I'm on my way," Helen said immediately. "I'll be on the next flight out. Don't even think about not pressing charges, you hear me? That fucker belongs in jail."

"I hear you," Rebecca replied, gratitude washing over her at her friend's instant, unquestioning support. "Thank you."

After promising to text her flight details, Helen ended the call with a fierce "Hang in there, Rebel. I'm on my way."

The second call was harder. Rebecca took a deep breath and dialed Jodie's number. Her daughter answered immediately.

"Hi Mom!"

Rebecca closed her eyes, steeling herself with false bravado. "Hi honey," she said, trying desperately to sound normal, but the words came out in a small voice. "Something's happened."

"What's wrong?" Alarm sharpened Jodie's voice.

Slowly, carefully, she told Jodie everything—the ambush, the mask, Vince's intervention, the police. Jodie's initial shock gave way to devastation as the full picture emerged.

"Dad did this?" she questioned, her voice small and broken. "I don't understand. I talked to him yesterday. He was getting on the plane."

"He must have gotten off, or never boarded. Jodie, I'm so sorry."

"Don't you apologize," her daughter said fiercely. "You didn't do anything wrong. Dad needs help. Not just counseling—like, real help. Anger management or... or something more. This isn't normal, Mom. This isn't him. Can you put him on the phone please? Is he there?"

"No, honey, the police have him. And I know he needs help," Rebecca agreed, though part of her wondered if this had always been inside Don, kept in check by his need to maintain appearances.

She ended the call, settling back against the pillows, exhaustion washing over her in waves.

Calling Luke was even harder—growing up, he had idolized Don, always doing things to try to please him. His reaction was different than Jodie's but no less intense.

"I'm flying out there," he said immediately, his voice tight with suppressed emotion. "I need to see you. To make sure you're okay."

"Luke, no," she insisted. "Helen is already on her way. I'm safe. And I need you to do something more important for me."

"What?"

"Be there for Jodie," she said. "This is hitting her hard. She needs her brother right now."

There was a long silence before Luke spoke again, his voice heavy with rage. "I don't know how to process this, Mom. Dad's always had a temper, but this? Attacking you? It's like... it's like finding out your whole childhood was a lie."

"Not a lie," Rebecca said softly. "Just... incomplete. We only ever see parts of the people we love."

The emotional toll of these conversations was leaving her even more exhausted than the physical trauma of Don's attack, and she wrapped up the call quickly, laying down and closing her eyes.

A knock at the bedroom door preceded Vince's voice. "Rebecca? The police are here."

"Coming," she called, summoning her remaining energy to sit up and smooth her hair, mindful of the bandage at her temple.

The next hour passed in a methodical haze of questions. Two officers took her statement, their manner professional but compassionate. Vince gave his account in the living area while Rebecca spoke with an officer in the bedroom.

"Mr. Morley is being charged with assault and battery," the officer informed her when they'd finished. "Given the previous incident at your hotel room and the witness statements, it's a solid case."

"What happens next?" she asked, curious despite her physical and emotional exhaustion.

"There will be an arraignment, likely tomorrow. The DA's office will contact you about moving forward with prosecution and will likely request restrictive conditions."

She found herself wondering about the legal implications. The divorce papers had been filed, but it was not yet complete. Would this assault affect that process? She made a mental note to ask Justine later.

One thing was certain—any lingering doubt about her decision to end the marriage had been extinguished. If there had been moments when she had questioned whether anything could save their marriage, those questions were now permanently answered.

"You should sleep," Vince said, noting her drooping eyelids. "I've arranged for a doctor to visit around noon. How did your calls go?"

"Good. My friend Helen is flying in," she said. "She should be here later this afternoon. Can I text her your number in case I'm asleep?"

"Of course," he replied, a concerned look still showing in the lines of his face.

She nodded. "Thank you, Vince. For everything."

He shrugged, uncomfortable with her gratitude. "Right place, right time."

As she drifted toward sleep, she contemplated the strange hollowness she felt. The attack had carved something out of her—not her newfound strength or independence, but perhaps the last vestiges of who she had been as Don's wife. The last tendrils of connection, of shared history that might have eased her memories of their marriage.

Don had severed those final threads himself, with his own hands, his own violence.

He does not get to break me, she thought with sudden clarity. This violence—this attempt to reclaim control—would not define her. With the same determination that had carried her through this past month, she would transform even this trauma into fuel for her journey forward.

CHAPTER 36

T HE BATHROOM MIRROR WOULDN'T lie. Rebecca winced as she dabbed antiseptic to the scrape along her cheekbone. Steam from the shower clouded the edges of the glass, but the center was clear enough to reveal the damage: a purpling bruise at her temple, a deep cut near her eyebrow, and an angry red scrape running from cheek to jaw where Don had repeatedly slammed her face into the alley wall. In the absence of the adrenaline that had carried her through the police questioning, a cold, hollow feeling spread through her.

Her hands trembled as she tore open a bandage. She'd slept solidly for two hours before she felt Vince gently shake her awake to check on her, letting her know that the doctor would be arriving in about an hour. Rather than sleep, she said she'd like to have a shower, and he assured her that he'd be in the next room, and to yell out if she needed anything.

She examined the scrape on her forearm, a ragged track where she'd hit the rough concrete wall. The memory flashed through her mind—Don's hands grabbing her hair, his strength manic as he smashed her against the wall, the shocking force of the impact—and her breath caught in her throat.

The first sob erupted from somewhere deep and primal. The second followed immediately, and then she couldn't stop them. She sank to the floor of the bathroom, her back against the cool tile wall, and let the tears come. They weren't dignified tears. They were hoarse, violent sobs that shook her entire body, gasping sounds torn from her chest, each one sending fresh waves of pain through her bruised ribs and throbbing head.

Her scrapes stung as salty tears tracked over them. The physical pain mingled with the emotional, each intensifying the other as she dragged in breath between sobs. She pressed both hands to her heart, trying to contain the hurt that seemed to radiate from her very core.

Twenty-five years of marriage. Two children together. And it had come to this—violence in a dim alley, police officers, witnesses, strangers intervening. The humiliation of it burned almost as much as the fear and pain. The knowledge that somewhere, in police reports and witness statements, the intimate details of her assault were documented, categorized, filed away—that strangers now knew more about the end of her marriage than her friends.

When the worst of the tears subsided, she pulled herself up using the edge of the sink. Her face in the mirror looked worse now—eyes red and swollen, nose running, bandages askew. But she couldn't summon the energy to fix it.

She heard Vince calling her name, and wrapping herself into a robe, she stepped out of the bathroom.

"Aww," he shushed as he moved forward to engulf her in a hug. "Rebecca, you're okay. You're safe now. Don's not coming back. He won't hurt you again." His soothing words came out in a rush as he guided her over to the bed.

She thanked him, and then mumbled, "Justine. I should let Justine know."

She sat on the edge of the bed, phone in hand, staring until the screen blurred. Then typed to Justine:

I need help.

The response came almost immediately:

I'm on my way.

She hadn't even known Justine was in Vegas. She'd mentioned coming up for the weekend, but Rebecca had assumed it would be afternoon at the earliest.

She curled onto her side, clutching the phone, and closed her eyes. The tears had stopped, but the hollowness remained, along with a different sensation—a strange detachment, as if she were floating somewhere near the ceiling, looking down at the battered woman on the hotel bed.

Fifteen minutes later, a light knock sounded at the door, followed by a text message:

It's me at your door.

From the bedroom, she heard Vince greeting someone and the low murmur of voices. Sitting up made her head swim, her bruised body protesting each movement. She steadied herself against the nightstand, waiting for the room to stop tilting.

She drew in a deep breath, wrapped her robe more tightly around herself, and forced herself toward the door, each step thudding in her skull.

Vince noticed her emerging from the bedroom and moved quickly to her side, offering his arm for support without making it obvious he was doing so. "Justine's here," he said quietly.

Justine stood inside the entry, her handbag clutched in one hand, the knuckles white with tension.

"Oh my God." Justine's professional composure faltered as she took in Rebecca's appearance. Eyes widening, her hand came up to cover her mouth for a brief moment before she recovered. "Rebecca, what happened?"

Without another word, she wrapped her arms around Rebecca, careful to avoid the injured areas. The simple contact broke through the strange numbness, and Rebecca was suddenly crying again, though more quietly this time.

"I'm so sorry," Justine said, guiding her to sit down on the sofa. Glancing at Vince, she knelt down in front of Rebecca, taking both of Rebecca's hands in hers. "Tell me what happened."

Rebecca shook her head. "I never thought he would—" Her voice cracked. "I never thought he'd actually attack me like that. Not once in twenty-five years."

Justine's expression hardened. "Don did this? When? This is completely unacceptable. Didn't he fly out yesterday?"

"It was Don. He didn't fly out. The police came and took him away," Rebecca said.

"And?"

"Apparently he's being charged," Rebecca's voice caught. "How do I face my children after their father ambushed me and, and—" She couldn't finish the sentence.

Justine squeezed her hands gently. "We'll figure it out together. One step at a time."

Rebecca nodded, drawing strength from Justine and Vince's stable presence.

"I'm going to give Greg Thompson a quick call, although maybe Don has already reached out to him from the station."

She scrolled through her iPhone and dialed, asking to be put through to Mr. Thompson as a matter of urgency.

"Mr. Thompson," Justine's tone was brusque. "Are you aware that your client physically assaulted Mrs. Morley this morning?"

She paused, and Rebecca assumed that Greg, Don's long-term colleague, was responding in his usual patronizing manner.

"No, I do assure you it was a physical assault. He's apparently in police custody," Justine asserted. "Mmhmm. Yes, she's right here."

She held the phone away and whispered to Rebecca, "He'd like to speak with you. Are you okay with that?"

She closed her eyes, holding out a hand to accept Justine's phone.

"Rebecca, is this true? We've known each other a long time and this whole situation has been rather difficult. It would be easy for you to misunderstand—" he began.

"No, Greg, it's true. He tried to force his way into my room the night before last, and then this morning he attacked me on a morning jog, wearing a mask and all black. I don't know how far he would have gone if someone hadn't helped me."

Greg was silent on the other end. Eventually, he spoke again. "Rebecca. I am so sorry. For all of it. Don's not just my client, he's also been my friend for twenty years, and this is not like him. You know that."

The familiar justification—*this is not like him*—struck her with unexpected rage. How many times over the years had she made similar excuses for Don's controlling behavior, his temper, his subtle undermining? Greg had been at their dinner parties, their holiday celebrations. He'd witnessed their marriage for two decades, but had he ever really seen it?

"I don't know what I know anymore, Greg. Here, I have to give you back to Justine," she said abruptly as a wave of nausea overtook her. She held the phone out to Justine, unwilling to engage further with the man who had helped Don craft the divorce papers that had so blindsided her.

Justine ended the call and exhaled. Before she could say more, there was a knock. Vince opened the door to a tall man in a navy jogging suit, a medical bag slung casually over his shoulder.

"Rebecca, this is Raj," Vince said, clasping the man's hand. "Old friend of mine. He's a doctor—came by as a favor."

"Happy to help," Raj said, his manner calm and unhurried. He gave Rebecca a quick but thorough once-over: checking her pupils with a small penlight, testing her grip strength, and lightly probing the bruises.

"You've taken a few hard knocks," he concluded, straightening. "But I'm not seeing anything that looks serious right now. Whoever patched you up did a solid job." He glanced at Vince with a small nod. "Just keep an eye on her for a day or two. If anything worsens, get her checked properly at the hospital."

Rebecca let out a shaky breath she hadn't realized she was holding. "Thank you," she murmured.

Raj squeezed her shoulder lightly. "Rest, fluids, and no heroics for a while. You'll mend." With that, he shook Vince's hand again and slipped out.

They sat in silence, the weight of everything that had happened that morning settling around them. Then Justine straightened her shoulders.

"Given no prior record, Don will likely face probation, a fine, or court-ordered counseling—but the protection order will hold."

Rebecca nodded mutely, still unable to believe this was happening.

"You should get some rest," Justine said, standing.

Having no energy left to argue, Rebecca mutely walked back to the bedroom, allowing Justine to help her settle into bed.

"One of us will stay right out here in the living room if you need us," Justine assured her.

Rebecca doubted she would be able to sleep, but the moment her head touched the pillow, exhaustion overcame her, and she drifted into a fitful slumber.

She woke sometime later to the sound of Justine's quiet voice. The room was still dimly lit, but the quality of light around the edges of the curtains suggested it was late afternoon. Aching in every muscle and joint, she slowly eased her way out of bed and over to the living room doors.

"Yes, she's resting now... No, the police were very responsive... I've already filed the protection order... We could ask for a complete reassessment of the settlement terms given these developments..."

Justine saw her and wrapped up the call. "You're awake. How are you feeling?"

"Well, like I've been smashed into a brick wall," Rebecca admitted, wincing as she sat down on the sofa. Every muscle in her body ached, and her head throbbed dully. "And I don't want a reassessment of settlement terms. I just want it over with, and Don out of my life. Where's Vince?"

"Fair enough. I understand. Vince headed out for a bit, to the pharmacy to get you some more bandages and run some other errands," Justine said.

"What time is it?"

"Almost four. You've been asleep for quite a while." Justine moved to sit on the edge of the sofa beside her.

Rebecca checked her phone, noting that Helen had texted from the air.

Relief washed over her waiting for Helen's imminent arrival. As much as she appreciated Justine's practical support, there was something about Helen's particular brand of fierce loyalty that she needed right now.

"Helen's landing early, should be touching down in about 30 minutes," she told Justine. "I think I'll get myself cleaned up and call the kids. Check in and let them know I'm okay."

Justine nodded. "Why don't you do that, get changed, and then we'll go down to meet Helen? A bit of a walk might do you good? We could get something to eat?"

The thought of facing people, of being seen with her bruised and bandaged face, made Rebecca's stomach clench with anxiety. She gave Justine a skeptical look, waving a hand at her face. At the same time, she knew that hiding away in her room would only intensify the feeling of being a victim.

"You'll be fine," Justine insisted with a smile. "If anyone stares, we'll tell them you were on last night's fight card."

"Alright," she agreed with a hint of laughter, reaching for her phone. "I'll call the kids quick, while you organize a bag for me to put over my head."

Getting both kids on a three-way call, and deliberately keeping the camera turned off, the check-in was brief but painful. The ongoing shock and rage in their voices was unmistakable.

"I still think I should fly out there," Luke insisted. "I can book a flight for tomorrow morning."

"Well then you're booking two flights," Jodie broke in.

"No, my sweethearts," Rebecca countered. "Helen is already on her way, and Justine is here. I'm okay, really, and I don't want you guys to see me like this. I just need some time to heal."

"Mom, you were attacked," Luke's voice cracked. "That is so *not* okay."

"I know," she agreed softly. "But I'm safe now. What I need from both of you is to take care of yourselves. This is a lot to process."

By the time she hung up, she felt drained, but determined. The conversation with her children, difficult as it was, had helped ground her in reality. A terrible thing had happened, but life continued. She was still a mother, still herself, still moving forward despite Don's attempt to violently reclaim control over her.

What he had tried to take from her wasn't only her physical safety, she realized, but her sense of self—her identity beyond being his wife, her right to choose her own path. It was the same pattern as always, escalated to a terrifying extreme. His rage had been triggered by her thriving without him. The bruises would heal in time, but she wouldn't allow him to bruise her spirit, her newfound independence, or her resolve to create her own life. She moved toward the bathroom to get ready, feeling only slightly dizzy.

Further shocked by her appearance as the bruises had darkened to hideous shades of purple, yellow and black, she almost laughed. They say anything goes in Vegas, but it wasn't yet the season for a Halloween mask.

Twenty minutes later, having changed into fresh clothes and put some make-up on the worst of her wounds, Rebecca stepped into the elevator with Justine, heading down to the casino floor. The bruise at her temple was unmistakable, but the butterfly bandage near her eyebrow and the larger adhesive on her cheek were neat and professionally applied, thanks to Justine's steady hands.

The moment the elevator doors opened, Rebecca felt exposed. She instinctively turned away from passing guests, her pulse quickening as she imagined everyone staring. Irritated by her instinct to hide, she forced herself to straighten, recognizing that old habits die hard.

"Chin up," Justine murmured, positioning herself slightly in front like a shield. "You have nothing to be ashamed of."

Vince was waiting near the bank of elevators, his solid presence a welcome sight amid the sea of strangers. He looked at Rebecca, a silent question asked with a raised eyebrow. She nodded to let him know she was okay, feeling a flush of gratitude toward the man who had essentially appointed himself her protector.

They made their way toward the high-limit poker room. Justine and Vince flanked her on either side, creating a buffer between her and the curious glances. She observed how people's eyes would widen at her injuries, then quickly look away when they noticed her companions' protective stances. She saw Vince nod toward a table with several players, some of whom nodded in greeting.

"Any news?" he asked Justine in a low voice.

"Yes," Justine answered when Rebecca hesitated. "I've filed for a temporary protection order. The assault charges, combined with the previous incident at the hotel, make Don a clear danger. However, since he's never done anything like this before, he'll most likely have to pay a fine and return to Savannah, rather than serve time."

Vince nodded, satisfaction evident in his expression. "Good. That's good. Get him out of Vegas."

Rebecca's phone chimed with a text message. "It's Helen," she said, checking the screen. "She's in the taxi."

"How about a drink while we wait," Justine suggested.

Despite the circumstances, ordering drinks provided a strange comfort. Justine and Vince spoke of neutral topics, including Rebecca in their conversation without forcing an obligation on her to participate. The normalcy was like a salve. She felt herself relaxing as she settled into the sofa, surrounded by her friends. She was safe. Don was in custody. Overwhelmed with gratitude, she reached out and grabbed one hand of each of her friends, silently thanking them.

When her phone buzzed again, she looked up to see Helen striding through the casino entrance, pulling a small carry-on behind her. Her friend's gaze scanned the room intently until she spotted their group at the bar.

"Rebecca!" Helen quickened her pace, weaving through the casino patrons with determination. As she approached, Rebecca watched her friend's face transform—first relief at seeing her, then shock as she registered the injuries, followed by something that made the color drain from her face before flooding back in a rush of crimson. Helen's free hand was clenched into an unrelenting fist, her knuckles white with tension, her jaw working as if she were physically biting back words too dangerous to release in public.

"That bastard," she finally managed, her voice a low, controlled tremor. "That absolute bastard."

She sat gingerly on the couch and enveloped Rebecca in a careful hug before gently pushing her to arm's length to better examine her face. "Are you okay? And don't say you're fine, because I can see that you're not."

"I'm better now than I was," Rebecca answered truthfully.

Justine leaned forward, and Rebecca jumped, "Oh goodness, sorry Helen—this is my friend and attorney that I've told you so much about, Justine Avery." Justine reached across to shake Helen's hand, telling her that she'd heard lots about her.

Helen's attention then shifted to Vince, and something interesting happened. The fierce protectiveness in her expression didn't fade, but it was joined by something else—a flash of awareness, a subtle shift in posture. For his part, Vince straightened almost imperceptibly, his casual stance becoming a fraction more attentive.

"I'm Helen," she said, extending her hand. "Rebecca's friend."

"Vince. Vince Callahan," he replied, taking her hand. "Also Rebecca's friend."

Their handshake lasted a beat longer than necessary. Rebecca and Justine exchanged glances, both registering the sudden, unexpected current that seemed to pass between Helen and Vince.

Helen had never believed in love at first sight, but it was hard to deny that something immediate and powerful had sparked between them.

"Vince is my guardian angel. He quite literally pulled Don off me this morning," she explained, breaking the moment. "He was passing by when... when it happened." Tears sprang into her eyes as she said, "I don't know what would have happened if—well, if he hadn't been there."

Helen finally released Vince's hand, but her eyes didn't leave his face. "Thank you for being there for her."

"Anyone would have done the same," he said.

"No," Helen contradicted firmly. "They wouldn't have."

Rebecca shifted in her seat, a sharp twinge radiating from her ribs as she turned to watch their interaction. She winced slightly, the pain medication taking the edge off but not eliminating the constant reminder of what she'd endured. Still, there was something comforting about witnessing this moment of connection between two people who'd each become important to her in such different ways.

They settled at a table and filled Helen in on the morning's events. Throughout the conversation, Rebecca noticed Helen and Vince finding reasons to engage directly with each other—passing a drink, asking questions, commenting on what the other said. It was subtle but unmistakable.

Helen laughed at something Vince said, the sound genuine and unguarded in a way that made Rebecca smile. Justine caught her eye and waggled her eyebrows slightly, the corner of her mouth quirking upward in a grin.

Rebecca leaned back and closed her eyes, letting the familiar casino sounds wash over her—the distant chime of slot machines, the murmur of conversation, glasses clinking against tabletops. Her body still ached, her face was still bruised, but she was here, breathing, surrounded by people who had dropped everything to be by her side.

Tomorrow would bring more healing and difficult conversations. But tonight, watching Helen's hand brush against Vince's as they both reached for the same appetizer, Rebecca felt the knot in her chest loosen. Life continuing, changing, evolving.

CHAPTER 37

R EBECCA STIRRED IN BED. Her body ached, a painful reminder of the attack. When she reached for her phone, her ribs protested with a sharp twinge. Her wrists were still tender, and even simple movements sent pain radiating up to her shoulder. 8:15 AM. She'd managed to sleep mostly through the night, though her dreams had been chaotic.

The events of the previous day came back in fragments—the police questioning, Vince's support, Justine's arrival, her breakdown in the bathroom, and finally, Helen's fierce protectiveness upon landing in Las Vegas. Helen had stayed in the suite, taking the sofa in the living area despite Rebecca's offer to book her a separate room.

She eased tenderly out of bed. In the bathroom, she examined her injuries. The bruises had continued to darken overnight, and the cuts and scrapes remained raw. She turned away, unwilling to dwell on Don's handiwork any longer than necessary.

After a careful shower, she dressed in comfortable clothes—gym shorts and a loose T-shirt—and made her way gingerly to the living area. Helen was already awake, sitting at the mahogany table by the window with a cup of coffee, reading something on an iPad.

"Morning," Rebecca said quietly.

Helen looked up, her eyes showing concern as she took in Rebecca's appearance. "How are you feeling?"

"Like shit," Rebecca admitted, eyeballing the coffee that Helen was sipping. "But better than I was this time yesterday."

"Hungry? I ordered breakfast. Should be here any minute."

As if on cue, a light knock came at the door. Helen went to answer it, checking the peephole first—a security check that now felt necessary in a way it hadn't been before Don's break-in attempt.

The waiter wheeled in a cart of covered plates. When Helen removed the covers, Rebecca found her usual breakfast, alongside fresh fruit and a pot of tea.

"I remembered—bagel, cream cheese, tomato," Helen rattled off, catching Rebecca's startled look.

She felt a rush of gratitude for her friend's thoughtfulness. "That's perfect, you're the best, Helen."

They ate in companionable silence for a few minutes before Helen spoke. "Vince texted earlier. He wanted to check on you."

Rebecca looked up. "That was kind of him. How did he get your number?"

"You gave it to him yesterday, remember? It was nice of him to check in. You're not? I mean, are you—" Helen babbled, a slight flush coloring her cheeks.

"Interested?" Rebecca supplied, suppressing a smile. "No, nothing like that. Vince is more than just an ordinary friend though—he's been an unwitting lifeline and an accidental hero to me. He's not what you might expect from a professional poker player."

"Oh? And what might one expect from a professional poker player?" Helen teased, trying to play casual.

Rebecca raised an eyebrow, recognizing the hint of interest in her friend's tone.

Helen waved dismissively. "Not important right now. What matters is how you're doing." She leaned forward. "Have you thought about what comes next? With the protection order in place?"

Rebecca took a careful bite of her bagel, considering the question. "I know what *doesn't* come next. I'm not running away, and I'm not letting him derail what I've been building here. And I'm not going to Savannah yet."

Helen nodded approvingly. "Good. That's what I wanted to hear."

"I'm going to continue writing," Rebecca continued, amazed by the certainty in her voice. "It's the one thing that's been anchoring me these past few weeks. When I'm writing, I'm not Don's ex-wife, or the victim of an assault. I'm just ME."

"So what have you been writing? Can I read something?" Helen asked, pushing her empty plate aside and refilling their cups. "You've been pretty vague about it."

Rebecca hesitated. She felt protective of her writing, still unsure of her voice, reluctant to share until she felt more confident. But if she couldn't tell Helen, who could she tell?

"Uh... trying different things. Some articles, a few stories."

"Fiction?"

"One about a woman who's run away and is trying to find her way home again. It's been stuck in my head for weeks." Rebecca curled her legs up on the sofa. "And fragments of other things that don't seem connected."

"What happens to her?" Helen asked, settling into her chair.

"I don't know yet. I haven't written enough to find out."

Helen laughed, the sound warm and familiar. "You always said that—that the stories tell themselves and you're just along for the ride. What else are you working on?"

"I wrote an introspective piece about fear after Don tried to push his way past my locked door. Maybe I can work that into the story. Maybe not."

Helen's eyes crinkled in a smile. "Give me a hint at least—what's the next scene?"

"I have no idea."

"Well, I guess I'll have to wait and read it to find out."

Rebecca smiled. "If I ever finish it."

"You will. You've always been a writer."

They were interrupted by a call from Justine with an update on the legal proceedings. The protection order had been granted, and once released, Don would be prohibited from contacting Rebecca or coming anywhere near her.

Rebecca felt a familiar restlessness settling over her. Despite her injuries and the emotional toll of the past two days, she couldn't bear lying in bed another day.

"I need to do something," she said abruptly.

Helen nodded in understanding. "The pool? The casino? Name it."

Rebecca shook her head. "Actually, I'd like to write. The story has been circling in my head since we started talking about it, I'd like to get some words down on paper before I need another rest. Do you mind?"

"No, that's perfect," Helen said, brightening. "Actually, Vince mentioned, once you're feeling better of course, he'd like to take me on a motorcycle ride out to Lake Mead. But I don't want to leave you alone if—"

"Go," Rebecca insisted, surprised by how much she meant it. "I'll be fine. The hotel has security watching out for me, and honestly, I could use some time with my laptop."

Helen studied her face. "You're sure, Rebel? Because we haven't made firm plans yet."

"I'm positive," Rebecca assured her. "Have fun. Get to know him better."

Helen left shortly after, and Rebecca settled at her writing desk, laptop open before her. She returned to her story, finding Margaret standing on the side of a long stretch of dusty highway, one thumb cocked at a passing car. She placed her fingers on the keyboard, closing her eyes to see what happened next, and—nothing.

No words came. Not even a feather of a breeze lifted Margaret's hair. Annoyed, Rebecca sat back, wondering where the story had gone.

She stretched out carefully on the sofa and closed her eyes, wary of exacerbating the pain from her various injuries, willing the threads of Margaret's story to reappear. Instead, an entirely different image formed behind her closed lids.

A mansion materialized stone by stone, perched precariously on a windswept cliff. The slate roof was missing tiles; ivy climbing the eastern wall toward a dimly lit window where a silhouette stood watching. Below, a narrow road wound its way up the hillside. A woman in an old-fashioned dress stood at the bottom, one hand shading her eyes as she gazed up at the house. The wind whipped her skirts around her ankles, and beside her sat a blue leather suitcase, its brass corner fixtures catching the afternoon sun.

The image wasn't just a picture—it carried weight, atmosphere, history. Rebecca could almost smell the salt air, hear the cry of gulls overhead, feel the tension between the watching figure and the woman below. It was as if she'd stumbled upon a scene already in progress, characters with lives and conflicts waiting to be uncovered.

She sat bolt upright, ignoring the protest from her aching body. The vision was so clear, elements of the story slamming into place like puzzle pieces finding their homes.

Moving to her laptop, she opened a new document and started typing—ideas flowing through her fingertips so quickly that she didn't even take the time to form complete sentences. Page after page, she lost herself in writing, the story racing from her fingers as if it had been waiting to be told. A sad writer struggling with some sort of tragic loss, a mysterious woman who challenges him, the harsh landscape whipped by bitter winds—all took shape on the page.

Hours passed unnoticed as she wrote, pausing only when the pain forced her to rest. She'd lay on the couch, gathering the strings of her imagination, and then return to the laptop to write more.

When she finally looked up, the afternoon light had shifted, casting long shadows across the room. Her phone showed several text messages from Helen, updating her on the day out with Vince—they'd enjoyed a long bike ride, and a casual lunch, and were now at the poker tables in the Palisade, where Vince was teaching her the basics of Texas Hold'em.

Rebecca grinned, picturing a focused expression on Helen's elfin face as she learned the game. Her friend was a quick study, competitive in the most charming way.

Rebecca shot back a message: *I've been lost in a story all day. What's for dinner?*

Let's check out that Library in the Monarch? Have you been?

Yes! It's fabulous. I'll make a booking for 7?

Helen's response came immediately: *Perfect! Can't wait to hear about the story! Vince says hi and he thinks you need some poker in your story.*

Rebecca chuckled.

She sent a quick reply: *Glad you're having fun! Tell Vince the only poker in this story is likely to be a fireplace poker! See you at 7.*

By the time she arrived at the restaurant, makeup carefully applied to cover the worst of her bruises, Helen and Vince were already seated at a corner table, deep in conversation. She paused to observe them—Helen gesturing animatedly, Vince watching her with undisguised interest, his face lit by a smile.

They spotted her, and Vince rose, his smile now including her, though it remained brightest for Helen.

"How are you feeling?" he asked, his eyes taking in her visible injuries with concern.

"Better," she said truthfully. "Thanks to you."

He waved this away. "Right place, right time."

"No," she insisted with a laugh. "You have to stop saying that! What you did for me yesterday—pulling Don off me, making sure I got back to my room safely, staying with me until Helen arrived—that went far beyond 'right place, right time'. I owe you. So, dinner is on me."

"You don't owe me anything," he said firmly, "but I'll never refuse a dinner offer."

They ordered drinks and food, the conversation shifting from the attack to more neutral topics. She watched with curiosity as Helen and Vince discovered shared interests. What struck her wasn't only what they discussed, but how they communicated. Helen, normally quick to interrupt, would fall silent when Vince spoke. Vince leaned forward when Helen was speaking, his poker face replaced by expressive reactions. Despite their different backgrounds, an undeniable connection was forming—a rhythm that seemed to exclude the rest of the room.

Watching her friends light up in conversation, Rebecca felt something shift within her. Witnessing their enjoyment in discovering each other reminded her that life's surprises weren't always painful. After Don's brutality, there was something deeply reassuring about seeing such attraction bloom between two people—like spotting the first green shoots after a harsh winter.

The attack, Don's intrusion, the fear and doubt of the past days—those things hadn't disappeared, but they had receded slightly, making room for something else. Something peaceful, even hopeful. If Helen could open herself to unexpected joy after years of cynicism about relationships, perhaps Rebecca too could embrace unforeseen paths in her own life.

"So, Rebel," Helen said, turning her attention to Rebecca. "Tell Vince about your writing. How did today go?"

Rebecca nodded. "It went well, actually, but I totally lost the story I had been working on. I didn't write one line. But a new story came crashing in—a tragic guy in a cliffside mansion. Once I caught that thread, I wrote all day," she said.

Helen nodded. "She's basically set up shop at that table by the window," she told Vince. "It's like she's become the writer-in-residence at the Monarch."

"Writer-in-residence," Rebecca repeated slowly. "Hey, that's a great job title."

"I like it! It fits," Vince said, raising his glass. "To our Writer-in-Residence."

Rebecca couldn't help but grin as they clinked glasses. The title felt too grand for what she was actually doing, but there was something appealing about it—defining herself by what she was creating rather than what she'd lost.

"I like it too," came another voice. They looked up to see a tall, distinguished man with silver-streaked hair standing a short distance from their table.

"Forgive the interruption," he said, a hint of interest breaking through his professional demeanor. "I'm Anthony Delaney, Communications Director here at the Monarch." His gaze lingered with particular interest on Rebecca's face, a brief glimmer of recognition flickering in his eyes.

He extended his hand. "Mrs. Morley? I'm glad I caught up with you. I wanted to personally check on your wellbeing after the other night's unfortunate incident at your room, and of course the terrible attack out on the Strip yesterday. I understand there's now a protection order in place, and our security team has been briefed. If you need anything, I do hope you reach out to me personally, or any of our staff."

Rebecca shook his extended hand, touched by the gesture. "Thank you, Mr. Delaney. I really appreciate your concern."

"Please, call me Anthony," he insisted. "I couldn't help overhearing your toast. Are you a writer?"

"Well, to be honest, I'm just starting," she admitted, "but I was telling my friend Helen earlier—it's like the hotel has been my muse—the atmosphere is so conducive to creativity."

"We aim to inspire," Delaney confirmed, glancing around at the sophisticated atmosphere of the bar. "Well, congratulations—'Writer-in-Residence' has a nice ring to it."

"It's just a nickname my friends gave me," Rebecca explained, hiding her embarrassment with a short laugh.

He hesitated, then reached into his pocket for a business card. "It's given me an idea. When you're feeling up to it, I'd love to discuss how we might fit into your writing journey." He handed the card to Rebecca. "In the meantime, your dinner is on me."

She felt a flutter of excitement at his words. Not just the implied validation of her work, but the suggestion that her writing might have a place, an audience, beyond her hotel room.

Later, after three delicious courses and lingering over coffee, she touched the edge of Anthony Delaney's card in her pocket, feeling the raised ink beneath her thumb. Upstairs, a chapter waited; across the table, Helen giggled at something Vince whispered, their hands finding each other without ceremony.

For the first time in days, Rebecca felt the shape of tomorrow—clear lines, open doors. She leaned forward, palms flat on the table, pushing herself up from her chair.

"All right," she said, grinning. "I'm glad we were all here. And now I'm going upstairs to write."

They rose and folded into a gentle hug, mindful of her bruises, before she stepped away, catching Anthony Delaney's eye at the bar and offering a small wave.

Outside the windows the Strip shimmered; inside, the story moved forward.

CHAPTER 38

Two weeks had passed since Don's attack. Rebecca sat cross-legged on the sofa in her suite, laptop balanced on her knees, a mug of tea cooling on the side table beside her. The bandages were gone, though a faint line remained where the cut above her eyebrow had healed. The bruising had faded to a yellowish shadow that makeup could almost completely conceal.

Through an arrangement with Anthony Delaney, she had extended her stay for another month, including rental of a glass-fronted library alcove tucked into a quaint corridor of the Monarch. The space was a bibliophile's dream: walls of bookshelves housing leather-bound classics, their gilded spines catching the light through the glass wall. At the center stood a magnificent desk of burnished walnut, its surface worn smooth by decades of use, surrounded by literary curiosities—antique inkwells, bronze statuettes, a nineteenth-century globe.

Rebecca had made the space subtly her own. Each morning, she'd arrange her things in the same order—laptop centered, notebook to the right, pen across the page, a carafe of water within reach. She'd developed a habit of running her fingertips along the edge of the desk before sitting down, occasionally tracing indentations in the wood—evidence of those who had worked there before her.

A small copper plaque affixed to the glass door bore the simple inscription 'Writer-in-Residence: Rebecca Morley'. Here she sat for hours each day, letting the tragic yet hopeful story of the sad writer and the mysterious woman unfold beneath her fingertips. Occasionally, she would glance up to find hotel guests observing her through the glass—inquisitive onlookers drawn to this unexpected tableau of creativity on display. Despite her initial discomfort, she'd grown accustomed to their attention, now responding with a smile and a wave.

She'd settled into a routine that felt more intentional than anything she'd had in years. Morning runs—short at first, gradually building as she healed. Breakfast at Arbor, followed by hours spent writing, losing herself in the expanding world of her cliffside mansion story. The simple rhythm of it—*run, write, explore, repeat*—had become both anchor and freedom.

Her phone chimed with a text from Helen: *Just landed. Grabbing my bag, then heading to the hotel. See you soon!*

She smiled. Helen had flown back to Savannah a few days after the attack, reluctantly returning to her business responsibilities, but had immediately booked a flight to return. Rebecca knew that she herself wasn't the only reason for Helen's visit—she suspected that Helen and Vince had been chatting on FaceTime almost every day, and she worried that they might be moving a bit quickly.

Setting aside her laptop, she stretched, feeling the pleasant ache of awakening muscles. She'd been writing since breakfast, the hours slipping by unnoticed as her fictional world took shape. She was excited to show Helen the small 'Writer-in-Residence' plaque that Anthony Delaney had made for her—a gesture that had made her laugh but also filled her with a strange pride.

Her phone rang, Justine's name flashing on the screen.

"Perfect timing," Rebecca answered. "I need a break."

"How's the novel coming along?" Justine queried, the smile evident in her voice.

"Slowly but surely. Some days the words flow, others it's like pulling teeth. But I'm making progress. Renting the alcove makes it feel real, though I still wonder whether I'm just playing at being a writer."

"I think a lot of writers feel that way," Justine assured her. "Even the most successful ones sometimes have impostor syndrome."

"Maybe that's it," Rebecca conceded. "How are things with you?"

"Busy as always," Justine said. "But that's not why I'm calling. I have some updates regarding Don."

Rebecca's grip tightened on the phone. "What kind of updates?"

"He's in Savannah, as you know. The Nevada charges were reduced to simple assault as part of a plea deal—he has a hefty fine to pay, a year of probation, mandatory anger management classes, and of course, the protection order remains in effect across state lines."

"I see."

"There's more," Justine continued. "I heard through the legal grapevine that he's been placed on extended leave from his firm. The official story is that he's taking time off for personal reasons, but the reality is that the partners wouldn't have been thrilled about one of their own being arrested for assaulting his ex-wife in public."

Rebecca absorbed this information, feeling a distinct lack of satisfaction at Don's professional troubles.

"Regardless, that doesn't affect our proceedings. The divorce is moving forward as scheduled. You should have the final decree within the next two weeks, and the property transfer will be completed shortly after."

She thought of Don, her fingers lightly tracing the rippled scar on her forearm. She felt no regret—no longing for what they had once shared. Her stomach didn't flutter with the old anxiety that once accompanied thoughts of Don's displeasure. Instead, a certain hollowness spread through her chest, a sadness not for what she'd lost but for what had never truly existed—the man she had thought he was, the partnership she had believed in for twenty-five years. Her jaw tightened briefly before she consciously relaxed it, exhaling slowly as she let the news settle within her.

A knock at the door interrupted her thoughts. Checking through the peephole—a habit now firmly ingrained despite hotel security—she saw Helen standing in the hallway, small weekend bag in hand and her face bright with anticipation.

"Rebel!" Helen strode through the open door, enveloping Rebecca in a heartfelt hug. "God, it's good to see you. You look much better than last time I saw you."

"And you look happy and eager," Rebecca said, noting the healthy glow in her friend's cheeks. "The desert air here must agree with you; you can't seem to get enough of it."

Helen laughed, setting her bag down inside the door. "I think it's the company rather than the climate." She examined Rebecca's face closely. "The bruising has almost completely faded. How are you feeling?"

"Better," Rebecca said truthfully. "Writing has been a godsend. It gives me somewhere to put all the... everything."

"Good." Helen nodded in satisfaction. "Now, tell me what I've missed while I was away."

They settled on the sofa, and Rebecca filled Helen in on developments with her novel, the Monarch staff's kindness, her writing space, and the update about Don.

"Extended leave?" Helen raised an eyebrow. "Is that code for 'we're figuring out how to quietly get rid of you'?"

"You think?"

"I hope not, for Don's sake," said Helen. "But it's not your issue to worry about."

Rebecca contemplated this. "I don't wish professional ruin on him, but..."

"But actions have consequences," Helen finished for her. "And speaking of consequences, how do you feel about him trying to get back with Annette?"

"Indifferent," Rebecca admitted. "I hope for her sake and the baby's that he's truly changing, but I have doubts. I wouldn't wish what I went through on anyone—not even the woman who had an affair with my husband and got herself knocked up."

"I have doubts too," said Helen, her tone hardening slightly. "Men like Don don't change overnight. The counseling is promising, I suppose, but..."

"But it's not my problem anymore," Rebecca concluded. "Annette is a grown woman who can make her own decisions. And Don will only change if he decides that is what's best for him. Like I chose to. Well, to be honest, I had to, in order to 'right my own ship'—otherwise I'd still be wallowing in self-pity."

Helen raised an eyebrow at her. "Look at you, all detached and wise. The Writer-in-Residence has come a long way from the woman who arrived in Vegas a couple of months ago."

"Maybe," Rebecca conceded. "But enough about me. Tell me about you and Vince. Things seem to be progressing quickly there."

Helen grinned sheepishly, a slight flush coloring her cheeks. "They are. He's not like anyone I've ever met before. On paper, we shouldn't work at all—a card shark who lives in hotels with almost no physical possessions, versus an interior designer firmly rooted in Savannah with three houses, all filled with beautiful things. And yet..."

"And yet?" Rebecca prompted, enjoying her friend's uncharacteristic bashfulness.

"And yet, I can talk to him for hours and never get bored. He listens—like he *really* listens—when I speak. He's kind and thoughtful and unexpectedly profound." Helen paused, her expression turning more serious. "But I worry about the logistics. The cross-country relationship, the different lifestyles. Is it sustainable?"

"I don't know," Rebecca admitted. "But maybe that's not the question to ask right now. Maybe it's more about enjoying whatever this is becoming, for however long it lasts. You've only known the guy for two weeks, and most of that time was over FaceTime, for heaven's sake. It's not like there's a lifelong commitment hanging in the balance."

Helen nodded thoughtfully. "You're right. When did you get so worldly, Rebel?"

"Around the same time I started calling myself a writer without immediately feeling like a fraud," Rebecca replied with a small smile. "Speaking of Vince, what are the plans for tonight?"

"He's booked a restaurant at the Wynn—some place with a terrace overlooking their lake. Then there's a jazz trio playing at a club he knows for after." Helen hesitated. "You'll join us, right?"

Rebecca considered the offer. "For dinner, yes. But maybe not for the jazz club. Three feels like a crowd for that sort of venue, and besides, I've been writing in the evenings the past few days. The scene I'm working on is at a critical point."

"Ah yes, how is our tragic and lonely man? Has he fallen off the cliff yet?" Helen asked, only minimally familiar with the work-in-progress.

Rebecca burst into startled laughter. "Well, no, I don't think that's quite where the story goes. I'm at the point where he meets a mysterious stranger—but it's like untying a difficult knot."

"And? Don't leave me hanging!"

"You'll have to wait and read it like everyone else."

"Cruel," Helen accused, though her eyes sparkled with amusement. "Fine, keep your secrets. But dinner at the Wynn is non-negotiable."

Rebecca leaned back, mock-sighing. "Concussion, black eye, busted ribs...and you're *still* bossing me around?"

Helen chuckled. "Of course. That's what friends are for."

CHAPTER 39

T HE TERRACE FOUNTAINS THREW golden light across the lake at the Wynn's lakeside restaurant, as Rebecca sat enjoying the company of her friends. The night was pleasantly warm, a light breeze stirring the air without chilling.

Vince was dressed in a sport coat rather than his usual casual attire, looking both distinguished and slightly uncomfortable. He had winked at Rebecca when she raised her eyebrows at his appearance. "Feel like I'm playing dress-up, but Helen has a dress code."

"You do clean up nicely," Rebecca told him with a smile. "Who knew there was such elegance hiding under all that leather-clad gruffness?"

He laughed, his weathered face creasing with amusement. "Don't tell anyone. Bad for my image."

Rebecca observed the easy rapport between her friend and Vince with a mixture of joy and wistfulness. They moved together naturally, picking up each other's sentences, sharing private jokes, touching casually in the unconscious way of people growing more comfortable with each other's physical presence.

It wasn't envy she felt. She didn't resent Helen this happiness or wish herself in her place. But watching them, she acknowledged a quiet longing for that kind of connection someday. Not with Don—never again with him—but perhaps, eventually, with someone else. Someone who would see her as she was now, not as the person she had been molded into during twenty-five years of marriage.

"Earth to Rebecca," Helen's voice broke into her thoughts. "Where did you go?"

"Sorry," Rebecca said, returning her attention to the conversation. "I'm thinking about my story."

"The sad man on the cliff?" asked Vince. "Helen tells me it's quite the tale."

"Well, Helen hasn't read it," Rebecca laughed. "Though I still have moments of doubt. Is it any good? Will anyone want to read it? Justine says I have Impostor Syndrome."

"Everyone feels that way a bit," he revealed, surprising her. "I've been playing cards professionally for twenty years, and I still have days where I wonder if I'm just a guy who is occasionally lucky."

"Really?" she asked, touched by his candor.

"Really," he confirmed. "Success isn't never doubting. It's playing the next hand anyway."

"That's... actually very helpful," said Rebecca.

"Vince is full of unexpected wisdom," Helen added, her hand finding his on the table. "It's part of his charm."

Melancholy strains of a saxophone drifted across the man-made lake as Rebecca stood and said her farewells, insisting that Helen and Vince enjoy the rest of the evening without her.

"I've got a scene that won't wait," she explained before heading up the escalator.

Back in her suite, she changed into comfortable clothes and settled at her desk, twisting her hair up with a pencil into a messy bun, a ritual that helped free her mind. The blank document no longer intimidated her—it beckoned with unwritten words.

She closed her eyes for thirty seconds—another part of her evolving creation process—visualizing the scene before attempting to write it. When her fingers touched the keyboard, they moved with certainty, finding the rhythm that had become familiar over weeks of daily practice.

The words came easily, flowing as if they had been waiting to be released. She rarely stopped to edit as she drafted, having learned that momentum mattered more than perfection. Those critical voices that used to interrupt her mid-sentence had been trained to wait their turn, relegated to the revision phase.

Occasionally, she'd pause, fingers hovering, head tilted as she listened to the cadence of a sentence. Then her hands would descend again, sometimes deleting paragraphs with decisive keystrokes before rebuilding them—not with frustration but with confidence in her instincts.

"You wrote me," the woman had said when she appeared at the Writer's door. Now, weeks later, he finally understood what she had meant.

She had not come from one of his stories, as he had first feared—some fantastical manifestation of his own imagination. Rather, she had recognized herself in his work—the melancholy girl in 'The Lighthouse

Visitor', the mysterious stranger in 'A Breath of Winter', the silent observer in 'Midnight Train'.

He had written her essence, scattered across a dozen stories, never realizing he was creating portraits of a real woman he had yet to meet. Or perhaps, more accurately, a woman he was destined to meet.

"Your stories found me when I needed them most," she told him as they walked along the cliffside path, the sea churning below them. "They spoke directly to me, as if you knew exactly what I was feeling. As if you'd looked into my soul. You saved my life."

"I had no idea," the Writer admitted. "I just wrote what felt true."

"That's why your words resonated," she said. "Truth recognizes truth. Like calls to like."

She stopped walking, turning to face him fully. The wind caught her hair, lifting it like a banner against the grey sky. "But now you have a choice to make."

"What choice?" he asked, though he already knew. Had known since she first appeared at his door.

"You believe that your gift comes from your pain. That your talent is fed by tragedy, by loneliness, and isolation. You've convinced yourself that any sort of joy or connection would dull your vision—that change would soften your insights. But you're wrong."

"It's not only my belief," the Writer argued. "It's been proven true. My best works were written in the dark."

"Correlation, not causation," she countered. "You wrote beautifully during those times not because of your pain, but despite it. Imagine what you might create from a place of joy."

The Writer shook his head. "I can't risk it. My writing is all I have."

"That," she said as she turned away, "is exactly the problem."

Rebecca paused, rereading what she had written. The conversation between her characters felt charged with something deeply personal—her own questions about creativity and happiness, about whether one needed to sacrifice for the sake of art, or if that was simply a convenient myth.

She continued, losing track of time as the scenes unfolded. Eventually, her eyes grew heavy. Glancing at the clock, she was startled to see it was past midnight. She saved her document and closed the laptop, stretching.

As she prepared for bed, her phone chimed with a text from Helen: *Don't wait up. Night was amazing. Details tomorrow. Sleep well, Rebel!*

She smiled, setting the phone aside. She wouldn't presume to interpret that cryptic message, but she was glad Helen was enjoying herself. Life was continuing to unfold in unexpected ways for both of them.

Sleep came easily that night, her dreams filled not with the chaos and fear that had haunted her after the attack, but with images from her story—the windswept cliff, the old mansion, the writer and the woman facing each other as the sea crashed below them.

When she woke the next morning, a line of dialogue from her dream still echoed in her mind: *"The choice isn't between happiness and art. It's between fear and opportunity."*

She reached for the notepad she now kept beside her bed, jotting down the phrase before it could evaporate. It felt important somehow—not just for her character, but for herself. A truth she was still in the process of discovering, one that might help her navigate the decision about Savannah and what came next.

After her morning run, Rebecca returned to find Helen already in the suite, looking simultaneously exhausted and exhilarated.

"Good morning," Rebecca greeted her, stripping off her running clothes on the way to the shower.

Helen chuckled, a sound of pure joy that made Rebecca smile in response.

"A very good morning indeed," Helen murmured, following Rebecca as far as the bathroom door, speaking loudly to be heard above the water. "The jazz club was incredible. The trio opened the night—then an accomplished pianist dropped in for an impromptu late set. We stayed until nearly three."

"For the music, I assume?" Rebecca asked innocently.

Helen's cheeks colored slightly. "Mostly for the music. Though after…"

"Oh God, please no details about the 'accomplished pianist'," Rebecca protested, making Helen laugh at the play on words.

"No, I want to," Helen said. "Not those details, obviously. But… Vince asked me if I'd consider sticking around a bit. For longer than a weekend. He pointed out that neither of us are kids, and while it's still so new, and it's all happening so fast, it does feel so right. We talked about whether I should open a second office of my design firm here."

"Whoa. That is a big step. And a fast one."

Helen handed a towel over the shower door to Rebecca. "Look who's talking, Miss Writer-in-Residence undertaking a complete life makeover in a matter of months. I know it's not a simple decision. My life is in Savannah—my business, my clients, my home."

"But?" Rebecca prompted, wrapped neatly to her ankles in the velvety bath sheet.

"But what else do I really have there? I haven't any family left there. My home is just a house. My rental houses are just investments that I can own from anywhere. My clients—well, there's that, I guess. But I feel something with Vince that I haven't felt in a very long time. Maybe ever."

Helen looked up, vulnerability clear in her eyes. "After so many years of keeping people at arm's length, there's something about him that fits. Like I am more myself than I've ever been." She shook her head with a small smile.

"And I'm not getting any younger, Rebel. If this is real—and it feels like it might be—how many more chances like this will come along? And what harm am I doing to this new and fragile thing if I'm away for weeks or months at a time?"

Rebecca caught her eye in the mirror. "You don't have to decide everything right now. And it doesn't have to be all or nothing. Maybe start with a longer visit, see how it feels to be here for more than a few days at a time."

Helen nodded, looking down at the tiled floor. "That's what Vince suggested too. A week, even a month. See if we can stand each other when it's not only the excitement of reuniting after being flung together during an unfortunate circumstance." She waved a hand vaguely at Rebecca's face, in case there was any uncertainty about what the unfortunate circumstance had been.

"Sounds sensible," Rebecca approved. "And who knows? Maybe you'll be the one 'in-residence' here in Las Vegas, and I might be back in Savannah myself. The final divorce decree should come through pretty soon, and the house transfer shortly after."

As she spoke the words, she was taken aback by the unexpected stab of jealousy that shot through her. The thought of Helen remaining here, waking each morning to the desert light while she herself had to return to Savannah, created a tightness in her chest that caught her off guard. It wasn't Helen's happiness she begrudged, but the freedom to choose this place that had unexpectedly become more than a temporary refuge.

The Savannah house, which she had once loved so dearly with its graceful proportions and shaded garden, now appeared in her mind as something entirely different—a museum of her former life, rooms filled with furniture chosen to please a husband she no longer had, spaces haunted by the ghost of the subservient woman she'd been.

Even the idea of returning to Savannah's humid air made her feel slightly claustrophobic after weeks of Nevada's dry heat. The weight of social connections there—people who knew her only as Don's wife, who would view her with curiosity or pity—pressed upon her even from a distance.

Yet it *was* still home—wasn't it? The place where she'd raised her children, where she knew every creaking floorboard and temperamental window. The contradiction pulled at her, this simultaneous longing for and resistance to the familiar place that was legally about to become wholly hers.

A flicker of doubt crossed Helen's face. "Do you still want to go back? You seem so different now, and so settled here, with your daily routine and your first novel coming along."

The question caught Rebecca off guard. She planned to return to Savannah once the divorce was finalized, once the house was officially hers. But now, with the actual moment approaching, she was hesitant to commit to returning.

"I don't know," she admitted truthfully. "I thought I was killing time here until I could go home. But now..."

"Now this feels a bit like home instead?" Helen suggested.

"Maybe," Rebecca agreed. "I'm not ready to make any permanent decisions. But I don't feel any urgency to get to Savannah."

"No rush," Helen assured her. "Take all the time you need. The house isn't going anywhere."

Early Sunday afternoon, she accompanied Helen to the airport, hugging her friend tightly before she passed through security.

"Two weeks," Helen promised. "I'll be back in two weeks. And if things keep going well with Vince, I'm going to stay for longer."

"I'll be here," Rebecca assured her. "Running laps up and down the Strip, working on my story about the sad writer, drinking too much tea, and answering to 'Writer-in-Residence'—whether I deserve the title or not."

Helen laughed, then grew serious. "You do deserve it, Rebel. You're finding your voice. I'm so proud of you."

Rebecca embraced her friend, grateful for the unwavering support. "And speaking of overwhelming gratitude, I might arrange an early Thanksgiving next time you're here, fly the kids out? And—if the divorce gets finalized on time and the house is transferred, I may fly back with you."

She watched as Helen disappeared through the security checkpoint and then returned to the Monarch, feeling a familiar mix of melancholy and anticipation. She missed Helen already, but she also looked forward to returning to her routine, to the peaceful focus of her writing hours.

Tucked inside the glass-fronted alcove office, she smoothed her hands across the desk's surface, wondering which room in the Savannah house could be repurposed into an office like this one. A desk like this was no longer a 'nice-to-have', but a necessity. While the desert hills inspired her and the Montblanc pen guided her words, the well-worn wood felt like her foundation.

Turning her attention to her laptop, the scene she had been struggling with earlier now seemed clear in her mind—the Writer and the Visitor standing on the cliff, an unspoken challenge looming large between them.

As her fingers flew across the keyboard, Rebecca felt the peculiar weightlessness of deep focus—hours passing unnoticed, the outside world falling away. A hotel guest paused at the glass wall, watching her work, but Rebecca barely noticed, too immersed in her fictional world.

Her sad fictional Writer stood on the cliff edge, the Visitor's challenge hanging heavy in the air between them. Rebecca paused, fingers resting lightly on the keys, knowing the choices her character faced mirrored her own in some ways. Stay in the comfort of familiar pain? Or risk the chance of the unknown?

Outside, she knew that the Nevada sunset would be painting the distant landscape in shades of amber and crimson. Inside, the desk lamp created a pool of warm light around her workspace. She reached for her Montblanc pen, jotting a note in the margin of her notebook: *His fear isn't of failing but of succeeding.*

The insight applied to her character, but she recognized it in herself too—that whisper of doubt about whether she could handle the freedom of a life entirely of her own making. She clicked the pen closed with decision, returning to the keyboard with renewed clarity. The words flowed until the night staff began their rounds, reminding her of the hour.

Rebecca gathered her things and locked the door behind her. Tomorrow would bring more words, more choices, more discoveries. Tonight, she carried her story with her—not just on the pages but in the certainty that she, like her characters, could choose something new.

CHAPTER 40

*I*T'S FINAL. *CALL ME when you're free.*

Rebecca stared at Justine's text, the words glowing on the screen. After more than two months of back-and-forth, her divorce from Don was officially complete. She was, legally and irrevocably, no longer the wife of Donald Morley.

She set the phone down on the table and looked out at the sun already high in the sky. The enormity of the moment was strangely anticlimactic—not the dramatic, emotional watershed she might have expected, but a silent acknowledgment of a transition already well underway.

All that remained were the practical details, the last threads to be tied up. She picked up her phone and dialed.

"Congratulations," Justine said when she picked up. "How does it feel to be officially divorced?"

Rebecca considered before replying. "Unemotional," she admitted. "Like confirming something I already knew."

"That's common when the emotional separation has already happened," Justine assured her. "The legal formalities are just catching up to reality."

"I suppose so. What happens now with the house?"

"The transfer paperwork is being filed today," Justine confirmed. "Should be completed within the week. The lump sum payment from Don should appear in your account within a few days."

Rebecca nodded, though Justine couldn't see her. The money itself was important for her, would provide some security while she established her own source of income, and give her some time to test the waters as a writer.

"When are you planning to return to Savannah?" Justine asked, the question hanging in the air like a challenge.

"That's what I need to figure out," Rebecca admitted. "I'd planned to go back once everything was finalized, but now..."

"Now you're not so sure?"

"Now I'm not so sure," Rebecca echoed. "I've built something here. A routine, a purpose. These past couple of months have been more than just marking time until I could go home."

"Sounds like you're leaning toward staying," Justine observed.

"I honestly don't know. I haven't decided yet." she paused. "The kids are flying over for an early Thanksgiving celebration next week. I thought I'd talk to them about it then. And speaking of, we'd love it if you'd join us for dinner, Thursday evening if you can."

"Thursday, sure! I'd be honored to join your family. Thanks for the invite. And your approach sounds sensible," Justine agreed. "There's no rush to make any major decisions."

After the call, Rebecca remained at her desk, gazing at the view she'd loved since she first noticed it. She reached for her journal—a new leather-bound Montblanc notebook that Helen had gifted her 'to match the pen'.

The leather cover felt smooth beneath her fingertips; the binding creaked as she opened it, the heavy pages demanding significance from whatever words she committed to them. The Montblanc pen balanced perfectly in her hand, its substantial weight requiring a different kind of attention than her usual quick scribbling.

Writing by hand still felt intimate in a way typing didn't, creating a more direct link to her inner self. The resistance of nib on paper, the flow of ink forming her unmistakable letters—it all created a sensory experience that slowed her thoughts.

The divorce is final, she wrote. *After 25 years, I am legally single again. The house in Savannah will be mine by the end of the week. Everything has gone as smoothly as possible. And yet... I thought I'd feel some sort of triumph, or at least relief. Instead, I feel untethered, as if I've been preparing for a journey only to find myself unsure of the destination. Savannah was always the endpoint in my mind—returning to the house, reclaiming that space as my own, rebuilding my life there. But what if the life I've been building here isn't just temporary?*

She paused, tapping the pen, considering her next words.

The hills beyond the Strip have become my touchstones. I look to them each morning, orienting myself by their distant presence. There's something about this uncompromising landscape that resonates with who I am becoming. Not the carefully curated lushness of Savannah gardens, but this stark, honest desert that makes no apologies for its nature. So the question becomes: do I go back because that's where I'm from, because that was the plan? Or do I stay because this is where I've found myself?

She closed the journal, no closer to an answer but clearer about the question. It wasn't simply about location, but about identity. Who she was now, versus who she had been. Who she might yet become.

The rest of the morning passed in the Monarch's writing alcove, forcing her attention away from her personal issues and focusing instead on writing, her novel flowing as her characters navigated their own difficult choices. By early afternoon, she'd completed a pivotal scene and decided to break for lunch.

Waiting for her meal, she pulled out her phone and composed a group text to Luke and Jodie: *Big news: The divorce was finalized today. Legally and officially starting my next chapter. Can't wait to see you both (and Sean!) next week for Thanksgiving!*

Jodie responded almost immediately: *Congratulations, Mom! Freedom looks good on you—we can't wait to see you too!*

Luke's reply came a few minutes later: *yeah I heard from dad that it was all done—he's doing better with the therapy*

Rebecca stared at Luke's message, caught off-guard by the short tone of the text, and the mention of Don. Even in divorce, he could still steal the headline. Her stomach tightened in a familiar knot—a complex tangle of emotions she still hadn't fully worked through. Of course, she knew the children still communicated with their father even after the attack—she would never want to disrupt that relationship—but it was jarring to be reminded of his ongoing presence in their lives, his continued evolution parallel to her own.

It made sense that Luke would maintain that connection, perhaps even take comfort in signs of his father's improvement. But the brevity of his response, the immediate pivot to Don's wellbeing rather than acknowledgment of a milestone, stung in a way she hadn't anticipated.

She took a deep breath, reminding herself that Luke was navigating his own complicated emotions about the divorce. His relationship with Don was separate from hers, as it should be. Still, she reread Jodie's enthusiastic response, grateful for its unambiguous support.

She set the phone down, telling herself that seeing them in person next week would be different. Text messages couldn't capture nuance or context, and Luke had never been particularly effusive in any form of communication.

She walked the Strip, enjoying the sun shining through the early November chill. The quality of light had changed with the season—sharper, more crystalline than the hazy summer heat. The desert breeze carried a crisp coolness unlike the heavy, wet chill she would have felt in Savannah.

While Las Vegas was entering its cooler season, it was nothing like the pronounced autumn in Savannah, with its carpeted streets of fallen leaves and the heavy scent of decay. Here, the palm trees remained green, the desert plants indifferent to the calendar. The seasons here were subtle shifts in temperature rather than dramatic transformations.

She breathed deeply, appreciating how the drier air filled her lungs completely, without the resistance of humidity. Even sound seemed clearer in this desert atmosphere—the traffic and the conversations of passersby.

Up in her suite, she was drawn to her laptop again, but not to her novel. Instead, she opened a browser and began researching real estate in Las Vegas, curious about what it might cost to establish permanent roots here. The prices were higher than Savannah for comparable square footage, but not prohibitively so, especially with the value of her Savannah house and the divorce settlement.

"But—" she declared aloud, "I sure as hell don't need a four-bedroom, double-storey house!"

Drawn to the city's downtown area, she clicked through photos of classy, open apartment spaces—so different from her Savannah home with its ornate decor and compartmentalized rooms that kept everyone in their proper place.

She imagined what life would be like in an open-plan apartment with large windows, modern finishes, and amenities that suited her new lifestyle—a dedicated writing space positioned to capture those essential mountain views, a kitchen designed for one or two people rather than family meals. No formal dining or living room, but instead, flexible spaces that could adapt to her needs rather than conforming to social expectations of what a 'proper home' should contain.

It was just research, she told herself. Exploring options. But as she bookmarked several properties, she knew she was doing more than idle browsing. She was seriously considering a future in Las Vegas.

Her phone rang—Helen's face appearing on the screen.

"I had lunch with Jodie today," Helen said without preamble. "So, it's official?"

"It's official," Rebecca confirmed. "Signed, sealed, delivered. I'm no longer Mrs. Donald Morley."

"Hallelujah!" Helen exclaimed. "We should celebrate when I'm there next week. Speaking of which, I've booked my flight. Arriving Tuesday, staying through 'til the following Monday."

"Perfect," Rebecca said. "The kids are landing Thursday afternoon and we'll do early Thanksgiving dinner that night, here at the Monarch. I arranged a limo to pick them up, Jodie will love that, and then I've reserved a private dining room. I keep forgetting Jodie's married now, is that horrible?"

"No, of course not, Reb. The wedding only happened a couple of weeks before you and Don went to Las Vegas, supposedly for only five days. I think it's safe to say, a lot has happened since then," Helen assured her. "Jodie's been settling into being married too—this has definitely been a big year of change for everyone."

"You're not wrong," Rebecca laughed. "Oh, and before I forget, do you want me to book one for you too, or..." she let the thought trail off, waiting for Helen to fill in the blanks.

"Vince invited me to stay with him," Helen said slowly, though her tone was light. "He might get sick of me though, so keep your sofa available."

They chatted a while longer about Helen's plans to scope out office space in Las Vegas and her increasing certainty about splitting time between cities. Rebecca listened with genuine happiness, marveling at how quickly life could change.

She disconnected from the call and returned to her writing desk, opening her novel file. She scrolled to where she'd left off earlier, reading over the last few paragraphs, searching for the thread of the narrative, as a fresh perspective on the scene suddenly crystallized in her mind.

She began to type, the words flowing freely:

"Your fortress of solitude here," she told him, gesturing to the mansion looming behind them. "Cold stone walls, empty rooms—you've arranged your life so carefully to exclude anything that might threaten change."

"It's served me well," the Writer argued. "My books—"

"Blast your books!" she interrupted. "I wouldn't be here if your books weren't meaningful. Beautiful, even. But your writing is so... so incomplete."

The Writer stiffened at this unexpected criticism. "What do you mean, incomplete?"

"You write eloquently of loss, of absence, of things missed or denied. But there's a whole vocabulary of experience that you never touch—joy, connection, the messy complications of being fully alive. There's never any resolution. There's no growth."

"And you think you can teach me those words?" he asked, his tone somewhere between defiance and hope.

"No," she said simply. "I think life can teach you, if you're willing to step outside these walls you've built. The question is whether you're brave enough to risk it."

Rebecca paused, rereading what she'd written. The parallels to her own situation were subtle, but they felt true. The Writer's fortress might be a literal mansion on a cliff, while hers had been a marriage that had ultimately confined rather than sheltered her. Both required courage to rise beyond—and like her fictional writer, she'd never even realized it, until change was forced upon her.

It's not about the change itself, she realized, stunned. It's about how you respond to it.

The rest of the week passed in a blur of writing and preparation for her guests. The money from the divorce settlement appeared as promised, and she squirreled it directly into a savings account—it represented both an ending and a beginning. The house transfer was completed with similar efficiency, the deed now listing Rebecca Fielding Morley as the sole owner of the Savannah property.

Her maiden name on the deed caught her attention. *Rebecca Fielding.* The name sat on the legal document like a visitor from another time—familiar yet strange, like running into a childhood friend after decades apart. She'd been Rebecca Morley for so long that the sight of her birth name felt like discovering a piece of herself she'd set aside and forgotten.

Rebecca Fielding. She whispered it aloud, testing how it felt in her mouth after all these years. The old Rebecca Fielding had had dreams of becoming a playwright. She had been independent, opinionated, ambitious, and had worn her hair long and wild. She'd stayed up all night talking about books and ideas and had believed in her own voice.

Somewhere along the way, that Rebecca Fielding had gradually disappeared, subsumed by the compliant Rebecca Morley. The transformation had been so gradual she hadn't noticed the complete substitution of one identity for another.

But now, seeing that name on an official document—Rebecca Fielding Morley—felt like an invitation. Maybe it was time to reclaim that part of her identity as well. Not to erase the years as Rebecca Morley—those years had given her the children, experiences that had shaped her, lessons that had ultimately led her here. But perhaps she could reintegrate the young woman she'd once been with the independent woman she was becoming.

Rebecca Fielding. Writer.

On Monday morning, she rose early and took a longer run than usual, pushing herself until her lungs burned and her muscles ached pleasantly. Showered and dressed, she made a decision. Instead of writing fiction today, she would make a concrete plan for her future.

She opened her laptop, intending to make sense of her conflicting feelings about Savannah and Las Vegas. But instead of lists or analyses, she found herself simply sitting with the question Helen had posed.

The truth was, she wasn't ready to leave. Not the desert light, not her writing alcove, not the version of herself she'd discovered here. But she also wasn't ready to close the door on Savannah entirely—on the house where she'd raised her children, on twenty-five years of memories that weren't all tied to Don.

What if she didn't have to choose? The house was hers now. She could keep it, maybe rent it out, while continuing to build her life in Las Vegas.

She closed the laptop without writing a word, feeling unusually settled. Some decisions didn't need to be made—they simply needed to be lived into.

Later, Rebecca joined Vince at the Monarch Bar. He had arrived early, rising to greet her with his warm smile.

"Congratulations on your freedom," he said, raising his glass in a toast. "Helen told me it was official."

"Thank you," she replied, clinking her glass against his. "It feels strange but right."

"Big weight off, I imagine," he said. "Even when you know it's the right call, ending something that lasted so long has gotta be a mindbender."

She nodded, appreciating his direct approach. "It is. Though the actual completion of the paperwork feels like just another box to check after so much of everything else that's happened."

"That's usually how it goes," he agreed. "The emotional stuff happens long before the legal stuff catches up." He regarded her thoughtfully. "So, what's next for our Writer-in-Residence? Back to Savannah?"

"That's the big question," she admitted. "I've been thinking about it all day." She outlined the plan she'd developed, watching Vince's face for a reaction.

"Sounds solid," he said when she finished. "Keeps your options open while you figure out what feels right long-term."

"That's the idea." She hesitated. "And if I do decide to stay in Las Vegas permanently, it's nice to have a friend here already."

"You got that," he assured her. "Me and Helen, we're not going anywhere."

"About that," she began, curious about the evolution of their relationship. "Helen mentioned she wants to look at office space while she's here. She seems pretty serious about splitting her time between Savannah and Las Vegas."

Vince's face lit up. "Yeah, it's moving faster than either of us expected. When you get to our age, though, you don't mess around with the small talk and games. You know when something's good."

"And it's good?" she prodded, though the answer was evident in his expression.

"It's good," he confirmed simply. "Never thought I'd meet someone like her, especially not under those circumstances." He shook his head slightly. "Life's funny that way. Sometimes the worst moments lead to good things."

Rebecca thought of her journey so far—how Don's betrayal had ultimately set her on a path to rediscovery, how the end of her marriage had created space for her creativity to reemerge.

"Very true," she agreed. "Do you think you'll ever get tired of hotel living?"

"Are you tired of it?" he countered with a grin before thinking through a proper answer. "Actually, I have been wondering about that. Nothing serious yet, but if Helen's going to be spending more time here, might be nice to have a real home base. But hey, I do have a storage unit that I call my own."

"What are you thinking?" she asked, wondering if their thoughts had been running along parallel tracks.

"Somewhere close to downtown, definitely," he mused. "Walking distance to some of my favorite places. Maybe a garage to tinker in."

Rebecca smiled. "I was looking at some high-rises close to downtown this morning. Maybe we're all starting to think about putting down some new roots."

"Great minds," he said with a wink. "Downtown is great. Though I'd have thought you'd want something quieter, more conducive to writing."

"Not necessarily," she said. "I've done all of my writing so far in the middle of a busy hotel. There's something about the energy of Las Vegas that works for me. As long as I can see those hills, I'm grounded and happy."

They continued chatting about the upcoming Thanksgiving gathering—it would be the first time her new circle of friends and her family would come together, a merging of her past and present that felt symbolically important. Their easy camaraderie reminded her of another advantage to staying—the new friendships she'd formed, connections unrelated to Don or her former identity as his wife.

Preparing for bed later that evening, Rebecca's phone chimed with an email arriving. Opening it, she found a message from Don: *So, the divorce was finalized today. I know congratulations isn't the right word, but I wanted to acknowledge the moment, and thank you for not contesting. It's helped with my situation. All transfers are complete on my end. I wish you well, Rebecca. And I'm sorry for everything.*

She stared at the message, unsure how to respond or whether to respond at all. The words—*'I'm sorry for everything'*—held no sting.

A calm detachment framed her reply: *Thank you for the apology. I wish you well too. All the best for the baby.*

It wasn't friendly, but it wasn't hostile either. A neutral acknowledgment of his message and the reality of their situation. She hit send before she could overthink it.

His response came quickly: *The therapist I'm seeing says closure is important. I know things ended badly between us, but I hope someday we can at least be cordial, for the kids' sake if nothing else.*

She considered this. Cordial seemed a high bar after what had happened, but not impossible given enough time and distance. *Maybe someday*, she replied. *Right now, I'm focused on moving forward. Take care, Don.*

Understood, came the response. *You take care too, Rebecca.*

She set the phone aside, pleasantly surprised by the lack of emotional turmoil the exchange had generated. She thought back over the past two months, reflecting on how most contact with Don had sent her into a spiral of hurt, anger, and confusion. Now it was simply a brief interaction with someone from her past, neither devastating nor particularly significant.

Progress, she thought as she turned out the light. Definite progress.

CHAPTER 41

REBECCA STOOD ALONE IN the private dining room, taking a final glance around before her guests arrived. The Monarch's staff had transformed the space according to her specifications—elegant but not stuffy, festive without being kitschy. The late afternoon sun streamed through the windows, bathing the room in golden light.

The door opened, and Helen entered, carrying a bottle of wine in each hand. "Vince'll be here shortly. Had to change after his afternoon game ran long."

Helen moved beside her, taking in the room. "This looks beautiful, Rebel. Very Rebecca *Fielding*."

Rebecca smiled at Helen's deliberate use of her maiden name. "You think they'll notice?" she asked quietly, not needing to specify that 'they' meant her children.

"How much you've grown? They'd have to be blind not to." Helen squeezed her arm. "They'll be happy for you."

"I'm worried about Luke," Rebecca admitted. "His texts have been so... brief, since what happened with Don. Almost formal. And after what Jodie told me about Don trying to run damage control with both of them..." She trailed off, unwilling to voice her deeper fear—that her son might have chosen sides.

"Give him time," Helen advised. "He's navigating a complicated situation. Finding out your father isn't who you thought he was—it can't be easy."

A knock interrupted them. Rebecca opened the door to find Justine, elegant as always in a rust-colored jumpsuit that complemented the autumn theme.

"Happy Thanksgiving," Justine said, embracing Rebecca before presenting a carefully wrapped bottle. "Single malt scotch—for after dinner. And I'm going to cut out early tonight—I have a date!"

"That's so exciting," Rebecca replied, sincerely pleased. The friendship that had evolved between them was an unexpected gift that had arisen out of this difficult year, but she still knew very little about Justine's personal life.

They had barely exchanged pleasantries when another knock announced the children's arrival. Her heart quickened as she opened the door. Luke entered first, tall and lanky in a grey button-down. Behind him came Jodie, radiant in a simple dress, her hand linked with Sean's.

"Mom," Jodie said, stepping forward to embrace Rebecca. "This hotel is incredible. Our room is amazing! Thank you for arranging everything."

"Of course," Rebecca murmured, holding her daughter close before turning to Luke.

He hesitated for a moment before stepping into her hug. "Happy Thanksgiving," he said, his voice flat. "You look great."

She searched his face for clues to his thoughts, but his expression remained guarded. She turned to Sean, welcoming him affectionately, then made introductions all around. The conversation moved in fits and starts, politeness masking the underlying currents of unfamiliarity and uncertainty.

"Vince should be here any minute," Helen said during a lull, her eyes flicking to the door.

"The poker player? Why is he invited to family Thanksgiving?" Luke asked, his tone hard to read.

Rebecca raised her eyebrows. "Vince is a good friend."

"He's the one who was there when Dad attacked her," Jodie explained to Sean, her voice dropping. "If he hadn't been there—"

The sentence hung unfinished in the air. Rebecca saw Luke's jaw tighten, his eyes darting away. Before she could address it, another knock came at the door.

Vince entered, looking snappy in a well-cut blazer. "Happy Thanksgiving," he said, kissing Rebecca's cheek before presenting a bottle of champagne. His eyes found Helen, a smile spreading across his weathered face.

"Vince, you remember Jodie," Rebecca said, making introductions. "And this is her husband Sean, and my son Luke."

"Good to see you again," he said to Jodie before shaking hands with Sean and Luke.

Luke's handshake was firm but brief, his expression revealing nothing.

"Shall we open the champagne?" Rebecca suggested, eager to move past the momentary awkwardness.

As Vince handled the bottle with expert ease, Rebecca noticed Luke watching him intently. The cork popped, and Vince poured glasses all around. They made a toast—to family, to friends, to Thanksgiving—and the first sip of champagne seemed to ease some of the tension in the room.

Conversations formed around the room—Helen and Jodie discussing interior design with Justine, Vince and Sean discovering a shared interest in local history. Rebecca sidled up beside Luke, who had drifted toward the window.

"Beautiful view," she said, joining him.

"Different from Savannah," he observed.

"Very different," she agreed. "But I've grown to love it."

Luke seemed about to say something, then stopped himself. Rebecca waited, giving him space.

"Dad says you and Vince are…" he trailed off, eyeballing Vince across the room, where he was deep in conversation with Sean.

"What? No! Not even close. Vince and Helen are an item," she laughed, almost relieved to have discovered one of the sources of his unease.

His face registered surprise, but he still looked uneasy.

"Luke, what is it? What's bothering you?" she ventured.

"Dad told me a different version of what happened," he finally said, his voice low enough that only she could hear.

Rebecca felt her heart sink. "What did he tell you?"

"That things got heated during a conversation, that you wouldn't let go of him so he pushed you away, harder than he meant to, and you fell against a wall." his eyes flicked toward Vince. "He said that guy was there and attacked him without provocation."

"That's not what happened, Luke." Her fingers tightened on the glass. She kept her voice even despite the anger building inside her.

"Yeah, that's what Jodie says too," he admitted, studying his champagne. "It's hard to know who to believe. Dad has been so… convincing. He said the police report was exaggerated. He said that guy's the reason why you won't come home. And why you wouldn't let me come out here when you were supposedly hurt."

"Your father was supposed to have left Las Vegas. He ambushed me during my morning run," she said, her voice hard. "He slammed my head against a brick wall repeatedly and kicked me. If Vince hadn't been leaving the diner in the same alley at that exact moment and intervened, I don't know what would have happened."

Luke's face paled. "Mom, I—"

"It's not your fault," she said quickly. "I know your Dad can be very convincing when he wants to be."

"I have something you should see, Luke," Helen announced, approaching with her phone.

"Helen, that isn't necessary," Rebecca protested.

"Yes, I think it is," Helen replied firmly, finding the photo and turning the screen toward Luke. "This is what I found when I arrived in Vegas. *This* doesn't happen just from *falling into a wall*."

Luke stared intently at the image, his expression stricken. The bruising was vivid, the cut above Rebecca's eyebrow angry despite the neat bandages, the swelling distorting half her face. His father had done this—deliberately hurt his mother badly enough to require medical attention. The comfortable lie he'd been telling himself crumbled in an instant.

"Maybe it looks worse than it was," he began, then faltered, staring down at the carpet. Helen continued to hold the phone where he could see the photo.

"Jesus," he whispered, looking up at his mother with new eyes. "I didn't realize. I need some time to wrap my head around this."

"I didn't show you this to make you feel bad," Helen said, easing off slightly. "But your father's been spinning quite a tale, and you deserve to know the truth."

"Why would he lie to me about this?" he asked, his voice rough.

"People create narratives they can live with," Rebecca said gently. "Your father included. But Luke—he's getting help now. You said the therapy seems to be making a difference. We can acknowledge what happened without letting it define our future."

He nodded, though conflict still shadowed his eyes. "I'm really sorry I believed him over you," he said finally.

"You're not responsible for your father's actions," Rebecca assured him, squeezing his arm. "Or his stories."

A staff member arrived to announce that dinner would be served momentarily, breaking the tension of the moment. As they moved toward the table, Rebecca noticed Luke hang back, his expression troubled. She gave him space, trusting that he would process this revelation in his own time.

The meal began with a butternut squash soup garnished with roasted sage. As they ate, conversation flowed naturally, initial awkwardness giving way to new connection. Vince was making a particular effort with Luke, noticing the young man's guarded posture and carefully selecting topics that might bridge the distance. Drawing him out with questions about his studies in architecture, Vince found common ground and a shared interest in sustainable design.

As the main course arrived—a modern interpretation of traditional Thanksgiving turkey with all the trimmings—Rebecca felt a subtle shift in the room's energy. The separate pieces of her life were fitting together, not perfectly, but with enough alignment to satisfy her. Her children, her friends, her sense of self—all present at this unconventional Thanksgiving table.

"So, Mom," Jodie said during a lull, "tell us about this novel you're writing. Helen says it's brilliant."

She felt a flush of self-consciousness. "Helen is biased," she demurred. "Not to mention she hasn't read it. But yes, I've been working on a novel. It's still very much in progress."

"What's it about?" Luke asked, surprising her with his interest.

She hesitated, unaccustomed to discussing her work beyond conversations with Helen. "It's about a writer who lives in isolation, believing his creativity was born from tragedy, and is fueled by loneliness and misery. Then a woman arrives—and she forces him to challenge his beliefs, offering him a choice between the talent he knows, and the possibility of happiness."

"That sounds cool," said Jodie.

"It will be," Helen confirmed. "Your mother's always had that voice—thoughtful, introspective, beautiful language."

"You wrote plays in college, right?" Luke asked. "I remember finding some in the attic once."

A pang of sadness touched Rebecca's heart as she realized how much of herself she had set aside during her marriage, parts of her identity that her children had never fully known. "I did, yes. Before I married your father."

"Were they ever performed?" Sean asked, curious.

"A couple of them. Small college productions." Rebecca took a sip of wine. "Writing was my first love, but life took me in different directions."

"And now you're finding your way back," Jodie observed. "Really inspiring, Mom."

Rebecca smiled at her daughter, touched by her support. "It feels right. Like I'm remembering who I was always meant to be. But of course I'm just starting out."

"She's being way too modest. She's the 'Writer-in-Residence' here at the Monarch. Has an office here where people watch her write. Your Mom is pretty remarkable," Vince told them, raising his glass to Rebecca.

"Wait, you actually have an office? And a title?" Luke asked, amused but not mocking.

"It started as a bit of a joke," Rebecca explained. "But Anthony, the communications director here, ran with it. PR gold for the Monarch, supporting the arts. I have a little plaque on the door of the library alcove where I write. It's an arrangement I made with the hotel, renting a little space to write in."

"You mean you have an actual office here?" Jodie asked, fascinated.

"I'll show you tomorrow," Rebecca promised. "It's the most beautiful space."

She noticed Luke watching her with a new awareness, as if seeing her clearly for the first time in years. When there was a natural break, he turned to her.

"So," he began, "what's going on with the house?"

The direct question created a momentary lull around the table. Rebecca set her fork down, considering her response.

"I've been thinking about that," she said carefully. "I'm planning to go soon to sort through things. But I wanted to talk to you guys this weekend. I'm thinking I might sell."

She watched Luke's reaction carefully, but instead of the immediate resistance she had feared, she saw only thoughtful consideration. Something loosened in her mind—permission she hadn't realized she'd been waiting for.

"It makes sense," he said hesitantly. "It is a big place for one person."

"It is," she agreed, relieved. "And while it holds many wonderful family memories, it also represents a chapter of my life that's closing now."

"You know," Jodie chimed in. "We attach so much meaning to physical spaces. But the memories don't disappear just because the house changes hands."

"Exactly," Rebecca said, grateful for her daughter's perspective. "The important things—the connections, the experiences we shared—those stay with us."

"Plus, the real estate market in Savannah is hot right now," Helen added pragmatically. "You could do very well on a sale."

"Always the businesswoman," Vince teased, his hand finding hers under the table.

"What kind of place would you want, Mom? Would you stay in Savannah?" Luke asked.

"I'm not sure, to be honest. For now, I really am loving Las Vegas. I might want to make this my home," she said hesitantly, gauging their reactions.

Finding no resistance, she continued, "In a place that has a view of the hills, and maybe the city. Modern, open, filled with light. A space designed for one person and her writing, and her guests, of course."

"Sounds like you've been thinking about this more than a little," Jodie observed with a wry smile.

"I might have," Rebecca admitted. "More than I realized until right now."

Dessert arrived—a deconstructed pumpkin pie garnished with chunks of dark chocolate and roasted coconut—momentarily diverting the conversation. As they ate, Rebecca was overwhelmed by a profound sense of gratitude. The evening had gone better than she had dared hope, her children embracing her evolution rather than resisting it.

Conversations continued to flow easily through coffees and scotch, breaking into smaller discussions that shifted throughout the evening. Rebecca sat beside Luke on a small sofa, watching as Vince taught Jodie and Sean a simple poker game.

"He seems like a good guy," Luke said, nodding toward Vince. "Not what I expected."

"What did you expect?"

"I don't know. I thought—I mean Dad said—that you guys had a thing. I felt a bit weird about it."

Rolling her eyes at Don's devious tactics to turn her son against her, Rebecca remained silent.

"What Dad told me about what happened in that alley, I pictured someone more..."

"Rough around the edges?" she suggested.

"Yeah, I guess. But he seems smart. Thoughtful."

"He's been a great friend. A lifeline for me," she said thoughtfully. "There's a lot more to him than meets the eye. I'm so glad he and Helen have connected like this."

Luke was quiet, watching the others. "You seem so content, Mom. Happier than I've seen you in a long time. I feel like twenty-one years have gone by, but I've never really known you. Like, the real you."

The simple observation touched her deeply. "I am happy," she admitted. "Despite everything—or maybe because of it—I've found my way to a kind of happiness I didn't know was possible."

"Good," he said simply. "You deserve that."

Rebecca studied her son's profile, so like her own yet with hints of his father. "How are you doing with everything? Really?"

Luke considered the question, taking his time to answer. "It's been difficult," he finally said. "Harder than I thought at first. Finding out Dad isn't who I thought he was. Now the lies about what he did to you. It's like..." he struggled for the words. "It's like the foundation shifted, and I'm still trying to find my balance."

"I understand that feeling."

"I guess you would," he acknowledged. "I want you to know—I am on your side, Mom. I'm on both of your sides. Even if I didn't always show it these past few weeks."

She felt tears prick at her eyes. "That means more than you know."

The evening continued, warm and convivial, until the energy began to wane. Justine left shortly after dinner, embracing each of the other guests in turn. Sean was the first to acknowledge fatigue from jet lag, followed by Jodie. As they prepared to leave, Rebecca hugged each of them, lingering with her children.

"Breakfast tomorrow?" she suggested. "Nine o'clock at Arbor? Just the four of us."

"Let's make it nine-thirty," Jodie suggested, keen to sleep in.

"I'll be there," Luke confirmed, his hug more heartfelt than when he'd arrived.

After they had gone, only Rebecca, Helen, and Vince remained. Rebecca sank onto the plush sofa that faced the window, feeling both emotionally full and physically tired.

"That went well," Helen observed, settling beside her.

"Better than I expected," Rebecca agreed. "Especially with Luke."

"He's finding his way," Vince commented, remaining standing as he finished his drink. "Good kid. Smart."

Rebecca smiled, touched by his assessment, and how similar it sounded to Luke's assessment of Vince. "Thank you both for being here tonight. It meant a lot to have you as part of this."

"Wouldn't have missed it," Vince assured her.

Later, after returning to her suite, Rebecca went straight to her writing desk. Though tired, she opened her journal, wanting to capture the emotions of the evening while fresh.

Thanksgiving dinner with my constellation of people, she wrote. *Not the family gathering I would have envisioned a year ago, or even six months ago, but somehow more authentic than many of the perfectly orchestrated holiday meals of the past. Luke and Jodie seem at peace with the changes, even supportive of my potential decision to stay in Las Vegas. They see me here—really see ME, the person I am becoming rather than the mother they've always known. That recognition is a gift beyond measure.*

She paused, tapping her pen against the page as she considered her next words.

I'm going to stay here. Not only for a few more months, but permanently. Las Vegas has become more than a temporary refuge—it's become the place where I rediscovered myself, where I found my voice again. The landscapes, the light, the sense of 'anything is possible' in the air—it suits me in a way Savannah no longer can, for all its beauty and history. The house in Savannah represents a chapter that's closing. And I've already begun writing the next one, here in this unexpected place that's become home.

She closed the journal thoughtfully, feeling the rightness of the decision settling into her bones.

Preparing for bed, she looked out at the nighttime view of Las Vegas, the Strip glittering below, the dark outline of the hills visible against the starry sky. She had been left here broken, lost, defined by what had been taken from her. Now she stood whole, found, defined by what she had created for herself.

CHAPTER 42

MONDAY MORNING DAWNED SUNNY after a chaotic weekend with family and friends, and Rebecca sat alone in her suite. The kids were out, and while the solitude felt welcome, she knew she would miss them once they flew home to Savannah the next day.

Her phone chimed with a text from Justine: *Property transfer complete. The house is officially yours. Congratulations!*

Instead of triumph, she felt a curious reluctance. Returning to Savannah, walking through those rooms filled with twenty-five years of memories, suddenly seemed not only daunting but unnecessary.

Thanks for letting me know, she wrote, setting the phone aside.

She turned to her laptop, opening a real estate website she'd been browsing for the past week. A new listing caught her attention—a corner unit on the top floor of a boutique building, slightly removed from the north end of the Strip. Walls of glass offered panoramic views in two directions, capturing both the glittering cityscape and the desert hills. The images showed the glow of sunset illuminating the space, the mountains golden in the late afternoon light. She could picture herself there, writing at a desk positioned by the windows, no barriers between her imagination and the vistas that inspired it.

She impulsively called the agent to request a private viewing, and the appointment was set for later that afternoon. She didn't want to tell anyone, not even Helen.

It felt important somehow to do this alone, to take this step based solely on her own judgment, her own desires. Not seeking approval or validation but following her instincts.

A knock at the door interrupted her browsing. She closed the laptop quickly before answering, finding Helen on the threshold with two takeout coffee cups.

"Thought you might need this," Helen offered, handing her one of the cups. "Vince and I discovered this little place three blocks away—puts even my own coffee to shame."

"Thanks," Rebecca said, accepting the coffee with gratitude. "Come in. The house is mine. Transfer completed this morning."

Helen settled on the sofa, kicking off her shoes with a comfortable familiarity and tucking her feet up under her. "Exciting times! So," she queried, "what's the deal with Savannah? Are you going to fly back with me, or wait a bit?"

Rebecca hesitated, turning the coffee cup in her hands. "Well. I know I said I'd go as soon as the house transfer is complete—"

"But?" Helen pressed, watching Rebecca's face closely.

Rebecca nodded, acknowledging that Helen deserved an answer after her years of unwavering friendship and support. "It's just... I'm finding myself reluctant to go, even temporarily. I might wait until the book is finished. I don't want to lose momentum, you know? And walking through all those rooms, sorting through all those memories..."

She trailed off, struggling to articulate the resistance she felt. Helen remained quiet, giving her space to find the words.

"I feel like I've made such progress here," she finally continued. "Found my voice again, established this new identity as a writer. I'm different, inside and out. Going to Savannah feels like it might pull me backward, into old patterns, old ways of seeing myself. It might derail the progress I have made."

Helen nodded thoughtfully. "I understand that. More than you might think." She paused, seeming to consider something. "What if you didn't have to go at all?"

"What do you mean?"

"What if I handled the house for you?" Helen suggested, the idea apparently forming as she spoke. "I could oversee the sorting, packing, shipping of whatever you want to keep. The rest could be sold or donated. I can help you put the house up for sale. If you want."

Rebecca stared at her friend, caught off guard by the offer. "Helen, that's a massive undertaking. I couldn't ask you to do that."

"You didn't ask—I offered. And I have staff to do the heavy lifting," Helen pointed out. "Besides, it makes practical sense. I'll be in Savannah anyway, and I know most of the things that truly matter to you. Everything else you can advise me on as we go." She leaned forward, eyes bright with conviction. "Let me do this for you, Rebel. Let me help you close this chapter cleanly."

"But still," Rebecca protested, "we're talking about an entire house. Twenty-five years of accumulated possessions."

"Which is precisely why you're dreading it," Helen said wisely. "Look, we do it all the time. People get transferred for work on short notice, we take care of the move. We can go room-by-room over video."

Rebecca felt relief wash over her at the possibility, at the same time incredulous at the thought of never going back to her home in Savannah. "You'd really do that for me?"

"In a heartbeat," Helen confirmed. "It'll give you the freedom to fully embrace your life here, to finish your book, without that looming obligation pulling you back."

"I don't know what to say," Rebecca admitted, truly moved.

"Say yes, if you really don't want to go," Helen urged.

Rebecca sighed, feeling as if a burden had been lifted. "Okay. I'll definitely think about it, but it's a solid maybe. Thank you."

"Good. Consider it done." Helen nodded decisively.

"I think the only truly important things I want to keep are the three boxes in the attic," Rebecca said without hesitation. "And my mother's things, some of the children's keepsakes, my old plays and stories. They need to come here so I can go through them for story ideas that might hold value. And a few pieces of my grandmother's antique furniture."

"And the house itself?" Helen asked.

"I think I'm going to sell it. The kids didn't seem particularly attached. Especially since they've both long moved out and started their own nests," Rebecca said, her certainty growing with each decision. "Know any agents?"

"Of course," Helen scoffed. "I know all the agents."

Rebecca pictured the Savannah house—the front porch with white columns, the formal living room where everything matched perfectly but reflected nothing of her taste, the kitchen with traditional cabinets and the granite countertops that Don had insisted upon. Every inch designed around appearances, fitting their social circle's expectations. How different from what she sought now—clean lines, walls of glass inviting the outside in. In Savannah, they had rooms they rarely used. Here, she wanted every space to serve a purpose, reflecting her actual life rather than the one she was expected to project.

"It's a good decision," Helen continued, pulling Rebecca from her thoughts. "The market's strong right now. It should sell quickly once it's cleared out and staged. I'll give you my professional opinion whether anything needs a quick refresh, but honestly, I'd avoid wasting money on renovations that people don't want. So many owners do quick last minute renos and then try to recover the cost in the sale price. Better to sell it as-is and let the new owners renovate how and what they want. Unless of course some parts of the house are in a shambles, which I know is not the case."

"It's in pristine condition," Rebecca confirmed, "like everything else in the life I built with Don. Perfect and empty." The words came without bitterness now, just a clear-eyed assessment of what had been and what no longer needed to be.

They created a rough inventory of what to keep, sell, and donate. With each item discussed, she shed another connection to the Savannah house, as if the mental sorting was already helping her let go.

"I've decided," she said,

"Decided what?" Helen asked, arching an eyebrow quizzically.

"Yes, I accept your offer to take care of the Savannah house," Rebecca grinned.

"We should celebrate this decision," Helen declared when they'd finished the preliminary list. "Dinner tomorrow night, you and me, after the kids have left? Vince has some games lined up with his cousin Nick so I'm flying solo today and tomorrow. There's a little place downtown that I think you'll love."

After Helen left, Rebecca prepared for the apartment viewing, changing into a simple black dress and low heels. She didn't tell the kids where she was going, mentioning only that she had an appointment before dinner.

The real estate agent, a poised woman named Elise, was waiting for her in the lobby of the building—a modern twelve-storey structure with a discreet entrance and an atmosphere of subtle luxury.

"The apartment is on the top floor," Elise explained as they rode the elevator. "Corner exposure, which gives you a slice of the Strip view and a wide expanse of the mountain view you mentioned wanting. It has a large outdoor area as well."

The solid French entry doors closed behind them with a satisfying weight—substantial and secure. Afternoon sunlight streamed through full-height windows, illuminating the dark hardwood floors and clean, architectural lines. To her right, the Strip stretched into the distance, while ahead, windows framed her hills, their silhouette etched against the clear blue sky—more textured from this height, creating patterns of light and shadow.

"Oh," she breathed, her footsteps echoing on the hardwood as she moved through the space—echoes of spaces waiting to be filled with a life not yet lived.

The living area flowed seamlessly into an open kitchen with high-end cabinets and appliances. A hallway led to two bedrooms, each with its own view and bathroom. But what captured her heart was the small alcove off the living room—clearly a home office, with ceiling-height bookshelves and a built-in wood-slab desk positioned to take full advantage of the mountain vista. She stepped to the desk, running her hand along its smooth surface, imagining mornings spent writing there, the hills visible whenever she looked up from her work.

"The terrace is through here," Elise said, opening a door off the kitchen to reveal a generous outdoor space with unobstructed views in three directions. Rebecca stepped outside, cooled by the desert breeze. The hills seemed closer, and she caught her breath as the late-autumn sunset began to paint them in shades of pink and gold.

"The building has excellent amenities," Elise continued as they moved back inside. "A lap pool, 24-hour concierge, secure parking. There's even a guest suite you can rent if you have visitors. And importantly, it's a permanent resident community, no vacation rentals. Many residents are professionals—doctors, lawyers, a few professors from UNLV."

"What's the asking price?" Rebecca finally asked, trying to prepare herself for disappointment.

Elise named a figure that was higher than Rebecca had anticipated—not entirely out of reach with the expected proceeds from selling the Savannah house, but it would require using a portion of her settlement money as well.

"If I were to make an offer," she said carefully, "it would need to be contingent on the sale of my home in Savannah. It should be on the market within the next couple of weeks."

"That's a fairly standard contingency," Elise nodded. "Though in this market, sellers typically include a 72-hour clause, which means if a non-contingent offer comes in, you'd have 72 hours to either remove your contingency or withdraw."

"I understand," Rebecca said. "I'd like to think about it overnight, if I could." In truth, she had already decided. This felt right in a way nothing in Savannah had for years. But such a significant decision deserved at least the respect of careful consideration.

"Of course," Elise agreed, handing her a folder with the property details. "Take your time. Though I should mention, in this market and at this price point, properties don't typically stay available long."

Rebecca nodded, doing one last slow turn around the living area to take in every detail. The proportions, the light, the view—everything felt exactly right, as if the space had been made for her.

That evening over dinner, Rebecca was unusually quiet, her mind processing the apartment viewing and Helen's unexpected solution for the Savannah house.

"Earth to Mom," Jodie teased, waving a hand in front of Rebecca's face.

"Sorry," she smiled, returning her attention to the conversation. "Just thinking."

"About what?" Luke asked, studying her with his perceptive gaze.

She hesitated, then decided to share at least part of what was on her mind. "Helen offered to oversee emptying the Savannah house for me. Sorting, packing, sending me what I'm going to keep, handling the sale of the rest."

"That's really generous of her," Jodie observed. "Are you going to take her up on it?"

"I am," Rebecca admitted. "Going back to the house, even temporarily... it doesn't feel right at the moment. Like it would be a step backward."

"I get that," Luke said, immediately understanding. "The house represents the past. We've all moved forward in different directions since leaving that house."

She looked at her perceptive son. "Exactly. I'm a different person now."

"I can help Aunt Helen too. I still have some stuff stored in the basement to go through," he added.

"What will you do? Stay here in the hotel?" Jodie asked. "Until when?"

"Well, I think at least until the book is finished. And like we talked about the other night, maybe I'll get a place of my own," Rebecca hinted, feeling the rightness of the decision as she spoke it aloud to her children. "This is where I found myself again, where I remembered who I was meant to be."

"I think that's perfect," Jodie declared. "And selfishly, I'm thrilled to have a reason to visit Vegas regularly. I love it here! Especially when flights are cheap."

"Well, you'll always have a place to stay," Rebecca promised.

She deliberately didn't mention her viewing that afternoon, wanting to be certain before sharing that development. Some decisions needed to be made in private, without the influence of others' opinions, no matter how well-intentioned.

The next day brought goodbyes as Luke, Jodie, and Sean prepared to leave. The morning was a flurry of packing and promises to stay in touch, with plans for visits in the new year.

"Proud of you, Mom," Luke said as they embraced in the lobby.

After they had gone, she looked again at the property listing for the high-ceilinged corner apartment. The photos couldn't capture what she'd felt standing in that space—the sense of alignment between who she was becoming and where she would live.

Her finger hovered over Elise's contact information. For a brief moment, doubt crept in—was she moving too quickly, making such a significant financial commitment without more deliberation? Her hand trembled slightly, and she set the phone down, taking a deep breath.

She walked to the window of her suite, looking out at the hills. The same hills she would be still able to see, but from a slightly different angle, and from a home that was truly hers. Not a temporary refuge, not a place defined by someone else's choices, but her own selection, her own space.

With sudden clarity, the hesitation vanished. This wasn't impulsive—it was decisive. The culmination of months of self-discovery and growth.

She returned to the desk, picked up her phone, and called Elise. Her voice carried a certain resonance—the sound of certainty.

"Hi Elise! This is Rebecca Mor—sorry—Rebecca Fielding," she said when the agent answered, the brief correction of her name feeling significant rather than awkward. "I'd like to make an offer on the top-floor apartment we viewed yesterday."

"Wonderful," Elise replied. "I had a feeling you might. Given the market, I'd recommend coming in at full asking price if you're serious about securing it."

"I am," Rebecca confirmed. "It's exactly what I want. And I'm willing to go ten thousand over asking to strengthen my position, given the contingency on selling my Savannah house."

"That's a smart approach," Elise approved. "I'll draft the offer right away, with the house sale contingency and a 72-hour clause. When would you want to close?"

"How about February 28th," suggested Rebecca. "Plenty of time for the Savannah house to sell, but can we add in flexibility to move it up if things happen more quickly, since the apartment is empty?"

They discussed the remaining details and Elise promised to email the offer paperwork through for Rebecca to sign. She ended the call with a sense of exhilaration. This was happening—she was putting down permanent roots in Las Vegas, committing to the life she had been building here, and she knew that nothing spoke more clearly than this: a desk by the window, views of the hills, and a future entirely her own.

CHAPTER 43

P ACING THE ROOM, NERVES jangling from the weight of her decision, Rebecca texted Helen: *Still on for dinner tonight?*

Helen's response came quickly: *Absolutely. 7 PM at Barry's. I have news!*

Helen's cryptic 'news' text was intriguing. Usually her friend was more specific, more detailed in her communications. This message suggested something significant.

Later that evening, Helen was smiling across the table at Rebecca in Barry's Supper Club, a chic steakhouse with an 'Old Vegas' vibe—deep leather booths and warm light.

"This place is fabulous," Rebecca said, savoring a bite of perfectly prepared sea bass. "How did you find it?"

"Vince," Helen admitted with a slight smile. "He knows all the hidden gems in this city."

"Speaking of Vince," Rebecca began, "is that your news? You've been grinning like the Cheshire cat since we sat down."

Helen's cheeks colored slightly. "Partly. I've decided to extend my stay through next week. We're working on some serious planning."

"That's wonderful," Rebecca said sincerely. "You two have really connected. So, let me guess—you're expanding your business to Las Vegas? Or has he found a place to buy?"

"Actually, neither. It's a bit different, and I've taken some inspiration from you." She took a deep breath. "I spoke with Melissa at the office today—about the business."

"Right," Rebecca nodded. "You mentioned you were going to ask her to take a bigger leadership role. What did she say?"

"I actually offered to sell her the business," Helen said, her eyes bright with excitement and nervousness. "The whole shebang—name, client list, reputation, office, warehouse, inventory. All of it."

"Helen!" Rebecca gasped. "That's... that's huge news. Are you planning to retire? Or start a business here? Is this because of Vince?"

"It's because of *me*," Helen corrected. "But yes, Vince is part of it. Watching you these past months—seeing you shed a life that wasn't serving you anymore, watching you embrace things so new and uncertain, but so true to who you are—it made me realize I've been living on autopilot. The business is successful, but I'm not growing anymore. I'm not challenged. I'm not excited to go to the office each morning."

"And Vince excites you," Rebecca observed with a smile.

"He does. *Life* with him does," Helen acknowledged. "We've been talking for weeks about life and purpose and what really matters. And then he got an offer..." She paused, looking down at the table between her flattened hands.

"What offer?"

Helen took a deep breath, her excitement bubbling over. "Vince's cousin invited him to join an exclusive poker tour—a six-month circuit of invitation-only tournaments—and he asked me to join him." Her eyes shone as she paused. "In Australia!"

"Australia?" Rebecca repeated, stunned. "For six months?"

She reached across the table, taking her friend's hand. She felt a momentary pang of loss—months without Helen's physical presence—but it was quickly replaced by a deeper understanding. This was Helen's turn to find herself.

"I know it sounds crazy," Helen said quickly, her words tumbling out. "Three days ago I was thinking about opening an office here and splitting my time half and half, and now I'm selling my Savannah business and going to Australia for six months! And after that, who knows? But when he asked me, my immediate reaction wasn't hesitation or worry or practical concerns. It was just... *yes*. Absolutely yes."

"Because you love him," Rebecca teased, her tone giving way to genuine tenderness as she recognized the transformation in her friend's face—the same lightness, the same certainty she felt about her own decisions.

"I do," Helen admitted, the thought clearly unfamiliar to her. "I know it's fast, but it's real. I'm forty-six years old, Rebel. I've never felt this way about anyone. And it made me realize I don't want to play it safe anymore. I don't want to split my time between two cities, trying to maintain separate lives. I want one life—full, adventurous, with the people I care about most."

"Then you should go to Australia," she said, shocking herself with the burst of joy she felt for Helen. "And I'm thrilled for you. Truly. We'll stay connected across the distance."

"FaceTime dates at ridiculous hours?" Helen suggested with a smile.

"Absolutely," Rebecca confirmed. "And who knows? Maybe I'll visit. I'm a free woman now, with a nearly finished novel and a bit of money saved up."

"But first, I *am* going to Savannah for a couple of weeks, to work out the details with Melissa, deal with your house and sort out my own house. Vince is going to fly over week after next to see me in my natural habitat." She wiggled in her seat in anticipation, eager to show Vince what she had built for herself.

"I really can't thank you enough for offering to take care of the house, but with everything else going on—"

"Don't even say it—absolutely not!" Helen interrupted with a protest. "I offered, and I'm doing it. We aren't leaving for Australia until late-January, so I have lots of time."

"Okay, okay," Rebecca laughed, distracted by her phone chiming with a text.

She looked at her phone and took a deep breath as a slow smile spread across her face. "Perfect timing. I have news too!"

Helen looked at her with one quizzical eyebrow raised.

"I made an offer on an apartment today. The offer was just accepted—with a 72-hour contingency on the sale of Savannah."

Helen's eyebrows shot up. "You did WHAT? When did you even look at places?"

"Yesterday afternoon," Rebecca admitted. "I've been browsing listings for the past week or so, to be honest. There was this new listing, a perfect corner unit with walls of glass and views of both the Strip and the hills. I went to see it alone—wanted to decide based solely on my own feelings about it."

Helen leaned forward eagerly. "I get that you're excited, but you need to look at a lot of places before deciding to *buy* one, Reb."

"It's perfect for me," Rebecca carried on, disregarding her friend's concerns. "There's even a dedicated writing room with a built-in desk and bookshelves, and a window seat overlooking the mountains. The moment I walked in, I just knew. It felt like home in a way the Savannah house never really did, even after twenty-five years."

"Well, we need to go look at a few more before you commit. That one's not going anywhere yet," Helen declared. "Hold off on signing anything. Vince and I can check it out, and we'll go see a few other places to compare."

Rebecca sank in the booth, her excitement fading.

"You're right." Her dejection was palpable. "And after that you and I will go hit some singles' bars, find some other men for you to test-drive before going off to Australia with Vince," she said, nodding sagely at Helen's shocked face.

Helen's mouth fell open, her eyes widening as the comparison sank in. She sat back in her chair, shaking her head with rueful recognition before breaking into laughter. "Touché. I sound ridiculous, don't I? So, you're sure about this place?"

"Yes!" Rebecca exclaimed, causing a few heads to glance in her direction. "I'm thrilled about it. The offer is contingent on selling the Savannah house. I set the closing for the end of February, but since the place is vacant, we can move it up if Savannah sells faster."

Helen reached across the table to squeeze her friend's hand. "This is huge! We need champagne to celebrate. I'll get Melissa and the crew into your house right away—if this place really is *The One*, you can't risk a competing offer knocking yours off the perch."

A profound sense of rightness settled over them as they toasted to change and embracing uncertainty for their futures.

"You know what this means, don't you?" Helen said, interrupting her thoughts.

"What?"

"You're going to need an interior designer," Helen pointed out with a grin. "And who better to help you furnish a new place than an interior designer who happens to be your oldest and very best friend?"

Rebecca laughed. "I hoped you might offer. It has a definite industrial loft vibe, so I want to keep the furnishings simple. Clean lines, nothing fussy. Bring the mountains inside, if that makes sense."

"I already have ideas," Helen admitted. "Darker tones to balance the natural light, lots of texture but minimal pattern. Open spaces for the eye to rest. What's the flooring? I have access to gorgeous stock—can I replace whatever's there?"

"No!" Rebecca was horrified. "It's herringbone! Dark-washed oak. It's fabulous."

The conversation shifted to design possibilities and color palettes, then over to Vince's poker tour in Australia—the cities they would visit, the adventures they were planning.

"I'll need to wrap up your house quickly," Helen mused, her practical side emerging. "We'll deck it out for Christmas—your house is so pretty dressed for the holidays, it'll move fast. I already have an agent in mind with a solid list of buyers."

"Even if it takes longer, the apartment will wait, I know it," Rebecca said, not wanting to get her hopes up too high. "Everything is falling into place exactly as it should."

Later that night, Rebecca opened her journal, uncapped her Montblanc pen and wrote—*Today was a Red Letter Day! I made an offer on a beautiful corner apartment with glass walls and incredible views, and it was accepted! Soon, I'll be sleeping under my very own roof for the first time in my entire life.*

With Helen handling the packing of the Savannah house, I don't have to return and sift through complicated memories. With that weight lifted, I'm free to move forward without constantly looking back.

And Helen herself is embarking on her own transformation—selling her business, following her heart to Australia with Vince—what a massive life change for her!

We're both reinventing ourselves, both finding the courage to claim lives that truly reflect our deepest desires rather than old familiar patterns.

The children are supportive of my decision to stay here permanently. No one is clinging to the Savannah house or what it represents—we all seem ready to embrace this change.

I never expected Las Vegas to become my home. Never imagined that at forty-five I would start over so completely, in a place so different from anywhere I'd lived before. But here I am!

My first novel has just a few chapters left to go. It won't be a simple happy ending, but a violent, difficult rending of old ways into new beginnings, with the courage to step beyond old limitations.

Like my own story. Still unfolding, still revealing itself page by page. And after this novel? For the first time, I'm allowing myself to imagine a future as a working writer—not just someone who writes, but someone whose identity is fundamentally tied to the creation of stories.

The possibilities stretch before me, limited only by my imagination and courage—both of which seem to be growing stronger by the day. The 'Writer-in-Residence' job title began as a joke, but now I wonder: what if it became my actual profession? What if this first novel opens doors to others? What if, at forty-five, I've not only found a hobby but a vocation?

Rebecca closed her journal, a feeling of peace washing over her. Outside, the lights of Las Vegas glittered against the desert night. Soon, she would watch those lights from her own home.

She thought of the Savannah house, trying to summon some grief at not returning to say goodbye. But all she felt was a gentle release, as if those rooms had already receded into the past where they belonged.

It was time to let go of what no longer served her, and claim this new life fully, without reservation.

CHAPTER 44

THE CURSOR BLINKED ACCUSINGLY on the empty page, marking time like a metronome counting beats of silence. The white expanse mocked Rebecca, sitting with her fingers poised over the keyboard, waiting for words that wouldn't come.

This had never happened so completely before. Since she'd begun writing her novel, the story had flowed as if the Writer and the Visitor had lives of their own, merely channeling their experiences through her. Each morning, she would find herself transported to the windswept cliff with the old mansion, where it felt like she was witnessing rather than imagining the interactions between her characters.

But today, nothing. The invisible pathway to that world had vanished overnight, leaving only an unsettling blankness where the story had been. Irony, then: just as life fell into place, the story slipped away.

She closed her laptop and wandered into the casino, weaving between slot machines and gaming tables amidst the jangle of electronic bells and occasional shouts of victory. The change of scenery did nothing to dislodge the silence in her mind.

Rebecca returned to her suite, setting up her laptop by the window. The familiar mahogany surface that had witnessed so many hours of productive writing now seemed to ridicule her silence, its polished surface reflecting her frustration.

It was as if a translucent barrier stood between her and her creativity—she could see the shape of her story but couldn't grasp the details. The page remained empty. For the first time since beginning her novel, she closed the document without having written a single word.

Tomorrow will be better, she assured herself, turning her attention to practical matters—responding to emails, paying bills, making a to-do list for the upcoming move. But a quiet unease lingered beneath her practical tasks, a fear that the sudden silence might not be temporary.

The next morning, she woke before her alarm, eager to return to the page. She performed her usual ritual with extra care—a longer run, a hotter shower, perfectly steeped tea. Physical preparations, but also a mental clearing, creating space for the story to reenter.

Yet when she opened her manuscript, the same foggy static awaited. The characters she'd lived with for weeks, whose voices she had heard as clearly as her own, had fallen silent. The cliff-top mansion, once so vivid she could have drawn its floor plan from memory, now seemed distant and indistinct, like a building glimpsed through heavy mist.

She scrolled back through earlier chapters, hoping to reorient herself, to find the thread of narrative that had slipped from her grasp. The words were there, sentences and paragraphs she had crafted over weeks of dedicated work. But reading them now felt like encountering someone else's writing—technically familiar, but emotionally distant.

Two hours passed with nothing to show for them. Not a single word added to her manuscript, not even a note or an outline for what might come next. The Writer and the Visitor remained frozen in their last interaction, their story suspended mid-arc.

By the third day of silence, anxiety had settled into her chest, a tight coil that constricted whenever she thought of writing. She avoided her laptop, instead spending hours wandering through the hotels along the Strip, as if physical motion might dislodge whatever was blocking her creative flow.

It didn't.

On the fourth morning, desperation drove her to call Helen in Savannah.

"I've lost it," Rebecca said without preamble. "The story. It's gone."

"Lost what, now?" Helen asked, the rustling of papers in the background suggesting she was in her office.

"The ability to write. The words won't come. It's like there's something between me and the story—I can sense it's still there, but I can't reach it." She paced her suite as she spoke, unable to sit still with the restless energy of frustration. "Four days, Helen. Not a single word in four days."

"Oh, writer's block," Helen said, her tone lightening. "That's normal, isn't it? With everything you're juggling—the house, the apartment—your mind probably needs a break. Hey, listen, the blankets and towels in your linen closet—"

"It isn't 'writer's block', it's like the story's severed the line!"

A pause on the line, then Helen's voice, gentle but firm—"Reb, you create the story. It doesn't *tell itself to you*; you write it. *You* decide what happens next, not some external force. Now, let's talk about your house—"

"That's not how it works," Rebecca interrupted. "When it's flowing properly, I'm not consciously deciding what happens next. It's more like I'm discovering it as I go. It's like the story already exists somewhere, and I'm the conduit for it to reach the page."

"So you're what, taking dictation from imaginary people?" Helen's laugh held no malice, only affectionate teasing.

"Not exactly," Rebecca sighed, struggling to articulate something she'd never had to explain before. "Helen, when you're faced with an empty space, is the design solely your idea? Doesn't the room have a say?"

"The room has a say?" Helen repeated, but her tone shifted, becoming more thoughtful. "Well, I suppose that's not entirely wrong. The space itself—its dimensions, the light, the architectural features—all of that influences my design, of course."

"Right," Rebecca said, frustrated but relieved to be understood. "It's the same for me with writing. Ideas come to me, but the story itself—its inherent nature, its internal logic—shapes how those ideas develop. And right now, I can't hear what the story is trying to tell me. It's like I've gone deaf to its voice. Or maybe it's stopped talking to me."

Helen was quiet, and when she spoke again, her tone held newfound respect. "I've never thought about creativity quite that way before. It's both imposing your vision and listening to what's already there."

"Right. And I'm listening as hard as I can, but hearing nothing."

"Maybe you're listening too hard," Helen suggested. "When I'm stuck with a difficult design, sometimes the worst thing I can do is obsess over it. I need to step back, let my subconscious work."

"I've tried that," Rebecca said. "I've tried not thinking about it. I've gone shopping. Wandered the Strip. And I've tried forcing it. Nothing works."

"What would your writer do when he's blocked?" Helen asked suddenly.

The question caught Rebecca off guard. "My writer?"

"The character in your novel. He's a writer too, right? What does he do when the words won't come?"

Rebecca closed her eyes, trying to visualize her character, to access his experience. "Ha! I don't know. Maybe I need to write in some writer's block for him. But he could walk along the cliff, I guess. Watch the sea. Wait for inspiration to return."

"And would it? Return, I mean? Would you write that in?"

"Eventually, yes I guess it would. But it wouldn't be predictable. Maybe ideas come to him after a particular encounter, or a change in the weather, or—" Rebecca stopped, a realization forming. "Or after a tragedy. A challenge. Something that forces him to look at things differently."

"So maybe you need a jolt—a new angle," Helen suggested. "Shift your perspective—not on the novel, but on anything. Go explore somewhere, see something unexpected. Or," her voice took on a teasing lilt, "meet a man, have a fun one-nighter."

"Helen!" Rebecca scolded. "You know I'm not even thinking of that kind of stuff yet."

"Well, maybe you should be. Just saying," Helen joked, changing the topic entirely.

The conversation wound down soon after, with Helen promising to call again soon to check on progress. But the idea she'd planted took root in Rebecca's mind. A challenge was required. A fresh perspective.

She left the hotel and took a taxi to the Neon Museum, a place she'd visited with Jodie—a graveyard for the massive neon signs that had defined Las Vegas in earlier eras.

As she wandered among the towering relics, she was captivated by their faded grandeur. Signs outliving what they signify. They had once blazed with light and color, demanding attention. Now they rested in dignified retirement, their stories preserved but transformed, their purpose shifted from advertisement to artifact.

She paused beneath a giant 'S', its bulbs clouded but proud against the darkening desert sky. It had once advertised a hotel that no longer existed, yet here were the remains of its marker, outliving the building it once heralded.

Something about this struck her as profoundly significant, though she couldn't immediately articulate why. She sat on a nearby bench, notebook in hand, and began to write—not her novel, but observations, impressions, the beginnings of thoughts that hadn't yet coalesced into a coherent whole.

Signs enduring beyond the realities they once described. The Writer's stories continuing to touch lives long after he—

Rebecca's hand stilled on the page. A connection was forming, a bridge between her current surroundings and the fictional world she had been unable to access.

The Writer's stories. His legacy. The impact of his words after he was gone.

That was it—the missing piece she hadn't been able to see, and the realization landed with the weight of truth. Her novel wasn't only about the Writer's choice between isolation and connection, between creativity and happiness. It was about his legacy. About what would remain when the creator was gone. About the stories that outlived their teller, like these neon signs enduring beyond the buildings they once adorned.

The Visitor hadn't appeared just to force a choice; she was there to show him the bridge he'd already built—his work reaching others despite his isolation.

The haze lifted all at once, the mental pathway to her fictional world suddenly clear again. Rebecca could see the cliff-top mansion, the Writer standing at his window, the Visitor approaching with a book in her hands—dog-eared and well-loved, carried with her through the years.

She taxied back to the Monarch, sentences forming faster than her steps, the next chapter unfolding with the momentum she had feared lost forever. By the time she reached her desk, her fingers were flying across the keyboard almost before she had fully seated herself.

"This is yours, isn't it?" the Visitor asked, placing the book on the table between them. Its spine was cracked, its pages yellowed with age and handling, its cover faded from years of exposure to sun and sea air.

The Writer recognized it immediately—an early novel, published under a pen-name nearly two decades earlier, one he had nearly forgotten among his more recent works.

"Where did you get this?" he asked, running a finger along its worn edge.

"It was given to me," she said. "Your book changed someone's life. They passed it on when mine needed changing."

The Writer looked up sharply. "Changed how?"

"Does it matter?" she countered. "The point is that these words—your words—traveled far beyond this cliff, this house. They weren't solely for you to pour out your pain. They lived their own life in the world, passing from hand to hand, heart to heart. While you sat here believing your isolation was necessary for your art, your art was endearing you to people you've never met, never seen, never imagined."

"That's not the same as—"

"Isn't it?" she interrupted. "You've convinced yourself that connection weakens your creativity, that your pain is the source of your insight. But what if the opposite is true? What if every story you've written has been a bridge? What if you've been reaching out all along, and just couldn't see it?"

The words flowed, hour after hour, making up for lost time. The story hadn't abandoned her; it had merely been waiting for her to discover this new dimension, this deeper understanding of what she was truly writing about.

When Rebecca finally stopped, the sun had fully set and was rising again, her tea had long gone cold beside her, and she had written more in one sustained session than ever before. She backed up the file twice and closed her laptop, watching the morning light illuminate the hills. The exhaustion she felt was the sweet fatigue of creation, of having given birth to something that now had a life of its own.

The experience of being blocked, painful as it had been, now seemed necessary—clearing the path for a connection with her story to emerge.

Maybe silence wasn't absence, but instead a cocoon—uncomfortable, but ultimately transformative. The fog wasn't obstruction but protection, shielding a fragile insight until it was strong enough to be born.

The silence had pushed her toward deeper understanding, like her divorce had ultimately pushed her toward a more authentic life. Like the neon signs repurposed from advertisement to art.

Everything, in its time, was reimagined, reborn, revealed anew.

Chapter 45

Outside, dawn painted the distant skyline in a line of rose and gold overlain by dark clouds, while fat raindrops pelted against her window. Rebecca had been awake since four, driven from sleep by the certainty that today was the day.

Today she would write the final chapter of her novel.

For weeks, she'd been approaching this moment, crafting the scenes that would bring her characters to their resolution. The Writer and the Visitor had evolved far beyond her initial concept, becoming more complex with each draft. Their journey had paralleled her own in unexpected ways, reflecting questions about identity, courage, and reinvention.

She took a sip of tea, savoring the momentary stillness. The words were there, waiting. She could feel them.

The Writer stood at the edge of the cliff, watching the sunrise break over the distant sea. Behind him, the mansion that had begun as his sanctuary and turned into his prison for so many years stood silent, its windows reflecting the golden light.

"You're still here," he said without turning, sensing her presence before he heard her footsteps.

"Did you think I wouldn't be?" she asked, moving to stand beside him. The wind caught her hair, lifting it like a banner against the morning sky.

"I wouldn't have blamed you if you hadn't. After everything."

She fell silent, her gaze following his out to the horizon where sea and sky melted into each other.

The Writer turned to her then, seeing her clearly for the first time—not as the mysterious catalyst who had disrupted his carefully constructed isolation, but as a woman who had made her own difficult choices, who carried her own complex history.

"What I've learned from you," he said slowly, "is that it was never truly a choice between creativity and connection. That was the false dichotomy I constructed to protect myself from fear."

"Fear of what?" she asked, though he sensed she already knew the answer.

"Discovering that my writing wasn't dependent on my pain. That I could create from joy as easily as from sorrow. Because if that were true—" he hesitated, the admission difficult after so long.

"Then all the years of isolation may have been wasted—all for nothing," she finished for him.

"Yes."

The word hung between them, simple and devastating in its truth.

"Then what now?" the Visitor asked, her eyes reflecting the rising sun.

The Writer looked back at the mansion one last time, acknowledging what it had been to him, what it had given him, and what it had cost him. Then he turned to the path that led down from the cliff, toward the village, toward whatever came next. He looked down at the suitcase by his feet; nothing but his ancient typewriter and a few meager belongings held within.

"Now," he said, offering her his hand, "we find out together."

Rebecca caught her breath. She felt as if she were standing on that cliff herself, poised at a moment of profound change. The emotions flowing through her belonged both to her characters and to herself—the grief of letting go, the vertigo of uncertainty, and the exhilaration of possibility.

The words had flowed seamlessly, her fingers dancing across the keyboard as if taking dictation from some deeper part of herself. When she reached the final line, she paused, rereading what she had written. It wasn't a typical ending—not a neat, conclusive finale that answered every question, but an opening, a beginning disguised as an ending.

Exactly right for this story. For these characters. For her.

Rebecca sat still, letting out a long breath. It was done. The first draft of her novel, complete from beginning to end. Imperfect, certainly—it needed revision, refinement, perhaps significant changes before it was truly finished. But the core of it, the heart, was there on the page.

She hit enter and typed: *The End.*

Tears filled her eyes—not just sadness at saying goodbye to characters who had become daily companions, but jubilation at bringing them to their resolution. For months, the Writer and the Visitor had lived inside her head, their voices sometimes clearer than the people around her. Now they belonged to the page, no longer hers alone. She had created something whole, something that hadn't existed before.

She saved the document, then saved it again to a backup folder, unwilling to risk losing even a word. She stretched muscles stiff from hours of focused work. The sun had fully risen now, burning away the last of the clouds. The city below was coming to life in the early-winter light.

She glanced at her writing space and ran her fingers along the edge of the mahogany table in silent farewell. Soon, she would be writing at the desk in her own apartment. Her next novel would be written in a space entirely her own.

Her phone chimed with a text from Helen: *Moving truck arriving at Savannah house today. Last chance—any other items you want shipped?*

Rebecca smiled at the timing. Helen and Melissa had been working steadily for two weeks, sorting through the contents of the Savannah house with remarkable efficiency. The sales agent that Helen had recommended had been generating hype about the upcoming listing.

I think you've covered everything, she texted.

I found your old journals from college too—sending those as well. Pretty racy stuff, Rebel!

She laughed out loud. Those journals documented her first serious relationship in college, written with the dramatic intensity of a twenty-year-old discovering passion. Helen had been her confidante then too, listening to Rebecca rhapsodize about a love that had seemed world-changing at the time—at least, until she met Don.

Don't you dare read any more of those, she replied, adding a laughing emoji.

Too late. Also found that play you wrote senior year—the one about the woman who reinvents herself after leaving her hometown. Seems prescient in retrospect.

Rebecca had forgotten about that play. "Chrysalis," she'd called it—a one-act piece about a woman who shed her provincial past like an outgrown skin, emerging transformed in a different city. Had she subconsciously remembered that story when she made her own journey of transformation?

Send that too, she texted. *I'd like to reread it.*

As she showered and dressed, she dwelled on names—her own, and those of her characters. The Writer and the Visitor in her novel remained nameless throughout, identified only by their roles. It had been a deliberate choice, allowing them to function as archetypes while still developing as specific characters.

But a different naming question had been nagging at her for weeks: what name would appear on the cover of her book? Rebecca Morley, the name she'd carried through twenty-five years of marriage, no longer fit. Rebecca Fielding, her maiden name that she was legally reclaiming, was closer to her authentic self but still didn't quite capture the person she had become through this journey.

"Rebel."

She spoke the nickname aloud, testing it in the quiet of her suite. Helen had called her that since high school, and always saw something in her that Rebecca herself had forgotten until recently—a streak of independence, of quiet defiance against imposed limitations.

"Rebel Fielding."

The name felt right, both familiar and new. A reclaiming of her origins combined with an acknowledgment of her evolution. Not a pseudonym exactly, but a pen name that represented her most authentic self.

Rebecca's mind kept returning to the publication question raised by Helen. She had been researching the process for weeks, trying to understand the complex landscape of modern publishing.

The traditional route—agents, publishers—offered legitimacy, but also meant waiting and seeking approval all over again. She'd had enough of waiting for validation from others. Self-publishing, on the other hand, had come a long way from the old 'vanity press' model. It offered her control: creative freedom, her own timeline, full responsibility. Success or failure would be hers alone. That, she realized, was the point; taking ownership of her life—its disappointments as well as its achievements—was the only path to authentic living. After twenty-five years of compromise, nothing felt truer than bringing her book into the world on her own terms.

She imagined working through the publishing process in her new apartment, seated at the desk capturing the mountain view. The space would witness not only the creation of stories, but their transformation into books. The glass walls would be the backdrop to this next phase of her career—a transparent boundary between her creative world and the landscape that had inspired it.

"Rebel Fielding—Author and publisher," she murmured, testing the name again. Yes, that was who would publish this book—not Rebecca Morley, wife and mother, not even Rebecca Fielding, returning to her origins, but Rebel Fielding, the writer she had hidden beneath those other identities, now finally free to emerge.

She spent the afternoon researching the practical aspects of self-publishing. By evening, she had compiled a detailed plan from manuscript completion through editing, publishing, and marketing.

Her phone rang—Helen calling from Savannah.

"Rebel Fielding speaking," she answered, expecting a witty response from Helen to her new name.

"The moving truck is on its way, and I am bloody exhausted," Helen announced. "Everything you wanted to keep is on its way to Vegas, and tomorrow, so am I! The rest of your stuff has been sorted for estate sale this weekend, with anything that doesn't sell going to charity."

Rebecca laughed, surprised that Helen had missed how she'd answered the phone. "Thank you for taking care of the house so quickly," she said, grateful once again for her friend's efficiency and generosity.

"Melissa was a godsend," Helen replied. "She has a real talent for organization. And she found a local estate sale company that handled all the pricing and setup. They think we'll clear at least twenty thousand for the furniture and household items."

"Wow! That's more than I expected," Rebecca admitted. "What about the house itself?"

"It's being staged and dolled up next week, and the first open house will be on the weekend. I wish you could come see it, in all its Christmas glory."

"Amazing! But we both know that's not going to happen. If I see it, I may never have the courage to leave it again. Oh, and I forgot to tell you—we've settled on a price, he's listing it at six-fifty," Rebecca said, the reality sinking in.

"Holy Rebel! That's significantly more than what you thought it was worth."

"It is significantly more than what it was worth even six months ago, but the agent says the market is booming right now," Rebecca confirmed.

"How does ending the 'Savannah chapter' feel?"

Rebecca considered the question, searching for any lingering regret or nostalgia. "Liberating," she said finally. "Like setting down a heavy suitcase I've been carrying for far too long."

"Good," Helen approved. "And how's the novel?"

"I finally wrote "THE END" on the first draft this morning," Rebecca said, unable to keep the pride from her voice. "It needs rework, of course, and editing. But the complete story is there. And there's a plot twist at the end that not even I saw coming. I'm going to weave it through the rest of the story now, some foreshadowing and what-not."

"Woo! That's incredible. Listen to you with all the fancy book terms. Have you decided on a title yet?"

"Not definitively," Rebecca admitted. "But I'll have one chosen by the time you get here. I've chosen my pen name though—Rebel Fielding."

There was a momentary silence on the line. "Rebel Fielding," Helen repeated, her voice heavy with emotion.

Rebecca waited, keen to hear her friend's honest response.

"Oh, clever monkey," Helen laughed. "That's why you answered the phone like that, but I was so caught up in my news that I missed the moment! Anyway, it's perfect. Absolutely perfect."

"You think so? It's not too... I don't know, presumptuous?"

"It's who you are," Helen said firmly. "Who you've always been, beneath all the layers that life—and Don—piled on top. Rebel is the essence of you, and Fielding is your birthright. It's probably the most authentic name you could choose."

Rebecca felt tears prick at her eyes, touched by Helen's validation. "I've decided to self-publish too," she added. "Complete creative control, my own timeline. I signed up for a course next week, and I've drafted a plan with all the steps I need to go through."

"That sounds perfect," Helen approved. "Independent publishing for the independent woman you've become."

They talked a while longer, finalizing plans for Helen's return to Las Vegas and Rebecca's upcoming move.

Ending the call, Rebecca returned to her laptop, opening the document containing her completed novel.

The Visitor, by Rebel Fielding, she typed on a blank title page, seeing the words together for the first time.

It looked okay, but not quite right. It didn't quite capture the essence of the story—transformation, the courage to leave the known for the possible.

The Fallacy of Solitude. She paused. Perhaps too academic.

The View from the Cliff. This resonated more deeply, encompassing both the literal setting and the metaphorical perspective that changed throughout the story. The cliff represented the threshold between isolation and connection, between past and future. From its edge, both characters had to decide whether to retreat to safety or step into uncertainty.

Rebecca leaned back, reflecting on her own cliff edges—the ones she'd already stepped off. Divorcing Don. Embracing Las Vegas. Selling the Savannah house. Buying the apartment. Each decision a moment of standing at the precipice, choosing the unknown over the familiar.

None of the titles felt definitively right, not yet. She needed distance from the manuscript first, time to see it with fresh eyes during revision. The perfect title would emerge when the story had fully revealed itself to her.

For now, she saved the document with the simple working title *The Writer,* closed her laptop, and turned toward the window. Outside, the mountains stood silhouetted against the darkening sky—constant, yet never quite the same from one moment to the next. Just like her.

CHAPTER 46

REBECCA ROSE EARLY, DRAWN from sleep by an unspoken urgency. Now that the first draft was complete, she thought of a million improvements and changes. She opened her novel file alongside a new notebook.

She began at the beginning, reading her own words as if they belonged to someone else. The Writer needed a stronger moment in chapter three, she decided. His backstory should be more prominent in the opening. The Visitor's arrival should carry less weight at first, increasing in impact gradually.

One passage in particular caught her attention—the first meeting between the Writer and the Visitor. She studied the lines, seeing now how they failed to capture the pivotal nature of this moment—the instant when isolation first confronted possibility. She began to rewrite:

The Writer opened the door, squinting against the unexpected sunlight. No one had walked the path to his door in over three months. The woman standing before him was windblown, her cheeks flushed from the climb, her eyes reflecting the vast sky behind her.

"Yes?" he asked, his voice rusty from disuse.

"I've come about the books," she said, her gaze steady, unflinching.

He nearly closed the door—had started the motion—when something in her expression made his hand still.

"Which books?" he asked instead.

Small changes, but they mattered. She sat back—satisfied, then horrified. Did the entire manuscript need a full rewrite?

She worked through the morning, losing track of time. When her phone chimed shortly after noon, she was startled to realize four hours had passed.

The text was from Vince: *Heard you finished the book. Congratulations! Dinner tonight to celebrate?*

Rebecca smiled, touched by the gesture. *Yes! Thank you! Dinner sounds wonderful, I can't wait to hear how your Australia plans are going. Let me know where and when.*

Grateful for the break, she pulled on her exercise clothes and joined the midday Strip hustle for a mind-clearing walk, second-guessing every edit she'd made.

That evening, over dinner with Vince at Joe's, Rebecca shared her publication plans.

"Self-publishing, huh?" he said, considering this. "Fitting. You've become quite the independent spirit. But if you find it's not right for you, I know a gal who's an agent. I could introduce you, if you like. No promises, and no strings attached."

"Thanks—I'll think about it. But this book grew up as I did; self-publishing feels right. Complete creative control, no compromises. But maybe for my second book, that might be a good way to go."

"I get that," he nodded. "Sometimes going solo is the only way to play your best hand."

She smiled at the poker analogy. "Exactly. And I think I'm ready to bet on myself."

"To Rebel Fielding, then," he toasted, raising his glass. "May her first book be the beginning of a long and successful career."

They clinked glasses, the simple toast acknowledging the significance of this milestone.

As they continued their meal, Vince shared updates about the upcoming poker tour in Australia with his cousin Nick, and his developing relationship with Helen.

"She's something special," he said, a gentleness in his expression that Rebecca had come to recognize whenever he spoke of Helen. "Never thought I'd meet someone like her, especially not at this stage of my life."

"She feels the same way about you," Rebecca assured him. "I've known Helen for thirty-five years, and this is the first time I have ever seen her like this—willing to reconsider her whole life structure for a relationship."

"You could have knocked me over with a feather when she said yes to Australia."

"Same," she laughed. "She hasn't sounded so excited about anything for a long time. I'm almost jealous of your trip, Australia sounds so fantastic! How did this even come about?"

"My cousin Nick lives up in Reno. He plays for the house up there. Got invited to play some private parties in Australia, so he invited me along."

"What do you mean, 'he plays for the house'?"

"Nick's a prop player. Casino stakes him to keep games running, but he's so freakin' good they pay him a cut of the rake."

She stared at Vince, completely baffled. Seeing her confusion, he continued to explain.

"He gets a cut of the house rake. The better he plays, the more tables run, the more rake everyone earns. Casino's happy, players stick, and Nick makes bank without risking his own cash. Steady gig—different path than my travel grind."

"Huh. Interesting," Rebecca commented, wondering how many of the players at the casino tables she walked by every day were 'prop players'. A tiny seed planted for her next novel.

"Australia is exactly what Nick needs. His wife died a few years ago. Cancer. Since then, he rarely leaves the tables other than to eat and sleep."

"And maybe it's exactly what you and Helen need too. A change of scenery for both of you, a bit of distance to get a clear view of where you're heading," she replied with a smile.

The week that followed settled into a rhythm: edits in the mornings, move prep and long walks in the afternoons.

The shipment from Savannah arrived, and she had it unloaded into a storage unit downtown. She'd pull from it after she moved in, choosing only what belonged in her new space.

Revising her manuscript, she reflected on both her journey and the Writer's, strengthening each paragraph until she herself was caught up in her own words. The more she worked with the text, the more confident she became that this story was worth sharing. Not because it was perfect, but because it was authentic, speaking to universal experiences of loss, rediscovery, and courage through the specific journey of her characters.

On a rainy afternoon, Rebecca found the box containing her old writing from Savannah. Inside were yellowed scripts, typewritten stories, and handwritten poems—her younger self's creative output. She spent hours reading them, recognizing the voice, silenced for too long but unmistakably her own.

Among the papers, she found the play Helen had mentioned—'Chrysalis', her project about a woman's self-reinvention. Reading it now, she paused at its opening stage direction: 'The mountainside represents both danger and possibility.' The image resonated with her novel's core theme. She was struck by both its naïveté and its foresight. The young Rebecca Fielding had somehow intuited a journey her older self would need to take decades later.

The final page of the script bore a handwritten note from her creative writing professor: *A promising exploration of female identity and reinvention. Your voice is emerging, Rebecca. Don't lose it.*

But she had lost it, or rather, had set it aside for the roles of wife and mother, for the person Don had wanted her to be. Finding it again, here in Las Vegas, felt like recovering a precious heirloom she had misplaced long ago.

That night, Rebecca added a dedication page to her novel: *For R.F., who waited patiently for this story to be told.*

She contemplated the title page again, dissatisfied with *The Writer* as her working title. It felt too simple, too direct for a story about transformation and courage.

A chime announcing an email drew her attention from the title page. Helen. Attached was a collection of photos—the staged rooms of the house, decorated beautifully and ready to sell.

Rebecca opened the images, bracing herself for a wave of nostalgia or regret. But as she clicked through them, she felt only a detached appreciation, as if viewing a museum exhibit of someone else's life.

The final image showed the front of the house from the street, framed by the oak trees she had once loved. Beneath it, Helen had astutely written: *Ready for its next chapter!*

Rebecca smiled at the thoughtful note. Yes, the house would have new inhabitants and its own continuing story. And she too was ready for hers.

The sun rose the following morning and Rebecca dressed for her run. The first open house was starting in an hour, and Jodie and Luke had both walked through the staged house the night before, sending her texts to say how incredible the house looked.

Mom, they totally should have done the open house at night, with it all lit up! Jodie had texted. Not a bad idea, she thought, flipping the text suggestion over to the agent.

Excellent idea! Let's plan that for mid-week, we'll get some munchies and mulled wine—a Christmas Open! he had texted back.

She felt only excitement, not nerves. She stretched in the elevator, eager to begin her run.

Helen stood waiting in the lobby, equally dressed for the occasion. "Ready to run?" she asked, linking her arm through Rebecca's.

"More than ready," Rebecca confirmed. "But since when do you run?"

"Since I'm going to be wearing a bikini on an Australian beach in less than six weeks," Helen laughed as they stepped out onto the Strip.

"I still can't believe how quickly it's all happening," Rebecca told Helen, disconnecting from a call with the real estate agent. The open house had exceeded expectations, a stream of potential buyers moving through the Savannah house all weekend, and an early offer coming in.

"I'm so glad it went well," Helen replied, satisfaction evident in her voice. "Christmas decorations, a fire in the hearth, subtle holiday scents—people aren't just buying a house, they're buying the image of what their life could be. But remember, you don't have to accept the first offer."

"The offer isn't bad—but such a long closing—end of May. I might wind up losing the apartment if I wait that long. The agent says I can counter-offer to bring the date forward."

"I think you should wait until after the open house tonight. The evening presentation will be absolutely magical," Helen said, thankful that Jodie had suggested it to show off the stunning lighting that her team had lovingly prepared.

"Jodie's going to FaceTime us at three, so we can see the house all lit up. Vince will meet us afterwards for drinks and dinner."

Rebecca smiled, remembering Jodie's hyper commentary as she'd walked through each room the night before the first showing, phone held high to capture the glow of twinkling lights, the elegant garlands on the staircase, a massive Christmas tree in the corner of the living room. The house had never looked better.

At three o'clock, comfortably seated in the Monarch Bar with a bottle of red and a bowl of hot mixed nuts, Rebecca's phone lit up with a FaceTime from Jodie.

"Hey Mom," Jodie's voice came excitedly over the line. "Mark is letting me pose as the 'agent's hostess' tonight, so I'll get to meet any prospective buyers."

Jodie toured them through the various rooms, showing people scattered throughout, while joyful holiday music played softly and a fire crackled in the wide stone hearth. Jodie frequently had to put the phone down to answer questions or greet people, while Rebecca and Helen enjoyed her play-by-play in the background.

"There's a young couple sitting in the living room by the tree. Mark says they were here for the whole two hours on Saturday," Jodie whispered into the phone. "He thinks they might be serious."

Rebecca laughed as her daughter gave her an exaggerated wink over FaceTime, promising to connect again when the open house had finished.

Hanging up the call, Helen laid a hand over Rebecca's. "Hey, you in there?"

"Me? Yes! Right here."

"What just happened? I saw your face change when Jodie said that young couple might be serious. No second thoughts?"

"No second thoughts," Rebecca confirmed. "A bit of nostalgia, I guess. It's all good. Change is what moves us forward in life."

Helen poured another glass of wine and leaned back in the leather-lined booth. "Always so wise."

Before Rebecca could respond, her phone rang loudly with an incoming call. "Helen, that's the agent!"

She answered, her pulse quickening slightly. "Hi Mark."

"Hi Rebecca, we have a second offer," said Mark, brisk with professional enthusiasm. "Lower than asking—five-ninety—but they're pre-approved, no contingencies, and they want to close in three weeks. They did mention this is their absolute highest offer. First home buyers. Young couple from the UK, expecting a baby—he works at the university and she's a nurse."

Rebecca's heart leapt. A fast closing would allow her to move up her own purchase timeline.

"What's your recommendation?" Rebecca asked, though she already knew her answer—it just felt right.

"I think we should work with this offer, without question. No contingencies, quick closing—it's a clean deal. We can ask them to meet us at a higher price, but we might lose the offer."

"Actually, I'm happy with their offer. It's still more than I was initially expecting, even though it's less than asking." She raised one fist in the air, pumping it in triumph.

Finality washed over her—not regret, but acknowledgment. The rooms where her children had grown up would soon belong to this young couple. They would fill those spaces with their own stories. The house would continue, transformed but enduring, just as she had.

Promising to sign the documents as soon as they arrived and ending the call, Rebecca turned to Helen.

"A few signatures and the house is sold. A lovely young English couple," Rebecca said, attempting—and failing—a British accent, lifting her glass of wine in salute. "Almost ten percent lower than asking, but they love the house. They're pre-approved and want to close in just three weeks!"

Helen's delighted laugh filled the room as she raised her glass to meet Rebecca's. "Three weeks! That's perfect! But ten percent less—why didn't you counter-offer?"

"I don't want to. It's their first home, and their best offer. Even if it's lower, I want the house to go to people who really love it."

"Rebecca Fielding, this is why you'll always be my ride-or-die—you have the kindest heart of anyone I've ever met. We better get out shopping for furniture for the apartment."

The thought sent a thrill through Rebecca. "I'm calling Elise. Let's see if we can move my closing date up!"

Rebecca closed her eyes, picturing herself at the built-in desk in her new apartment, morning light streaming through the windows, the hills in the distance. Her laptop open, her notebooks arranged just so, perhaps a small plant bringing life to the corner. Not simply a writing space but her creative sanctuary. No compromises for anyone else's taste. The thought sent a current of anticipation through her—writing in a space that was an extension of herself.

"New year, new home, new life," Helen chanted. "It's all coming together, isn't it?"

"It is," Rebecca agreed. "Faster than I ever imagined."

She turned to Helen with a smile. "Look at us two—you selling your business, heading to Australia with Vince; me finishing my novel, buying a new place. Who would have thought six months ago that we'd be here, with completely reimagined lives?"

"To parallel journeys," Helen toasted, raising her glass. "Different destinations, same courage."

"To courage, then," Rebecca replied, clinking her glass against Helen's. "And to whatever comes next."

CHAPTER 47

C HRISTMAS AT THE MONARCH was lovelier than she could have imagined. Brilliantly decorated trees stood in both her suite and the glass-fronted writing alcove where most of her book had been written. Quieter than she had anticipated, but no less meaningful for its intimacy, she joined her friends for Christmas Eve dinner.

Helen and Vince arrived in a rush of activity, having spent the afternoon finalizing details for their Australian adventure. Their departure was set for January 22nd, giving Helen plenty of time to help Rebecca settle into her apartment before they left.

"Ten days in Sydney, then Melbourne, Brisbane, followed by three weeks in Perth," Vince explained, his weathered face animated as he described the private tour that his cousin Nick had arranged. "Six major parties, plus some smaller matches. And then we head to the Sunshine Coast in Queensland. Nick'll be moonlighting as a house player at a casino in Brisbane while Helen and I do some sightseeing."

"And plenty of beach time between events," Helen added, her eyes bright with anticipation.

Luke was spending the holidays with his new girlfriend's family, with promises to bring her to Vegas in January. Jodie and Sean had sent their regrets, spending Christmas with his family in Vermont, but had sent a special delivery with Helen—a small box wrapped in silver paper with a card addressed simply to "Mom—call me before you open!".

FaceTiming Jodie right away, conscious of the time difference, Rebecca showed the little box to her daughter on the screen. Jodie's grin was wide as she called Sean over to watch Rebecca open her gift.

Inside the box, nestled in tissue paper, was a framed ultrasound image with a handwritten note: *Baby Miller, Arriving late July. Merry Christmas, Grandma!*

Rebecca stared at the grainy image, tears welling. "Oh my God," she whispered. "A baby. I'm going to be a grandmother."

Helen and Vince stood, rushing over to engulf her in a group hug, laughing with Jodie and Sean on-screen as Rebecca wiped tears from her face.

The double transition—from wife to independent woman, from mother to grandmother—struck her with unexpected force. Her child was having a child, life moving forward in its relentless cycle of renewal. Not sadness, not quite joy, but a profound awareness of life's continuous unfolding, layers of meaning and connection.

Rebecca sat alone in her suite later that night, the ultrasound picture propped on the bedside table. Her last weeks at the Monarch stretched before her—the final passage before the next phase of her new life.

Don had texted a terse *Merry Christmas* earlier in the day, which she had acknowledged with equal brevity. According to Luke, he was spending the holiday with Annette, their relationship tentatively reconstructed in preparation for their own baby's arrival.

Circles within circles, endings folding into beginnings. She traced the outline of the tiny form in Jodie's ultrasound. Another chapter opening as others closed.

Soon, she would sign the papers and receive the keys to her new home. Helen would help her move the few possessions she'd kept, along with the new items they'd carefully selected together. Her novel was nearing its first round of edits, the plot twist that appeared at the ending finally clear in her mind, after weeks of careful crafting.

The closing process was swift and uncomplicated. Signing her name—Rebecca Fielding—on document after document, until finally a shiny electronic fob and a small ring of keys were placed in her hand.

"Congratulations, Ms. Fielding," the escrow officer said. "The apartment is officially yours."

Outside, Helen hugged her tightly. "I'm so proud of you, Rebel," she whispered. "This is huge."

They drove directly to the building, Rebecca's heart beating faster as they rode the elevator to the top floor. She pushed open the solid wooden doors into the apartment—her apartment—and stepped in slowly, absorbing the reality that this space was now hers.

Sunlight streamed through the windows, illuminating the herringbone hardwood floors and clean lines. The mountains were perfectly framed through the north-facing windows, their solidarity a welcome constant in her changing life.

"Welcome home," Helen said softly, gazing around the space in appreciation.

Rebecca stepped into the empty living room, her footsteps echoing. Exhilaration and nerves rose—this wasn't just a purchase; it was a declaration of independence.

She inhaled the scent of fresh paint and polished wood—so different from the Monarch's subtle perfume of luxury. The acoustic quality of the emptiness surrounded her, a blank canvas awaiting her imprint.

She moved through the rooms, seeing them with fresh eyes now that they belonged to her. The sleek industrial kitchen, with its concrete countertops and dark wood cabinetry. The stunning vistas through every wall of glass. And most importantly, the little alcove that would be her writing space, with its built-in desk, bookshelves, and window seat overlooking the hills.

"The furniture won't be delivered until Thursday. Are you going to stay at the Monarch for the next couple of nights, or—"

"I'm staying here tonight," Rebecca interrupted, bouncing on her toes with a wide grin on her face. "My first night as sole homeowner, and it'll be in my new home."

Helen laughed. "I had a feeling you'd say that. That's why I brought this." She gestured to the large bag she'd carried up. "Air mattress, sheets, the basics. Enough to get you through until the rest of the stuff arrives."

Rebecca hugged her friend impulsively. "You think of everything."

"It's my superpower," Helen agreed with an earnest smile. "Now, let's go pack your essentials and get you moved in! Your Writer-in-Residence days are officially over."

"Not entirely," mused Rebecca. "I'll always be a writer-in-residence somewhere."

Back at the Monarch, as she packed her remaining belongings, Anthony Delaney appeared at Rebecca's door with a small, wrapped package.

"A going-away present," he said, handing it to her. "We'll really miss seeing you around here, Rebecca."

Inside was a framed replica of the copper plaque from her writing alcove, 'Writer-in-Residence: Rebecca Morley' now replaced with 'Rebel Fielding, Writer-in-Residence Emeritus, Monarch Las Vegas'.

Tears sprang to her eyes as she held it closely to her chest, thanking Anthony.

"So you'll remember where it all began," Anthony smiled. "You've become part of our story here."

"And the Monarch is certainly part of mine," she replied, truly touched by the gesture.

As they made their way through the lobby one last time, several staff members paused to wish her well. Small connections formed over the months that had helped make this temporary shelter feel like home.

Later that afternoon, after shooing Helen out, Rebecca was alone in her home. She stood by the windows, watching the lights of Las Vegas come alive as dusk settled over the valley, the mountains fading into silhouettes against the darkening sky.

She curled up on the built-in window seat and opened her laptop. Scrolling up to the first page of her novel, she deleted the title to make room for another.

The Writer-in-Residence, by Rebel Fielding.

Feeling like she'd finally nailed it, she saved the document and then opened her notebook, flipping to a clean page.

My name is Rebel Fielding, she wrote. *I am a writer, but I wasn't always. Writing has become my home, designed around words and light and the hills that anchor me. I own my apartment, where I'll build a life shaped by creativity rather than compromise.*

Tomorrow, my things will start to arrive—furniture, books for the bookshelves, a new bed to sleep in. Practical necessities. Even a massive hand-knotted Persian silk rug that Helen insisted was the best investment piece I could buy. But tonight, in this empty space full of possibility, I acknowledge the journey that brought me here. From Rebecca Morley, wife and mother, to Rebel Fielding, author and independent woman.

'Writer-in-Residence'. A title granted by my friends, a plaque on the door of a room in my favorite hotel, and an identity I've earned through daily practice, through showing up at the page and doing the work. And now, the title of my first novel!

Wherever I live, whatever I write, that is who I am now. Who I have always been, beneath the surface.

She capped her pen and closed the notebook. Tomorrow would start the practical bustle of moving in—furniture to arrange, boxes to unpack, a home to create. But tonight was for acknowledging the milestone, for savoring the solitary triumph of this moment.

Settled back into the window seat with a glass of wine, she looked out at the night. The hills were dark shapes against the star-scattered sky—the same hills she had noticed from the Solara when she first emerged from depression, aimless and unmoored. Once, they were simply geographic features; now, they were witnesses to her transformation, companions to her writing life. Once, she had believed that Don had left her here, abandoned her in this glittering, unfamiliar city; now, she understood that Vegas wasn't where she'd been left; it was where she'd been found.

CHAPTER 48

LATE AFTERNOON LIGHT WASHED over her desk as Rebecca stared at the screen, mouse pointer hovering over the 'Publish' button. After months of revisions, professional editing, with a cover design featuring a silhouetted house on a sunlit cliff, *The Writer-in-Residence by Rebel Fielding* was ready to enter the world.

She'd followed her plan meticulously. Now, on the first day of April, she finally felt ready to release her novel to the reading public.

She took a deep breath and clicked. Oddly calm, the click was almost anticlimactic. The real achievement had been the writing itself.

A progress bar appeared, then a confirmation message: *Your title has been submitted successfully and will be available within 72 hours.*

Done.

After a lifetime of writing in private, of setting her creative ambitions aside for the roles of wife and mother, of doubting her own voice, Rebel Fielding was officially a published author.

Outside her window, the familiar hills stood against the darkening sky. On her bookshelves—filled with favorites shipped from Savannah as well as recent acquisitions—a small space waited for the printed edition of her own book.

Her phone chimed with a text from Helen: *Did you do it???*

Rebecca smiled, typing quickly: *Just clicked Publish on the eBook. No turning back now.*

Helen's response came immediately: *CONGRATULATIONS! Opening champagne here in your honor. Vince says he's placing the first order the minute it's available.*

A glow of accomplishment spread through Rebecca's chest. She had done it—had not only written a novel but seen it through to publication. Whatever happened next—whether her book found hundreds of readers or only a handful—she had fulfilled the promise she'd made to herself in those early days at the Monarch, seated at the mahogany table by the window, rediscovering her voice word by word.

Rising from her desk, she stepped out onto the balcony, into the cozy outdoor space she had created with Helen's guidance—a lounge set, desert plants, and a small table where she sometimes had her morning coffee.

Las Vegas spread below her, spring sunset glinting off glass towers, the Strip preparing for its nightly transformation into a river of light. In just three months, this view had become essential to her daily life.

Her phone rang—Jodie's smiling face appearing on the screen.

"Did you publish it?" her daughter asked excitedly, without preamble.

"The eBook, yes. Just now," Rebecca confirmed. "How did you know?"

"I've been waiting for you to call," Jodie admitted with a laugh. "I thought you'd be hovering over the button all afternoon. Figured you might need a push before I go to bed."

Rebecca smiled, touched by Jodie's caring thoughtfulness. "You weren't wrong. It felt like such a momentous step, but then once done, it really was just the smallest thing."

"It *is* a momentous step, Mom," Jodie said, her voice filled with pride. "You wrote a novel. You're a published author. Do you have any idea how incredible that is?"

"It's still sinking in," Rebecca admitted. "Part of me can't quite believe it's real."

Luke had been equally supportive in his more reserved way, asking questions about her publishing process and offering technical help with her website.

The next three days passed in a curious mixture of anticipation and normalcy. Rebecca published the print and audio versions and continued her routines—morning runs, writing sessions devoted now to early notes for her second novel, afternoons spent on practical matters and social engagements. But underneath the familiar rhythm ran a current of expectancy, knowing her words were making their way into the world.

On the fourth morning, she woke to an email notification: *Your title 'The Writer-in-Residence' is now live.*

Her heart quickened as she opened her laptop and navigated to the page. There it was—her book, her name, her words, available for anyone to purchase and read. The cover design looked even better than she had expected against the white background of the webpage, the typography elegant and understated, the imagery evocative without being literal.

With a deep breath, she posted the link to her social media accounts with a simple message: *My debut novel, 'The Writer-in-Residence,' is now available! A heartfelt thanks to everyone who supported my journey.*

By mid-afternoon, she had received her first review—five stars from 'V. Callahan', with a brief but thoughtful comment about the novel's exploration of creativity and isolation. She smiled, recognizing Vince's gesture of support. Helen followed shortly after with her own five-star review, more effusive in its praise but equally genuine.

"Shameless friend reviews," she murmured, smiling, but she couldn't deny the pleasure they brought. These people knew her, had watched her struggle and persevere, understood what this achievement represented in the context of her life. Their support felt earned, meaningful.

Anthony from the Monarch called to congratulate her, mentioning that he'd ordered a copy and planned to display it in the hotel's library. "We're proud of our Writer-in-Residence Emeritus," he said warmly. "I can't wait to read it."

By the end of the first week, Rebecca had developed an embarrassing habit of checking her sales dashboard every morning with her coffee—a ritual that yielded mostly single digits but occasionally surprised her with a cluster of purchases from readers she'd never met.

The moment that made it feel real came when a book blogger reached out asking to feature The Writer-in-Residence. During their phone interview, the blogger mentioned a particular scene—the Writer's first glimpse of his old book in the Visitor's hands—and how it had reminded her of her own grandmother's well-worn copy of Jane Eyre.

"That's exactly what I was going for," Rebecca said, then paused, startled by her own certainty. When had she become someone who knew what she was going for?

When the feature went live, it brought a small spike in sales along with something more valuable: a review from a stranger who wrote, "This author understands the courage it takes to reinvent yourself."

She read that line three times, confirming that her story had reached someone she'd never met, in exactly the way she'd hoped.

"Your first real-reader comments," Helen remarked during their weekly video call from Brisbane, where she was sun-kissed and glowing. "How does it feel?"

"Like the difference between writing in my journal and actually being a writer," Rebecca admitted.

One morning, about ten days after publication, Rebecca received an unexpected email from Anthony at the Monarch:

Rebecca (or should I say Rebel?),

I finished your novel last night and had to write immediately. It's truly exceptional—thoughtful, beautifully written, and deeply moving.

I've already recommended it to several colleagues, including my friend Beth Warren, who runs a writers' retreat at Lake Las Vegas. She was intrigued when I mentioned your book and connection to the Monarch, and asked if she might meet you while she's in town.

Would you be available for lunch at the Library next Wednesday? My treat. Beth is well-connected in publishing circles, though this isn't a business meeting—just an opportunity to connect with someone who shares your passion for literary fiction.

Looking forward to hearing from you,
Anthony

Rebecca read the email twice, both flattered and slightly intimidated. She accepted the invitation, trying to keep her expectations modest. Just a casual lunch, not a professional opportunity. Still, the mere fact that her novel had impressed Anthony enough for him to recommend it to his friend was validation in itself.

That evening, she received a text from Luke: *Finished your book. It's good, Mom. Really good. The part where the Writer realizes his isolation was a choice, not a necessity—that hit hard. We so often think we need permission, that we don't get a choice in our next steps. Proud of you.*

Tears pricked at Rebecca's eyes as she read her son's message. Of all the reactions, all the reviews, all the unexpected connections, this one meant the most. Luke, usually so reserved with his emotions, who had struggled with the dissolution of his parents' marriage, had read her words and found something meaningful in them.

She texted back: *Thank you, Luke. That means everything to me.*

The following Wednesday, she arrived at the Monarch Library for her lunch with Anthony and Beth Warren. Returning to the space where she'd written so much of her novel, now as a published author, felt like completing a circle.

Beth, a woman in her fifties with short silver hair and an easy laugh, greeted Rebecca amiably, immediately putting her at ease.

"Anthony warned me not to turn this into a business meeting," Beth said as they settled at their table, "but I have to say, I was really impressed with your novel. There's a confidence in your prose that's rare in debut fiction."

Rebecca accepted the compliment graciously, and their conversation flowed naturally—favorite books, writing processes, the challenges of literary fiction. Beth shared stories from her years as an agent without making Rebecca feel evaluated.

Toward the end of lunch, Beth's tone became more personal. "Anthony tells me you came to writing later in life, after a significant change."

"A divorce, after twenty-five years of marriage," Rebecca confirmed. "I was like a fledgling, having to find my feet again after so long in that defined role."

Beth hesitated, then added, "I hope you don't mind my saying this, but your book deserves a wider audience than self-publishing typically allows. Have you considered traditional publishing for your next project?"

Rebecca explained her reasons for choosing independence—control and timeline.

"Completely valid," Beth assured her. "But traditional publishing offers wider distribution, professional support, potential for foreign rights. The trade-off is less control and longer timelines, but for the right project, it's worth considering."

As they parted, Beth handed Rebecca her card. "If you're working on a second novel, I'd be interested in hearing about it. No pressure—just an open door."

She tucked the card into her purse, resisting the urge to assign it too much weight. Still, the idea lingered—an open door she hadn't even known to knock on.

Back home, Rebecca flipped open a new notebook and uncapped her pen. When I clicked "Publish", I was hoping for connection.

The reality has been both humbling and affirming. My novel is finding its readers one person at a time. Each review represents a meaningful exchange—my words for their time. And that is all the validation I need.

My voice has finally been spoken, to a public audience. The Writer and the Visitor have left my private imagination and entered the wider world, as I have emerged from my former life into this new identity.

I don't know yet what the path for my next book will be. But I know this: I will write as honestly as I did before, following the story where it leads. The writing itself—the daily practice, the discovery—is the core of what it means to be a writer.

Her phone chimed with a text from Helen: *How are the book sales going?*

Rebecca smiled, typing back: *Modest but steady. Each sale feels like a small miracle.*

Helen's response was immediate and characteristically direct: *That's how it should feel. It was never about the recognition for you—it was always about the writing. Everything else is just noise. Call me as soon as you can. I have a proposition for you xx.*

Rebecca turned to her window and looked out at the hills beyond. Helen was right. No matter what came next, the essential truth remained unchanged: she was a writer. Had always been a writer, beneath all the other identities life had layered upon her.

She picked up her phone and called Helen.

Epilogue

WARMTH STRETCHED INTO THE Australian evening as the sun dipped toward the west. Rebecca stepped onto the balcony of her rented beachfront cottage at Sunshine Beach, cup of tea in hand, breathing in the salt air. Three weeks in, she was still captivated—the endless ocean, golden sand, and the rhythm of the tide.

It had been Helen's idea, of course. "Come join me in Australia," she'd said during a video call a month earlier. "Vince and Nick have another run of games lined up in Perth. I'm taking a coastal design intensive with a brilliant Queensland architect. Come and stay. Bring your laptop, work on your second book somewhere different and beautiful."

Rebecca had hesitated. Helen had pressed. "After everything you've gone through, Reb, you deserve this. Consider it research—a new landscape for new stories."

And here she was, although she'd insisted on her own accommodations. "I need solitude for writing, and if I'm going that far to work on a new book, I need to use the time wisely," she'd explained, knowing Helen would understand.

Her phone pinged with a text from Helen: *Vince and Nick are back! Dinner still on for tomorrow night at Periwinkle?*

Rebecca smiled, texting back: *Looking forward to it. Enjoy your reunion with Vince tonight!*

She slipped her phone into her pocket and took the wooden stairs down to the beach below. The sun had begun its descent over the land to the west, painting the sky in streaks of lavender that reflected on the gentle waves. A few people still lingered—couples strolling the tideline, the occasional fisherman casting into the trough where land met sea.

What had begun as a two-month writing retreat had become a pause—a chance to reflect on the whirlwind of the past year. The slow, quiet success of her novel, an upcoming indie book tour through the southeastern US, and seeing her pen name nudging onto the bottom of a bestseller list. Here, with the ocean as backdrop, she'd found the space to process it all while gathering threads for her next story.

At the water's edge, she let the surf wash over her feet as the first stars appeared above, her mind drifting between memories and thoughts of the future.

Not even a year had passed since Don had handed her a folder of divorce papers in Las Vegas. With that single act, the cycle of her life had been broken. Without it, she might still be moving through the same unchanging routines, mistaking survival for living. Twenty-five years had slipped past—children raised with joy, but also compromises that dimmed her spirit and left her dreams to gather dust. There was no changing the past, no reclaiming those years of stagnation. Yet the shock of the divorce, combined with the unlikely backdrop of Las Vegas, had jolted her onto a path she might never have chosen alone—the chance, at last, to begin again.

What she *could* do—what she *was* doing—was refuse to let another day pass without purpose, without growth.

Her second novel was taking shape, its characters wrestling with exactly this question: how to honor the past without becoming its prisoner, how to embrace the future without fear. Having turned forty-six earlier in the year, Rebecca had discovered that life could still surprise her, that her imagination hadn't abandoned her during those dormant years but had simply been waiting, patient as the tides, for the moment she would reclaim it.

The sun descending behind her cast a shadow forward toward the ocean—a reminder that time continued its steady march. But time itself was neutral; it was what you did with it that mattered. Rebecca looked out at the steely grey of the ocean and reaffirmed the promise to herself: no more living in waiting, no more days measured only by what others needed from her.

The darkness deepened, more stars appearing overhead, the moon casting enough light to illuminate the beach in silver. She continued walking, relishing the solitude, the rhythm of her steps matching the pulse of waves.

A figure appeared ahead moving easily toward her along the beach—a man—tall, with sandy hair.

They nodded to each other as they passed, a silent acknowledgment of shared space. Rebecca continued a few more paces, then paused, turning back. The man had stopped as well, looking out at the moonlit ocean.

"Beautiful night," she offered.

He turned, his face mostly in shadow but his smile visible in the moonlight. "It is," he agreed, his accent marking him as American, though with a different cadence than her own Southern tones.

"Are you visiting or local?" she asked, shocking herself with the initiative. The Rebecca of a year ago would never have struck up a conversation with a strange man on a beach.

"Bit of both," he replied. "I've been here a couple of months now for work but considering making it more permanent. You?"

"Just visiting," she said. "I came down to join a friend on her vacation."

She glanced at the book tucked under his arm, the cover distinctively familiar. Recognition hit hard. It was her book—here, on a beach half a world away from where she wrote it, in the hands of a stranger.

"What are you reading?" she asked with a smile.

He chuckled, holding the book out toward the darkening sky. "Oh. Fiction. Women's fiction, I think you'd call it." He had the grace to not look too embarrassed. "Not usually my thing, but my cousin recommended it—we're having dinner with the author tomorrow. To my surprise, I like it."

"You must be Nick Callahan."

Now it was his turn to look startled. "How—?"

"I'm the author you're having dinner with tomorrow. I'm Rebecca Fielding."

"You're joking. Good thing I said I like it," he laughed.

An awkward pause filled the space between them.

"Helen calls you Rebel."

"I know she does. She has for decades, but I mostly answer to Rebecca actually."

He reached out to shake her hand, his grip firm. "Pleasure to meet you, 'Rebecca actually'. And I'm guessing from your expression that this is as unexpected for you as it is for me."

"Completely," she admitted with a smile. "Though strangely fitting, somehow."

"The universe has a sense of humor," he agreed. Then, with a slightly embarrassed laugh, "I don't suppose you'd sign it?"

"I'd be happy to. I'm staying just up there." She gestured toward her cottage. "If you're walking this way, I have a pen on the porch."

They fell into step together, the conversation flowing with surprising ease as they made their way along the moonlit shore.

Rebecca's phone pinged in her pocket, and she leaned across to show Nick the message from Helen: *Vince and I can't wait for you to meet Nick tomorrow! You're going to love him!*

Their eyes met, then they both burst into laughter—honest, unrestrained laughter that resounded along the empty beach.

"Well," he said as their laughter subsided, "I guess we'll ruin the surprise."

"Or improve it," Rebecca suggested. "Now we won't waste time on awkward introductions."

They reached her cottage, climbing to the porch illuminated by a lantern. She found a pen, and Nick held out his copy of her novel—well-read, with a cracked spine and dog-eared pages.

As she signed her name—her real name, not her pen name—Rebecca felt a curious sense of completion, as if some invisible circle had been closed. Here she was, on the other side of the world from both Las Vegas and Savannah, encountering her own words in the hands of a stranger who was, through an improbable web of connections, not entirely a stranger after all.

"Would you like a cup of tea?" she offered as she returned the book. "Or a glass of wine?"

Nick considered, about to make an excuse to leave, and then smiled. "Wine sounds perfect."

"Take a seat," she offered, gesturing toward the chairs on the deck. As she went inside to get the wine, she felt at ease with this impromptu invitation.

She poured two glasses of an Adelaide Hills Sauvignon Blanc. Nick had settled into an Adirondack chair, his long frame relaxed as he gazed out at the moonlit ocean.

"I have some coral trout I was planning to grill for dinner," Rebecca heard herself saying. "And fresh vegetables from the farmer's market. Nothing fancy, but there's plenty if you'd like to join me."

Nick's eyes brightened. "Are you sure? I don't want to impose."

"I'm sure," she said, realizing she meant it. "It would be nice to have company."

An effortless evening unfolded, conversation flowing between them with a natural rhythm as she prepared the meal and he helped set the table.

Nick, she discovered, had studied literature before the poker world claimed him. "My grandfather taught me cards, my mother taught me Keats," he explained with a wry smile. "Made for an interesting childhood."

As they talked, Rebecca noticed how he'd occasionally stop mid-conversation to listen intently to the sounds around them—the rhythm of the waves, a distant bird call, the wind rustling through the palms.

"Sorry," he said when he caught her watching him with curiosity. "Occupational hazard. Everything's information if you pay attention. I got in the habit of listening to everything at once."

There was something endearing about this awareness, this subtle attention to the world's details that most people missed.

Sitting down to eat, the moon was high over the ocean. What astonished Rebecca most was her own ease—preparing a meal for a man she'd just met without nervousness. It felt natural, as if they'd known each other far longer than a few hours.

"This is incredible," Nick said, sampling the fish. "You're a woman of many talents."

"Only recently discovered," she replied, surprised by her own candor. "For most of my adult life, I thought of myself as quite ordinary. Limited, even."

"The woman who wrote that book," he nodded toward his copy of *The Writer-in-Residence* on the side table, "could never be described as ordinary."

The conversation continued through dinner and another glass of wine, ranging from travel to books to music. By the time they'd finished cleaning up the kitchen, she was shocked to discover that three hours had passed like minutes.

"I should probably call a cab," he said, glancing at his watch. "I don't fancy walking back in the dark through the park. That beachside staircase is treacherous enough coming down in broad daylight, let alone trying to navigate up it with half a bottle of wine under my belt."

She laughed. "That staircase claimed my dignity on my second day here. Broad daylight, completely sober."

They stood on the deck waiting for the taxi, the night breeze redolent with the scent of salt and frangipani. The sense of connection between them hung in the air, unspoken but undeniable.

Nick turned to her. "Thank you for dinner. For the conversation. For an evening I wasn't expecting but couldn't have enjoyed more."

Rebecca amazed herself by stepping forward to give him a brief hug. "Thank you for being such good company."

"Until tomorrow night at Periwinkle, then," he said, his eyes lingering on hers for a moment.

"Until tomorrow," she agreed.

After the cab disappeared, she walked out onto the deck, gazing at the silver-traced waves. The evening had unfolded in a way she never would have anticipated in her previous life. Inviting a stranger for dinner, sharing hours of effortless conversation, feeling completely at ease. It was a testament to how much she had changed.

She had come to Australia to join Helen, a space to contemplate her next creative steps. Meeting someone that sparked a romantic interest in her had been nowhere on the agenda. Yet here she was, still feeling the pleasant warmth of connection from a chance encounter on the beach.

What struck her most was the nature of that connection. It wasn't born from loneliness or need, but from curiosity and genuine interest. A meeting between two complete people, neither seeking fulfillment through the other. Just the recognition of something worth exploring, without expectation.

For the first time, Rebecca approached the prospect of a new relationship not as a rescue or a necessity, but simply as another enriching dimension of a life already full of meaning, purpose, and joy. It was a novel feeling—wholly complete in herself yet unafraid to explore connection.

She smiled, closing the cottage door behind her and settling onto the small sofa by the window. Tomorrow would bring an official introduction to Nick with Helen and Vince at Periwinkle, a chance to see if tonight's easy rapport would translate to a more conventional setting. There was a delicious irony to it—meeting Nick again for the first time, pretending they were strangers.

Whatever came next—friendship, romance, or simply a pleasant memory—Rebecca was looking forward to it with open curiosity rather than anxiety. Another unexpected gift from this unexpected year.

She opened her notebook. On a fresh page, she wrote:

A thousand years have passed since I arrived in Las Vegas to celebrate my 25th wedding anniversary, and there I was, left clutching the shards of a shattered life. I never imagined what would emerge from those fragments—not just survival, but transformation.

I've published a novel. I've bought a glass-walled apartment. I've transformed—the frightened woman stranded in Las Vegas would hardly recognize me—yet she remains, integrated rather than discarded.

And now I'm in Australia. The second book grows daily in the blissfully cool mornings and searing Queensland afternoons.

Helen and Vince will soon return to Las Vegas, while I'll head to Savannah for the birth of my first grandchild. My children are flourishing in their separate lives while remaining connected to mine in healthier ways. Even Don has found stability, according to Luke—a humbler version, focusing on fatherhood.

The Las Vegas hills witnessed it all—my tears and triumphs, my doubts and determinations. They became my constants, reminding me of my journey. While I love the ocean, I do miss those hills.

"The choice isn't between happiness and art," I once wrote. "It's between fear and possibility." Words that have become my compass.

I don't know what comes next, but I know this: I am home—in myself. In the person I was always meant to be.

The End

About the Author

J.A. Hoskins is a Canadian-born Australian author living in a small town on Queensland's Sunshine Coast.

With a lifelong love of stories and a career spanning engineering, technical writing, and ghostwritten works, J.A. Hoskins has written in many voices before stepping forward with her own. Shaped by life across two hemispheres, she brings a distinctive perspective to themes of resilience, reinvention, and identity.

Writer-in-Residence is her debut novel, marking the beginning of a new chapter in her creative journey.

ALSO BY J.A. HOSKINS

John

Release Date: January, 2026

After a shattering family tragedy, Jude escapes to the Adelaide Hills, a place filled with memories of childhood vacations. There she meets John, whose quiet devotion and steadfast friendship offer her the strength to start something new.

A novel of unconditional love, resilience in the face of hardship, and the courage it takes to embrace tomorrow, *John* is a moving reminder that even in life's darkest seasons, hope can still take root.